GROWING A FAMILY IN PERSIMMON HOLLOW

PERSIMMON HOLLOW LEGACY SERIES BOOK 3

GERRI BAUER

SPIRANTHES PRESS, LLC

Growing a Family in Persimmon Hollow

This is a work of fiction. Names, characters, corporations, institutions, organizations, events, or locales in this novel are either the product of the author's imagination or, if real, used fictitiously. The resemblance of any character to any actual persons (living or dead) is entirely coincidental.

Editor: Ericka McIntyre, https://www.erickamcintyre.com/

Cover art: SelfPubBookCovers.com/MU-Designs

ISBN
979-8-9866600-6-6 (general paperback)
978-1-7328711-37 (Amazon paperback)
978-1-7328711-20 (Kindle)
978-1-732-8711-44 (ePUB)

Published by Spiranthes Press, LLC
DeLand, Florida, USA

❀ Formatted with Vellum

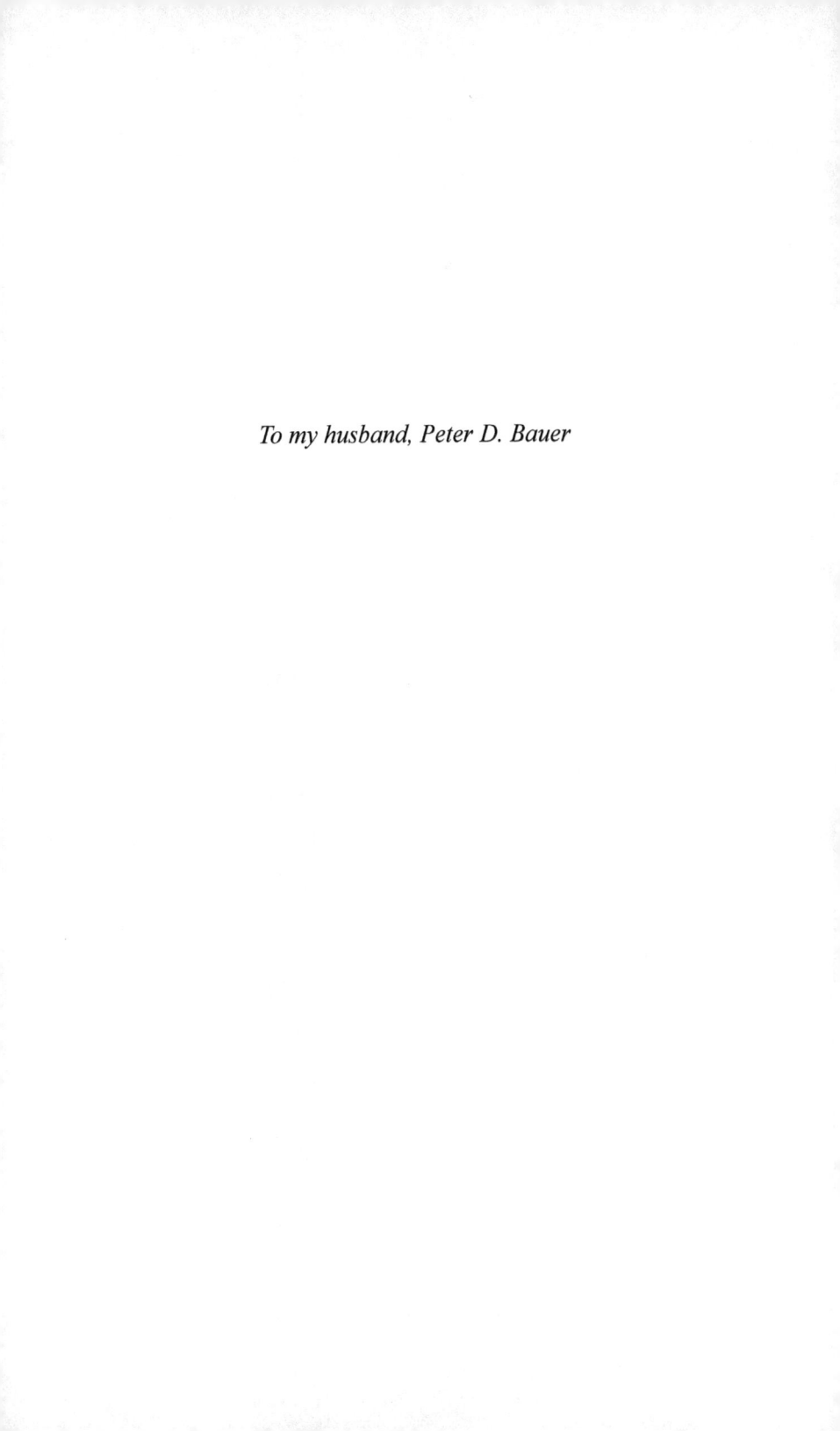

To my husband, Peter D. Bauer

CHAPTER 1

ersimmon Hollow, January, 1891

Penelope Gold stood by the window, cradled a hand over her abdomen, and swallowed. She had to stay detached. The life growing inside would be with her for only another six months. Then he or she would stay here at St. Isidore's Orphanage South in this hinterland town on the Florida frontier.

Penelope would return to Boston, and pretend to have absorbed a rich understanding of Italian Renaissance art after an extended trip abroad. Everyone at musicales and dinner parties would nod and make appropriate murmurings as though they believed her.

She stepped back and sat down hard on the wood-frame bed in her small but sunny room. Her travel guidebook bounced off the edge of the mattress and dropped to the bare pine floor with a thud.

A dizzy spell clamped down on her. The pinwheel patterns of the clean but faded quilt appeared to spin. She looked down and tried to focus on the guidebook's title print. The words, too, blurred and waved. She reached for the clean chamber pot just in time. The effluent barely missed Baedeker's *Italy Handbook for Travelers: Second Part, Central Italy and Rome.*

NATE RUSSON nearly leapt from the steps before the train fully came to a halt at the Persimmon Hollow station. Eager? Yes, indeed. He'd make a name for himself if this job turned out as promising as Professor Art suspected it would. And when had the prof ever been wrong? Nate drummed his fingers on the doorway's sturdy frame and then nearly lost his footing when the train lurched to a stop.

He grabbed his satchel and was the first one off. Actually, he was the only one off. The conductor picked up the waiting mailbag and waved farewell to Nate, and the train lumbered off.

Nate's hands itched to probe, sift, and dig through the ancient shell mounds he knew lay just a short distance from the small station house. Too bad it was in the opposite direction of his first destination. He tugged on his watch fob, checked the time, and tucked the timepiece back into the pocket of his trousers. Only a few minutes early. Not enough time to tramp over to the riverbank and return before his hosts arrived to pick him up. In fact, he could hear wagon wheels creak in the near distance.

With a good amount of will, he resigned himself to duty. He imagined he'd first have to meet every farmer, preacher, merchant, church lady, and schoolmarm in town. That's what the professor had alluded to when he wrote that his sweetheart—Professor Art with a sweetheart?—wanted to "introduce Nate to everyone" before the excavation got under way.

"We just need to explain things, my boy," Art had written. "Some around here don't even know the word *archaeology,* much less what it means and what we intend to undertake."

Nate hoped they'd be able to dispense with the niceties in short order. Darn propriety, he thought. Always getting in the way.

. . .

"IF THE WEATHER is always this nice, I might move here permanently," Nate said as he shook Seth Taylor's hand, and then Clyde Williams' hand, and was introduced to more people than he could remember at once. "I have to keep reminding myself it's January. Just look."

He waved in a general direction outward from the wide front porch of the Alloway Boarding House, which was crowded with people. Sharp, bright sunlight angled against the wooden buildings that lined the sandy road. The sun-shadow contrast emphasized the clean edges of false fronts, windowsills, and peaked roofs of the town's central district. They were clustered around the main intersection before giving way to a few blocks of businesses in each direction, followed by fenced homesteads.

The day's heat accented woodsy smells of cedar, pine, and oak from trees in homestead yards and along the middle of the main road. The heavy air captured the sweet scent of citrus that rose from gleaming orange globes on dooryard trees visible in every direction.

The large wood-frame Alloway House seemed a natural part of the surroundings. Bees droned amid pink camellia blossoms that blanketed a shrub in the yard.

"Near perfect breeze, yup, and a right nice dose of sunshine," answered Clyde, his thumbs hooked in his denim overalls.

"Tell me again, you are?" Nate asked.

"Owner of Clyde's Mercantile, the best—"

" 'The best mercantile in town.' *No*, the *only* mercantile in town," interrupted two youths who seemed delighted at their comment.

"It's a town joke," the girl explained. "Clyde always introduces himself and his store as the best, when it's the only one of its kind for miles around. You saw the country on your ride into town. Persimmon Hollow is surrounded by wilderness."

"Ahem," said Clyde to Nate. "Allow me to introduce Miss Polly Taylor and Master Billy Taylor, who think they are smarter than their young hides."

Clyde nodded toward the man named Seth Taylor. "They go with that fellow. Hey, Seth, your young'uns are at it again." Clyde half-suppressed a grin and ambled off.

"Ah, nice to see siblings get along," Nate said to Seth. "My brothers and sisters and me, we tussle as much as we hug. But our blood is thick. We stand by one another. Family always does."

"Same here," said Seth.

He grinned at the two youths, who beamed back at him before clattering down the porch steps and plunking down on the bottom rung.

Seth continued to sort out people and relationships for Nate's benefit. "My wife, Agnes, is the woman with the dark hair who's talking to Fanny Alloway and Professor Art." He pointed to a young woman whose smile filled her heart-shaped face. She chatted with the older couple while corralling an energetic toddler.

"The little one is our Seth Jr. My wife is the town's moral compass. She and the Sisters of St. Francis keep everyone in line, seeing as we don't have a resident priest yet in Persimmon Hollow."

"You have sisters in town?" Nate asked. "I'll have to be on my best behavior."

"Not in town, exactly," said Seth. "They run St. Isidore's Orphanage South. Agnes and I built the orphanage on my family land, Taylor Grove, two miles out from here. Long story behind how it all came about. You'll get an earful sooner than later from the ladies. You're welcome to visit out at the grove anytime."

"Excellent," said Nate. "I'll be sure to do so." He shook hands again, then moved to the next cluster of people on the porch.

Nate appreciated the roominess of the porch, which wrapped around all sides of the structure of a style he'd dubbed Florida Victorian Vernacular. The house had two stories and a generous number of tall windows that stretched almost ceiling to floor. The white building lacked the scrollwork and ornate embellishments he saw on similar houses up North. It was as clean and straightforward as the startup town that surrounded it and the people he'd met so far.

PENELOPE WATCHED the introductions from her perch at the far end of the porch. She tried to listen with care. After a week in town, she still didn't have names and faces straightened out. There were too many people intertwined in too many family and community connections.

Just trying to figure out the Taylors—the Seth-Agnes-Billy-Polly-baby Seth family—gave her a headache. She knew Agnes had come to Persimmon Hollow alone a number of years ago, seeking escape just as Penelope was now doing. From what, she couldn't remember.

Penelope adjusted her hat and wiped the sweat on her forehead with discreet dabs. Artfully folded watered silk and draped lace, accented by ostrich feathers, made for a fashionable hat. But it held in heat rather than warded off the sun she'd expected to be in. It was painfully obvious to her she was overdressed. This was no society tea.

Worse, she felt sicker with each passing minute. *Focus, Penelope,* she told herself. She steeled her mind back to the strangers around her. How did the Taylors fit together?

She did recall that Agnes's adopted daughter Polly had followed from the North soon after Agnes arrived. How had a then-unmarried woman adopted a daughter? Penelope couldn't fathom. She only remembered being told Agnes had nudged Seth onto a path toward redemption from his past. And that

Billy's was Seth's nephew, not his son. Penelope wasn't privy to details. She sensed she'd heard only part of the story about the Taylor family on whose land she now resided—temporarily —under the shelter of the Sisters of St. Francis at the orphanage.

Read Agnes and Seth's story in At Home in Persimmon Hollow

Penelope turned her gaze toward the late-middle-aged Alloway sisters, Fanny and Eunice. They owned the Alloway House where people had gathered, although only Fanny still lived in it. They seemed to know everyone. The daughters of the now-deceased town founder, they had long run the family home as a boarding house.

She knew Eunice had married the man in overalls named Clyde Williams not that long ago. Eunice and Clyde now lived across the street, above Clyde's Mercantile.

Right now, Fanny hovered around the man named Professor Art. Their relationship, as with Eunice and Clyde's, was a late-in-life love story. It's why Penelope remembered the details. The professor had known Fanny in their youth. They'd lost touch when separated by family relocations. Fanny and her sister had become missionaries and Art a university professor.

Art found Fanny in Persimmon Hollow when he arrived to do academic research a year earlier, and he'd vowed never to lose her again. He was now happily retired and helped Fanny with the boarding house. She could see how much Fanny enjoyed fussing over him.

Penelope sighed. In truth, she felt too sick to care any longer who was who and how they were related. She wasn't any more enamored of sleepy Persimmon Hollow now than she had been the first time she saw it, when her family had dragged her to town for a winter vacation.

Penelope nestled into her wicker chair and did her best to fade in the corner of the porch. She shifted the chair to position herself slightly behind a large potted fern whose fronds spilled from a tall urn. The movement made her stomach feel queasy. She closed her eyes, which made it worse. Near despair, she removed her hat and set it on the side table. The gentle air on her overheated head felt blissful. But it did little to settle her stomach.

She opened her eyes and forced her attention back to the talkative crowd. She made herself study the people. Anything to keep her mind off this queasiness. She focused on finding distinguishable features to help her differentiate one person from the next:

Seth, with dark hair, a firm step, strong build, and Stetson hat, one of the town's leading men;

Agnes, whose dark hair curled against her cheeks in a way that framed kind but serious eyes that took in everything;

Clyde, tall and thin and always in overalls, with a friendly word for all;

Eunice, also tall and thin, with sharp eyes and glasses perched halfway down her nose;

Fanny, with plump pink face, curly gray hair, and bouncy cheerfulness;

Professor Art, full of spry energy and sporting a shock of white hair and round glasses;

Polly, light-brown-haired, lively, and freckle-faced;

the slightly taller and blonder Billy, whose friendly eyes showed just a glint of mischief.

And the newly arrived fellow, Nate, an archaeologist if she'd heard correctly. He seemed like a spirited horse ready to run. She saw it in his alert movements and in the intelligence shining from his dark blue eyes. Even his glasses couldn't cover the interest that sparked there. If only she felt a hint of the energy he projected.

Of all of them, only Fanny Alloway was really familiar to Penelope. She'd been a kind hostess during Penelope's earlier vacation at the boarding house, the time she'd moped through her visit.

Penelope thought back to when she, her two brothers, and their wives had stayed at the Alloway House for that winter vacation. Her family had insisted she make the journey because they disapproved of her then-beau, Herman, and wanted to put distance between them.

She hated to admit they'd been right. At the time, she'd refused to listen. Her separation from Herman lasted as long as the vacation. They'd picked the relationship back up as soon as she returned to Boston.

Then Herman had shown his dark side, cornering Penelope in a way that allowed no escape. He'd assaulted her and she'd become pregnant. He was the reason for her current stay in Persimmon Hollow. But this time she'd made the trip alone—in disgrace.

Penelope almost regretted attending the welcome tea for the visiting archaeologist. She thought with longing of her quiet, sunlit room at the orphanage. But the weather had been so beautiful, the sky so blue, the breeze a caress that fluttered the window curtains and rippled across her skin.

The gentle wind had carried rich earthy scents on clean air that steadied her nerves and quieted her body. The camellia shrubs that dotted the landscape at Taylor Grove were flush with blooms in cardinal and crimson reds and angel whites. Hawks soared in the sky overhead. Sandhill cranes almost as tall as she was walked past her window with jerky-smooth movements that sparked wonder in her.

Everything had conspired to lure her out of her self-imposed shell. It was impossible to be somber or self-pitying on such a day. And the entreaties from the others to join them at the tea had been so earnest.

"Why, h-e-l-lo-! Hello!"

She looked up, a fraction too quickly, and let the hint of a dizzy spell pass. The archaeologist Nate stood before her. For the first time since the gathering began, he appeared at a loss for words.

"Who do we have hiding here?" he said, and stared as though not quite sure Penelope was really sitting there or if he was seeing a mirage.

His brown hair was lighter than her own dark chestnut tresses, so deep they appeared brunette in certain light. His hair was wavy, fine, and somewhat rumpled, whereas hers was thick, straight, and always pinned into a neat chignon. And his eyes, so clear and such a dark blue. Behind his round, wire-rimmed glasses, they held a momentarily stunned expression that soon gave way to appreciation.

"How do you do, miss?" He bowed, grinned, and held out a hand. She raised up hers, automatically, for after all that's how she'd always met men. He kissed the top of her gloved hand and set it gently back in her lap.

"The sun didn't get in my eyes and blind me with illusion!" he declared. "You are the most beautiful woman I've ever seen in my life. Your hair, my gosh, it glints in the sun. And your eyes— they remind me of amber. God has kissed you with abundant beauty!"

He half-turned away. "Professor Art, where have you been hiding this picture of perfection all my life?"

"Picture of perfection?" Penelope was in no mood. Who, really, was this man and why didn't he just go away? He had no idea how she looked when at her best, which certainly wasn't now.

Agnes Taylor walked up to them within seconds, holding her

squirming toddler with what appeared to be an effortless grasp. Fanny and Professor Art were inches behind.

"Are you feeling well, Penelope?" Agnes asked, and sat in the chair on the other side of the fern. Penelope took in the way Agnes perched the little boy on her lap and soothed his brow. She felt an unexpected twinge. She'd never get to do that with the child she carried.

"At the moment, yes," Penelope said with a weak smile.

Agnes nodded. She was one of the few people who knew the truth. "You let me know, otherwise."

"Penelope. A beautiful name," Nate said, not giving an inch of space to the others. "Are you one of Persimmon Hollow's sun-kissed denizens? Tell me you're not spoken for. My heart would shatter."

"Oh, pish, young man, settle down and don't railroad the poor girl," tsked Fanny, but her tone was kind. "Penelope is still learning everyone's names. She's only been with us a week."

"Perfect! We, two strangers, can get to know everyone together, can't we, Miss…uh, Miss?"

"Gold," Penelope said.

"And worth more than any amount of that precious metal, I'm sure," said Nate.

"And he's Nate Russon, over-confident smooth talker and up-and-coming archaeologist from my old university," said Professor Art. "He's here to conduct an excavation of the large shell mound out by the river, the one across from Hontoon Island. That island holds its own mysteries and mounds, too. But we're—he's, I mean—starting on the mainland."

"With a bit of luck this will make my career," said Nate to Penelope. "Are you staying here at the boarding house, too?"

Penelope shook her head no and fought off a fatigue that made her want to curl up in the chair and nap. She didn't want to talk to anyone. She was too tired.

The professor introduced Nate to another man who'd

wandered up. Someone slammed the screen door. Agnes made a comment to a recently arrived woman she called Lupita. A cardinal chirped from a tree. Little Seth Jr. started to fuss, people spoke too loudly, and Fanny yoo-hooed to a person walking down the street. Nate made quick work of more hellos and turned back toward Penelope.

"Would you mind taking a walk with me? If not now, perhaps later this afternoon or early evening, Miss Gold? With a chaperone, of course, if that's how things are done around here."

Penelope's hand flew to her mouth as bile rose out of nowhere. She bolted up, pushed Nate aside, and ran into the house. She prayed she'd make it to the wash basin in the upstairs bedroom Fanny had earlier invited her to use for resting.

The others on the porch stilled and looked at the door.

"Was it something I said?" asked a bewildered Nate. "I'm not that bad-looking of a guy."

"Penelope is a bit under the weather, that's all," said Agnes, with a quick, knowing look to Fanny. "Fanny, take little Seth, I'll go check on her after giving her a few minutes of privacy." The plump older woman held out her arms to take the toddler.

"She'll be back in good health in no time if I may help," said Nate. "I usually have a good effect on people. You ask anyone in my family."

"It's going to be a long winter," Agnes said under her breath to Fanny as she handed over little Seth.

"I certainly hope so," said Nate, and gave Agnes a cat's grin at having overheard her. Billy whooped approval from where he now sat nearby, on the porch railing. Nate winked at him before returning his attention to Agnes, who had rolled her gaze upward at Billy's antics.

"To receive a plum assignment in a land of endless summer and then find the woman of my dreams at the destination, well, the only thing missing is a spectacular scientific discovery out in those shell mounds," Nate said. "And I'll find that soon enough. What could go wrong?"

He whistled as he walked over to where some of the other men had clustered.

The two women watched him amble off, tall, lean, toned, and filled with buoyant energy edged with bright confidence.

"Wherever did Art find him?" Agnes asked.

"At the university," Fanny said. "Art stepped up to be his mentor after noting his intelligence and discovering he's first in his immigrant family to pursue higher learning. Art says he's a good man, a hard worker eager to advance, and has the brains to match his ambition."

"And more than a bit of brashness," mused Agnes.

"At least it's good-natured," Fanny said, and planted a kiss on the sniffling little Seth. "Unlike this little man right now."

Agnes smoothed the toddler's hair and kissed his head. "He gets crabby when he's overtired," she said. "Just like his father. I better get them both back to Taylor Grove. I can tell just by looking at Seth that he's had all the small-town talk he can handle for one day. Let me go check on Penelope first."

Upstairs, Penelope splashed her face with cool water from the wash basin. She'd heaved up nothing, because nothing would stay down to begin with. How could everything have gone so wrong, so quickly, and ended in this forced exile? She blinked back tears of anger and frustration. It was going to be a long winter.

CHAPTER 2

$\mathcal{P}$enelope relaxed in the sitting area outside the orphanage and dared to hope. For two days now, she'd hardly suffered any morning sickness. *Morning!* Ha, she'd succumbed in the afternoon and evening, too. She'd hardly had strength to even sketch, let alone paint the unusual scenery of Florida. She'd even let her habitual morning hour of Italian language exercises languish. But her body had settled down, finally.

She set her art book beside her on the wicker settee, put a protective hand over her belly, and drank in the beauty of the Florida day. She counted off the weeks in her mind. In a couple more days, she'd be at the twelve-week mark of her pregnancy, a word no one used around her. Yet one she couldn't forget. She'd experienced three months of nausea, fatigue, anger, fear, stress, and a jumble of conflicting emotions underneath the calm demeanor she worked hard to maintain.

Since arriving in Persimmon Hollow, though, she had started to feel calmer. More than any time since she'd been so horribly violated. She stopped, took in a breath, and felt a different kind of sickness lurch inside her. Herman—the reason she was in her predicament—hadn't made any attempt to contact her since before her departure from Boston. He knew she was now in Persimmon Hollow. He knew why.

He had forced himself on her. Then tried to blame her for his aggression. Then had grown angry at her refusal to consume a potion he'd procured, a noxious mixture of unnamed ingredients. He'd claimed it was for women who were "indisposed," as he worded her condition, and that it would cause the termination of what he called "her burden." He'd even forced her to see a doctor she soon learned was an abortionist. She'd refused to stay, incensed at the effrontery.

She told him she wanted an apology and for him to accept his responsibilities.

She was still waiting.

The longer the silence continued, the clearer the picture became. And the longer Herman remained silent, the less she wanted to hear from him.

Penelope wasn't one to shirk reality. Her current path was her best option. Despite keeping up her genteel appearance, though, she was unsettled. Everything had happened so fast: the attack, the further unraveling of Herman's façade, the disapproval of her family, the changes in her body, the exile to Persimmon Hollow. She prided herself on being sturdy and strong-minded, but it was a lot for anyone to endure within a few months.

The fragile calmness Persimmon Hollow had started to instill in her fled. It left as fast as the flock of ibis, rooting around the yard for bugs, skittered away when the orphanage door opened. The birds resumed their explorations somewhat farther away, but she wasn't as easily settled.

Penelope pulled her shawl closer around her shoulders and picked up her book as she waited to see who'd come outside.

"The temperature is dropping quickly, Miss Penelope," said Cornelia Carr. Like Penelope, the young woman was a guest in the convent rooms of the orphanage, but one who was discerning religious life. The mother superior, Sister Bridget, had assigned Cornelia the job of lady's companion to Penelope.

Cornelia settled into one of the wicker seats across from Penelope, who'd smiled a welcome despite wishing to be left alone. The young woman arranged a bulk of fabric underneath an embroidery ring. Penelope corralled her emotions into compliance with her controlled appearance of serenity.

The settee and chairs were set around an oval wicker table. They formed a seating area to the side of the orphanage front door. An arbor laced with dark green jasmine vines anchored the space and made it feel like an outdoor room. Nearby, azalea shrubs were coming into early bloom. The bold magenta color of the blossoms belied each flower's delicate structure.

"Do you need anything?" Cornelia asked. "Another shawl? A lap quilt? We should go in soon, you don't want to catch a chill."

"You fuss too much," Penelope said. "Lady's companions back in Boston aren't nearly as solicitous."

Cornelia bent her head over her fabric and stitched a stem motif that framed the embroidered letters *JHS*. "You're our guest here, and my responsibility is to keep you company and make sure you're comfortable at all times."

If only Cornelia knew the comforts she'd left behind in her Boston home, Penelope thought. She studied the novice, who looked younger than her twenty years. Penelope was only five years older, yet sometimes felt younger in the face of Cornelia's quiet serenity.

Cornelia had shared with Penelope that she was discerning the Lord's will. She was at the convent and orphanage to determine whether God truly was calling her to join the sisters and devote herself to a life of prayer and service.

Penelope knew that, to Cornelia, the plain, sturdy orphanage was palatial compared to the riverside cabins she'd lived in not far from Persimmon Hollow. Fever had claimed her parents and siblings and she'd then lived with relatives and neighbors before settling at the convent.

Penelope's mind darted to the luxuries she'd left behind. Plush carpets, velvet drapes, electricity, steam heat, sumptuous clothing, fine china, expensive furniture, and servants to attend to every bit of it.

She thought of her small room here. Unvarnished wood floor, rag rugs, clean but worn quilt on a bed half the size of her one at home, an unembellished pine armoire, pine desk with cane-seat chair, a rocking chair with a quilted seat cushion, and wash-stand with blue-flowered basin and pitcher.

She'd been told with some pride, by Fanny, that all the furniture had been made by the orphanage's previous maintenance man, who'd moved to town with his family and opened a furniture shop.

A chasm separated the material comforts of the orphanage and the Gold family's Boston mansion. Yet Penelope was discovering that this quiet country retreat, her place of exile, was snug and satisfying. It was like she had feathered a tidy nest. Her next thought came unbidden: how the foppish Herman would laugh at her description and her ability to find solace in these spare surroundings.

Why hadn't she noticed vainglory about him before? At least his pretensions had been on the surface, unlike his vicious side. He was a smooth talker, a practiced flatterer.

The day suddenly became chillier.

"You do more than enough, more than many others would do, and I'm appreciative," Penelope said to Cornelia. "You even quiz me on my lessons in Renaissance art."

For, heaven knew, she had better be fluent in art history upon her return to Boston.

"I have a long way to go before noting the finer distinctions between the use of rough and finishing gessoes," Penelope added. A laugh escaped, surprising her.

"You're feeling better, aren't you?" Cornelia said, her corn-flower blue eyes widening with hope. "We've been praying mightily for your, um, *illness* not to be a burden for you."

A wind gust startled them before Penelope could answer. "You best get inside," said Cornelia, who rose and gathered her sewing and Penelope's book.

A colder, stronger blast bit into them.

"Agnes had invited me to the Taylor house for supper," Penelope said. "I want to walk over there, but I better get another wrap first."

"Oh, no, you mustn't take a chill," clucked Cornelia. "Sister Bridget and Sister Rose would be horrified, and you don't want to cross both a mother superior and a prioress at the same time, believe me. Plus, Agnes Taylor would back them up in a heartbeat. Maybe you could go tomorrow."

Cornelia turned toward the lane that led from the orphanage to the main sandy roadway that wound through the Taylor Grove homestead. The lane passed the orphanage before winding up a barely discernible incline toward the Taylor family's log cabin, visible in the near distance. There, the road branched out to other parts of the homestead including the compound where the resident caretakers, Alfredo and Lupita Gomez, lived. Between the Taylor and Gomez housing areas were a smokehouse and other outbuildings.

Acres of orange groves surrounded the central living areas and branched out for a good distance beyond. On one side of the housing areas, the land opened out onto the Taylor Grove's farmland, fronted by a barn. On another side, beyond a cluster of citrus trees, a pine- and oak-forested woodland loomed tall.

"I hear someone coming," Cornelia said. "Whoever it is can give you a ride up to the Taylor house. I'll run and get you a cape and be back in a minute." She hurried inside.

Penelope watched as a wagon creaked into view and moved toward her. Drapes of Spanish moss hanging from oak tree limbs, and deep afternoon shadows, obscured the driver until he grew closer.

It was the new fellow in town, the archaeologist.

"Hellooo! Going my way?!" Nate halted the horse, jumped out, and covered the distance between the cart and Penelope's chair in a few long strides. "So this is where they're hiding you. My lovely Miss Gold, I've been searching for you since the afternoon I made your acquaintance. Now fate brings us together again." He bowed with exaggerated movements.

A small gurgle escaped Penelope at his theatricality. "I give you points for making me smile," she said.

The door reopened and Cornelia came out with a cape in her hands and with Sisters Bridget and Rose behind her. Bridget stepped forward and introduced herself and the others from the convent to Nate.

Nate bowed to them with seriousness this time. "Nate Russon, archaeologist, at your service," he said.

"I'm afraid we have little use for your specialty," said Sister Bridget. "But we'd be obliged if you'd drive Miss Gold to the Taylor house for supper. The coldest night of winter appears to be bearing down on us. But she is quite determined to keep her engagement."

"That's my destination, too," Nate said. "I'm happy to escort Miss Gold." He took the cape from Cornelia and draped it around Penelope. He then stretched out his hand to her and helped her up into the wagon's plank seat as though the vehicle was a barouche. Penelope gingerly settled herself on the hard seat. She remembered sinking into plush cushions in her family's carriage. She'd never given the comfort a second thought until now.

Another blast of wind whipped around them and Penelope was grateful for the cape. "You're right, sister, about that forecast," Nate said. "I'm part of the advance crew sent to help Seth set up small wood fires to protect citrus from the cold. This part of the country is new to me, so I've no idea what lies ahead. But I'm game. Plus, they're feeding me first."

He glanced at Penelope as he jumped up and sat beside her. "Do you have any idea how they protect an entire citrus grove?"

She shook her head no and adjusted the cape's hood so that it closed more snugly. The sisters and their novice huddled in the protection of the doorway.

A small figure barreled around the side of the building. "I know! I know! I can tell you, sisters."

A thin, dark-haired boy skidded to a halt when he saw the wagon and Nate and Penelope. His eyes widened, then narrowed. His lips clamped shut and his expression changed from helpfulness to suspicion.

"Who are you? I thought it was Billy talking to the sisters," he said to Nate.

"Onofrio, you should be inside with the others, preparing for mealtime," Sister Bridget said. "Since you're here, say a proper hello to Mr. Nate and Miss Penelope. They're our guests and one is always attentive to guests."

He grunted, shoved his hands into his pockets, and looked downward. He then shuffled over to Cornelia, who had walked out to meet him. She put an arm around his shoulders.

"May I present Onofrio, our newest resident," Sister Bridget said. "He just arrived today, a few hours ago. Penelope, you were resting when Billy and Clyde drove him here from the train station."

"*Ciao*," said Penelope, guessing his heritage from his name.

The boy looked up, surprised, but wary.

"Hi, yourself."

"*Quanti anni hai?*" she asked. It felt good to speak the language instead of recite her book lessons aloud in the quiet of her room.

"I'm ten. *Comu semu?*"

"Oh, gentlemen never ask ladies their ages."

He shrugged and appeared to lose interest in her. Instead, he focused on Nate.

"Are you going to set fire to the wood piles?"

"Soon as I find out how they're organized, yes sir," Nate said. "Maybe you can explain it to me."

Penelope noticed that Nate didn't talk down to Onofrio. He seemed to sense the same fragile toughness in the boy that she noted. One look in the little one's guarded eyes spoke volumes.

Sister Bridget narrowed her eyes and fixed her gaze on the boy. "Onofrio has just been removed from a tough city environment. Of course, he wouldn't lie and pretend knowledge about something he knows nothing about."

"I no lie!" The boy's demeanor changed in an instant. He wriggled out of Cornelia's embrace, drew himself up, and dared to almost glare at the Mother Superior.

"Billy and *Signore* Clyde, they talk about how to keep trees warm and how much wood to chop down and how many fires to make," Onofrio said. "They talk the whole trip here from the train." He looked at Nate again. "I tell you what they say, okay? Man to man."

"It's a deal," Nate said. The boy stood a bit taller. He ran over to Nate's side of the wagon and stuck out his hand. Nate looked momentarily perplexed but he took the boy's proffered handshake.

"That's how you make a solid deal," the child informed Nate with adult seriousness.

Penelope's heart pinched at how grown-up he sounded.

A blast of chilly wind reminded the group the reason their conversation had even started.

"I suggest you delay the discussion," Sister Bridget said. "Onofrio, it's time to eat. Nate, you best get to the Taylors' right away, both to get Penelope out of this wind and to help with the trees."

Onofrio ran to Bridget and tugged on her sleeve. "I go too, yes, lemme go. I help. *Si?*"

Nate spoke before Bridget had a chance to reply. "I'll keep an eye on him and make sure he's fed."

Penelope gave him a sidewards glance. Not every man would volunteer to take on a potentially troublesome boy, even just for an evening. She couldn't think of anyone within her circle who'd have given Onofrio more than a passing look, if that. Perhaps the overly confident sheen Nate projected toward her masked a deeper, more complex man.

"Or you can suffer the scrutiny of that sad expression for the rest of the evening," Nate said.

Onofrio immediately deepened the mournful, pleading look he directed toward Bridget. Nate turned sideways so the boy wouldn't see his grin.

"I've managed worse," Bridget said. But her gaze assessed the boy and she appeared to make a decision that went beyond granting permission to leave the property.

"You will obey Mr. Nate, Miss Penelope, and Mr. and Mrs. Taylor, do you understand?"

"Oh, *si, si, si,*" yelled Onofrio, and he scrambled into the back of the wagon as he shouted. Cornelia went inside and returned momentarily with an extra jacket for Onofrio.

"Put that on and cover yourself with those blankets back there," Nate said. He leaned back to get the boy situated. Onofrio resisted the help. "As you like," Nate said with a calmness that caused the boy to stop his struggling.

Nate looked at Penelope. "And you scoot right over next to me if you need more warmth," he said, and patted the seat beside him.

"Good thing Onofrio has joined us, so I don't need to ask the sisters to assign a chaperone," Penelope said.

The boy immediately bounded up from the wagon bed and

leaned over the back of the seat. His head and shoulders wedged between Nate and Penelope.

"I protect you, lady," he said. He drew his eyebrows together and stared at Nate.

Nate and Penelope's gazes met with the humor neither allowed to show on their faces.

"Thank you, young man," Penelope said to Onofrio as she turned to look at him. "I'll let you know if I need any help."

"Okay you do that," Onofrio said, and plopped back down on the wagon bed.

An inner warmth penetrated the chill that surrounded Penelope. Nate's brightness and his rightness with the child were toasty antidotes to the bleakness of her situation. She had no real worries about Nate's intentions. He seemed an open, honest book. And something about Onofrio had touched her heart. In addition, the Taylor house was so close it was almost within sight.

"Good thing is right!" Nate said. "Without Onofrio, Mother Superior might have ordered some of her sisters in Christ into the wagon with us."

He looked over toward the doorway. "You know I'm joking! Do any of you want to join us? Let me help you into the wagon." He set down the reins and made as if getting out.

"We trust you with a woman and child, Mr. Russon," said Sister Bridget. "A good Catholic boy like you – oh, yes, I can tell —wouldn't go back on his word to the Sisters of St. Francis. Especially when his companions are a woman of good family spending time here to recover her strength, and a boy in need of nourishment on many levels. And, especially, when Christ is already in the wagon with all of you, as He is with us at all times."

"You know me too well already," said Nate, with mock sadness.

"That Mother Superior, she's a tough one," Onofrio confided

in a whisper loud enough for all to hear. "You don't want to mess with her."

"We know young men and women, is more like it," said Sister Bridget. Her eyes reflected a mirth she wouldn't let show on her lips.

Penelope relaxed amid the easy banter. Was it their shared faith that broke through conventions? Nate was at ease around these religious women whom Penelope had yet to figure out. He hadn't known them any longer than she had. Yet it was like he'd known them forever. The child, too, was comfortable around them.

She liked the atmosphere of contentment she was absorbing at the orphanage, Taylor Grove, and in town. Surely, somewhere in the vicinity lived people who weren't as happy as the ones she'd encountered. But the ones who surrounded her were content with life and satisfied if they had their needs met with a bit leftover.

She thought again of what luxury had meant to her in Boston. In addition to all the physical comforts, it also included annual visits to the Continent and a calendar that revolved around museums, music, social calls, and dinner parties. Even the art studio adjoining her bedroom suite was lavish and housed an abundance of equipment and supplies.

None of those trappings had followed her to Florida. She initially felt almost as unmoored by that as she did by her condition. Even her conception of fine dining had been forced to undergo a metamorphosis. Now it meant foods like sun-kissed citrus picked from dooryard trees. And fresh vegetables harvested from the kitchen garden, warm from the sun and with dirt still clinging to their roots. It meant gumbos and stews, cornbread and risen potato bread, and other foods new to her.

Her Florida calendar was filled with unpretentious people, family-style meals without servants in attendance, walks in the winter air, and daily prayers in the orphanage chapel.

There was no denying that Penelope Gold, Boston society miss, had become Penelope Gold, Florida pioneer nester, in quick order.

She looked over at Nate, and again sensed the restrained eagerness she'd noted at the Alloway House get-together. He sat next to her on the wagon seat and watched her, waiting.

"Ready?" he asked. "You were lost in your thoughts there. Do you still want to go?"

"I'm more than ready," she said.

She waved goodbye to Bridget, Rose, and Cornelia as Nate picked up the reins.

"Send Billy or one of the workers down to get us if you need more hands," Bridget said. "We'll be free after Vespers."

"I'm sure we'll be fine," Nate said. "How many trees could Seth Taylor have out here?"

Penelope laughed out loud.

"What?" said Nate.

"Mr. Taylor has hundreds, perhaps thousands, of trees," Penelope said. "As I've felt able, I've taken to strolling among the ones closest to the orphanage."

"That many?" Nate asked. The wagon rolled at a steady, even pace.

"Yes," said Penelope. "I was surprised when I learned the extent of his grove."

"The Lord provides," Nate said. "Look how much more time I'll get to spend with you." He inched the horses forward.

Penelope hid curved lips. She didn't want to encourage this quirky scientist, not in any way. But his optimism was a balm. She was short on it, herself, right now.

"It's quiet back there," she said, to change the subject. She and Nate both glanced into the wagon bed. Onofrio, wrapped in his coat and burrowed under the blankets, was sound asleep.

CHAPTER 3

"Gosh, this wind is biting," Penelope said. "I thought Florida was always warm."

"Yeah, me too," Nate said. "But it could be worse. It can always be worse."

"Are you permanently cheerful?"

"I try to make a habit of it, yes. But I get tongue-tied at times around a lady of quality like you, and then I blather and make no sense."

She stiffened. Smooth words rolled off his tongue with ease. Cheery or not, she'd be wise to stay on guard. Not that he'd be eager to be around her when she really began to show her condition. When he knew the truth.

They rolled up to the Taylor house, a large rectangular log cabin with an addition on the rear that was the most lighted section of the house. The sharp air carried a savory aroma that wafted from the chimney and mixed with the scent of burning wood.

Penelope tensed automatically, then let her muscles relax when the smells didn't make her feel nauseated. In fact, the savory one made her realize she was hungry, for the first time, it seemed, in weeks. Until now, cooking odors often sent her flying out of the room.

The front door opened and Agnes Taylor came out onto the porch and down the outside steps to meet them.

"Come inside," she urged Penelope. "I thought you might have changed your mind, with the weather turning so quickly."

"I welcomed the diversion," Penelope said, and gave her hand to Nate, who'd hopped down and come around to assist her from the wagon. "I hadn't realized it would get so cold."

"Neither did we," Agnes said. "Thank you, Nate, for coming. Let's get you both inside for a bite to eat."

"Hold on a minute," Nate said. He leaned into the wagon bed and gave a gentle shake to Onofrio. "Wake up call, little man!"

The boy awoke with a start, tensed, and put up his fists before his eyes had opened.

"Whoa, you're safe here, son," Nate said, his voice calm and even. "Hop out. You must be hungry."

Onofrio jumped out and looked around. Penelope could see his mind working to place everyone in context. Part of him seemed poised for flight, part for fight.

"Who do we have here?" Agnes said. She made her voice soft and musical.

"Onofrio, lately arrived at the orphanage," said Nate. "He volunteered to help."

"Why, thank you," Agnes said gently. "Please come inside. We feed hearty meals to all our volunteers."

A now slightly less wary Onofrio walked with them toward the house, but kept his distance. He seemed to have lost his voice.

"I hope you don't mind, but the others have eaten already and are out working," Agnes said to Nate. "We don't have a minute to lose. If frost arrives and lasts more than a few hours, we could lose our middle- and late-season citrus crops. Thank goodness the early ripening fruit is already harvested."

Penelope saw figures moving among the near trees. Some people carried wood, others positioned logs into stacks, and still others started low, smoky fires. The small wood piles were equidistant from one another along rows of trees. The fires popped, sizzled, and fizzed.

Earthy smells and crackling wood sounds followed Penelope and the others into the roomy log cabin. The house's front-room parlor, the first room they entered, was nearly as chilled as the porch had been. Agnes urged them toward the back-room kitchen addition, where warmth and brightness were welcoming beacons.

"Sit here," Agnes settled them at a large wood-plank table. The back door opened and Seth stepped inside as Penelope and Nate got comfortable and settled Onofrio between them.

"Any more coffee ready?" Seth asked. "We've got hours to go and most are chilled to the bone already."

"I'll make more," said Agnes. She poured liquid from the largest enameled coffeepot Penelope had ever seen into a smaller one, identical in shape.

Nate had started to take off his coat but stopped as Seth spoke. He re-buttoned it so that it hid half his chin as he got up from the table. Onofrio mimicked his every action.

"I can tell I'm needed out there straightaway," Nate said to Onofrio. "You eat first. Penelope, Agnes, just leave me a bite. I'll come back and eat when I take a break for warmth."

"No, I eat later with you. I'm not hungry," Onofrio insisted. Seth glanced from Onofrio to Nate and back again, but kept silent.

"Okay, but bundle up," Nate said.

Agnes and Penelope wrapped the boy in extra layers of clothing until he squirmed out of their grasp.

Seth grabbed the smaller coffee pot and started toward the door. Agnes pulled a pile of folded kitchen towels from the dry sink and gave them to Nate. "Wrap these towels around that pot to help keep the heat in," she said.

Seth, Nate, and Onofrio hastened out and Agnes closed the door behind them. She looked at Penelope with an expression of doubt. "Our housekeeper Lupita and I made a big pot of chili. Are you able to stomach such a meal? I'm not sure I would have been able to. Would you like something lighter?"

Penelope wasn't accustomed to such frank conversation, especially between strangers. But she was in a different place now, a kind of wilderness in more ways than one.

"Actually, for the first time since I learned of my condition, I have an appetite," she said.

"Wonderful," said Agnes. "You do have more color in your cheeks, but I wrote that off to the wind and cold. But still—how about some chicken broth with noodles? I've some leftover from lunch. It'll heat up quickly. And some hot tea."

Penelope agreed and watched in surprise as Agnes took a bowl out of an icebox.

"Where do you get ice?" she asked. "Unless I'm mistaken, Florida doesn't have cold weather long enough for blocks of ice to form. Although that's hard to believe tonight."

Agnes's wide smile filled her face. "The ice is the most amazing thing." Then she frowned. "Only not tonight. The ice blocks come from Mr. Stetson's ice plant. He opened it not that long ago. Perhaps you've heard of him? The hatmaker from Philadelphia? He winters here, has a large orange and pineapple grove west of town. Yes, you could say it's a challenge keeping anything cold in summer. The insulated box and the ice blocks make life easier."

The conversation dwindled as Agnes prepared the meal and Penelope prodded her memory about the name Stetson. She wasn't familiar with Philadelphia society. She remembered learning at the orphanage that the Philadelphia hatmaker had been friends with the now-deceased town founder. And that Stetson was an important investor in Persimmon Hollow.

Agnes set a bowl of soup in front of her, along with slices of homemade bread, butter, a teapot, and teacup. Penelope thought she'd never smelled food so enticing. She dipped in her spoon and had to restrain herself from slurping.

Agnes sat down across from her and first sipped, then drank quickly from a cup of coffee. A crease formed in Agnes's brow.

"Penelope, I don't mean to be rude, but would you mind if I left for a while to help the others? Every extra hand is a Godsend."

"Oh, by all means. I've no fear of solitude," Penelope said. "I kind of like it."

The crease smoothed on Agnes's face. "Then I'll ask one more favor. No, two. Please keep an ear tuned to the bedroom. Little Seth is a good sleeper but if he fusses give me a call from the back door. I'll work close enough to hear you if you call. And, if you could assist anyone who comes to eat before I'm back, I'd greatly appreciate it."

"Of course, I'd be happy to," Penelope said automatically. Her social skills masked the fluster inside her. It wasn't that she didn't want to help. She'd never tended a child nor cooked or served food, other than pouring tea or presiding over a table staffed by servants.

Agnes bustled out moments later. Penelope hoped the toddler stayed asleep and that she'd be spared cook and waitress duties. She had little clue how to act in a kitchen. And she wasn't ready to take care of a cherub-faced youngster. She was afraid of the feelings it would stir.

Penelope had just drained the last drop of her tea when the door was pushed open and a red-cheeked Nate came in. He stood by the wood stove and rubbed his arms with brisk motions.

"Feels good in here," he said. He started to peel off layers of outerwear. Penelope saw they included a couple more than he had started with.

"Where's Onofrio?" she asked.

"He found Billy and acted like he was a long-lost friend. Hard at work by his side, helping distribute the smaller chunks of wood. He told me he wasn't ready to come in. Said the coffee and biscuits out there are keeping him filled up."

"Coffee? At his age?"

"Right? That boy has had a harder life than he's let on. Makes me want to do what I can for him while I'm here. In town, I mean, not just here at the grove. I tell you what, they're prepared out there. But unlike Onofrio, I discovered that hauling wood and tending fires makes me hungry for more than coffee and biscuits. Mrs. Taylor says you're the keeper of the chili? Can I beg a bowl?"

"Happily." Penelope rose as Nate flopped into a chair at the table. She saw the Dutch oven on the wood stove and assumed it contained the chili. A soup ladle rested on a small plate on the counter beside the stove. Next to it were stacks of bowls and plates.

Ladling chili couldn't be more difficult than pouring tea, she decided, as she stood before the stove. How did one hold the ladle for the best grip? Like a pen? A hairbrush? She kept her back to Nate. For some reason, she didn't want him to see her hesitancy. She was smart. She could figure out something this simple by herself.

She picked up the ladle and tested a few holds until one felt right. With her other hand she reached for the Dutch oven's lid.

"Aaiiiieee, wait!" Nate jumped up and grabbed her wrist seconds before she made contact with the lid. She dropped the ladle, and it clanged on the stove. *Oh, please, don't let the little one awaken,* she thought.

"What?!" She stepped back, away from Nate, but not before

feeling a funny heart-flip at his closeness. How odd. She hardly knew him.

"You'll burn your skin off, you touch that without a potholder or towel or something," Nate said. "Your ill health must be addling you. I don't mean that as an insult. You gave me quite a jump just then. I doubt this tiny town has the latest in medical care."

Penelope grew mortified at her *faux pas*. How could she have forgotten such a thing? Even when pouring tea, she used a crocheted tea towel if the teapot handle was too hot.

"I know, you were flummoxed at being so close to me," Nate said. "Yeah, all the girls react to me like that. You sit down. I'll get my chili. My mother made sure her boys knew their way around the kitchen. 'You never know what you'll have to do in this strange land of La Merica,'" she'd say. "That's how she says America from the day she stepped off the boat."

Ah, Nate is Italian, an immigrant, Penelope thought. He must be from a fine family, a Northern Italian family, she assessed, given his blue eyes, education and job, and how he carried himself and spoke. And, right now, his words smoothed over an awkward moment for her.

"Thanks, Nate. I better go check on little Seth. I can't believe the clatter in here didn't wake him."

Nate followed, carrying an extra blanket he'd picked up from a stack piled at the end of the table. "Is he sleeping in a cold bedroom? The kitchen is the warmest room in the house. Here, wrap this around you or put it on the little fellow."

But the bedroom wasn't as cold as they'd expected. A small, closed stove behind a locked fire screen barrier kept the room— if not toasty—at least not chilled. They gazed at the small figure asleep under layers of quilts.

"This little man is deep in dreamland," said Nate.

"He sure is," Penelope whispered, relieved. "Let's get out

before he wakes." Before they left, she made sure the toddler was still snug and tucked under his quilts.

"Sure thing," said Nate. "I don't want him awake and cranky. He was the one causing a fuss at that introduction shindig for me."

"They're a bundle of energy at this age," Penelope said. A thought about what her own little one would be like at that age darted into her mind before she had a chance to block it.

Back in the kitchen, Nate ladled himself a bowl of chili. He opened the stove oven door. "Cornbread? Any cornbread? I'm calling for ya."

Penelope found the squares of pone on a towel-covered plate on the warm shelf above the stove. She took undue pride in serving Nate two pieces.

"Honored, miss," he said as he accepted the plate. "Don't think I don't know you wouldn't even be civil to the likes of me in other circumstances."

She shook her head no but he stopped her. "It's okay. But this boy has plans to make something of himself. Someday your kind will talk to me. Invite me to your homes, even."

Penelope drew her brows together as she sat down across from him. "You don't have a thick accent. How old were you when you immigrated?"

"Oh, I was born here, five months after my parents arrived from Sicily. There are eleven of us—mom, dad, my grandfather, an aunt, four sisters, two brothers, and me. I'm in the middle of the pack. All work in the family grocery except me. My dad and grandfather started with a pushcart and now they have their own storefront on Mulberry Street—that's in New York where I'm from—and are planning to open a second one."

Sicily? Nate—this smart, talkative scientist with wit and personality—was from the type of family that filled the immigrant neighborhoods on Boston's North End? The streets she never ventured into, the loud, unruly, incomprehensible streets where—she'd been told—women gossiped and argued and had too many babies, men were violent, and children dirty. At least that's what she'd heard. That imagery didn't fit with Nate.

Nate continued explaining between shoveling food into his mouth, chewing, and swallowing. "My family pinned hopes on me ever since a nun noticed my aptitude for science in fifth grade and pushed me to continue my education. I'm lucky to have the job I do. And to have the family I have."

"Talent and hard work are always recognized and rewarded," Penelope said. It was an automatic reply, the kind she used at social mixers to be polite. Because at the moment her thoughts were whirling.

Nate stopped with his spoon mid-air. "You keep believing that if you like."

"Believing what?" Her mind still grappled with conflicting assumptions and realities.

"That talent and hard work are always recognized and rewarded. Maybe where you come from. Me and my kind? It's a hard slog. But I'm not one to back down from a challenge."

He took a bite of cornbread. "Want some?" he asked, and pushed the plate toward her.

"No, no thanks, I'm full." The soup and some crackers had settled well in her stomach, still a little delicate from the past weeks of unrest.

"But you don't have an Italian name," she blurted. "*Russon* isn't Italian."

Nate set down his cornbread. Penelope intuited a dip in his buoyant demeanor.

"But *Russo* is," he said in a quiet voice. "I'd never have gotten my job had I applied using the name Russo. Professor Art suggested I Anglicize it."

His tone etched down a notch. "I never told my family. I let them think the name on my credentials was a paperwork mistake that was too late to fix."

Something flared in Penelope at the unfairness.

"I understand, in a way," she said, and took a sip from her cup of tea, which she had refilled. "I was denied entry to the Boston Art Club because I'm a woman. The leaders were quite astonished when I showed up on their doorstep. You should have seen their faces. But one had encouraged me to visit based on a few paintings I'd shown him through an intermediary. Male, of course. I'd signed my work with my initials. Anyway, the gentlemen suggested I return home and paint on china."

"Cheeky guys, with a lot of nerve," Nate said.

"They soon discovered how much my family supports the club financially. They grudgingly allowed me on the premises at certain times and days, provided I stay out of sight. I couldn't even take group classes. They were unpleasant to me in ways small and large. It taxed me, made me uncomfortable, and drained the joy from making art. I only went for two months."

"I wouldn't have lasted that long," Nate said. "I know what you mean about those so-called minor unpleasantries. Nothing minor about them. Early in my school years I switched from using *Natanaele* to Nate as my first name."

He and Penelope's gazes met and a bond of understanding—and something deeper—flickered between them.

Their conversation waned. Penelope sipped her tea and Nate finished his chili and got up and helped himself to another serving.

Penelope could hardly think of two people further apart in society than she and Nate. Yet she felt more relaxed and more herself with him than with most other men of her acquaintance.

Certainly she'd never felt totally relaxed with Herman. With him, she always had a tense awareness of herself and how she performed in her surroundings. He was so focused on appearances. She hadn't realized the depth of his emphasis on superficialities until now, in the warmth of a cozy kitchen where she didn't have to keep her guard up.

"I'm impressed at their process here," Nate said, gesturing in the air with a square of cornbread before dunking the edge of it into his chili. "A big money crop still hangs on those trees. These folks will be up all night tending the fires. They try to build one at the intersection of every four trees but the limited time is forcing them to stretch beyond that kind of ideal placement."

He took another bite and swallowed. "The steady fires keep temperatures up a few degrees in their near areas, I'm told. It's enough to prevent major cold damage unless the weather dips into what Seth called a 'hard freeze.' Still not sure of the specifics on that. But every last person is pitching in. Raises my respect for them. I'm in it for the long haul, until sunrise and later if necessary."

Penelope tried to imagine the men from her past life staying up for anything except cards or billiards.

Nate slurped down the last of his second helping. "That sure was good and it warmed me up," he said, and stood. He started to pick up his plates and utensils, but Penelope signaled for him to let them be.

"Keeping things tidy here is the least I can do, since I can't be out there," she said. "I'll clean up."

"Thanks, much appreciated," Nate said. "I tip my hat to you." He made a comical attempt to tip the knitted cap he'd just pulled snugly on his head, making Penelope chuckle. He bounced up and down a few times on his toes, swung his arms, donned his layers of outerwear, and dashed back outside.

Penelope picked up the dishes and took them over to the sink, where a long-handled pump stood in the spot where, back home, she'd see a spigot. She'd wash and dry the dishes herself so Agnes wouldn't have to. Even if it took her all night to figure out how.

CHAPTER 4

*P*enelope awoke with a start from the rocking chair she had pulled close to the wood stove. She'd only meant to sit for a few minutes after she had finished neatening the kitchen. She discovered she was wrapped in two more shawls than she'd sat down with, and a small quilt was draped across her lap.

Coming more fully awake, she saw part of a figure closing the kitchen door behind him or her. The latch made a soft click. She wondered what time it was. She considered walking into the living room to look at the grandfather clock she'd noticed when going to the bedroom. But she was too snug to move.

All was quiet in the house, including the toddler's room. From outdoors came muffled sounds of voices, the plunk of logs being dropped, the crackle of wood burning, and the scrape of saws being drawn across timber. Hints of smoke pushed through invisible cracks and mingled with the indoor air. She was thankful to be inside.

Penelope fingered the indigo yarns of one of the shawl's fringes. With a light hand, she traced the stitches in the quilt's calico and gingham pieced triangles. They were neat and evenly spaced. Her eyes grew heavy. It was surely the middle of the night. She readjusted and covered herself fully again, leaned her head back, and closed her eyelids.

"Hush, you'll wake her!" A girl's whisper was anything but.

"I'm trying to be quiet! You hush. Where did you say the coffee beans were?"

"In the pantry. Tiptoe around her chair, will you?"

Penelope half-listened to the exchange in a haze of semi-wakefulness. A blast of smoke-scented cold air came from the direction of the voices.

A crash brought her fully awake.

"*OW*. Ouch." A boy's youthful voice cracked.

"You clumsy oaf!" the girl cried.

Penelope opened her eyes. An adolescent boy was on the floor next to an overturned kitchen-table chair. Onofrio stood next to him and couldn't quite stifle a laugh. Soon it was a guffaw.

The girl stepped around them in a huff and opened the pantry door.

Penelope ran through her mind the many people she'd met or heard about. The two young people with Onofrio were the adopted Taylor siblings.

A small voice cried from the bedroom. "Mama? Mama!" Sniffles followed.

"Oh, great, you even woke up little Seth," the girl wailed, no longer attempting to keep her voice down. "I'm coming, little man. Polly is coming."

"Will you three bring it down a notch." Nate stood in the doorway. He stepped inside and quickly pulled the door closed behind him. He, too, carried a scent of pine smoke.

"I see they managed to wake you," Nate said to Penelope. "Why am I not surprised? Wait. I know. Because I feel like I'm back home with my siblings. Get back out there, all of you. I'll see to the coffee."

Billy scrambled to right the chair. Onofrio helped him. Polly returned carrying a sleepy and cranky little Seth wrapped in a quilt. She kissed the toddler, smoothed his hair, and set him on Penelope's lap. Penelope's arms instinctively drew the youngster close. He looked at her suspiciously for a moment but didn't balk. She felt his weight soften and relax into her.

The trio of youngsters apologized to Penelope and scooted back into the inky night. Penelope drew more of the quilt over the sleepy little boy and draped part of one of her shawls across his shoulders and the back of his head. The bottom rungs of her chair squeaked against the wood floor as she rocked him back to sleep.

Nate checked to make sure the door was tightly closed. "I originally came in to say that, if you bundle up extra well, the stars are worth the price of a few minutes of cold," he said.

He studied Penelope with the toddler. A tender look crossed his face and was gone almost before Penelope registered it.

"But I see you're occupied. And it's really cold."

"After I get him asleep and back to bed, maybe, just a peek for a minute," Penelope said. "I love to look at stars." She rubbed the little boy's back in small, gentle circles. His eyelids drooped.

"The night sky glitters with so many stars it's hard to look away," Nate said. "Folk's livelihoods are at stake and the skies put on a show of brilliance. No fog, no clouds, no mist. Just bold twinkling lights, millions, billions of them. It's like they mock our small attempts to fight back against nature's force."

"Or shine light on them, in an effort to say all is not lost."

Nate gave her quick glance.

"Why, exactly, are you here, if I might ask?"

"Because I don't want to disturb anyone to bring me back to the orphanage."

"No, why are you here, alone, in Florida, spending the winter at a convent? Don't people, especially your kind, travel with companions even when going away for health reasons? And don't they sequester in more fashionable places?"

"Mr. Russon, such personal questions." Penelope was momentarily taken aback. "Why are you here, alone, in Florida, spending the winter in a boarding house?"

"Because I plan to secure my future based on the archaeological findings in the ancient mounds by the river. Success here will be the springboard I need to get past the competition and the bias. Oh, the bias is there, despite my name change. Olive skin has a way of raising suspicions among some people of lighter skin coloring. No one else thought this Florida exploration had any potential. That's why I had a chance. I jumped at it."

He looked around. "Now, where is the coffee?" He moved toward the open pantry door.

Penelope heard sounds of boxes and bags being pushed and moved on shelves as Nate dug out the coffee. Yes, she was securing her future, too, she thought. A slight and unwelcome bite of bitterness flickered.

She could just imagine herself telling Nate her story: *Why yes, I'm here to give birth to my illegitimate child, now that I have brought ruin to myself and chipped my family's gilded name and reputation. They don't seem to care that I was assaulted.*

Instead, she rose, taking care she didn't jostle little Seth, who was asleep again. She was surprised at how natural her movements felt. She carried him to the bedroom, laid him back in bed, and drew his covers close. "Sleep tight, little one," she whispered, and placed a wisp of a kiss on his forehead.

She walked back into the kitchen just as Nate emerged from the pantry with a sack of something.

Penelope took the sack from him.

"Careful, it's heavier than it looks."

That was an understatement. She plopped it on the table and untied the strings.

"Oh. This isn't coffee. It looks like some kind of cooking bean."

Nate looked over her shoulder and snickered. "No, those are coffee beans you're looking at." He sniffed. "Lucky for us, they're already roasted."

Penelope let her gaze travel around the kitchen. She had a vague idea of what a coffee grinder looked like, having once seen a servant using one.

She went into the pantry after having no success in the kitchen proper, and found the grinder right away. She didn't look at Nate as she carried it out to the table, reached into the bag, and poured a scoop of beans into the bowl atop the contraption.

"Here, let me." Nate started to turn the lever. "I'll grind. If you can make the coffee, I'd appreciate it. That way I can get back outside while it brews. You've no idea how hard people are working to keep those fires going. Don't know if it's gonna work, either. It's as frosty as a Northern winter night."

Penelope opened the grinder's small bottom drawer and withdrew the ground beans.

"You'll need a bigger fire," Nate said. "Better stoke it soon. And don't lift the big kettle after the water's in it. Put it on the stove first, and then put the water in."

Penelope gripped the grinder drawer's small knob. She'd have been irked at his orders if she wasn't secretly grateful for the advice. Stoke the fire? Make coffee? She didn't want to show her ignorance.

"Might want to grind some more beans after these are brewing. It's going to be a long, hard night. Hard to believe it's only ten o'clock. You're going to have a steady stream of people in and out to catch some warmth and gulp a cup of coffee."

He looked long at her, still standing with her hand gripped on the small drawer knob.

"Did I say something wrong again?" he asked. "Seems to be one of my specialties around you."

She shook her head. She took a deep breath and pulled her shoulders back.

"I'm here all winter for my health. I don't know how to make coffee."

He looked hard at her. Then his face softened.

"Florida is already having a good effect on you, from what I can see," he answered, as though they had just exchanged pleasantries at a soiree. "I wish you success in regaining your health. But I've got to say I've never met a woman who couldn't brew coffee."

"There's always a first, then," Penelope said. Why did she care what he thought? His behavior bordered on rudeness.

"I've never met a man who presumed to ask so many personal questions and make so many judgments on such early acquaintance."

"Point taken," Nate said. "For my penance, I'll show you how to brew coffee. Then I'll leave you alone. Until I need more coffee." His quick grin was never far from his face and it was hard to resist.

Nate showed her how to measure a level amount of ground coffee and determine how much to put in the kettle. He placed the kettle on the stove, explained the proportion of water to coffee, and poured in the water.

"Let it boil, and then slide it to a warming spot until the grounds settle to the bottom. Don't attempt to lift the full pot of coffee and pour it into the smaller kettles. Not if you're feeling poorly. I or whoever comes to get something to drink can do that."

Nate stoked the fire, added a few more pieces of kindling, and assessed the flame in the firebox. He nodded to himself and closed it. "That should do fine," he said.

"Tell Agnes I'll keep coffee ready, for as long as everyone is out there," Penelope said.

"Much obliged," he said, and made for the door.

"I can speak three languages," she called, as he shut the door behind him.

"Can you say *coffee* in all of them?" came the reply, followed by a guffaw.

Penelope hadn't expected him to hear her. She smiled as the sound of his footsteps faded.

She kept a close watch on the kettle until the liquid boiled. Nate hadn't said how long to let the coffee boil. After a couple of minutes, she tasted a spoonful, let the liquid boil awhile longer, tasted again, and proclaimed it acceptable. Quite good, actually.

After the grounds settled, she ladled the dark liquid into the smaller kettles and set them on a warm corner of the stove. She then started another round in the big pot. Oddly, she felt content in her rustic busyness. Better than she used to feel when seated in the parlor back home, playing charades or having bland after-dinner conversations with family and guests.

Once in a while, Herman had shown up and livened the gatherings for her, although not for the others. Had she been so bored she welcomed any diversion? No, Herman had gone out of his way to make himself agreeable in ways he must have sensed mattered to her. And apparently made no such effort with others in her family.

A knot twisted in her stomach as she gingerly fed more kindling into the stove as Nate had done. Distance was making her vision clearer. Like Nate, Herman was a smooth talker. But Nate had an open honesty and rough edges, while Herman was masked and polished. She hadn't realized until too late that his veneer covered a sour core. It had been a rare mistake in judgment for her.

Her shame at his flat refusal to marry her still made her cheeks burn. He'd not only refused. He'd disappeared without word for three weeks. Then returned and tried to make her get rid of the baby.

She slammed the cookstove's door closed harder than she'd

intended. If only Nate knew the details. He'd drop his flattery faster than the temperature was plummeting outdoors.

A short while later, she served coffee and brewed more as quickly as she could to a glum cluster of folks grouped around the table.

"I've never seen anything like this," said Agnes, and wrapped her hands around the coffee mug. She leaned her face over it to capture warmth from the steam. "It was in the low sixties this afternoon, just hours ago. Now here it is, near freezing."

"I knew it, I just knew it," said Billy. "The wooly worms had really wide dark stripes on 'em. I knew we were in for a cold winter."

"Wooly worms? What's that?" Onofrio asked, and he and Billy soon started a side conversation.

Seth ran a hand through his hair. He had dark circles under his eyes. "I noticed the corn shucks were tighter than usual back during harvest, but didn't give it much thought at the time. Should have. Would have laid in more wood."

Agnes reached a hand over and covered his with her own. "You've done all you possibly could. Between us and the rest of the helpers out there, we'll keep the fires going all night."

Penelope took a quilt from a pile Agnes had carried in from another room and covered Polly, who'd lain down on the bench against the wall and fallen asleep.

"You expecting significant damage?" Nate asked Seth, and took a sip of coffee and bite of Dried Apple pie Agnes had removed from the pie safe and set on the table.

"Maybe thirty percent," Seth said. "Unless things get worse before morning."

"Ouch," said Nate.

"I can absorb it with some belt-tightening," Seth said. "Some others in Persimmon Hollow don't have any cushion. If the fruit freezes on the tree, it'll be good only for juice. The market will be overloaded and prices will plummet. That, and nobody will have any fresh citrus to ship North. That fresh fruit is what commands the best prices."

The grandfather clock in the parlor chimed twelve times. Penelope looked at the weary faces. She read determination in them.

Seth got up slowly. "I've faced worse. We'll get through it."

Agnes blessed herself. "Yes, we'll get through it. Please, all, a quick prayer before we go back out."

Penelope had never been around people who prayed openly. She hesitated. Should she join in? Prayer and church were as regimented in her family life as everything else was. They had their time—once a week—and place—the church building.

The others at the table—including Nate—blessed themselves the way her family's Irish Catholic maids did back home. She bowed her head. Agnes started a prayer with the words "Hail, Mary," and the others chimed in. They recited in unison a prayer unfamiliar to Penelope.

That came from me, too, God, Penelope added silently. Perhaps the extra petitions would help her little baby. And she could benefit from a few of them, herself.

CHAPTER 5

$\mathcal{T}$he next morning dawned bitterly cold. Penelope had caught winks of sleep but was weak with fatigue when Nate dropped her off at the orphanage in the gray early morning light.

"I never did get to see the stars last night," she said, as the final twinkles faded in the sky.

Nate was somber as he helped her down. "I promise you will. And I keep my promises." He bade her farewell in a tired voice. Both knew the crop situation was serious.

The grass crunched with frost as Penelope walked to the orphanage door. All around her, the smell of wood smoke hung in the air.

She knew Sisters Bridget, Rose, the three other sisters who helped run the orphanage, and Cornelia were already up. They rose at dawn each day for a prayer time they called Lauds.

She pushed opened the door, after noticing small icicles hanging from the top of the window recesses. Silence greeted her. Eyes heavy with sleep, she fumbled for paper, pen, and inkwell on the table near the chapel door, and penned a note for the sisters. Onofrio had worked all night and was now asleep at the Taylor house, she wrote. Billy would bring him back after breakfast. Then she stumbled to her room.

Never had a refuge been so welcome. She saw that someone had added extra covers to her bed. She crawled under the quilts with gratitude and without changing.

As sleep hovered, she felt weary but calm. No frayed nerves jangled her, as they sometimes did after a late-night ball. She'd been useful, had joined in a small way a community united in their quest against a foe. She fell asleep with her hand resting on her abdomen.

Penelope awoke with a heaviness and blinked at the brightness of the room. For a moment she wondered where she was. Everything flooded back. She was so tired. And she smelled like smoke.

A light tap sounded on the door.

"Miss Gold, are you awake?"

"Yes, come in. And Cornelia, please call me Penelope."

Cornelia pushed open the door as Penelope shifted to a sitting position. "Since it's too cold to be outdoors today, I wondered if you'd like to sit in the chapel awhile and pray."

That was the last thing Penelope wished to do at that moment. Cornelia drew strength from her daily devotions on a level beyond anything Penelope ever felt called toward.

"You go ahead, Cornelia. I'm still waking up. Being up and down all night fatigued me. And I wish to wash away some of this smokiness."

"We heard of everyone's heroic efforts. Sister Bridget offered our services but Agnes said you had enough help. And, you are said to brew a fine cup of coffee."

Penelope smiled. "My first kitchen skill."

Cornelia made haste to wipe the shock from her face.

"I'm glad I learned," Penelope added. "I also washed dishes. Imagine! And fed kindling into a stove."

Cornelia looked uncertain whether to laugh or nod in sober agreement.

"I'm poking fun at myself, Cornelia. It's all right to laugh. Surely the women in the religious life you're studying for know how to laugh."

"Why, yes, of course we do!" She adjusted her veil, which Penelope had noticed was different than the ones the sisters wore. Theirs were dark-colored, while Cornelia's was light.

"I'll be back in a while to check on you," Cornelia said as she left.

Penelope rolled over and went right back to sleep. She dreamt of setting a towering mound of pancakes, with sausage, biscuits, and gravy, in front of a hungry Nate.

When she woke again, she was refreshed—and hungry—and determined to remove every vestige of pinewood smoke that clung to her. She freshened up thoroughly but quickly in the day's chill, put on a clean dress, and wandered out toward the kitchen.

The orphanage was too quiet. The kitchen was empty. She didn't hear any sounds from the dining room, the classrooms, the dormitories upstairs, or the section of the house that comprised the convent quarters. Odd. It was a weekday. That meant it was a workday.

The older orphans should have been at practice at things like cooking, coopering, sewing, and woodworking. Or they should have been at academic study, but classes didn't seem to be in session. She should be hearing the youngest orphans reciting their diction exercises. The sisters must have taken them all somewhere. Penelope couldn't imagine where, on such a cold day.

She peeled a tangerine, found a chunk of Sister Brigid's sourdough bread, and drew a dipper of water from the large crock on the counter. As she ate, the image of scrambled eggs, bacon, toast, and coffee arose in her mind. Oh, stop, she thought. Unless you plan to fix the meal yourself.

She finished, bundled up and went out in search of someone. Anyone.

The day was crisp, but the sky was as bright as the blue of the birds she'd learned were Florida scrub jays. The early azalea flowers she'd admired were wilted and frizzled from the plunge of temperatures. Their magenta coloring had been transformed to brownish purple.

Cornelia came into view on the path from the Taylor cabin, carrying a sack of something.

"I meant to get back before you got up," Cornelia called as she neared. "Every available person is helping pick the frozen oranges, even the youngsters. I've a bag of fruit here. I came to drop it off for us to juice later. Do you need anything before I go back?"

"No, but I'm going with you."

Cornelia looked hesitant.

"I'm feeling stronger," Penelope insisted. "I can at least brew the coffee, remember?"

As they reached the Taylor house and grove beyond, Penelope understood the breadth of "every available person." People were everywhere. Some climbed up and down ladders and picked fruit off trees, others carted bagfuls to central points, others were already juicing mounds of fruits. She saw Onofrio directing other orphans as though he'd worked at the grove for years.

Smoke drifted from an outdoor bread oven, atop which sat coffee kettles. People on break clustered around a small table piled with coffee cups, fruit that had been harvested before the freeze, and chunks of bread. The group included Fanny Alloway and Professor Art, and Clyde and his wife, Eunice.

Nate clamored down a ladder with a full harvest bag over his shoulder, plunked it down and walked over to the refreshment area just as Penelope and Cornelia got there.

Nate's normal liveliness was muted. He nodded hello but otherwise focused on the coffee.

Fanny watched him with sympathy and nudged the professor.

"Fanny tells me this coming together is how people in Persimmon Hollow act in times of crisis," Professor Art said to Nate.

"I get it," Nate said. "I do. My family and neighborhood act the same. But every single person? All of them?" He sounded exasperated. "Every able-bodied person in all Persimmon Hollow is out in a grove somewhere pulling frozen oranges, grapefruits, and tangerines from trees? It's hard, prof, to understand there isn't a single man available to help me start digging. Time's wasting."

"Too cold to be out at the mounds today, anyway," the professor said. "The wind off the river would run you off within minutes."

"You're getting soft in your dotage, prof," grumbled Nate.

Penelope stifled a gasp at his audacity but the professor grinned.

"Nate, any artifacts out there have been undisturbed for hundreds, maybe thousands, of years," replied Art. "One more day won't make a difference."

"I can tell none of you are trying get ahead in a tough world," Nate said.

"Except perhaps people whose livelihoods depend on getting frozen citrus to market as juice," said Agnes. She'd walked up behind the group and had listened for the last few moments.

"Even the youngest orphans are helping," Penelope added.

Nate looked at her, then Agnes, then the other adults.

"I guess I'm being a horse's behind," Nate finally said.

"Hey! Who is a horse's a—?" Ornofio had come running

when he saw Cornelia and Penelope. He didn't get his last word out before Nate clamped a hand over his mouth.

"A gentleman never uses curse words," Nate said.

Onofrio jerked himself free. "Okay, okay! I come to see if Miss Cornelia or Miss Penelope need help."

"We're fine but thanks for offering," Penelope said. "You're doing a good job and your excellent help is most needed in the groves."

Onofrio straightened under the praise and then bolted back to where youngsters were sorting picked fruits.

"Sometimes I forget other things can be more important than me and my projects," Nate said.

"We all do," said Penelope, and thought suddenly of her baby. *Not now.* She turned toward Agnes. "Did all the citrus freeze last night?"

"Most, yes," Agnes said. "We had a hard freeze." Nate and Penelope exchanged quizzical looks. "That's when temperatures drop below freezing for longer than five hours," Agnes explained. "We were in the twenties for about six hours."

"Word in town is that a lot of people were hit hard," said Clyde. "I reckon we'll all need to pitch in until spring crops come up. Lot of people in need."

Fanny, Art, Eunice, and Agnes murmured agreement. Nate and Penelope's glances met again. No one was that altruistic, thought Penelope, much less an entire town. People helped each other through an immediate crisis but soon drifted back to their own concerns. At least that was her understanding. She saw from Nate's expression it likely was his, too.

But she accepted the conviction she read in the faces of the townspeople. "Anything I can do here?" she asked. "I wouldn't be of much assistance with the fruit, but I can brew coffee."

"I vouch for her—she got pretty good after all that practice last night," Nate said, in a hint of his former self. Penelope was glad to see him happier, and then wondered why.

"You, Penelope, should be indoors," Agnes said, and gave Penelope a questioning glance. "Are you feeling well?"

Before Penelope could answer, Nate did the favor.

"She tells me she's here for her health and it looks like Persimmon Hollow is doing her a world of good," he said. "Her eyes shine. She has good color. She's not thin or frail. Whatever ails you, Miss Gold, the Florida climate seems agreeable for you. That, or, like I said before, being around me could be what cheers you."

Clyde chuckled. But Fanny and Agnes exchanged worried looks.

"Illness isn't always apparent on the outside," Agnes said. "I think it's best that Penelope stays indoors today." She, Fanny, and Eunice gathered the dishes and mugs, handed some to Penelope to carry, and started toward the house.

"When Florida becomes Florida again, I'd be honored to show you my archaeology project, Miss Gold," Nate called after them.

"I'd be delighted," Penelope said over her shoulder. "Antiquities fascinate me."

Nate broke into a wide smile. And worry grew on Agnes and Fanny's faces.

CHAPTER 6

A few weeks later, Penelope joined the Taylor family and the Alloway sisters, the professor, and Clyde for a ride to the river to see Nate's excavation site. Cornelia insisted on accompanying her. Agnes had left little Seth Jr. with Lupita at the house. The weather was perfect, springlike and sweet with the scent of early citrus blossoms. It was hard to believe a harsh freeze had blown through less than a month earlier.

Her melancholy had lifted. Penelope had expected it to worsen—given how her body gave constant reminders of her circumstances. But something about the Florida sun—even when cold outdoors—cheered her. And all this sky. Everywhere, all around her, the Florida sky stretched and embraced her with bright blues and whispery clouds of pearl and ivory.

Best of all, the people who surrounded her made her feel welcomed and at ease. Their lack of pretension was refreshing.

Her days had fallen into a familiar pattern. She rose early, attended prayers with the sisters and orphans, joined them for breakfast, and took a morning walk. She then returned to her room, studied Italian for an hour, and then went outdoors when the weather permitted, to read her books about Italy's history, art, and culture.

After lunch, she napped, and then sketched, painted, or went calling on the handful of people she knew. She joined the sisters and orphans at evening prayer, dinner, and quiet conversation in the orphanage anteroom that doubled as a sitting room. She'd even joined them for Mass in town when the priest was able to visit Persimmon Hollow. She'd found peace in that Mass and in her daily prayers and routines.

The only thing she'd been recalcitrant about was writing letters. She'd sent a couple to family and none to social acquaintances or Herman. No one had written to her. So be it. She wouldn't let their silences ruin her days.

"Here we are," Clyde said, as he guided the wagon off the narrow trail they'd traveled through riverine woodland. He stopped in an open area that paralleled the riverfront.

Penelope stared.

"Everyone told me Florida didn't have any hills," she said. Yet before her, at an angle to her at the edge of the river, was a sandy mound a good ten or twelve feet tall. It rose with a rounded shape a few feet back from the water's edge, and appeared to stretch for a good hundred or more feet. Clyde's wagon couldn't have traveled any farther without running into it.

The mound sloped down to the level ground at the river's edge. Beyond was the tannin-colored river and opposite was a small island. Penelope saw another large mound hug the perimeter of the island.

She heard Nate and a handful of support workers and looked upward. They were high atop the mound in front of her. The hill was so old that trees, shrubs, and tangled undergrowth had taken firm root along its slope and even on top of it.

Nate saw them, stuck his shovel in the ground, leaned on it, and waved down at them. "Take that path through the woods and come around the back side of the mound," he called. He pointed toward a break in the trees and thickets at ground level. "You'll find a gentle incline that winds its way up here. Just follow the trail."

Penelope felt she were in a magical world as they entered the tangled hammock vegetation of the mound. It was lush, shady, and degrees cooler than the ambient air of the wagon ride. Unfamiliar flora surrounded her, but she soon learned names from the others.

Tall palmetto trees grew steps away from bare-limbed cypress trees from which Spanish moss dangled in wispy gray tendrils. Lichen-covered oak tree trunks shared territory with hickory, persimmon, and sweetbay magnolia trees. Lower-growing yaupon holly bushes, spiky palmettos, and wax myrtle shrubs bordered the leafy, sandy path. Tangled vines grew up and across trees and shrubs, and ferns carpeted crevices. At times the visitors had to walk single file.

Penelope inhaled the tangy smell of the river that greeted them when they rounded curves adjacent to the placid waterway. She was amazed to see full-grown trees show up as they followed the path upward.

"How old is this hill?" she asked.

"Tustenuggee says it's called a mound and it's hundreds of years old," said Billy Taylor as he led the group.

"Who?"

"Seth's closest friend," said Agnes. "He's part Seminole, hence the name. He lives at the grove when he's in this part of the state."

"In a chickee," added Polly. "That's what his house is called. Wow, look at this fern." She halted the whole group, stooped, and inspected the soft lime fronds of a young bird's nest fern growing on the bank of a moist depression just off the trail.

"Take notes for a science lesson," suggested Agnes, ever the former schoolteacher. She home-schooled Polly and Billy in most academics, sent them to the orphanage for religious education, and had them enrolled them in Persimmon Hollow Academy for music, art, and advanced science.

Penelope was glad for the break. She felt well, but had to admit she tired more easily than normal for her. She was also very aware of her growing size, hide it though she still tried.

"A chickee is what? A type of tent or house?" she asked Polly.

Billy and Polly talked over themselves in explaining Tustenuggee's housing in more detail than Penelope needed to hear. She tried to visualize an open-sided wood platform with a roof made of palm fronds. It would make a lovely sketch, she thought, a unique shelter set amid the semi-tropical flora of the region. She was glad she'd brought her pencils and a pad out with her today. Even more glad that Billy had offered to carry them on the trail.

Penelope made a mental note to send for more watercolor paints and better paper and brushes. The request for supplies would force her to write again to her silent family. She wondered what stories they were sharing in society regarding her "overseas travels."

They reached the top of the tree-covered mound. Penelope was surprised at how level the ground was and how large and overgrown the space.

Nate stood in a roped-off clearing in a large rectangle of earth dug from a section of the mound. He and his crew had dug a pit about twelve feet wide and three times as long. She guessed it had a depth of about six inches near where she stood. But Nate and his crew were gradually digging much deeper in other sections. Some squared-off pits within the larger rectangle were several feet deep.

Nate looked so different in workaday denims with sand and leaf debris clinging to the fabric. He wore an old white shirt with sleeves rolled halfway up to his elbows, and he'd tied a band of fabric around his forehead to keep sweat from dripping. Nearby, his assistants measured off another rectangle of ground and prepared to mark and rope it.

Amid the hellos, Nate zeroed his attention onto Penelope.

"You're looking well today," he enthused as he bent his leg over a low barrier rope and walked over to meet them. His gaze drew Penelope out from the group. She saw him scan her figure and she gave thanks for what her voluminous cloak and shawls could still mask.

"This Florida sun and air can cure anything, I'm convinced," Nate said. "Come, let me give you a tour."

He climbed out of the pit, started to take her hand, thought twice about it, and instead indicated that she follow him toward his nearby study and worktable area. Penelope suddenly found Cornelia pasted to her side. Agnes and Fanny proclaimed sudden interest in the archaeology project they'd hardly mentioned to Penelope, and clustered on her other side. The others in the excursion group also gathered.

"Of course, yes, I mean all of you," Nate said. He spread his arms wide and launched into a lengthy explanation of the project.

Polly soon interrupted. "Did you find any ancient stuff yet, Nate? Bones? Hey, what kind of ferns are those?" She grabbed Nate's arm and pulled him to the edge of the rectangle, where another fern bank beneath a hickory tree was visible just outside the work area.

Agnes sighed and turned toward the Alloway sisters. "Fanny, I know you and Eunice have told me that ladies on the frontier need multiple skills that go beyond traditional roles. But Polly is becoming a handful. Even something acceptable such as fern study becomes a wilderness expedition for her. I'm almost at my wits' end with her forward behavior."

Penelope listened as she unpacked her sketchpad and pencils. Her opinion was that Polly would turn out just fine. She looked around for a place to spread her blanket. She noticed Cornelia already seated beneath a tree, at prayer while holding a string of beads evenly spaced on a circular string. A crucifix and a smaller cluster of beads hung from a short piece of straight string attached to the circular one.

"Polly is excited about ferns, and botanical subjects are one of my interests," Penelope said to Agnes. "Would you like me to teach her to sketch and perhaps create watercolors of them? I'm more skilled at art than I am in the kitchen."

"I'd appreciate that," Agnes said. "I'm always reminded how much I still don't know about Polly, despite having tended her from babyhood at the orphanage. Polly has considered herself an adult since about age ten. Now that she's getting older her head-strong ways are surfacing more and more."

"You were raised at the orphanage here?" Penelope asked Agnes.

"On, no," Agnes said. "The orphanage was in New York. After I was already in Florida teaching school, the orphanage lost its property and was forced to close. That prompted Seth and me to help them resettle a branch of it here."

"Ah, I wondered how the orphanage came to be here," Penelope said. "As for Polly," she said and glanced at the energetic teen, "as she matures, she'll likely face the same hard lessons the rest of us have encountered."

"Would that I could protect her," Agnes said. "Polly!" She raised her voice and called her.

"Yes'm?" Polly came back over with Nate.

"Miss Gold has offered to give you art lessons."

Polly cast an unimpressed look at the art materials.

"Your ferns," said Penelope. "Art is a way to preserve them."

"I already do that," Polly said. "I dry them, press them, and mount them on paper. Why bother painting a picture of them?"

Penelope had a hint of clarity about what Agnes faced. What must it be like to have a daughter on the edge of womanhood? She thought again of her baby and wished she knew whether it were a boy or a girl. Her constant attempts to remain detached grew more difficult by the day. Especially now that her body was thickening rapidly. Her secret would be out soon, no matter how tightly she laced her maternity corset and no matter how many cloaks and shawls she draped around herself.

"You're an artist?!" Nate walked closer, as happy as Polly was dubious. "Wow, thank you, Lord Jesus, this is my day, my month, my year!"

All heads turned toward him.

"I need an artist to record my finds," he said. "Come! Look at what we've unearthed already!"

He led them back to tables in the shade beyond the main area of work. On one were buckets and wood-frame sifters fitted with screens of different sizes. Next to them were small shards and chips of objects unrecognizable to everyone but Nate. Another table contained more of the objects.

He pointed to a small dark square that had a burlap-type weave etched on it. "Pottery shards," he exclaimed. "And this," he indicated a slender bone, "was likely a bone pin." Down the collection of artifacts he went, one by one, describing a chip of an arrowhead, another broken bit of pottery, seeds, a few dried berries.

Penelope was underwhelmed. The others appeared to feel the same, except Professor Art. His eyes were large and alight.

"You've found all this, already?!" He and Nate bent their heads over the items.

Polly scampered off to inspect more ferns. The other adults wandered off to watch an excavation section being expanded, except for Cornelia, who remained seated under the tree, eyes closed and hands moving over the beads in a rhythmic pace. Billy stood off to one side, where he'd been the entire time. Interested, watchful, but stand-offish.

Penelope stayed put. Antiquities intrigued her, but she equated them with Roman ruins and Egyptian pyramids, not two-inch pottery shards. Yet the professor and Nate's professional interest told her something important was taking place. It was one of the most interesting things she'd encountered in Persimmon Hollow and she planned to learn more.

Before she asked for more details, Billy came forward, took his hands out of his jeans pockets and seemed to be scrounging up courage.

"You ain't found any bodies yet, I hope," he said. "No human bones?"

Nate looked up in surprise. "No, not yet. I hope to. What an impressive find that would be. Even loose bones can advance study. I'd measure them and record differences and similarities. And to find a complete skeleton? Wow. Analysis could tell us much about the primitives who once lived here."

"They weren't primitives," Billy shouted. The conversations going on around them stopped. The small party coalesced around the table again. Seth put an arm on Billy's shoulder.

"Everything all right, son? It's impolite to shout at a man doing his job."

Billy shook his shoulder free.

"Tustenuggee says his ancestors are buried here. Says it's not right for other people to dig them up for fun."

"Not fun," Nate shook his head. "It's an attempt to understand. But rest easy. I don't think we'll find human remains right here. This section seems to be where food remains and daily-use items were discarded. No one would bury their dead with food refuse."

He gave Billy a serious look.

"I mean no disrespect to anyone's ancestors," Nate said.

Billy slouched off.

"May I ask what Tustenuggee's role in Persimmon Hollow is?" Nate said to the others.

"We'll explain while we eat," said Agnes, taking charge. Cornelia sprang up to help her, Fanny, and Eunice set out the picnic foodstuffs. Penelope discovered she was, once again, famished.

Nate received the full rundown of who was who in Persimmon Hollow as they savored cold chicken, coleslaw, pound cake, and lemonade. The explanations helped refresh Penelope's knowledge, too. Afterward, Nate stretched out beneath the massive canopy of the live oak tree against which Penelope had sat down and leaned against. He watched as she adjusted her sketchpad on a small laptop desk.

"I was serious, before," he said. "Would you be interested in sketching my finds? You could make a little money. I have a small discretionary fund."

"Money's not an object," she said, while making a few sketch lines to test the sketch pad's incline.

"Of course. I forgot."

"No, I meant, there's no need to pay me. I'd be happy to draw them. I'm thankful for ways to fill up my time here."

"The fresh air would be good for you and could help heal your ailments," he said.

"If this excavation is as rich in artifacts as you hope, I'll get many good doses of this healthful air," she said.

"There might be enough to warrant an illustrated essay," Nate said, reading the cue from her circumspect reply.

She looked up, intrigued. "Publication in an academic journal would benefit your career."

"Without a doubt."

"Nate, I can't commit to sketching enough to accompany an in-depth research report, at least I can't commit right now, but I'll take it under consideration."

"That's all I ask," he said. "Your health comes first."

Penelope focused on her pad. She began to sketch the luncheon group mingling on the main blanket. She had a firm hand and good eye, and the image took shape quickly.

"Have you ever thought of drawing professionally?" Nate asked.

She glanced up, surprised.

"No, never. Why would I?"

"To be independent," Nate said.

"Ah, as in, not dependent on anyone," she said. "Really, it's not anything I need to worry about. My family isn't evil or mean."

And I don't have a husband, she thought. Yet. Unless someone forced Herman to accept responsibility and ask for her hand. The idea grew more distasteful by the day. The chasm created by his silence—and hers—was growing cluttered with newfound awareness and convictions. The more she observed the couples around her, the more she understood what a partner-ship of marriage could really mean. It wasn't anything she and Herman shared.

"May I ask why there isn't anyone here with you?" Nate asked. "If anyone in my family gets sick, a crowd gathers around them. Not even an invading army could get through. It's amazing the ill person doesn't suffocate for lack of air circulation."

Penelope's pencil stilled. How to answer? It wasn't his busi-ness. She could sense the concern behind his inquiry. And she minded his question less than she had the last time he started to pry. But they were still only acquaintances.

A part of her didn't want him to know, wanted to keep him at bay about her condition as long as possible. She swallowed as she realized why. She didn't want to lose their budding friend-ship or his admiration.

"My family knew I'd be in good hands with the Sisters of St. Francis," she said.

Nate had sat up and let his arms dangle over his drawn-up knees. "Not even a companion? Or a maid? A woman like you? I can tell quality. You're the real thing."

He flopped back against the tree. "Shut up, Nate, mind your own business," he grumbled to himself.

A chuckle escaped Penelope. "Cornelia was tasked with being my companion and she does a good job," she said. "The sisters thought it'd be a good interlude for her as she discerns whether a vocation to religious life is real or a false ideal."

"She's a quiet one, Cornelia is."

"But a true warm spirit," Penelope said. "Sister Bridget said she rivals Agnes and Agnes's friend, Sarah Bight, in her knowledge of scripture. Mrs. Bight, her husband, and family were the orphanage caretakers but they live in town now. Sarah's husband opened a carpentry and furniture shop. I haven't met them yet."

"I'm still getting everyone sorted out myself," Nate said. "Every time I think I have the network of people in town figured out, more show up."

"I know what you mean!"

"I'm glad we can sort it out together," he said. "Makes me feel less like an outsider."

When she didn't immediately answer, he rose. "The ancients are calling me. Back to my shovel and trowel." He looked down at her sketch. "You were serious about considering doing illustrations of the finds, yes?"

Penelope nodded.

"It could be a daily task, if the pace of discoveries keeps up," Nate said. "Maybe you could come out again tomorrow, any time you like? I'm here from just after sunup to near sundown."

She looked up, and with her hand shaded the sun from her eyes. "I look forward to it."

Nate's eyes so reflected his happiness that he hardly needed to add the, "I do, too."

CHAPTER 7

A return letter from Penelope's family contained both surprises and a dull constancy. It arrived tucked in a parcel of paints, watercolor paper, camel's hair brushes, and a new Italian language book. All of it the best money could buy.

Penelope sat at her desk and read in the sunlight that streamed through her corner bedroom's windows. In the past, a letter with such a chill tone would have tugged at her melancholia. But recently, she'd rarely felt blue. How different from when she'd wintered before at the Alloway House with her two brothers and their wives.

That had been a forced vacation. Even watching drama unfold around her in the love triangle of seamstress Josefa Gomez, her wealthy but disagreeable suitor, and the patient carpenter Ben Stillman hadn't shaken off her lethargy during that visit.

Herman's impassioned letters during that period were in sharp contrast to his current silence. She was glad, now, that she'd burned all his correspondence before leaving Boston. Her head must have known before her heart that he wasn't the upright man she'd tried to imagine him to be.

She wondered what had become of the three lovers in the Persimmon Hollow drama, and hoped the outcome had been happier than her own. She made a mental note to ask Fanny Alloway for an update.

Thinking about the seamstress reminded Penelope that her dresses needed to be let out. Her corset stays were tied as loosely as possible, but her clothes were strained to the breaking point. Florida agreed with her. Apparently, so did being *enceinte*.

She turned her attention back to the letter from her stepmother:

"Your grandmother and I saw Herman at the opera with another woman. He took pains to avoid us, but we were able to observe them with our glasses. He is quite despicable. We also spoke with the woman who leads the Ladies' Improvement Society—her name escapes me. She insists you present a program on your European travels when you return home. Use the enclosed materials wisely to prepare appropriate watercolors of ruins and vistas of the Italian countryside. Be diligent about Italian language practice and inquire whether any others—quality winter visitors perhaps?—have knowledge of the language. You could converse and hone verbal skills."

Penelope lowered the letter for a moment and smiled. She pictured Onofrio talking circles around her in Italian. *Yes, my dear stepmother,* she thought, *I have found someone with whom to converse.*

She picked up the correspondence again.

"I have no need to repeat to you the seriousness of your situation and the discretion that must be entertained so our name and standing aren't compromised and your position in society remains secure," her stepmother penned. "A presentation before a small, reputable gathering is exactly the type of quiet assurance needed for us to retain dignity in the face of questions. Your sudden departure has raised suspicions. So far we have been able to counter them with vague excuses about your health."

On and on the letter went with remonstrations, reminders, and reprimands about her inexcusable behavior. Penelope had tried to explain everything that had happened, on the day her situation exploded into the open. She'd fled home from the abortion facility Herman had tricked her into visiting. She'd been so distraught her words had tumbled out in a jumble. Perhaps her story hadn't made complete sense. Even she still questioned, sometimes, how Herman had managed to compromise her virtue. Memories of the day he'd forced himself on her were foggy, as though she'd experienced what happened through some kind of mist.

Enough, she thought, and rose. *This sunshine calls for a walk.* She wished Nate would find more artifacts so that she'd have reason to visit the excavation more frequently. She decided to stroll to the Taylor house. The homestead was always alive with activity. That, and the sunshine and exercise, would dispel the dark thoughts that troubled her. She checked her watch. If she left now, Cornelia—busy assisting at religious education class—wouldn't feel compelled to accompany her. The young woman did enough.

But the disturbing memories lingered. Agnes greeted Penelope at the door of the Taylor house with a smile soon followed by a look of concern.

"If you'd like to talk, I'm a good listener," Agnes said. "Come in."

But Penelope had already sunk into a cushioned rocking chair on the porch. "I'm not usually so transparent," she said.

"My past has made me sensitive to others who may have experienced harsh situations," Agnes said. She appeared to choose her words carefully as she sat down in a chair opposite Penelope. "Plus, I'm aware of your situation. It is, shall we say, *unusual?*"

Penelope inhaled deeply, closed her eyes for a few seconds,

but didn't speak. Agnes filled the breach with a murmured prayer.

REMEMBER, *most loving Virgin Mary,*
never was it heard
that anyone who turned to you for help
was left unaided.
Inspired by this confidence,
though burdened by my sins,
I run to your protection
for you are my mother.
Mother of the Word of God,
do not despise my words of pleading
but be merciful and hear my prayer.
Amen.

PENELOPE OPENED HER EYES. "What a beautiful prayer."

"The Memorare," said Agnes.

"I could do with some mercy," said Penelope.

"Our Lord grants mercy without question, and his mother helps guide you closer to him," Agnes said.

"Extra help is welcome," Penelope said. "My past is haunting me today."

She dove in without further preamble. "Herman, the man who wronged me, was smooth and urbane. Sometimes his wooing pushed boundaries. I'd always resist. And he appeared to accept the rules of decency."

She gazed out over the landscape, to settle herself before revealing the details.

"Everything changed the day of an autumn hayride to an apple farm in the Massachusetts countryside," Penelope said. "It started as an enjoyable time. We didn't know our companions in the wagon but all were friendly. We were driven through the orchard, stopped to pick apples, then returned to a clearing for refreshments. I got out and mingled with the others while Herman went to get beverages."

She inhaled and let out the breath in a long swoosh.

"I remember becoming woozy after drinking the cider he brought me. All of a sudden, I felt thick and slow and had difficulty talking. And walking. As though my balance were off. I tried to step away from the crowd to find more air, and almost fell."

Florida receded as the past loomed in Penelope's mind.

"Herman quickly propped me up. He insisted we take a walk so I could breathe in the country air. Promised he'd aid me."

She gave a strangled half-laugh.

"Instead, he half-dragged me away from the others and into the open door of a barn that was some distance away. A dim bell of warning penetrated my fogged brain but my limbs couldn't respond. I needed Herman's support just to keep from collapsing."

Agnes kept her kind gaze on Penelope.

"A short time later—or maybe a long time?—the warning alarm in my mind signaled again. I realized, from the faraway sound of bells jangling on a horse, that the hay wagon was departing. It was probably headed back toward the farmhouse on the far side of the orchard, where the ride had started. The wagon was leaving and were weren't on it.

"I panicked when I found myself incapable of calling out for the driver to wait. I couldn't move with any kind of coordination or speed. My tongue was thick and I had trouble forming words. I tugged on Herman's arm and tried to gesture. He kept up a low flow of platitudes and flatteries that made no sense to me.

"The next thing I remember, he half carried, half dragged me deeper into the barn. He shoved me into the back of an empty wagon like the one we'd been on."

Penelope's well of reserve faltered. She gripped the arms of her chair and looked directly at Agnes instead of out into the yard.

"Oh, Agnes, I was so addled and confused. I fought, or tried to, but my resistance was ineffective against his strength. He pushed me down and I sank in a strange dizziness. It's odd, but I remember little things, like how thin streams of sunlight penetrated the barn slats and how dust from the hay swirled in the beams. I smelled the horses and hay and then got a strong whiff of alcohol as Herman's face moved into close view. His weight pressed on me.

"I must have fainted. The next thing I recall is that I awakened with a headache, mussed clothes, and a painful soreness. My horrified realization quickly followed."

Penelope bowed her head and sob escaped her, the first she'd ever shed over what happened.

Agnes was out of her chair. She stood behind Penelope and placed her hands on her shoulders. "Perhaps you'd wish to continue later?" she asked. "How about some tea now?"

Penelope's training kicked in. She straightened up. "Yes, to the tea, but no to stopping. I feel relieved getting this out. Unless you're tired of listening."

"No, of course not," Agnes said. "You rest for a moment and I'll be back soon with tea and some pound cake."

Penelope rocked and listened to the chirp of sparrows. A rhythmic pecking sound drew her gaze to a red-tufted woodpecker on a tall, remnant stump of an oak. It was twice the size of any woodpecker she'd ever seen. Closer to her, a red geranium bloomed in a container on the porch steps. *Someone must have protected it from that freeze,* she thought.

By the time Agnes returned, the Florida warmth and beauty had started to restore Penelope's equilibrium.

"Even tea and pound cake are more flavorful in this setting," Penelope said, and soon felt able to resume her story.

"My dismay grew as my mind cleared. Herman had the audacity to act solicitous as he helped me out of the wagon in the barn. But he grew irritated when I accused him of violating me. He insisted I'd been a willing participant. Even tried to place the blame on me. Gone were his flattery and concern. He barked at me to make myself presentable while he thought up a story about why we'd been left behind when the wagon rumbled off. Anger started bubbling atop my dismay but I thought it best to stay calm until we were back among other people.

"As he hastened me out of the barn, we both saw a driver and wagon coming toward us. Our absence must have been noticed and a rider sent back for us. The bored adolescent driver didn't look at us as we climbed aboard and Herman made lame excuses. The boy hardly seemed to listen. Herman prattled about how I'd been sick to my stomach and how he tended to me and gave me privacy from the others.

"A week later, seemingly contrite, Herman showed up at my house seeking forgiveness. I wasn't willing to extend it. A week after that, I missed my normally very regular monthly flow. Worry began to flood me. A month later, when I again failed to menstruate, I confronted him with the news."

A small voice from inside the house interrupted. "Mama. Mama? Mama! I'm hungry."

Agnes got up and cast an apologetic glance at Penelope. "Little Seth. He's awake early from his nap."

"Maaaammmmaa."

"I've taken enough of your time," Penelope said, and also rose.

"No, please stay," Agnes said. "Come inside. Seth won't pay us any mind as soon as I put a snack in front of him. He'll have as much fun studying his food as eating it."

True enough, the little boy was fascinated with the peeled tangerine sections Agnes gave him. Penelope watched as he inspected each piece, squished some of them, poked others, and got as much on him as in him.

Her heart tugged when he gave her and Agnes the widest smile after making a show of chewing and swallowing. "Hooray!" he called out, and waved his arms.

"He knows he's cute," Agnes said, and Penelope saw the mother's love in her eyes.

The sound of a wagon rolling up in front of the house caught their attention. Footsteps on the porch were followed by a knock on the door.

"Hello! Anybody home?"

"Josefa!" Agnes said. "She and Ben are back!" She picked up Seth and headed toward the front door. "You remember them? Come say hello."

Penelope followed. So, Josefa and Ben were a couple. Here was her answer about the love triangle she'd seen on her earlier visit. Penelope automatically put a hand up to check her chignon. She stood a few steps apart as Agnes and little Seth greeted Josefa and Ben with hugs and kisses.

Read Josefa and Ben's story in Stitching A Life in Persimmon Hollow

---

"Josefa, you remember Penelope Gold?" Agnes said, waving Penelope closer. "She stayed at the Alloway House on a previous visit. She's back in town for another stay."

"Why, yes, Miss Gold!" said Josefa. "It's so good to see you. I'm happy you've returned to us."

They hugged, and Josefa drew back. "You look in good health," she said. "I know, it's Persimmon Hollow. It works magic on us all. You remember my husband, Ben? I mean, he wasn't my husband then, but he is now."

Josefa looked up at Ben. Penelope could almost feel the intensity of the love-filled glance that passed between the young couple. A sense of loss tugged at her, loss for something she'd never had and no longer saw on the horizon.

"We've been visiting Ben's family in St. Augustine," Josefa said as Ben bowed and said hello to Penelope.

"We returned soon as we could when we heard the freeze had reached this far south," Ben said. "We've all got a lot to do now."

"What are your plans?" Agnes asked.

"Aside from coaxing my damaged nursery stock to health— although I'm lucky, most of mine were protected or are dormant —we want to help neighbors and townsfolk who took the hardest hits," he said.

"Aunt Lupita wrote me that Agnes wants to stage a theatrical to raise funds," Josefa said to Penelope. "I'm going to make the costumes. Penelope, did you bring your sketchpads and paints with you? I remember how much you sketched and how little you spoke when you last visited. Perhaps you could paint the backdrops?"

Josefa warmed to her idea.

"I'm sure others would help," she continued. "You'd need only supervise if you wish. No need to tax yourself. Are your brothers and sisters-in-law in town with you again? Do you think they'd like to be involved? It's quite an undertaking, what Agnes is proposing. But that's never stopped her from anything."

Ben rose from where he'd squatted to show little Seth a toy he'd brought him. It spun across the floor after being twirled in place.

"Miss Gold, be forewarned," Ben said. "When the Persimmon Hollow women get busy on a mission, nothing stands in their way."

"And where is my Aunt Lupita?" Josefa asked Agnes, and

looked around and behind her. "I expected her to be here with you."

"She's at the orphanage today, teaching embroidery," Agnes said. "She loves guiding the little ones through their stitches."

"Ah, I'll see her there," Josefa said. "We plan to stop there next." She twirled toward Penelope. "I'm sure the children would love to paint the backdrops for a theatrical."

Tracking the shifting conversation forced Penelope to focus beyond her own woes.

"My family isn't here with me this time," she said, her first chance to get in the answer. "And, if I can fit scenery work around the sketching I'm doing for Nate, I'd be glad to help."

"Nate, who's Nate?" asked Josefa.

"He's a visiting archaeologist who's excavating a shell mound on the riverside, near Hontoon Island," Penelope said.

"See, see how much we've missed," said Josefa, with a tug on Ben's sleeve. But Ben was staring at Penelope.

"Is Professor Art involved?" At Penelope's nod, he looked at Josefa, his face alight. "I need to get up there and explore any botanical discoveries."

Josefa laughed. "Yes, we must. I knew you'd say that. Penelope, when are you next going? Why not now? After we stop at the orphanage, I mean. You can introduce us to Nate."

Agnes answered for them all. "It's too late for the journey there and back this afternoon. Penelope's already had a long day. A better idea would be for you to give her a ride back to the orphanage with you. She's staying there."

"At the orphanage? Not in town?" blurted out Josefa, then covered her mouth with her hand. "Forgive me. Not my business. We'd be delighted to give you a ride."

Agnes smoothed the moment by drawing attention to little Seth. He chortled every time he managed to spin the toy the way Ben showed him.

"It's good to be back," said Josefa, and sighed. "Only one

thing could make this homecoming better." A shadow crossed her olive-skinned face as her glance followed little Seth. "One of them."

Penelope's hand unconsciously went to her abdomen. Her life would be much easier if she could trade with Josefa. She opened her mouth then closed it, astonished. She'd come within inches of saying it aloud.

Seth toddled to pick up the toy that had spun out of reach, stumbled, stubbed his toe, sat down, and started to howl.

"That's my cue to say good-bye," Ben said.

Penelope hugged Agnes. "Thank you. I feel as though a weight has been lifted."

"Anytime," Agnes said, and waved the trio off.

Penelope explained more about Nate's project on the short trip to the orphanage. By the time she veered off toward her room while Ben and Josefa went in search of Lupita, the sisters, and the orphans, Penelope felt she'd gained new friends. Even more, she yearned to see Nate. He was quickly becoming the closest new friend of all.

But none of these new friends knew her secret. Yet.

AN UNSMILING CORNELIA stood in the doorway minutes after Penelope sat down at her desk and removed her hat. Cornelia obviously wrestled with whatever she was about to say.

Penelope came to her rescue. "I should have told you what I was doing. I will, in the future."

Cornelia planted herself in the rocking chair in the corner of the room. "We worry about your health."

"I'm fine, really," Penelope said. "I'm just going to rest awhile." Agnes had been correct. It had been a long afternoon. She felt drained of energy.

"You do that," Cornelia said. "I'll sit right here and recite my rosary."

Fatigue settled on Penelope as soon as she sat down on the bed. She removed her shoes and laid atop the covers and closed her eyes.

In the silence, Cornelia's murmured prayers ebbed and flowed with a quiet regularity. Penelope grew calm listening to the repetitions. She'd have to ask Cornelia to teach her this rosary, this prayerful meditation that had such power to soothe.

CHAPTER 8

"There, what do you think?" Penelope held up the sketch of a bone Nate was certain had once been used as a hairpin. "I still can't figure how they twisted it to stay in their hair."

Nate shielded his eyes from the sun with one hand and closed, in a few quick steps, the yards that separated the two of them.

"Another fine example by the talented Penelope Gold. Are you sure you don't want to illustrate the paper I'm writing?"

"Maybe. I'm still thinking about it," Penelope said, but followed her words with a smile. She'd come to appreciate the comfortable relationship they'd developed. She wondered if Nate realized how much his optimistic outlook and cheerful perseverance did for her spirits. She felt better able to face life's troubles just being around him.

"Actually, Nate, I'm drawing so much out here, you'll have more than enough to choose from for your paper," she said.

Nate's eyes brightened. "True. But as I develop the text, I might need overview sketches or specific details." He hesitated for half a beat. "And more opportunities to be with you."

She glanced up and caught the admiration in his gaze.

"Just wanted to see if you were listening," he said. "No, not really. That's an excuse. I meant what I said."

"Oh, Nate," she said, but she'd felt a shiver of warmth at his flirtation. Then steeled herself against the emotion. She focused on her art to break the exchange between them.

Nate loped back to the corner of dirt that was his current focus. He was certain that if he just dug long enough, he'd uncover the one artifact that could advance the world's knowledge of past civilizations.

He was adamant that everything be handled with respect and recorded for prosperity. She'd detailed each shard, broken bit of bone, and cucurbit seed cluster that came up in the pails of dirt. Nate etched faint, neat lines in the corner of each illustration and jotted down artifact name, number, and field notes. He had a strong, even hand. No doubts, no uncertainties.

"Hey! I think I might have something!" Nate hollered. Penelope didn't immediately reply or even lift her gaze. Nate became euphoric over everything his trowel encountered.

The riverside mound was a place of tranquil beauty, she admitted as much, but the St. Johns River valley was no Italy. The "valley" was a slight incline. No Forum or Roman Colosseum dotted the landscape, no frescoes adorned church walls. The archaeological finds were small and broken and, for the most part, seemed rather uninspiring.

His exclamations finally got her attention. Nate and the townsmen he'd hired to help with the project were clustered around a chipped piece of a something, she couldn't tell what. She rose and walked the short distance from shade to sunny worksite.

The object was a jagged shard of wood, perhaps four inches long, with hatch marks that might have been meant to mimic feathers. It was hard to tell.

"By the sounds of you, I expected to see something along the lines of a buried village, like Pompeii," Penelope said.

"No, but what a piece!" Nate said, all seriousness. "Looks like a wing to a bird effigy. Or possibly the stem of a pipe. Or part of some kind of totem? With luck, the rest of it won't be far away. I can sense it!"

His face spoke of hope and excitement. She took the piece with care. "Let me sketch it while you keep digging," she said.

She settled back in her spot and inhaled the warm air awash with the scents of citrus blossoms and jasmine flowers. Her hand went again to her abdomen. Love and protectiveness surged in her.

She quickly figured numbers in her head. Just past five months now. As her body thickened and rounded, she'd begun to feel an even deeper bond with the baby. She was thankful most people attributed her growing rotundness to regained health...or seemed to accept it as that. She dressed carefully to give that impression. Everyone knew she was in town for her health. They'd seen other recovering invalids grow stout as they healed.

Her routine had become so pleasant. She dreaded the inevitable upheaval that would occur when her stoutness was seen for what it was.

Would Nate still ask for her assistance then, she wondered as she peered at the latest discovery. She drew the shard, taking care to record every detail of the etching that indeed looked to her like a bird's feathers. She set down her pencil after she finished and leaned back in her chair. The focus and the ambience had lulled her into a relaxed heaviness.

More shouts from the excavation pit roused her.

"Penelope! You gotta see this!" Nate hollered.

He and the workers were grouped in a corner of the pit, now about four feet deep. Penelope got up and moved closer. This time even Cornelia walked over.

"What is it?" Penelope called. She shook off Nate's offer of assistance to step down into the work area. The last thing she wanted was for his hand to encircle her now-thick middle.

Penelope stepped downward into the pit on an incline carved in the sand, gasped, and stopped. Movement! The baby moved! She opened and closed her mouth, swallowed, felt tears in her eyes, and then tried to get a grip on her unexpected reaction. She closed her eyes for a moment. She couldn't, just couldn't, get too close to this little one. Yet another part of her shouted that it was already too late.

"Are you okay?" Nate asked, an urgent note in his voice. He was beside her in seconds and put a hand on her arm to steady her. "Careful. You seemed to be doing so well these past weeks. Here, sit down over here. No, wait."

He grabbed a canvas cover from another section of the excavation pit and draped it over the soil at the edge, so Penelope could sit at ground level with her feet in the pit. He and Cornelia eased her down.

"Truly, I'm all right," Penelope said with a weak laugh. "Don't mind me. I rose too quickly and walked over here too fast. Please, let me see what you discovered."

Nate bolted back to where he'd been digging.

Penelope knew she was fiercely attached to the life growing inside her. She refused to look ahead, to when she'd have to leave her infant behind. At the same time, she'd started judging every person she met in Persimmon Hollow as to their worthiness as an adoptive parent, should her baby end up with one of them.

From what she remembered of her stepmother and grandmother's explanations, the sisters at the orphanage would keep the baby until he or she was settled in a secure home—with generous financial support from the Gold family, she was sure. Penelope wondered how much of a donation her grandmother had already made to St. Isidore's. It was an orphanage, not a home for unwed mothers.

"Wow!" Nate's voice was a welcome intrusion. "Penelope, this has to be seen right here, before the pieces are removed. It's amazing. I'll call out what I see. Try to visualize everything."

"I can walk over there," she insisted. She planted her feet with firmness and got up with Cornelia's help.

"Careful. Polly, Billy, help her and Cornelia," Nate ordered the two youths who'd just arrived at the work site. The two self-proclaimed Persimmon Hollow Excavation Assistants made haste to get to the excavation each day after their studies.

"Sure, what's up?" Billy asked, as Penelope waved off the extra hands.

"I'm fine," she said. "Go assist Nate." Nate and his workers were methodically yet quickly clearing a section of a flat piece of wood set across sawhorses. It functioned as a dig-adjacent work-table and was covered with artifacts, screens, brushes, and trowels.

"Careful, don't let anything get out of order," Nate said. "Billy, get Miss Gold's stool. If she can, she must make a quick sketch of this finding *in situ*."

"*In situ*, what the heck does that mean?" Polly asked Billy.

"Dunno, but I aim to find out. Keep an eye out for any kind of human bones or skulls or stuff like that."

"I will. Do you think Nate knows we'll tell Tustenuggee?"

Billy shrugged. "Don't know and don't care."

"Nate's a nice guy. Mom and Dad really like him. So do the Alloways and Clyde 'n all. Penelope really seems to like him."

Billy shrugged again. "Don't care. Tustenuggee's ancestors are more important. How many times did we hear in religion class that cemeteries are sacred places? This is kinda a cemetery, near as I can figure."

"Your hero the professor brought Nate here, you know," Polly prodded.

"Whose side are you on anyway?"

Polly pursed her lips. "Maybe there's a way not to take sides. Maybe this can work for everybody. That's what Mom would try to do, find a way to make everybody get along."

Billy didn't answer. Both turned their gazes back toward the unfolding excavation drama. "It is exciting, though, being like a spy and making sure no bones pop up and get taken away," Polly said, as she helped Billy fold up and transport the stool. They then zeroed their attention on the adults.

Penelope's hand flew to her mouth as she stood at the edge of the pit and looked down at the section of ground Nate pointed out. Nate looked up at her with a grin of satisfaction. He pushed his glasses higher on his nose, wiped a sleeve across his forehead and left behind a smudge of dirt, then leaned a hand on a shovel propped in the dirt nearby.

The excavation layer was studded with large broken shards of what appeared to be earthenware vessels. Far too many to count with ease. Beside them, more than half buried lengthwise, lay what appeared to be a carved bird perched atop a post. Possibly the carving on which the smaller, broken piece she'd sketched had once been attached.

Penelope met Nate's gaze and felt his happiness. After weeks of unearthing only minuscule pieces, he had hit upon something of significance.

"Nate, this is magnificent!"

"You're telling me! Can you do a quick sketch so we can remember later where everything was and how it was positioned and label all the items appropriately?"

"Absolutely, let me get my—"

"No, I'll do it!" He hopped out of the pit with a nimble climb. "Nobody touch anything! Take a break. We'll get back to work after Miss Gold sketches. No, on second thought, that's enough for today. Everybody gets the rest of the afternoon off, with pay!"

Nate was back in seconds with Penelope's sketchpad and pencils. His hired workers cheerfully gathered their tools and headed out. Cornelia, Polly, and Billy all helped Penelope maneuver down the sand incline into the pit while Nate set up her art materials and made sure the stool was level and on firm ground in front of the work table.

"Here, sit right there." Nate placed a hand under Penelope's elbow and guided her to the seat. His light touch meant more than it should have, and his hand lingered seconds longer than necessary.

A thrill coursed through her at being so close to him. She wanted to be near him. She had a sudden, dawning awareness. So much about him was right. His sunny personality, his mixture of buoyancy and steadfastness, the fine bearing she couldn't help but notice, his sharp intelligence, and his consideration of everyone despite his focused ambition.

He was the type of man she'd been looking for, for a long while. And he was all wrong, for so many reasons.

He released her, but didn't move. Penelope was glad she had on the frightful maternity corset she initially had vowed she'd never wear. It at least made her appear somewhat smooth.

She wanted Nate to continue seeing her as the image she'd crafted: an educated Bostonian artist temporarily residing in Florida for health and relaxation. She had to make that image endure. She couldn't bear what would happen otherwise.

Nate remained close. Their gazes locked. Cornelia cleared her throat.

"My art things." Penelope turned this way and that, searching for them, uncommonly flustered.

"Uh, right here, I brought them over." Nate grabbed her material from the edge of the table and repositioned the stool. He took Penelope's hand.

"Careful. Don't lose your balance." He helped her get settled. "I'll be just over there." He pointed to a canvas-covered work area on the opposite corner of the excavation pit. "I want to jot down my field notes."

After a while, Cornelia began urging Penelope to pack up. "We should get back," she said, and then repeated the request. "Especially because we arrived so early this morning. You must be tired."

Penelope demurred. "Soon," she replied. She was too immersed in the scene before her. First, she had sketched a quick overview of the site. It showed where the artifacts were positioned in the sandy loam mixed with shell. She notated the strata of the pit wall and recorded the layers of sand, shell, and loam. Then she drew a separate rectangle and filled it with details of the bird carving. She was recording every scratch of feather marking.

Cornelia spoke again.

"Sister Bridget and the others won't be happy we're still here this late in the day," Cornelia said. "You're missing your nap time."

Penelope had to chuckle. "Please, I'm not a child."

"Well, Billy and Polly always get here at two o'clock and that's usually our time signal for departure. It's an hour past that now."

"Soon," Penelope said, and continued drawing. A few moments later, she heard Cornelia move away and begin a soft recitation. It was her afternoon prayer, she knew. Penelope had become accustomed to the timing of the canonical prayers the sisters and Cornelia called the Divine Office.

Finally, fingers cramped, she set down her pencil and flexed her hands. An umbrella Nate had angled over her work space no longer shielded her from the sun. She was suddenly aware of fatigue and thirst. Cornelia had finished praying and was now packing up their paraphernalia.

"I get the message," Penelope said to Cornelia. She looked then for Nate.

"I've done as much from this vantage point as possible," Penelope called out to him.

Nate leapt up from his paperwork and bolted over to her. He looked at her sketches and whistled. "Impressive!"

"My mind buzzed," she said. "Look, the small sketches show parts of vessels, coiled pottery shards, and pieces with fiber-tamped markings." She pointed out each detail. "Here are pieces of animal effigies. And Nate, that was just on the surface!"

Their shared zeal energized her.

"Now we get to pick them out and inspect them," Nate said, and looked over the ground with near reverence. He stooped and began to scoop out the smaller artifacts that surrounded the bird carving. One bowl shard was larger than the wooden wing piece that had previously emerged. Penelope watched as he brushed away sand that clung to its crevices.

Cornelia cleared her throat. She walked over and removed all Penelope's art supplies and packed them. Billy and Polly stood a distance away but watched every move Nate made.

Nate put the shard on his collection table and then crouched down. He moved close to the day's prize, the bird carving. First, he brushed away leaf debris and dirt. Penelope stared with intent as feather etchings became evident, plus wings, a beak and eyes.

Gently, oh so carefully, he dislodged the carving inch by inch, picked it up, and carried it to her sketch table. Their fingers touched as she helped him set the object down. His hands were strong yet gentle. Penelope forgot that others were nearby. It was as though she and Nate were in their own world.

"Look, there is where the wing piece broke off," she exclaimed, as they studied the artifact. She didn't realize until she spoke that she'd been holding her breath.

"Yes. And look, here, at the precision of these wing etchings."

She leaned forward even more as Nate lifted the carving so

that it stood vertically. "A good seven inches tall, I'd say," he guessed.

"It has a proud look about it," she said. "What kind of wood is it?"

"Not sure," Nate said. "Pine or cypress." He inspected the piece and ran his fingers over its curves and carvings. Penelope rose and fetched the broken wing piece. She held it up to its proper place on the carving as Nate held it still.

"To think, an ancient man stood right in this exact spot maybe thousands of years ago, right where we are today," Nate said. "Somebody who spent hours making this."

"I've always associated antiquities with places like Rome and Egypt," Penelope said. "I'd never expect to find evidence of past civilizations in a place like this."

"Goes to show just how much we don't know," Nate said. He carried both the carving and its broken wing to the artifacts table. "And how much I aim to move the knowledge forward," he said when he returned to her. His eyes shone. Penelope could feel his aspiration.

"I believe you will." Her voice was low and fervent.

"Thanks for the vote of confidence. Don't forget your contribution. Your drawings will make my words take shape. We make a good team. We could go places."

Penelope didn't reply. The glow in Nate's eyes dimmed.

He'd had his back to the excavation pit, but now turned away from her. He was still close to her and she almost felt him stiffen.

"Hey! What are you two doing?" he called out.

Billy and Polly were on their hands and knees inspecting the dirt where the bird carving had been and where other artifacts remained. They both gave a start at Nate's words, and leaned back on their heels.

"Uh, nothing, just looking," Polly said.

"There's something underneath where that wooden bird was," Billy said.

"You were digging?" Nate asked, incredulous, and already standing next to them.

"Just poking around a little," Billy said.

"Look, I appreciate help but you can give this kind of help a rest, permanently," Nate said. It was the closest to ill humor Penelope had observed in him. "This may look like play but it isn't. It's a scientific excavation that follows protocols. One has to record where and when an artifact is found, what else is in proximity, what the stratum is."

Polly and Billy exchanged guilty glances.

Nate blew out a breath.

"If you want to do something, help form a work line. You, too, Cornelia, if you want." He waved to Cornelia, who'd quietly watched everything going on.

"We should return to town," Cornelia said. "Now."

"Just a bit longer," Penelope said. "Please."

Soon, Nate unearthed and brushed clean each piece, Polly and Billy transported them to one of the larger work tables, and Cornelia and Penelope arranged and labeled the items in the order of receipt and location.

Shadows lengthened and river breezes cooled the air by the time Nate dug around the last item. It was the one Billy had pointed out. Only a fraction showed, a sharp edge. The piece was wedged amid a wad of organic debris.

"Maybe it's the light, but it appears different than the other pieces," said Penelope, who'd straightened from her work to stretch her back, and walked closer to him.

"That's because I think it is," came Nate's reply.

"May I?" asked Penelope, intrigued. She indicated a wish to go closer.

"Absolutely," said Nate. Billy, Polly, and Cornelia joined them, and they stood in a semicircle to watch the past emerge from the soil.

Nate scooped away the sand, leaves, root hairs, and leaf

mold. Then he stopped digging, stopped talking, stopped everything. It seemed the day had come to a sharp halt. She stared, as
much in awe as Billy, Polly, and Cornelia, whose mouths were
agape. Nate, still kneeling, rested back on his heels, and gazed at
the find. His usual smiling face had fallen into grave lines.

Penelope blinked. Then drew in a sharp breath.

CHAPTER 9

*N*ate brushed away stray grains of sand as though the artifact were a fragile leaf instead of what it appeared to be: some kind of metal. Penelope studied the small, square, crusted object that had been unearthed.

"That's not wood. What is it?" Penelope asked.

"Underneath the tarnish, silver," Nate said. "I'm almost positive. Where would the aboriginals here have acquired silver?"

His enthusiasm rebounded with vigor. "This indicates trade networks existed. Yes!" He pumped a fist in the waning afternoon light, then resumed careful cleaning of the item.

Penelope peered at the artifact.

"Look how precise these marks are," she said, and traced, in the air, small indentations that paralleled the border.

"And look here," Nate pointed at a spot he'd wiped clean. "A crosswise incision that's evenly spaced. This could have been a piece of jewelry or a talisman or other sacred object. See the hole, where a chain or rope or thread could go."

The afternoon shadows grew even longer as they pondered the surprise finding. Then Nate let out another whoop.

"Pay dirt! I finally hit pay dirt!"

He continued talking as though to himself. "There's no context. Yet. It could have been carried here by some long-ago flood or debris from a hurricane or other storm. Or perhaps it's post-Columbian and they got it from the Spanish explorers. But, no, it's lying here with stuff I'm certain is pre-Columbian."

He looked at Penelope. "Something this important is rarely an isolated find. This is the start of something big. I can feel it."

He handed the pendant to Penelope. She carried the artifact over to the table, and Cornelia labeled and recorded it. Billy and Polly had drawn back from the others and were having their own quiet conversation.

Nate paced the excavation area and continued to think aloud. "This is a huge breakthrough. People who made bird carvings and adornments or ceremonial items like that silver piece weren't primitive beings. They must have had some kind of organized society. Leaders. Workers. Class levels. They clearly didn't have to devote all their time to sustenance. We could be looking at a shift from hunter-gatherer to a more settled agricultural society. Look at all the seed remains we've been finding."

He stopped. "I'm getting way ahead of myself."

"We won't be able to see unless we get out of here before it gets full dark," Billy said as he and Polly drifted closer again. Penelope noticed the two youngsters were subdued.

Shadows sliced hard into the site by the time they'd tidied up the work area and packed artifacts Nate wanted to study that evening. Billy and Polly worked without comment and remained silent as they started to lead the way out.

"You expect to find a lot more stuff?" Billy finally asked Nate after they'd reached the two wagons at the bottom of the mound. Their descent had been quiet, in contrast to the chorus of frogs and insects that grew louder the later the day became.

"I hope so," Nate said. He helped Cornelia and Penelope into his wagon, while Billy and Polly got into their smaller one and set off. Nate climbed in his wagon and handed the pendant to Penelope, who sat between him and Cornelia.

"Would you mind holding this one? I want to keep it near me. And, listen, I can't thank you enough for coming out here with me and staying all day. See, I told you, being around me would be good for you. Even I can see the healthy bloom in your cheeks. You must be feeling better. Yup, this is a day I'll long remember, for many reasons."

He cast her a meaningful glance that she ignored.

"It'll stay with me, too," Penelope said. "Imagine, someone wore this pendant so long ago. It makes me wonder who she was —for it had to be a she, don't you think? Was she young, old, a princess, a queen, a healer, a priestess? Who were her people and how did she get here?"

"Questions of my own soul," said Nate. "Just wait until the prof hears about this!"

Penelope kept the conversation focused on impersonal chat about the artifact for the rest of the ride back into town. Cornelia was quiet and Penelope knew she was perturbed at the lateness of the hour.

"Do you want to come out early with me again tomorrow?" Nate asked, an eager look on his face as he rolled up in front of the orphanage door. "Time out there obviously does you good. And with better health comes more energy and a need for more diversion. Right? I can hope."

But Sister Bridget, trailed by Onofrio, had come outside and reached them in time to hear Nate's parting words.

"Where have you been, Miss Cornelia? Miss Penelope, I was ready to go search for you until..." Onofrio started to say in rapid speech until Bridget put a hand on his shoulder.

Cornelia spoke volumes to Penelope with a slight raise of a shoulder and eyebrows.

"Cornelia?" asked an unsmiling Bridget.

"Our late return was my fault," Penelope spoke up before Cornelia could.

"No, mine," Nate said, and hopped out.

Onofrio ran and stood next to him and mimicked his stance. "Wot happen, Mr. Nate, that you keep these ladies past dinner and Sister here she worries and says extra prayers?"

"I didn't have you to keep us on track," Nate said, and tousled the boy's hair.

"*Si*, right, you're a smart man," Onofrio said, and his brightness softened the mood of the others. "Next time, I go too."

"After school and chores, and if you maintain good behavior, then maybe you can go," Bridget said.

The lives of the ancients faded as reality brought Penelope her back to the present and the life she carried. As if the baby heard, she moved. Penelope sighed. She couldn't help herself. Out of the blue, she had taken to calling her baby a "she."

Her little one would enter the world no matter how ready Penelope would be. No matter how Nate, the rest of Persimmon Hollow, or her family felt about it. Or Herman. Her heart grew colder each day toward him. To think, in her shock, she'd begged the man who'd violated her to marry her for propriety's sake. If nothing else, time in Florida had cleared her mind.

Penelope was apprehensive and somewhat excited about the future. The one thing she wasn't was detached. She'd received stern counsel before coming south. Told to be indifferent, to stay aloof from polite society, and to keep any feelings toward her baby to a minimum. And to practice her Italian with diligence. She needed to return to Boston sounding like she'd just spent a year in Italy. Not with dirt on her gloves from sifting through Florida history.

Penelope looked at Onofrio. Daily translation and reading exercises had helped her expand her Italian vocabulary over the past few months. But she really needed to converse in the language to perfect her fluency.

"And, if sister allows it, I'd like to talk with you in Italian, so I may practice the language," she said to the boy. "We could set up a schedule."

Onofrio, who'd looked as though he were weighing whether or not to protest Bridget's last directive, gave Penelope his full attention.

"You pay?" he asked.

Cornelia gasped. Bridget frowned. Nate looked up and tried to suppress a smile. Penelope met Onofrio as an equal.

"We'll discuss the terms, you and I and Sister, all right? In the next couple of days."

"*Si*. I no rob you," he said, and bounded away before Bridget or anyone else could admonish him.

WORD SPREAD about Nate's discovery of the pendant, animal effigy, and pottery pieces. The excavation site started to become a tourist attraction. Soon it seemed that anyone with a few hours to spare found their way to the riverside mound.

"If only their wallets opened up as much as their mouths do," Nate said to the Taylor Grove group gathered around the largest artifact table one Saturday morning.

Billy guffawed. "They sure do have opinions." His suspicions about the excavation work had diminished as the findings returned to their previous, more mundane levels of pottery shards. No other carvings or precious metals had been unearthed. No human bones were found among the animal remains.

"Opinions, indeed," said Agnes. "Especially from some who aren't from Persimmon Hollow." She and Lupita, the Taylor Grove housekeeper, had driven out from town to bring a picnic lunch to Penelope, Cornelia, Polly, Billy, Nate, and Onofrio, who'd been granted leave to join the group on Saturdays.

"You can say that again," said Polly. "Where are they coming from?"

"From what I hear at Clyde's Mercantile, some are from Jacksonville, St. Augustine, Palatka, and Orlando," Lupita said. "They're making sightseeing journeys in groups."

Penelope sat a few feet away from everyone and half-listened as she sketched. She had developed a system of preliminary field sketches in pencil. From them, she made detailed ink drawings. She'd even started to copy some of her ink drawings and tint them with watercolors.

She heard the murmured words as Cornelia, closer to her and apart from the others, began her midday prayer:

O GOD, come to our aid.
  O Lord, make haste to help us.
  Glory be to the Father and to the Son and to the Holy Spirit,
  as it was in the beginning, is now, and ever shall be,
  world without end.

THEY'D all do well if God would come to their aid, Penelope thought, especially her. In the three weeks since the discovery of the pendant, she'd puffed out to a point that her maternity corset was no longer an option. Just that morning, when she'd arrived at the site, she'd noticed Nate cast a quick, perplexed glance along the length of her figure. He wasn't the first to do so. *Yes, God*, Penelope found herself praying, *please come to my aid*.

Accustomed to crowds from social events, Penelope was able to tune out the noisy onlookers. Not so, Nate. He blew out a puff of air as he sidestepped eager questions and opinions and carried over to Penelope a handful of newly dug shards.

"At least they're not jumping in the pit," Nate grumbled. "Shards, bits of pottery and bone tools, and you'd think I'd found the Holy Grail," he said. He'd been forced to put more rope around the excavation station to prevent people from trampling the site and pressing in on his volunteer force of cleaners and cataloguers—Cornelia, Billy, and Polly—and his artist, Penelope, and all-around helper, Onofrio.

"You're not going to let a few crowds diminish your cheer, are you?" Penelope said, and looked up at him. She suspected his grumbles were caused by more than noisy onlookers.

His eyes softened and some of the tension drained from his face.

"Still no more precious metal or effigies or impressive pottery?" she asked.

He shook his head no.

"That's what's really bothering you, isn't it?"

"If I don't make another spectacular find, my funding will run out at the end of the summer," he said. "Can't help but have that sticking in the back of my mind. Yeah, I might be glad to find something else big. And if some of the gawkers donated to the effort."

She wanted to get up and stand next to him but didn't want to draw attention to her shape and size.

"I even set up a sign and a donation jar," Nate said. "You see how much isn't in it."

A few coins and a couple of bills that she knew were donated by Seth Taylor nested at the bottom of the near-empty jar on a small table where the path reached the top of the mound. Every visitor had to pass by in order to get to and from the excavation site.

"They're paying as much attention to that as to Polly's plea," Penelope said. Next to the donation table was a piece of wood on which Polly had painted a request that visitors stop trampling on the ferns.

"Yeah, she and Professor Art are deep in some kind of comparison between the structure of the living ferns and the few spores and fossilized imprints I've dug up," Nate said. "I cart her field notes back to the Alloway House every day. The professor has taken over the dining room table with a pressed plant apparatus and what looks to me like an herbarium."

"I know. Fanny told Agnes she's not raising a fuss because he's doing his best not to whine about his knees not allowing him to make the hike up here."

Nate nodded. "Kind of makes me feel like I'm whining. When I'm darn lucky to be here."

"At least the tourist season is almost over, from what I've been told," Penelope said. "Fanny said the Alloway House guests have left, except for the professor, of course. These people," she waved a hand toward the dozen or so onlookers who'd made their way to the excavation, "will probably all leave Florida soon."

"Along with whatever funding they might possess," Nate said. "And then, you'll be leaving too. Make my day brighter, why don't you?"

She patted the empty stool next to the chair she sat in.

"Take a break for a few minutes?"

Surprisingly, Nate agreed. Which gave Penelope cause for alarm. Where was the Nate of the night of the freeze or the Nate of the day of the big discovery? He'd been on top of the world, or at least of Persimmon Hollow. In a fever of energy, he'd rarely slowed down.

She set aside her sketchpad and pencil.

Nate sat and gazed up at the sky.

"We expected—the professor and I—that something major would turn up here. I get a taste of it and, poof, nothing else but broken pieces of pottery." Nate laughed without mirth. "Listen to me. Already jaded about finding chips of pottery. They're important by themselves. But no more silver, no more carvings."

"We were all excited when they first turned up," Penelope said. "Have you tried to reassemble anything yet?"

"No. I've been focused on finding more precious metal or a larger effigy. Something that'll help me secure me more funding."

Penelope looked at her hands folded over her midsection and hoped Nate didn't notice. She guessed he was too polite to say anything about a woman's weight or figure. And right now, he wasn't seeing her. A thought flashed, of how easy it would be for her family to write a check that would cover Nate's research funding for a year or more.

She stayed quiet. When Herman had first learned of her family's wealth, he started to find ways to ask for it—for some project or another. He'd also grown more attentive to her. Certain actions and requests had finally started to nag at her but she'd pushed aside the hints. On one hand, he escorted her to lectures, musicales, and other gatherings, albeit on a scattered schedule. On the other, he found reasons to avoid joining the family for holiday outings or dinners. Work, he always said, as an excuse for his absences.

He'd seemed almost desperate the day of the hay ride, when she told him her grandmother had denied her request to finance his latest business scheme. She'd held back the information that she'd agreed with the decision.

"Penelope?" Nate's voice called her back to the present.

"Sorry," she said. Nate was not Herman. He was a dreamer, yes, but he was also a hard worker with an education, distinct goals, and a carefully thought-out plan. Still... she'd learned her lesson about how people acted around money.

"Feeling okay? You look like everything in Florida agrees with you."

She girded herself but he said nothing else. "Actually, I do feel much better," she said.

"I'm both happy and dejected at that news," he said. "The better you feel, the sooner your time here will end."

"Yours will end soon, too," she pointed out. "When are you due back at your job?"

"Start of the fall semester," he said. "A good result here could secure me a spot as a faculty member instead of an assistant researcher making a pittance of a salary. But I have to find something worth writing about beyond one pendant and one bird effigy. I need more evidence to support my theory that these so-called 'primitives' were more advanced than we give them credit for."

"Or maybe more advanced than some people are now," Penelope said, as her stomach turned at the sight of an unkempt visitor spitting tobacco juice.

Nate grimaced.

Cornelia walked over to them as Penelope and Nate stared at the disarray that had taken over the once-tranquil excavation site.

Penelope could almost feel the serenity emanating from her younger companion.

"Does your prayer make you so calm, or is it something else?" she asked Cornelia. "You're always serene after you pray the Daily Office. I remember being chilled by ministers droning about the fires of hell. I never left church feeling anything other than fearful of God."

She had both Nate and Cornelia's attention.

"Penelope, prayer is a most powerful way for me to feel close to Our Lord," Cornelia said earnestly. "Afraid of God? Oh, gosh, no. The rosary and the Divine Office are contemplative practices that put me at peace. That's true whether I pray alone, like I did just now, or with the sisters or at the Taylor house or at Mass in town. You're welcome to pray with me at any time."

"Thanks, Cornelia. I may do so, if you'll teach me."

"We can start right now, with the rosary."

"I'll leave you women to the praying for now," Nate said. "This man has to battle the hordes keeping me from the field of my destiny." At least his cheer seemed restored.

Penelope waved him off as Onofrio clamored for his attention by waving a thin, broken tree limb around.

"How did your lesson go with Onofrio last week?" Cornelia asked her, after she'd given Penelope a lesson on the mysteries and prayers of the rosary. "It was the first one, right?"

"Yes. He speaks the language beautifully. But he made a hasty exit when I tried to discuss penning an agreement. Something bothered him, I could tell, but he didn't say what."

"He held his tongue? That's a good sign," Cornelia said. "I've been hoping he's absorbed some lessons about manners. We're trying hard to teach him. He's a handful and a fighter. Likes to talk tough in English. He was living and boxing—at his age!—on the streets of New York City until the sisters from Mother Frances Xavier Cabrini's new mission rescued him. They asked to send him here temporarily, to get him far from the streets. They say he's intelligent and they have hopes for his future. But he gets in one scrape or another fairly often, all minor, thank God. He fancies himself my protector, and now yours, too, I think, when he can escape school lessons and chores. Or *in order to* escape them."

They both laughed as they watched Nate squat down to Onofrio's level and give the boy some kind of advice or explanation.

"Nate is so patient with him," Cornelia said.

"I've noticed," Penelope said. "He'll make a good father."

She felt a shift in her abdomen. Followed by a vague fear that startled her with its urgency.

With each passing day, she felt more strongly that she couldn't—and maybe wouldn't—leave her baby. She had to protect her from the world's harshness. From conditions that led orphaned urchins to box on the streets for survival. She had to shelter her. Raise her. How could she go home and attend a concert or preside over a dinner party, not knowing what her child was doing or where she was?

Penelope noticed Cornelia watched her. The younger woman spoke in her usual gentle way. "God walks with you, Miss Gold. Always."

He'd be the only one who would, if her family reacted the way she expected to the nascent idea taking shape in her mind, Penelope thought. She reached for another one of the delicious biscuits the Persimmon Hollow ladies had brought in their picnic baskets. Gosh, she was hungry.

Raised voices grabbed her attention. Minutes later an aggrieved-looking Nate headed toward her and Cornelia with a mutinous Onofrio in tow.

The boy tugged to release Nate's grip on his arm as soon as they stopped.

Penelope swallowed the last of her biscuit in surprise. "What's wrong? A few minutes ago you two were deep in conversation."

"I'm no staying here another *minutu*," Onofrio declared, and folded his thin arms across his chest. Penelope saw he was almost hugging himself. "I want to go fishing or back to the grove." He hitched up his pants and scowled. "I'm not staying here. I ain't free labor and I ain't gonna dig ditches for nothing cause this four-eyed professor don't want to do it himself."

Penelope almost gasped. Even patient Cornelia sighed. Nate kept a level gaze on Onofrio.

"I assigned him a job, like the other workers have jobs," said Nate, and wiped sweat from his brow. He spoke as much to the boy as to the women.

"Onofrio, apologize to Mr. Nate for insulting him," Cornelia said in the sternest voice Penelope had heard her use. "Then help us understand what upset you. We thought you wanted to be here today."

The boy swallowed, hard. "Okay, sorry. I thought Mr. Nate want me. Not just a free ditch digger."

Penelope understood in an instant what really bothered him.

He'd misread Nate's attempt to make him one of the excavation crew.

She met Nate's gaze, and saw his eyes widen in understanding. He squatted down. "Onofrio, I wasn't clear. I'd be honored if you'd join my work crew. I pay the going rate. I don't invite just anyone to join me, you understand? Only special men."

The boy eyed him, but held back. "Okay maybe next time. Now I make sure nobody bothers Miss Cornelia and Miss Penelope. I stay here with them."

Both Nate and Cornelia started to protest but Penelope spoke over them.

"*Grazie.*"

The boy turned his suspicious glance toward her. "You are, what is the word? Welcome."

Penelope studied the thin, wiry boy, so old for his age, so suspicious, and trying so hard to be a man. For the first time in her life, she felt a glimmer of understanding of how poverty could shape a person at a young age. She'd never ventured into poor neighborhoods back home. And here, she usually saw the orphans in orderly groups under the watchful eyes of the religious sisters.

She wanted to refocus his attention, so Nate could get back to work. "Perhaps you can take a few minutes to discuss our contract for language lessons," she suggested. "We haven't signed a contract yet."

To her surprise, Onofrio's scowl deepened.

"What's wrong?" she asked. "We'll be making a business arrangement. We write up a contract for a certain number of sessions devoted to conversation in Italian."

He shook his head no with vigor. "No, uh, uh, no contract. I don't sign no contract! No! You hear me!?" He almost shouted.

"Oh, I've heard enough," Cornelia said. "Onofrio, go sit by yourself for a while. Think about your behavior, say an Act of

Contrition, and prepare yourself to make a Confession when Father Kenny visits."

He shrugged and swaggered off.

"I apologize for him."

"No need. I'm curious as to what prompted such a vehement reply," Penelope said.

"Me, too," Nate said. He had started walking to the work area but had circled back when he heard Onofrio's raised voice.

"Regardless, his behavior is unacceptable," Cornelia said. "I know for a fact he doesn't act this way in the classroom. He generally says nothing at all there."

Onofrio sat under a nearby tree and looked mournfully at them until Cornelia nodded that he could rejoin activities. He scrambled up, reverted to his age, and scampered over to where Billy and Polly sat. Soon, all three looped back to where the three adults gathered. Billy nudged Onofrio toward Nate.

"*Amicu* again?" Onofrio asked Nate as he reached out for a manlike handshake.

"Friends for life," Nate answered as he returned the handshake. "Friend to friend, I recommend you hear what Miss Penelope has to say about business. After you get the Italian lessons straightened out, you and I will talk about your job for me. Not bad, young man, lining up two jobs in one day."

Awareness lit in Onofrio's eyes. "Hey, yeah, not too bad."

Penelope saw his shoulders relax ever so slightly.

"We will draft business papers the way professionals do," she said carefully as she saw Onofrio start to scowl again. "A business arrangement means both parties benefit, not just one side."

He stared at her as if assessing her truthfulness. With Billy and Polly within earshot, and Cornelia's recent reprimand, he also seemed to be considering his words.

He drew in a sharp breath. "Business papers. That's what they told my poppa. He sign the papers and then they take him away and leave me all alone. He no come back. Never!"

Onofrio no longer sounded tough. He sounded like a frightened little boy. He stood very close to Nate, who put a hand on his shoulder and gave it a squeeze.

"We don't allow that kind of thing to happen in Persimmon Hollow," Nate said. "People who cheat others aren't welcome here."

Onofrio digested the information.

"Why don't you at least listen to what Miss Penelope has to offer? A man of the world has to listen and then make his decision. I'm willing to offer advice if you need any. Man-to-man, you understand?"

Penelope's heart warmed at the way Nate protected Onofrio as though it were the most natural action in the world. And as though he had nothing else to do. She knew how much Nate itched to be digging. Yet he'd set aside his ambition to calm the fears of a child he hardly knew. What a good father he would make. She closed her eyes for a long moment. Why was she thinking of Nate as a father?

Nate leaned down to Onofrio's level and lowered his voice. "We won't tell the women what we discuss. Deal?"

Onofrio grinned and punched Nate on the arm. "Deal!"

Nate's eyes widened at the gesture and he glanced at Penelope with raised eyebrows. She smiled her approval. She wasn't surprised to see him treat Onofrio this way, not really. It fit everything she'd come to learn about him.

Onofrio turned a brave face toward Penelope. "I will discuss the business arrangement. No signing any papers, okay?"

"We'll shake on it," Penelope suggested, and Onofrio responded with a grip that belied his age.

"You come see me after you're finished here," Nate said. "I've got to get back to digging. I'm starting to see tourists hovering over there." He bounded off.

Penelope and Onofrio soon settled on payment, hours, and duties, and he ran off to help Nate again. The day's site work on the excavation fell in to its familiar pattern. More inquisitive tourists soon arrived.

Onofrio soon started giving tours and leading visitors around as though born to the business.

"What did you say to him?" Penelope walked over to Nate to ask.

Nate chuckled. "Look how he's got them in order," he said. "I made him assistant project manager and offered a salary that almost made him gulp. He caught himself, though, and tried to act as though he routinely received such offers. His duties include giving tours and keeping visitors in line. He appears to be a natural."

Nate watched him with pride in his gaze.

"They're not even trampling the ferns anymore," Penelope said. They watched Onofrio gesture and explain about ferns.

Cornelia wandered over to join them. "Thank you both for whatever you did to transform that young man. I saw him stop tourists from picking up and handling artifacts on one of the specimen tables."

"What Nate did was become a father figure," Penelope said, her gaze direct and on Nate. "A good one."

"Never too early to start," Nate said, with an equally candid look at her.

Cornelia physically moved between the two of them, causing Penelope to take a step back. "I came over to ask you to rest awhile with the other women in the shade," Cornelia said to Penelope. "The day is becoming overly warm. Your skin is flushing."

Penelope resisted the notion to disagree. Her flushed skin had nothing to do with the weather. But Nate tensed and urged her to listen and rest.

As they walked away, Penelope and Cornelia passed Polly and Billy working at the labeling table. Polly chattered as much as she worked, but Billy was bent over his task, intent on wiping sand from a fragment of pottery. His lips were pressed in a thin line.

"Billy's being awfully quiet, don't you think?" Penelope asked. "He and Polly banter back and forth all the time."

"Focused on his work, I guess," Cornelia said.

But Penelope wondered. She remembered his resistance to the archaeological dig and his loyalty to Seth's friend Tustenuggee. And she prayed trouble didn't loom on the horizon.

CHAPTER 10

*P*enelope had looked forward to the fitting session with Josefa. She needed her dressmaking expertise. She guessed that by now the seamstress had either figured out her secret or been made aware by the other women.

But when Penelope emerged in her chemise from behind a dressing screen in her room a few days after the weekend picnic, she questioned her assumption.

Josefa bounced up from the chair she'd been seated in, her eyes round and her measuring tape dangling from her hand. She stared at Penelope's protruding belly.

"It's okay, you can measure me. Just be careful."

Josefa shook her head, shock still evident in her expression. "It's not that." She looked away. She fussed with her pile of sample fabrics and dressmaking patterns laid out on the bed and fiddled with items in her sewing basket.

"You didn't know?" *So Agnes Taylor and Josefa's own Aunt Lupita hadn't told her?*

"No," Josefa whispered. She neatened the already crisp corners of the fabric choices she had pulled from the pile as suggested options.

"It's a long story," Penelope said.

"Oh, no, *senora*, it's none of my business, that's quite all right," Josefa spoke in a rapid flow of words. She began to measure Penelope's height, arm length, leg length, everything, Penelope noticed, except her baby bump. Her large baby bump.

"But where is your husband?" Josefa blurted out as she stopped measuring. "I'm sorry but I have to ask! He should be with you! And why has this been such a secret? A baby is a joy."

"I, ah, he…" Penelope took a breath. The baby shifted inside her. "There is no husband."

Josefa sat down on the bed, speechless again.

Penelope pushed aside a pile of lace cuffs and collars and eased down next to the younger woman.

Did she tell Josefa the truth? Or make up some story? Living in the orphanage had shown her how much the sisters valued truth and honesty. The Taylors and Josefa's aunt and uncle and the core settlers in Persimmon Hollow were all the same. Nate— oh, why think of Nate now—was one of the most upstanding men she'd met.

In society, back home in Boston, her "rapid health decline" was branded a mystery and not discussed openly. Even if her social acquaintances showed up in Persimmon Hollow and physically bumped into her abdomen, they wouldn't spurt questions as Josefa did. They'd ask Penelope about the weather she was encountering on her travels.

She told Josefa the truth.

"Dear Lady of Guadalupe, please watch and look over our dear Penelope." Josefa was back on her feet, walking back and forth in Penelope's small room. She prayed aloud, her hands clasped. "Keep her safe from harm and from the evil intentions of others."

She tossed her long braid over her shoulder and sorted through the fabric on the bed again. "This one is perfect," she said, and held up coral-colored silk fabric. "It goes nicely with your hair and skin color. Miss Penelope, we will make you the most beautiful lady in waiting that ever visited Persimmon Hollow!"

Josefa became all business as her dressmaker side emerged. "We cannot hide what God has allowed to be set into motion. But you will be dressed in a tasteful manner. Are you going to stay inside for your last couple of months? Many ladies do."

"Pregnancy is not a disease and I don't want to hide," Penelope said. She knew the social proprieties. But she was beginning not to care. "The fresh air does me a lot of good. And I help Nate with drawings at the excavation site. I hope to do that as long as I'm able to move around freely. At that time, well, I can still sketch here."

"I think he's sweet on you, that's what I've heard Agnes say," Josefa said as she pinned fabric around Penelope.

Their glances met. Josefa blushed.

"I guess we'll have to wait and see how he feels after…" Penelope said, and cast a downward glance at her body. "After he sees the real me."

She tried to sound nonchalant. Yet, inside her grew something besides her precious baby bundle. Her feelings for Nate grew.

She felt good being around him. She liked his mix of optimism and pragmatism. She liked the way his wavy hair flopped over the bandanas he tied around his head and how his blue eyes intensified when he was impassioned about a subject. She liked his strength and action as much as she appreciated his intelligence. The two of them shared interests. And, there was no denying, the two of them shared an unspoken attraction.

What was happening to her? Would she feel the same if she had met him in Boston society? Silly. She never would have met him in Boston society. She never would have gotten to know him, even if he did live in Boston instead of New York. The

Italian Catholics lived in one part of town. The Protestant Beacon Hill gentry lived in another. More than physical distance separated them.

Josefa shook out her fabric and refolded it. "Okay, Miss Penelope, I will add an extension panel to one of your walking skirts right away, within a day. Then I'll sew a new walking skirt and shirtwaist for you—I can complete the set in four days, fewer if I get my aunt and Agnes to help. Then I'll make a second set for you."

"I can help sew," Penelope said. "I've already let out seams on my chemises and on two shirtwaists. If you pin the new panel into the walking skirt, I'll stitch it together. That way you can start the new items right away."

"Wonderful," Josefa said.

Then, she added, "If you don't mind me saying so, Miss Penelope, you appear much happier than last time you were here. I worried about your melancholy then. We all did. Fanny Alloway especially because she saw you daily and saw how much you were affected."

"I was upset that my family had separated me from the man I thought I loved, a man whose true nature I wasn't able to see at the time," Penelope said.

Josefa pursed her lips. "Men can be most difficult to figure out. My Aunt Lupita says a woman should watch for certain signs when she can't figure out a man: how he treats his mother, and how he treats those weaker or less important than him. And, this is a strange thing, to be sure, how he acts when untangling a pile of rope that has gotten into a jumble of knots."

Penelope raised her eyebrows in question.

"Lupita said if he has no patience, loses his temper, and quickly throws down the rope in disgust, he might lose his temper or give up too easily when he faces challenges in life."

"Your aunt is a wise woman," Penelope said. She remembered how Herman lost his temper, loudly, when he couldn't secure the front-row seats that had been promised at the theater. They had gone to someone more important. And how he'd once impatiently thrown a wrinkled, knotted cravat into the trash basket moments after attempting to untangle it.

"If you think about it, that's not so strange a piece of advice," Penelope said. "I could have used it a while back."

"*Si*," Josefa said. "But sometimes we don't always listen, no?"

She let out a dramatic sigh. "I wish I were carrying a baby. We thought, Ben and I, my aunt, everyone, we all expected I would be with child already. My aunt is praying novenas for me. I am, too."

She looked curiously at Penelope, who didn't know what to say. There weren't any routine social answers to such a subject.

"Soon, I hope," Josefa said.

"Yes, I hope so too," Penelope said. She helped Josefa gather her sewing accouterments.

"I can't wait to hold your baby!" Josefa said.

Penelope thought of the counsel she'd received, months ago, from everyone from her mother to her doctor to the sisters at the orphanage: *Don't hold your baby when it's born. Don't even see the little one. It will make leaving the child behind more manageable for you.*

At the time, she had nodded her agreement dully, shamed and distraught. Now, she saw things differently. No way would she let anyone take her baby before she, Penelope, was good and ready to let the infant leave her arms.

A firm knock at the door was followed by Cornelia's voice. "May I come in?"

"Of course," Penelope said, and opened the door. She took one look at Cornelia's expectant gaze. "Has something happened?"

"It appears so," Cornelia said. "I've been asked to bring you to the Alloway House in town if you feel able to make the journey. It's a lovely day for a ride."

"Let's go, then," Penelope said. She was glad for the diversion. Plus, she had skipped a visit to the excavation because of her fitting session. She missed the time outdoors.

"You, too, Josefa," Cornelia said, as the seamstress picked up her wares. "I don't know what the fuss is about, but I'm told several people are already there."

PENELOPE HEARD Nate talking as she and the others entered the Alloway House dining room. It was crowded with people. All the Taylors were there: Seth, Agnes, Polly, Billy, and even little Seth. And the Gomezes— Josefa's Aunt Lupita and Uncle Alfredo. The entire Taylor Grove clan wore work clothing, as though they'd stopped what they were doing mid-step.

She noticed the same workday garb on the townfolk—Eunice and Clyde Williams, and Fanny and Professor Art. Onofrio, shadowing Nate's side, looked like he'd just climbed out of an excavation pit.

Estelle Wade, the Alloway House's now-occasional cook, came in from the kitchen, wiped her hands on her apron and sat down at the table. Her son, Bernie, dressed in his schoolteacher clothing—he must have dropped by to visit his mother—followed and pushed in her chair before taking one himself.

Everyone focused on Nate while snacking on cookies and pound cake and helping themselves to coffee and tea from the sideboard. He stood with Billy, Polly, and Onofrio, who shifted from foot to foot and pressed his lips together. The little boy looked like he would burst with whatever the news was.

Chatter quieted as Nate began to speak. "It was so crusted and covered with dirt that at first I thought it was another piece of bone," Penelope heard, after missing his first words amid the noise and movement in the room.

"Then we cleaned it up and saw—" Polly butted in.

"Polly," Agnes called over her shoulder from the sideboard. "Let Nate speak."

"She's right about the cleaning," Nate said. "Polly, Billy, and Onofrio were at the site after school to clean, sort, and tag items. I wouldn't be this far along without their dedication."

His gaze searched the room and found Penelope. "Or without the assistance and support of Miss Penelope, who wasn't able to join us at the mound today."

Her heart quickened at the expression in his eyes.

"So," Nate turned back to his audience, "after the artifact was cleaned, we saw it was made of silver. I suspect that, like the item found earlier, it was made specifically for ceremonial use. Either the actual artifact or the silver required to make it was likely acquired in trade. Finding that first pendant wasn't just a fluke. This second artifact adds weight to my theory that the ancients in this area were far more advanced than scholars have imagined."

A few murmurs of surprise rippled around the table. Penelope caught her breath. She eased down in a chair. This was indeed big news.

"This isn't just any piece of silver." Nate dug in the pocket of his pants and held up a small item about two inches in size. Everyone stared at the small object.

"See how it's shaped like a crescent moon?" Nate asked. He pointed. "And note this pattern of small holes incised neatly around the edge. Three of them go all the way through, making an opening for a thread or cord to go through. What we have here is another pendant. The first was smaller, but also silver. This one is larger. Both exhibit signs of artistic rendering."

He stopped to catch his breath. "Also, note this indentation in the center. I'm convinced it's a thumbprint, put there deliberately in an attempt at ornamentation. Something was used to press the silver into shape. Close inspection leads me to think the person who crafted this used his hand."

"Or hers," Polly muttered.

Nate spoke with restraint but his excitement was evident to Penelope by the intensity of his gaze. This discovery, coupled with the earlier ones, could bring Nate the success and professional security he craved.

Suddenly everyone at the table was talking at once.

"I told 'em they were wrong to turn up their noses at this excavation," Professor Art crowed. "Yup, this botany professor's archaeology hat remains in fine working order. Like I've always said, the two fields are cousins and I'm glad I specialized in both. I told those colleagues they'd be sorry. Keep digging, my boy. What a remarkable discovery, this and the other silver piece and the effigy. I'll write to the dean tonight."

He rubbed his hands together. "This makes up for me not being able to hobble up to the top of the mound."

"We need to think about posting guards up there," Seth said. "Word will get out about this faster than it did about the excavation itself."

"Seth Taylor, this is Persimmon Hollow." Fanny tapped his arm with her fan. "No need to worry."

"Doesn't hurt to be cautious," he answered. "You know me. And I know that ruffians are drawn exactly to this type of intrigue."

"I was cleaning it when, poof, like magic, it started to shine," an excited Onofrio repeated to anyone who would listen.

"Never heard of any precious metal veins in these parts but I reckon we need to start looking," Clyde mused. "Imagine me selling mining equipment at the Mercantile. Spanish explorers who came through way back yonder thought Florida might yield gold and silver riches. Searched far and wide."

"And they didn't find any," said Eunice, who pushed her glasses up the bridge of her nose and looked all the world like the Academy principal she was. "I for one am glad. Imagine Persimmon Hollow as mining town. That's not how my and Fanny's father envisioned his settlement. He founded it as place of education and culture."

"And being that one part of town is just getting started on that, I'd like to bring my pupils on a field trip to the site," said Bernie, speaking up for the first time. "You good with the idea, Nate? I want them to see science in action and learn about possibilities."

"Name the day," Nate said. He and Bernie started a side conversation while several others argued the merits and detriments of mining and mining towns.

Penelope rose and edged through the noise to reach Nate after he and Bernie shook hands on their conversation.

"May I take a closer look?" she asked.

"Sure!" he said, and turned toward her to hand over the pendant. The oversized shawl she'd wrapped twice around her torso and draped to her knees slipped as she reached to take the artifact. She couldn't grab the shawl quickly enough. It slid and crumpled to the floor. Oh, how could she have forgotten to pin it closed, the way she'd pinned it every time before?

Nate automatically bent down and grabbed the shawl. As he rose, his gaze locked on her abdomen and then went in a line up to her face as he straightened. The glow in his eyes dimmed. Instead, a slow, dark spark grew from confusion into realization.

"Let me explain," she whispered as she pulled the shawl around her and held it closed in front of her. "Later."

Nate pressed his lips together. He appeared not to have heard. Spots of color appeared on his cheeks. He gave her the silver pendant without comment.

She tried to recapture the joy of the gathering but it was now overlaid by anguish. Of all people, she wanted Nate to understand. Needed him to understand. Of all people, she most worried about judgment from the kind, smart, funny man she'd come to know…was coming to love.

"It's beautiful, Nate," she said. "May I borrow it overnight to sketch it?"

"I'd rather you did so at the site tomorrow," he said, with a stiff edge to his voice. "I prefer to keep all artifacts together."

"Of course," she said, but her nerves tightened.

He reached into his other pocket and pulled out a folded piece of paper. "When it became obvious you wouldn't be out there today, I made a sketch of the placement. Perhaps you could make a better copy and return it tomorrow."

He handed her the paper and took the pendant before she had a chance to fully inspect it. Sunny Nate was gone. In his place was a stranger—a stiff, professional Nate.

She blinked back tears that threatened to become obvious. They surprised her so much she nearly stumbled back to her chair. She sat with her gaze down for a few moments to compose herself. She looked up and saw Nate quickly shift the stare he'd fixed on her. Nobody spoke. Penelope became aware of the silence. Even Onofrio held his tongue, although he stared at her with saucer eyes.

Penelope summoned her will and regained her decorum. She stood and walked to where Nate had moved. *So her secret was out. So what.* Part of her was relieved.

"Nate, where did you find it, what part of the excavation area?" She tried to keep her tone conversational.

His face stiffened and a flash of hurt crossed the expression in his eyes. Then the professional Nate returned.

"About twelve to fourteen centimeters from where the first silver pendant was unearthed."

"This is the break you've been waiting for, working for," she said. She tried to muster enthusiasm. This was Nate's moment. Not hers for self-pity.

"It's enough to garner more funding," she added. "Who knows what you'll discover next."

She meant every word, yet felt as though they were forced and artificial.

Nate looked at her with an anguished expression. "I've made all the discoveries I can handle for one day," he said. "If you'll excuse me, I need to discuss next steps with Professor Art."

His face spoke the question his mouth didn't say: *Why didn't you tell me?*

Nate turned away from her. Penelope's heart pounded. She felt a little faint.

"I need some fresh air," she said to Agnes, who, along with everyone else in the room, had listened to the exchange.

"Come onto the porch." Agnes guided her outside. Cornelia was close behind.

As they stepped outside, Penelope heard Onofrio cry out in an amazed voice. "Did you see? *Signorina* Penelope—she having a *bambino!*" The door clicked closed behind them.

The fresh air cooled the hotness of Penelope's cheeks and face.

Agnes's gaze rested on Penelope's figure before lifting to meet her eyes.

"From now until the end of your confinement, you may wish to curtail your activities outside Taylor Grove," Agnes counseled. "Not only because of wagging tongues in town. You'll be uncomfortable at times, particularly as the weather grows hotter. You may want to reconsider the daily journey to the excavation site. Cut back to one day a week and then reassess. The walk up the mound is a gentle incline, I know. But you have to adapt your pace—with everything—to what your body dictates."

Penelope sat glumly in a cushioned wicker seat. Cornelia sat down across from her, gaze down as was her wont, and Agnes remained standing.

"I have to go out there tomorrow, to sketch the silver piece. I'm not ready to admit defeat," Penelope said.

"It's not admitting defeat, it's listening to your body and your baby," Agnes said. "You can copy the sketch Nate made, as he suggested."

Penelope pressed her lips together.

"You knew this moment would come," Agnes added.

Penelope knew she didn't mean the size of her body or the physical changes she was experiencing.

"I've grown to like Nate quite a bit," Penelope said. Then wondered why she'd blurted that out.

"And he, you," Agnes said. "Yes, we've been watching. At least, the women have been watching. You're on delicate ground."

Penelope sighed. "I've been cushioned in a dream world, I guess. I got caught up in the excitement of the excavation. I guess I'd hoped things would just continue as they were, indefinitely."

"We know this isn't an easy situation for you," Agnes said. "But wonderful changes of the heart can and do happen in Persimmon Hollow. My life is proof of that. Give Nate time to absorb what he learned today. Talk to him."

"Why? So he can regret time spent with me?" Penelope asked in a sharper tone than she normally used. "I've seen him glance at my empty ring finger more than once during times we spent together." She gave a pained laugh. "Yes, I imagine he will have plenty of questions."

"That only you can decide whether you'll answer."

"I've never been a person that shies from difficulties," Penelope said. "So much so, that I may as well tell you I've had second thoughts about leaving the baby for adoption."

Agnes's brows drew together.

"The arrangement between your family, the orphanage, me as the Taylor Grove representative, and Sister Bridget as the orphanage representative, is for you to reside in Persimmon Hollow until able to travel home after the birth," Agnes said. "The baby will remain with the orphanage until a good home can be found."

"Yes, I know about the arrangement my family paid for," Penelope said, with emphasis on the word *paid*. "All I'm saying is I may decide to keep my baby."

"Have you discussed this with your family?" Agnes asked.

"No."

"Have you thought it all the way through?"

"I'm working on that, right now. I assure you I can afford to support myself and a baby. Where, I don't know yet."

"Single mothers face many tribulations," Agnes said. "Penelope, I was raised in an orphanage. Cornelia lived in foster homes. We've seen the struggles many families face even when there is a married couple determined to stay together."

"I do nothing on impulse," Penelope said.

"Yes, I understand. But there's a hard truth to swallow. What happened inside may, no, *will* repeat itself elsewhere in the coming weeks. You were focused on Nate. You didn't see the shock on the faces of the others in the room. Apart from the sisters and Cornelia, only Fanny, Lupita, and I knew the truth."

Penelope didn't want to hear what she was saying.

"Remember you are always welcome—here at the Alloway House and everywhere at Taylor Grove," Agnes said. "Let your temporary home at the orphanage be your personal haven. But prepare yourself for the, shall we say, *less charitable* people you will encounter."

Penelope thought of Nate's expression. She closed her eyes. Bumpy roads were ahead. Some of the prayers she'd heard all around her for months now sprang to her lips. Especially words from the evening prayers she often joined.

God, come to my assistance.

Lord, make haste to help me.

Lord, make haste to help me, please, she murmured. Please, heed my prayer.

THE DOOR to the porch squeaked open and hit the wall with a thud.

"Fanny says please come back in so we can talk about the theatrical," Polly announced. She practically danced in anticipation. Her natural ringlets swung as she struck an exaggerated stage pose.

"I await my call to stardom," she emoted, one arm slung across her forehead and the other out in supplication.

"We're not staging a melodrama, Polly," said Agnes, as she and Cornelia helped Penelope up from the soft cushions of the wicker chair. "And you'll never be a stage actress, if I have my say about it. They're hardly respectable women. Although I'm sure many are nice enough people."

Proper society rates unwed mothers low on the respectability scale, too, thought Penelope as she trailed the others inside. She wondered if her situation ranked above or below the profession of stage actress, then despaired at even thinking about it.

Fanny already had the group's attention as they entered the dining room, all except Nate's.

"Since we're already gathered, Agnes and I want to propose that we stage a theatrical as part of our Fourth of July celebration."

Penelope's gaze went straight for Nate, who toyed with the silver pendant. He turned it over and sideways, studied it, and nudged the professor. The white-haired scholar was also more focused on the artifact than on his late-in-life sweetheart's stage plans.

"I have reason to bring up the topic now even though some of you are more focused elsewhere," Fanny said. She stopped talking and stared pointedly at Nate and Art until they looked up with sheepish expressions.

"We want to stage a performance to raise funds for townsfolk hit hard by the freeze a few months ago," Fanny explained.

Rippled murmurs of assent circled the room.

"Between information Clyde has heard at the store and what Seth has gleaned from other citrus growers, we know of at least five families who had all their savings tied up in their crops," Fanny continued. "They've lost everything."

She let her words sink in before continuing. "People from miles around attend our Independence Day festivities. Crowds that day will be thick. We'll be able to raise a generous amount to distribute. But we'll need many hands so I hope you'll consider participating. I know you will."

Fanny phrased her last statement as a command, not a question.

"There's too many teachers in this room, telling folks what they ought to be doing," protested Billy from where he leaned against the wall. "I don't wanna work on some stupid play. There's a rumor going round that acrobats are coming through town this year for the holiday as part of a circus. That's way more exciting. And what about the parade? I'll work on the parade. I'm not getting up on any old stage."

"A circus!? A circus! I want to join. Swing on the ropes!" Onofrio crowed.

From opposite sides of the table, Seth and Agnes turned level gazes toward Billy. Nate put a gentle but firm restraining arm on Onofrio and shook his head no. "Can't just walk off the job, Onofrio. I need you. I'd miss you." Penelope caught the adoring look the boy darted at him.

"And you, Billy, you want to rethink your statement, son?" Seth asked. "Good. I'm glad you agree with me," he added, without waiting for an answer.

"Don't worry, we won't make you go on stage, Billy," Fanny

said. "You can help behind the scenes, on the set. And rest assured, the parade will still take place."

"But you can forget the circus because that's an old rumor," Clyde interjected. "They had to cancel this year."

Billy scrunched his face and Onofrio followed suit, but they both attempted to listen.

"Your play is a worthy cause," Cornelia said. "I'd be happy to assist, behind the scenes of course."

Penelope, meanwhile, tried in vain to catch Nate's attention. He refused to look at her.

"Our biggest question right now," resumed Fanny, "is what play to stage?"

"*Othello*," mumbled Penelope under her breath, in keeping with her mood. But she'd spoken louder than she'd thought.

Eunice, seated diagonally across from the table, glanced at her over the top of her glasses. "Perhaps something a bit lighter, dear."

"What did you say, what? I couldn't hear," Fanny asked, cupping her hand to her ear. "Lighter than what?"

"I believe the lady mentioned *Othello*," said Nate, who had sat down in one of the chairs against the wall. He pushed the chair back onto two legs and crossed his arms. "I can't imagine why."

"Well, then, Nate, what do you think we should stage?" Penelope asked.

The room quieted to listen to the exchange.

His gaze did meet hers this time. It was a hard look. "*Richard III*," he said, as though no one else was in the room. "You know, a cautionary tale about what happens to schemers."

Penelope winced internally, but kept her face passive. How dare he make such a veiled, harsh comment.

"My choice is more appropriate," she replied. "You know, a cautionary tale about rumors and innuendos believed and acted upon before truth has a chance to emerge."

Their gazes locked, but his eyes widened slightly at her explanation. Neither gave way or backed down.

"My, my, can't we find anything cheerier than Shakespearean dramas?" Fanny objected, and her cheeks started to get pink. She reached for her fan on the table. "It will be a celebratory day, after all."

She waved her fan. Penelope and Nate remained locked in their staring match.

Polly yawned. "Didn't anybody else write plays except Shakespeare?"

The room grew increasingly warm. Little Seth, who'd been napping, awoke with a cranky cry when crows landed on the porch railing and cawed as though they were inside the house.

"That's how I'll sound if I have to sit through a play in the heat of a Florida July," said Seth as Agnes tended little Seth. "Can't a parade be enough? We can sell ice cream to raise money."

"But can we raise enough on ice-cream sales?" asked Fanny. "What about a short theatrical scene, instead of a full play?"

Nate and Penelope, meanwhile, continued to watch each other until Penelope finally looked away. She squared her shoulders, tilted her chin upward, and shot a defiant glare just past Nate and looked out the window beyond. From the corner of her eye, she saw that he continued to scrutinize her.

"We need to raise funds for others," Agnes added. "This isn't about us."

"Dad's right," Billy said. "Nobody's gonna sit long in the heat. Look how hot it is already, and June doesn't start until next week."

Penelope was aware of the intensifying heat. But her discomfort had less to do with the weather and her growing bulk, and more to do with the stiff-necked creature on the other side of the room. She should have guessed that underneath that cheery façade, Nate would act just like the stuffy science lecturers she'd had many occasions to hear back home.

She'd been silly, she told herself, to let feelings take root for Nate while they lived in this charming but isolated bubble of Persimmon Hollow.

She made a concerted effort to enter the conversation.

"Last summer was warm in Boston, so we changed plans we'd initially made for lengthy orations on Independence Day," Penelope said. She forced her focus onto the discussion, despite how aware she was of Nate.

"Instead, we had a short program," she continued. "It consisted of a reading of the Declaration of Independence, a singing of the national anthem, and the recitation of a few poems."

Her suggestion hung in the room's thick air.

"You could tell folks that unless they donate, they'll be forced to sit for a longer program," Seth said. "Possibly an entire play by Shakespeare."

The men guffawed. Onofrio watched them, then slapped his thigh and did the same. Even Nate made an attempt to grin, but fell short.

"I say we vote on it," Clyde said.

Nate raised his hand in favor of the short-program idea, but it was a grudging effort, Penelope was sure. He wasn't smiling.

"It's unanimous, then," said Fanny, chirpy again.

"Can I recite one of the poems?" Polly asked.

"Yes," said Fanny, "And Billy, there still will be set construction. We'll have a short program but the setting must be theatrical, to draw people in."

"As if they'll have somewhere else to go," Billy retorted, and jumped out of the way before Agnes or Seth could reach him. He bumped into Cornelia's chair, lost his footing, scrambled to gain it, and ran out the door. Polly and Ornofio were quick to follow.

Fanny and Agnes grilled Penelope for particulars on the

Boston short program. Nate pushed back his chair with a loud noise and stood up.

"I'm happy to assist," he said. "Just assign me to a job. Right now, I need to get back out to the excavation site. The daylight lasts long and I don't want to miss any more time."

Good-byes waved him off. Penelope's was tempered, but she saw that it didn't matter. He still refused to acknowledge her.

"Well, that worked out well," said Fanny. "We wouldn't have been able to produce a full staging anyway. Not enough time for rehearsals. How did that happen, Agnes? We discussed this so long ago."

"Time got away from us, again," said Agnes. "Here, little guy, sit with Miss Fanny for a few minutes," she said to her son and handed him to the other woman. Little Seth snuggled into Fanny's lap.

Agnes walked over to Penelope and guided her to a corner of the room as others filed out amid chatter.

"Here's my advice, even though you're not asking for it," Agnes said. "Go out to the excavation tomorrow with Cornelia, as usual, and before you're physically unable to do so. Get everything out in the open. Better to do that than to let anything fester unsaid."

Penelope nodded her agreement. Cornelia had come to stand behind her like a hovering guardian angel.

"Don't look so glum," Agnes said. "Truly, all will be well."

Penelope had thought she'd masked her feelings. Apparently not. Just like she'd thought she'd spoken low when mentioning the play. What was wrong with her? She was starting to feel miserable in so many ways. As though on cue, her legs started to ache.

"Come to Vespers today," Cornelia said. "We'll get to the orphanage chapel in time if we leave now. Place everything that troubles you into the hands of the Lord and focus on your prayers. I promise you will feel soothed and supported."

"She's right," said Agnes. "And you look like you need more rest, too." She took Penelope's hands. "I recognize the signs. Your baby has taken over your life and will make his or her presence known a lot. Get ready for a wonderful—but sometimes challenging—ride."

Penelope was skeptical that anything could or would help her right now. She'd just lost a giant chunk of her foundation. Nate's withdrawal made her feel as though she'd been abandoned by a close friend. The pain was sharper than she could have imagined.

CHAPTER 11

gnes is right. Clearing the air with Nate is the only solution, come what may of the encounter, Penelope thought. She took another break on the walk up the excavation slope. The incline was gentle as it wrapped around the mound, yet it seemed to have grown steeper in recent weeks.

"Just need to catch my breath," she told Cornelia, who stopped and waited with her. Billy, Polly, and Onofrio had gone ahead the first time she'd rested, and this was the third. With school over for the season, the youngsters were even more engaged in Nate's project.

The incline was smooth, with the sandy causeway already worn into a gentle groove by so many footsteps. But every step was leaden to Penelope. Her body had seemed to grow heavier overnight. Heat had settled in for the half-year summer and the humid atmosphere was becoming oppressive. She was restless at night and lethargic during the day.

Finally, the two women reached the level ground at top. A crestfallen Onofrio waited there. "No tourists!" he complained. "Why no tourists?" He scanned the majestic view they had, of the placid river, tangled woods, and the sandy road that led back into town.

"Nobody coming on the road or the river," he said.

"The winter visitors have all gone back North," Penelope said to him in Italian. "The winter tourist season has ended."

"How'm I gonna make any more money now?" He looked dejected.

"You still earn cash from our conversations, remember? And I'm sure Nate will find another job for you now that tourists aren't taking up as much of your time."

"Small change," he grumbled. "The tourists, they tip me sometimes big coins, once even a dollar bill! I gotta think of something big. This could take a while." He ran off toward the main excavation pit.

Penelope followed at a sedate pace. Cornelia busied herself with setting up a sitting area in a shady spot. Polly and Billy were at work in a corner of the excavation.

"Cornelia, I can do that," Penelope said when Cornelia started to unpack the art supplies.

Cornelia waved Penelope away. "Helping others is one way of serving our Lord. It brings me peace and contentment."

"I envy you that peace and contentment," Penelope said. "But I fear only annoyance and impatience would arise in me if I were to emulate your path."

Cornelia stood up and brushed sand off her novice's habit.

"True, this isn't for everyone," she said. "But I can't wait until I can take my formal vows and become a Sister of St. Francis." Her face shone.

They turned together toward the excavation area and discovered that a ragtag group of strangers had arrived.

So, the tourists hadn't all gone home.

"Oh, Sister Bridget expected this would happen," Cornelia said. "She said now that spring crops are harvested, summer crops are still young, and schools are on break, local people from the surrounding areas would come to see what all the fuss is about."

Onofrio was delighted. Penelope listened as he spouted the spiel he'd perfected. She knew he'd even arranged a point where Nate stopped working for a few minutes and offered an explanation of the day's finds.

But today, that was the only time Nate spoke, other than a few words here and there of instruction to others. He worked at a feverish pace with his lips pressed together, and he continued to ignore Penelope.

Polly and Billy picked up on his mood and were quiet as they tagged and labeled artifact shards. Onofrio started his own mini-square excavation outside Nate's work area when he wasn't guiding the sporadic visitors.

Penelope returned Nate's silent treatment for a couple of hours. She grew hot, then irritated, when her third attempt to sketch the precise design on a pottery shard went awry again.

The small group broke for an awkward lunch more oppressive than the sunlight of the afternoon. As the day warmed, visitors drifted off. The chill between Nate and Penelope remained pronounced. He hadn't even sat with them for lunch, but had taken his food and gone to his work table to eat.

"I'm going hunting for ferns in the shade," Polly said and wiped her mouth. "Me too," echoed both Billy and Onofrio. The three couldn't escape fast enough. Cornelia tidied up the lunch remains and offered Penelope a hand to get up. When Penelope shook her head, Cornelia took her prayer book from her bag and walked a short distance away.

Penelope saw Nate start to move back toward the dig area.

"Not so fast, please." She lumbered to a standing position.

He froze but didn't turn toward Penelope.

"Are you going to stop speaking to me forever?"

He turned, at that. His face was guarded.

"Maybe?"

"Why?"

His eyebrows arched. "Maybe I should be the one asking that question."

"Then ask it."

"This isn't some stupid game, Penelope. Why taunt me?"

She was surprised. She was vexed, but not trying to be coy or secretive.

"Nobody said anything about games," she said.

This wasn't going well at all. She eased herself back down in her chair.

Silence dangled between them for long minutes. The afternoon heat hung over them and Penelope wished for a breeze.

Nate suddenly took large steps that led him to her side in seconds. He stood rigidly beside her chair, looked down and met her gaze with eyes masked of emotion.

"I have to spell out the game?" He seemed genuinely perplexed. "What else accounts for whatever fanciful idea you had in mind? When, Miss Gold, were you going to tell me you are married? Was I supposed to guess, even though you don't wear a ring?"

The space between the two of them felt sharp and pressed on Penelope. *Just get to the point,* she told herself. *Get this over with.*

"The reason I don't wear a wedding band, Mr. Russon, is because I'm not married."

Nate's mouth dropped open, then closed. He stared at her with shock plain on his face. She kept her back straight and chin up. The time for embarrassment was long gone.

He wiped a hand on his forehead's bandana and through his hair. He scratched his neck. His glance darted at her protruding abdomen and just as quickly moved away. Finally, he blew out puffs of air.

"Okay, it's obvious you insist on keeping this some sort of

guessing game," he said. His eyes were bright. "I'll be the fool and play. You're engaged and soon to be wed."

Penelope shook her head. She knew she should say more, but how? No handy words came to mind. She'd never trained in the niceties of social dribble over such a topic. How, oh how, could she tell him what really happened? Her throat constricted.

"You're a widow, then?"

"No."

Nate blew out a puff of air. Penelope continued to cast about for a way to push the conversation where it needed to go. She had to determine how to dance around a delicate topic that wasn't what it appeared to be.

"I think it's obvious, from my answers, and you can figure out..." she started to say.

"See, you leave me no alternative but to guess," he said at the same time.

They both shut up.

"Go ahead," she said, almost in a whisper.

"No, you," he said, in two snapped words. "I don't think you want to hear what I think."

"Oh, but I do," she said. "I do want to hear how you judge me before you know the facts and circumstances."

Penelope rarely lost her temper, but her discomfort fueled by irritation, heat, and humidity made her testier by the minute.

"As you would judge, were you to see the same," he retorted.

"Not true." Although, possibly very true, a tiny voice inside her admitted.

"I didn't take you for that kind of woman."

"Oh, please stop, Nate. That's enough! What kind of woman do you think I am? A harlot? A fool?"

"The kind of woman who needs to go away 'for her health,' for nine months," he said.

"My choices were limited."

"Obviously."

"I'm the same person I was last week and last month."

Nate gave her a cool glance. "I want to believe that. But it's hard. So, where's the happy father?"

"I wish he were in jail." The words burst out before she was fully able to comprehend how true they were to her. They hit hard as soon as they bounced into the air. Herman was waltzing free while she paid a life-altering sentence of societal retribution for a sin she hadn't committed.

Penelope burst into tears, a rarity for her. She squeezed her eyes shut but had trouble controlling herself. Months of pent-up emotion spilled out.

"Hey, there, hey, now." Nate knelt down on one knee to make his face level with hers. He took one of her hands in his and patted it. His exasperation, confusion, and anger vanished. She saw only concern and care through her blurred gaze.

Cornelia came running over.

"I think you should go back to work now," she said to Nate without looking at him.

Penelope shook her head no, and stuttered a reply, while her mind registered that Nate was in the position a man took to propose. She almost laughed, but it would have come out as hysterics.

"We need to finish." She hiccupped and gulped. "Our conversation. We need to finish."

Cornelia looked dubious. Polly, Billy, and Onofrio had moved closer to investigate but stayed clear of the adult drama. They kept a good distance away and soon disappeared again.

"I insist," said Penelope, inch by inch regaining her composure. Nate still patted her hand as though uncertain what else to do.

"I come from a large family and I've been around ladies in this condition," Nate said to Cornelia. "It's best to do as they say."

Cornelia considered his words but didn't step away until Penelope urged her to return to her prayers.

"I want to know more about this fellow who belongs inside a cell," Nate said in a lowered voice after he and Penelope were alone again. "Anyone who causes you trouble is no friend of mine. I'd go after him if I could."

The cloud over Penelope's heart parted a little. She dabbed her eyes with her handkerchief, and Nate awkwardly let go of her other hand and straightened up. Then he sat down next to her, on the ground.

"From what you're not telling me, I think the bloke had better keep his distance," Nate said. "I'm no stranger to standing up to bullies. If you need someone to defend your honor, I'm your man."

Sweet, sweet Nate. "Thank you," she whispered. "I hope to settle things in as civil a manner as possible, should it come to that."

But she'd left Boston in such a hurry she wasn't sure what that meant. The reality of the baby hadn't sunk in yet when she left. What exactly did she now want from Herman, if anything?

"Fair enough," Nate said. "Just give me the word." He lifted her chin with his hand, gently. "But look. Try and understand. Do you blame me for being surprised?"

"No," she said, with a sad smile. He released her chin, but not before she thought for a sudden moment that they would kiss.

"Why didn't you say anything before? I mean, your, uh, *condition* is somewhat difficult to hide."

"It wasn't hard to hide at first. I just didn't want to deal with the way people would treat me differently when they knew. I don't believe in hiding."

"You're hiding here, in Persimmon Hollow."

"Because my family made me."

"Come on, Penelope. I didn't just crawl out from under a rock."

They looked at each other. Nate, who spent hours each day doing exactly that? Crawling around in the sand and muck and under rock-like protuberances of coquina shell and sand that stuck out from the sides of his excavation pit?

They both laughed, small, tentative laughs. The pain around Penelope's heart eased a bit.

"This isn't easy for me to discuss," she said.

Nate held up a hand. "Can I apologize first?"

"For?" She gave him an expectant look.

"For misjudging you." He looked down at his hands, then up and across the work area. "For being angry with you. For being angry with myself."

He turned to face her directly. "I see you're in an unfortunate situation but let me tell you, I'm mighty relieved you're not married. I hardly slept last night, for thinking I'd lost you forever, for thinking I'd been taken for a fool."

"Nate! Why think that?"

"Penelope, I took the liberty of thinking you enjoyed my company. Of liking yours. Of liking you. I've never known a woman like you, a cultured woman, the type of woman who generally doesn't notice I exist. I guess it went to my head. Then all of a sudden I see you're on the verge of motherhood."

"You noticed nothing over the past few months?" Penelope asked. "I've been gaining weight steadily."

"I know. I thought you were regaining your health. I kept telling myself people gain weight in different ways, different places on their bodies." His words had a sad tinge.

"I don't understand why you felt you'd been taken for a fool."

Nate scratched the back of his head. "You would if you came from an immigrant family accustomed to being shunned by people who consider themselves better. I felt I'd misread our companionship, that in reality I was just a handy fellow here to amuse you in your temporary boredom."

"Oh, no, Nate," she said, and placed a hand on his arm. "I enjoy being with you, more than you know. Our talks, this project, our work together. Doing the drawings and paintings kept me from slipping into despair, many times."

He placed his hand over hers. "I knew your interest in the artifacts was real when I saw you out here day after day. I thought we'd been growing closer, like good friends. That's another reason I was surprised you hadn't mentioned anything was out of the ordinary."

"My situation hardly makes for polite social conversation."

"But it's a reality. Your reality."

"Yes, I'm aware of that."

"We're beyond society's conventions, or so I thought."

"We are, Nate, or at least I hope we are."

They lapsed into silence but the tension had evaporated. Penelope felt the friendly Nate had returned, at least a little bit. His guard was up, though, in a way it hadn't been.

"I'm willing to share the full story if you care to hear it," she said.

"Only if you're comfortable doing so," he said. "I figured out a lot when you said that fool belonged in jail."

She wanted to lean into him, to feel his protective arms around her, and almost did.

"I assume he's not in any danger of seeing prison walls?" Nate asked.

"Probably not. It's not fair."

"I know about unfairness, Penelope. Anybody who isn't sitting pretty atop the halls of power knows about it." He kept his hand over hers, which stayed on his arm.

She felt the baby move. After a few more minutes, she withdrew her hands to her lap and started to talk.

"I questioned how my judgment about the man—his name is

Herman—had been so wrong," she said. "I've come to realize during my exile that he'd been superb in his con game. He'd learned what I favored and played into those feelings. He pretended to care about me and my opinions and desires."

Despite the day's warmth, she gave a shiver.

"Don't put yourself through this again," Nate said. "*You* are what matters. Not the past. Do you want a shawl? Should I call Cornelia over?"

"No to both questions," she said. "And talking about the past helps release its grip on me. Helps me realize it wasn't my fault. I know you understand."

He nodded and stayed close but didn't touch her.

She told him about the day of the hay ride, the assault, and the aftermath. She noticed Nate's fists clench and unclench more than once.

"I shudder when I remember the day Herman's mask came off for good," Penelope said. "My mind was clouded the day he took advantage of me. But his future actions allowed me to see him with clarity."

"How could he act worse than he already had?" Nate grumbled.

"He did. He asked me to see a doctor friend of his. He said the doctor would provide special pills to calm me so we could discuss my situation, as he said, 'in a rational way.'"

She gave a short laugh while Nate snorted.

"I was still assuming Herman would step up and accept his responsibilities, so I agreed. But I was wrong. He took me to a seedy, dangerous part of the city. It was a chilly day, but he was sweating when he told the carriage driver to stop in front of a rundown building. I remember it had a dirty, battered door. The street was filthy, with debris and unkempt buildings. Many had broken or boarded windows."

She struggled to keep her emotions level. Nate noticed, and

gently took her hand again. She gripped it. His hand felt solid and steady. She felt strength flow from him to her.

"The doctor was an abortionist," she said. "I suspected as much as soon as I walked into the dimly lit waiting room. No reputable doctor maintains such ill-kempt premises. I knew for certain when the doctor—wearing a soiled operating smock— beckoned us into the inner chamber. Herman had a tight grip on my arm so I had to enter the room. One glance told me all I needed to know. I found some kind of superhuman ability. I shoved Herman away the second he loosened his hold when the doctor beckoned me toward a dirty examination table. Herman was so surprised he stumbled backward and lost his balance. I ran, and somehow made it outside and into the carriage before Herman could catch up with me. The driver took one look at my face and had the carriage wheels turning by the time Herman got outside and shouted at us."

She realized she was digging her fingernails into Nate's hand. He sat, rock solid, his gaze on her face. His eyes revealed concern but his jaw was clenched.

"Thank God you got away," he said. He raised her hand to his lips, kissed it, and set it down gently atop the other hand she rested on her lap. She felt her fingers relax.

"You're safe now," he said. "It's over."

She flexed and arched her wrist. Nate stood up and paced in a small oval in front of her.

"But I'm ready to do what your family obviously isn't," he said.

"No, Nate, think about what you're saying. The laws, the social net, the prejudices, all would work against both you and me. I'd rather you help me move forward."

"What are your plans?" Nate asked. "From what I know, women in situations like yours go away as you did until they give birth. Then they leave their newborn baby in the care of someone else and return to the life they left."

She couldn't help but see the shadow of sadness that passed over his face. "Is that what you will do?" he asked. He had stepped away a few paces, as though to shield himself from her answer. But he faced her squarely, thumbs hooked into the back pockets of his denims.

Penelope fingered a fold in her skirt for a moment.

"Had you asked me that months ago, I'd have said yes, that was the plan. But I've done a lot of thinking and praying. I've decided to keep my baby."

He let out a low whistle. "That's brave. Is your family okay with that idea?"

"They don't know it yet."

"Ah."

"You think me unwise?"

"No, brave. You're choosing a tough road. What if your family resists?"

"They won't. They'll accept the inevitable."

"But if they don't? How will you support yourself and the little one? You have to consider everything. You don't need me to tell you that, either."

"Money has never been a concern."

"I see."

"It's just something I've never had to worry about. I expect my family to be difficult and to disapprove. I don't expect them to cut me off. They may insist I live elsewhere. Appearances are very important to them."

"Penelope, you're being naïve. People who control wealth can be cruel. Even to relatives. You've had only a taste of it," he added as she started to protest. "Living away from family, thrown onto your own resources—it would be a big sacrifice."

"Leaving my baby would be, too. I know the road ahead will be difficult. I've thought about what I'll give up in terms of culture, city life, fine dining, art excursions, all that."

"Those are externals, Penelope, the frivolous things, not the essentials," Nate said. He was by her side again, one knee on the ground, the other propping up the arm he leaned across his bent thigh. His face was earnest, as though he was trying to will his message into her.

"Well, I can't imagine myself doing any of those things again, if my baby was being raised elsewhere. I've never been the fluttery debutante type. I've always preferred solitude, and especially my art, because it helps me battle melancholy."

"I already had a great deal of respect for you, Penelope," Nate said. "And it's going up as we speak. But you're not going to have time to sketch if you're tossed out to make your own way in the world while raising a child. You told me to think about what I was saying, a few minutes ago. Now it's your turn."

She swallowed, but didn't speak for a few minutes.

"And what would you have me do, Nate? Succumb to my family's wishes and leave my baby?"

He blew out a breath. "No, I hate that idea as much as you do."

"I'll figure something out," she said.

"With my help," he said. "You can rely on me for anything, today, tomorrow, in the far-off future, always. Even if I'm off on another continent chasing long-lost antiquities. I'll make sure you always know where I'll be and how to find me."

"Your words mean more than you know," she said.

He kissed her hand again and she felt like a schoolgirl.

Just then, the fern-hunters trooped back into the dig site with noisy exuberance. Penelope waved Nate off, back to his work. She didn't let on how much she'd read into his last words. She didn't want to think of a future without Nate. She wanted to keep the status quo indefinitely—and knew she couldn't.

"Look at all this!" Polly called from one of the worktables and held up a giant clump of ferns. "What 'til Professor Art gets ahold of these! New ones, never saw them before. The spores are different."

"They all look the same to me," said Billy, and plopped down a handful.

"We sell them?" Onofrio asked, and dropped a clump atop the others. "No? Then why waste our time? What you gonna do with them?"

"Study them, press them, and maybe arrange them on paper and use them for decorations," Polly said. "I'm making a fern book."

Onofrio shook his head as though Polly spoke nonsense.

Nate surveyed the scene.

The three youngsters were clustered around the table where uncategorized pieces and small artifact finds awaited labeling. "Move the pottery pieces off to one side and put the ferns at the end of the table," Nate called. "Carefully!" he added, as Billy knocked something off the table. Nate bolted over and picked up the piece. It had fallen beside a knapsack Nate carried to and from the site each day. He grabbed the sack, too.

"Whoa, Penelope, I forgot to show you this!" he said as he set the fallen piece back on the table and loped over to her, knapsack in hand.

"Look at this. Finished it yesterday, after days of wrestling with a jigsaw puzzle of jagged pieces. A complete bowl, reconstructed."

He sat the sack down, opened it, and withdrew something cocooned in wadded sheets of newspaper. He unwrapped each sheet as though the item it covered was in danger of collapse. Finally, he removed the last sheet.

Penelope leaned forward for a closer look. Nestled in the pile of wrinkled newspaper was a small oval bowl in the shape of a turtle. Around the rim, Nate had re-affixed squat, thick pieces that resembled a turtle's head and legs. The leg protrusions bore incisions that indicated claws, and the head atop the slightly thicker neck featured eye and mouth markings.

She lifted her gaze to meet his.

"Nate, this is incredible." She air-traced her finger over the bowl's markings. "Look at the intricacy of the decorations."

"I know, nothing primitive about it," Nate said.

"Not at all. What would it have been used for?"

"Not sure. Ceremonial is my first guess."

"Any idea of its age?"

"Pre-Columbian. But I can't pin down a specific date range without doing more research."

"I can't wait to sketch it," Penelope said. "I'll make several copies. If you want, I can help mail them to museums and universities with requests for comparison to their antiquities."

He appeared momentarily startled. "Thanks, but Penelope, I can't ask you to do anything beyond sketching. The rest is my responsibility. And you have more than enough going on."

His gaze slid over her swelling body and quickly back up to her face.

She placed a hand on his arm. "Please, let me help. Writing, sketching—they're among the things I'm still able to do easily. And they keep my mind occupied."

He looked at her for a long moment.

"I can think of nothing I'd like better than your help." He placed his hand atop hers and squeezed it, then released it. "Everything will work out in the end."

She didn't ask if he referred to his work or her situation. She felt only relief and a renewed flow of friendship between them. The edginess that had marked the start of her visit had evaporated. They were almost—almost—back on the solid ground that had buoyed her for so many weeks now.

Her lifted spirits must have shown on her face. Because she noticed delight written all over Nate's.

"Let me get this piece back to the table and get back to work," he said.

"Cornelia and I need to return to town," Penelope said. "I'll come back tomorrow to do the illustration. My energy may be flagging, but it's not gone yet."

He started to walk back to the collections table, turtle bowl carefully in his hands, when he stopped and turned back toward her.

"Penelope. Thanks."

She lifted her hand in reply, but her eyes spoke what she couldn't find the words to say. "Thank you for listening, for really hearing what I had to say," she murmured, too low for the words to carry to him. She watched as Nate sat the turtle bowl atop the table and hopped back into the excavation with a carefree maneuver that spoke of a man who'd just shed a burden.

Penelope noticed handfuls of random sightseers straggle through as she neatened and packed her art supplies and Cornelia stored them in the carrying case. She half-listened to Onofrio talk about stratum levels and marveled at how much he'd learned. She heard Polly explain more about ferns than the visitors likely wished to hear, although some young men did show marked interest in the table where ferns and artifacts shared space. *Must be admiring the turtle bowl,* she thought idly.

THE NEXT MORNING, Penelope was anxious see if any more archaeological surprises were being unearthed. She and Cornelia joined the youngsters for an early journey out to the river. During the ride, she admitted to herself that she was equally anxious to know if her relationship with Nate had really been repaired. Or as repaired as it could be as they traveled their very different paths.

Nate, bent over a task in the excavation, straightened as they arrived. Joy spread across his face. Penelope grinned. The day was bright, indeed. In contrast to the humid stickiness that already pressed around her, Penelope's heart felt as light as an early morning breeze.

Nate climbed out of the pit and loped over toward where Penelope was arranging her art supplies. Polly finagled the boys and even Cornelia into taking a quick look for ferns along a new path she'd made.

"Look, another treasure!" Nate exclaimed as he neared Penelope with a small object in his hand. "Just unearthed it. Haven't even gotten it over to the collection table yet for labeling. Look how it bears a decorative resemblance to the turtle bowl."

He rubbed the side of an almost-whole bowl clean with the edge of his shirt. "See the etchings?"

Heads close together, Nate and Penelope inspected the smallish bowl. "It's missing only this V-shaped chip on one side," he pointed out. "See how the decorative incisions are similar to the turtle bowl?"

Penelope studied the artifact. "It's like the same artist's hand was at work," she said.

"Yeah, that's what I thought, too," Nate agreed. "This and the other piece reflect a distinct artistic style."

"These ancients—they focused on beauty as well as survival," Penelope said. "Can you get the turtle bowl? I'll draw each one alone and then positioned side by side. We can compare the etchings."

"Sure thing." He scrambled up and over to the collection table just as the youngsters and Cornelia returned with fern specimens in hand.

Nate halted abruptly and whirled back toward the group.

"Did one of you move the turtle bowl that was right here?" Nate asked them and pointed to an empty space amid the clutter. "When picking up ferns or putting them down?"

Polly, Billy, and Onofrio shook their heads no. "I haven't put anything there yet today," Polly said, and held up the new ferns in her hand. "And we don't need much space for ferns. We don't touch anything else unless we ask you first or are doing tagging for you."

Cornelia's nod vouched for them.

Nate took long, quick steps over to the group. "The turtle bowl is missing." He studied one youngster after another. "Did you take it to sell, young man?" he asked Onofrio.

The boy's eyes went round and wide.

"No, sir! I no touch anything that belongs to Mr. Nate! We shake hands, we are partners! You remember, yes?" He looked both worried and innocent, with a touch of defiance mixed in.

"I believe you," Nate said.

The little boy visibly relaxed. "Maybe somebody steal it? I help you find it."

Penelope couldn't imagine anything had been stolen from this remote place. The idea didn't fit the homey picture she had weaved in her mind about Persimmon Hollow. Surely the bowl was simply misplaced.

"Billy?" Nate asked. The youth's serious expression answered as much as his words of innocence did. Polly shook her head when Nate looked at her.

Cornelia pulled out her rosary beads. Nate appeared like he might ask even Cornelia if she'd taken the bowl. He opened his mouth but closed it before speaking.

His face was grim. He clenched and unclenched his fist and muttered about how he should have repacked the bowl the previous day.

"I'm not accusing anyone here," he said finally. "But unless some animal wandered through and took a fancy to one particular artifact, we have a theft on our hands."

CHAPTER 12

$\mathcal{T}$he atmosphere inside the Taylor cabin the next afternoon was as gloomy as the grayness of the sky outside. On an ordinary day, the drip of gentle but steady raindrops on palm fronds outside would have lulled Penelope. Not today. Yesterday's upsetting news had put Persimmon Hollow on edge.

Seth sat at the edge of a chair by the fireplace and whittled the figure of a man on a horse for his young son. The shavings fell on the drop cloth he'd spread on the floor. Billy, stretched out on the floor, idly picked at the slivers of wood. Agnes rocked little Seth on her lap.

Polly, Cornelia, and Penelope sat on the settee. Nate paced the room, with his shadow Onofrio close by his side.

"I appreciate you opening up space in the barn for the artifacts," Nate said to Seth and Agnes. "We got everything moved in short order."

Seth nodded. "Still, doesn't solve what looks to me like a crime."

"True," Nate said. "But I'm glad we've hauled everything from the site to here. Billy, a big thanks to you and to you,

Onofrio, and the other boys at the orphanage. I'll stop there later to say my thanks to them in person."

"The Alloways are asking around town about any sightings of suspicious people," Agnes said.

"I wish I'd paid more attention to the people who came to the dig site," Polly said.

"Or the people I saw near the table," Penelope said.

"They couldn't lift anything with us right there," Billy said.

"No, but some of them—they ask a lot of questions, so many I lost my place and almost got confused," Onofrio said.

"What kind of questions?" Nate asked.

"Stupid ones," Onofrio said. "Like why we put the work tables in one place and not another. They distract me with stupid questions."

Everyone paid attention.

"At first I suspected the thief acted at night," Nate said. "Now I wonder if somebody out there yesterday didn't lift the bowl. Thank God I hadn't left the silver pieces in view. Onofrio, Polly, Billy, you were around the visitors the most. Do you remember anything specific?"

Their blank expressions gave him the answer.

"I'd guess the people there yesterday were country folk, judging by their clothing," Penelope said.

"Which tells us, at least, that a slick visitor didn't steal it and then slip away from town," Nate said. "It's a start, anyway."

"Whoever has it will probably try to sell it far from here," Seth said.

Little Seth slid off Agnes's lap, toddled over to Billy, and joined the exploration of Seth's wood shavings with joyful abandon. Curls and slivers of wood scattered.

"Acts more like his father every day," Agnes said.

Penelope knew she was trying to lighten the mood but no one could muster a laugh.

Agnes adjusted the wick of a kerosene lamp on the side table.

A dim glow cast a pool of warm light. She reached for the Bible that was set beside the lamp.

"The only place to turn in a time like this is to God," she said.

Billy let out a groan under his breath. No one spoke as the sound of thin pages being turned mingled with the patter of raindrops outside.

"Cornelia, do you have a suggestion?" Agnes asked, to Penelope's surprise. Everyone knew Agnes had memorized chunks of the Bible and knew the order of books in both the Old and New Testaments.

"When I was younger and fearful about anything, I always found solace in the Gospel of Matthew, where he tells of Jesus offering peace to souls who take his yoke," Cornelia said. She spoke with an authority Penelope hadn't observed in her before.

"It's just two simple lines but they bolstered me," Cornelia said. "Look in Chapter 11."

Agnes studied the pages for several moments. "I think I know which passage you mean. Yes, here it is, Matthew 11:28–29:

Come to me, all you who are weary and burdened, and I will give you rest. Take my yoke upon you and learn from me, for I am gentle and humble in heart, and you will find rest for your souls.

"There's been no bloodshed, and no one was hurt," Agnes said. "As serious as this is, I'm thankful we're all here, safe and in good health."

"I'm all for having a peaceful soul, but I've got an excavation site to protect," Nate said. "Last thing I need is pothunters out there."

"Put guards on the site," Seth said.

"Funds are stretched thin," Nate said. "There's almost nothing left."

"I'll do it!" Billy said.

"When would you sleep?" Agnes asked. "You have chores in the grove and on the farm that take up a chunk of your day, especially in summer."

"I'll do it after them and for part of the night. You could pay me later, Nate."

"What does Professor Art have to say?" Penelope asked.

Nate shrugged. "The idea of posting a guard didn't come up when I talked to him last night. We spent most of our time reviewing possible thief candidates put forth by people in town. If they weren't thugs passing through, who are they? Where would lowlifes hide? I thought Persimmon Hollow was next door to Eden, the way you all talk about it."

Seth stopped whittling. "We don't have a lot of what you call 'lowlifes.' I bet most of the names that came up were regular folk down on their luck, but honest enough not to steal."

Nate stuck his hands in his pockets. "Yeah. Eunice and Fanny knew every person named and their history back to the Flood."

"There are some known bandits who live out by the river," Seth said. "They come and go, and tend to stay out of sight or leave town when it's this hot out. Can't hurt to send someone out to check."

"Clyde's been saying Persimmon Hollow is getting big enough to need a marshal," Billy said.

"You mean this place doesn't have one?" Nate asked. "Okay, we have to come up with a plan for security ourselves then. I need to talk to the professor."

"He and Fanny, along with Eunice and Clyde, are due out here any minute," Agnes said. "We're all having supper at the orphanage so we can plan how to include the children in the holiday theatrical."

The Independence Day theatrical. Penelope had forgotten about it. She'd offered to help create the scenic backdrops. Well, she certainly couldn't crawl around the floor and paint canvas. But she would create a design and supervise the painting. More things to keep her busy. The act of thievery had unsettled her more than she let on. She felt as though something were trying to crack her protective shield and shred the dream she was spinning.

A short while later, a wagon squeaked up the sandy drive. Fanny, Professor Art, Eunice, and Clyde soon crowded into the parlor with the others. The conversation rallied again and rolled from one idea to the next, without solution.

"Seth, Agnes, okay if I bunk out in your barn with my artifacts if I'm not staying overnight at the site, until all this is settled?" Nate asked.

"Absolutely," Agnes and Seth answered at the same time.

"Come on, son, there's no need for that," Professor Art started to protest.

"Says the man lucky enough to leave his books, papers, and dried plant material strewn across Fanny's dining room table," said Eunice.

"It's a good thing I didn't have all my finds out at the site," said Nate, in no mood for levity.

"Honey," Fanny said, and tapped Art on the arm with her fan. "I really do need my dining room table back. I need space to make decorations, invitations, and programs for the holiday."

"I surrender," said Art. "Temporarily. I use that space to research the flora Nate unearths. My small input can help convince others of the advances in science my protégé is making."

"No need to convince us, we're proud of Nate's achievements," Agnes said. "I'm honored he wants to set up a field station at Taylor Grove."

"A what?" Polly, Billy, and Onofrio all perked up. Penelope glanced up. It was the first she'd heard of the idea. From the expressions around her, it was the first many of them had heard.

"A permanent outpost for ongoing exploration," Nate explained.

Others started to speak at once, but Penelope realized she and Nate still had much to repair in their relationship. A month ago, he would have told her first. In time, she prayed. In time. *You knew in your heart it would take more than a day's conversation to repair the breach. You just didn't want to admit it.*

Penelope closed her eyes and listened to the conversations. She wondered how the explosive letter she'd recently written had been received by her family. In it, she'd laid out her revised plan, which went counter to the one they'd devised for her. She hadn't told anyone she'd written. Not even Nate.

Her relatives should have fully digested it by now, she thought. Perhaps even replied already. She hoped a wire transfer would arrive in return mail. Even if it came with a lecture. They'd probably command her to justify the loss of standing they'd suffer due to what they'd call "her selfish decision." So be it.

A memory nagged at her. The memory of how Nate thought it naïve of her to expect her family to give up without a fight. She pushed the intrusion away.

As the talk continued around her, she thought maybe she could help Nate pay for security. Just a small loan, after she received new funds. Yes, the shock of her secret had temporarily unraveled their tight bond. But he still cared. It was obvious. And she cared for him. She couldn't bear to lose the closeness between them. Anything but that.

NATE KEPT a polite distance between them in the following weeks. Penelope saw that he grew tenser by the day as the pothunter trail grew colder. He threw himself into daytime explorations and nighttime sorting, tagging, and writing.

Penelope reluctantly gave up her trips to the excavation site as she grew more ungainly. She continued to sketch, but sat in her room or outside in the wicker chairs near the arbor. Nate or

Cornelia or Onofrio delivered artifacts to her from the barn and work site.

The silence from her family was ominous. She swallowed her doubts and stayed busy.

One afternoon, she was seated outside and inking in the details on a rendering of an incised bowl fragment when a shadow loomed over her. She looked up and blinked.

Nate looked thinner and more haggard than he'd ever appeared.

"Oh, Nate, please sit," she beckoned a chair near her. "The sun has almost claimed my shade but it's still nice out. You look like you need the rest."

"No time," he said. "I came myself to put this one securely in the barn." He held up a bone. "Just unearthed it."

Penelope carefully put down her pen. "Is that what I think it is?"

Nate looked around to be certain they were alone. "Yes. A tibia, I think. I found it today when I dug a new layer. There are a lot of smaller bones, some pieces of femur and maybe humerus. Everything's jumbled as though the site was disturbed centuries ago."

"Whew," said Penelope. "I don't even know what to say." She glanced at his tired eyes. "Please, rest a few minutes," she urged again. "I'm almost finished with this sketch. If you can wait about ten minutes, you can take that shard with you to the barn." She indicated the bowl fragment she modeled her sketch upon.

Nate put the bone on the table, sat down, and leaned his head against the back of the chair. The gentle scrape of Penelope's fountain pen against the thick paper filled the quiet space.

"I miss my trips to the site," she said, without looking up.

"I miss them too."

She did gaze up then, and met his eyes. His were guarded. Yet he was here, wasn't he? Had sat down and stayed. She returned to her task. The gentle and methodical scratching of her crosshatch lines calmed her, too.

"You're so beautiful, Penelope."

Her ink line went jagged and she lifted her hand with a start.

Nate rubbed a hand over his eyes. "I don't mean to be so forward, even though I meant what I said. You're right, I'm over-tired. Not watching my tongue."

She blotted out the erratic line of ink before it dried.

"Nate, thanks for the compliment. But honestly, I feel about the size of one of those manatees the Taylors took me to see months ago in the spring run."

He chuckled. "Every newcomer is taken to see the manatees."

Their gazes touched for a moment. Penelope felt her cheeks grow heated. She looked away.

"I mean it, Penelope, you're beautiful," Nate said. He leaned forward in the chair, put his hands on his thighs and stretched his arms. "Maybe it's the way the light shines on your hair or in your eyes. Your soft heart and gentle ways. Your delicate hand and the way it holds the pen or the way you angle your head when you work. All I know is, as I sat here and watched you, the thought screamed at me. And you deserve to hear it."

Penelope tried to keep her expression light. She wanted to wrap her arms around him. Be close to him. Hear him tell her again she was beautiful and desirable.

"Your words mean more than you can imagine, especially now," she said, her voice hardly above a whisper.

She thought for a moment he was going to reach forward and kiss her. Instead, he leaned back again in his chair and gripped his hands together.

"I wish I could do more for you," he said. "If my career were more advanced, more settled, I could—no, I should be able to find a way now. You need me."

She lifted a hand to stop him. "I do need you, Nate. But

you're already doing enough. Look who's talking now of shouldering more than they should. You look like you're not getting enough sleep already."

"I'm not. Doesn't matter."

"Yes, it does. You'll buckle under the strain unless you pace yourself. I've watched you grow feverish in search of treasures. You always find time to guide Onofrio. You shape theories and theses mentally all day long, then stay up late writing and updating field notes. And I know how much the unsolved theft troubles you. Did I miss anything?"

Nate shook his head. "But I haven't come up with other treasures. There's nothing out there right now a thief would want. Chipped tibias and femurs don't interest them."

He picked up the tibia bone from the table. "But this adds a new dimension to the project. New meaning that I haven't figured out yet."

Nate studied the bone. "It doesn't look like much. But I'd be leaping with excitement if I wasn't exhausted. You're right about my being rundown."

"I wish I had suggestions to make," Penelope said. She shifted in her chair in search of a more comfortable position and felt a fatigue come over her. "But I've reached a point where I must rest whenever my body and my baby dictate a slowdown. Kind of like right now."

Nate was on his feet in seconds. "You need to get inside? Here, lean on me. I'll come back and get your art stuff."

She let him help her up. "You could force yourself to take daily breaks, too," she said, as he escorted her toward the door. "Stop driving yourself so hard."

She glanced up at him and read stubbornness in his face.

"It's almost July," he said. "I have to organize my notes. Secure more funding. Have to. Especially now." His free hand fisted for a moment and Penelope felt the tension in his body. She stopped walking.

"Nate, would you be amenable to a loan?"

"I sure would. Point me in the right direction."

"I mean from me."

"Your family is in banking?"

"No. But I have some family money and can request more funds at any time. My family is interested in the sciences."

"Your family that doesn't know you're planning to defy them?"

She drew in a breath. "In fact, I'm awaiting a letter from them as we speak. I wrote to them about my intentions."

Nate drew her gently around so that she faced him. He took her hands in his.

"My sweet Penelope, you're the last person I want to borrow money from. Mark my words, you're going to need every cent if you follow through with your plan. The folks back home won't be pleased. The checkbooks and ledger books will slam shut."

She let a brief acknowledgment of his words fly over her, then brushed it away.

"I hope to prove you wrong," she said

"I hope so, too. Why are you refusing to consider they might react harshly?"

"Because they're my family. They might be difficult but they're not hateful. I see the skepticism in your face, Nate. I promise I'll think about alternatives. Just not right now. I don't want to worry about anything right now. It might upset my baby."

As if knowing it was the subject of discussion, the baby kicked.

"Ouch."

"What's wrong? Did I grip your hands too hard?" Nate instantly released her.

"No, it's the baby. He—she—just kicked."

His eyes widened.

"Oof, the little one just did it again."

Penelope grinned. Nate did too.

"C'mere, give me your hand," she said. Penelope didn't know what came over her. She wanted to share this incredible joy. Shyly, she took Nate's hand and place it atop her mounding body. He barely touched the top of her gown, just let his hand graze there.

"Whoa! I felt it!" he almost shouted a few seconds later and pumped the air with his fist.

"I'm astonished every time it happens," Penelope said.

"Wow, I feel like the happy dad and I didn't even know the little tyke existed until a short while ago," Nate said.

The orphanage door opened and Cornelia peered out from inside. "Everything okay out here?"

"Yes, Cornelia, come if you want to feel the baby. He or she is v-e-r-y active right now." Penelope beckoned to her.

Cornelia's eyes glistened as she hurried out. She crouched and placed her ear close and her hand atop Penelope. Sure enough, she didn't have to wait long.

Cornelia straightened and clasped her hands together. "A gift from God."

Funny, that's not how Penelope had thought about this baby for months.

"Yes, it is, indeed," Nate echoed.

Penelope looked at the two of them watching her with silly happiness on their faces.

"That's why I want to keep her. Or him. But I think it's a her."

"God works in wondrous ways, that's what Sister Bridget always says," Cornelia said. "Now, excuse me, I want to go share the news if that's okay with you, Miss Penelope. Your baby is kicking and that must mean he—she—is healthy. Oh, happy day!"

"By all means, share the news," Penelope said. It wasn't as if her secret was hidden anymore. Cornelia ran inside with a light step.

"I think my family will come around and will be as full of joy as we are right now," Penelope said to Nate. "I'm sure everything will be fine."

Nate's expression showed he didn't believe that any more than she did.

CHAPTER 13

*P*enelope read and re-read the letter before folding it and placing it back in the envelope with slow, precise movements. Her relatives would curb her funds if she followed through with her plan. No discussion. No understanding. Just a curt directive and a pointed reminder that she remember her—and their—status and station in life.

Well, there it was. Was she really surprised? Even before Nate's warnings, a stone of doubt had lodged in a corner of her mind. She'd ignored it after being unable to dislodge it. Hoped that her belief in the essential goodness of people would prove correct.

But the harsh tone of the letter was as loud as the midday lull outside her window was quiet. Into the silence filtered recollections of her family's stiff behavior and attitude. She gazed out at the still landscape until movement in a cedar tree caught her attention. From the safety of its branches, two young cardinals made short, wobbly forays into flight. "Go safely, little ones," she whispered, "and please survive."

"And how am I—we—going to survive?" She spoke aloud to herself and the baby inside her. She swallowed a swell of anxiety, rose from her desk, and tried to stretch. Her back ached and she felt every prickle of the June heat. Indigestion had become her constant companion. Penelope moistened a tea towel in the water from her pitcher and dabbed her face and hands. The cool liquid did little to relieve the rising heat of distress.

The sharp refusal from Boston, her growing fears as childbirth neared, and doubts about the future pressed hard from all sides. Melancholia seeped through the cracks.

Agnes, Sister Bridget, and the other women had insisted she stay off her feet until the Boston doctor hired by her family arrived for her final days of confinement. But Penelope knew that getting out and being around people were her best tools for fighting the rising sadness.

She glanced at her bed. It'd be so easy to just lie down and sleep for the rest of the day.

But then she'd awaken to the same mess. No, she wouldn't give in. Doom and gloom were bad for her and worse for her baby. She laid a hand over the giant mound her body had become. "We *will* find a way through this, little one," she whispered.

And how will you do that, her inner self screamed at her.

A prayer she'd learned from Cornelia rolled off her lips with soft urgency. She'd come to understand how the sacraments, prayers, and rituals of Cornelia's religion drew believers closer to God. She'd discovered she had a devotion to the Blessed Mother, to whom she now prayed. "Please, Mother Mary, take my petition to your Son, Our Lord. May He give me the strength to walk my path."

The path's direction remained veiled but her anxiety eased as she prayed. She said an Our Father and a Hail Mary, followed by several recitations of the Jesus Prayer: "Lord Jesus Christ, son of God, have mercy on me." She prayed until she was able to swallow her fear, at least temporarily.

Yes, she was scared. But she wouldn't crumble. Her family

might be abandoning her, but God and hew newfound kin in Persimmon Hollow wouldn't.

Thudding footsteps and laughing voices deeper in the orphanage bounced off the silence. Penelope straightened her rounded shoulders. It sounded like young amateur thespians were assembling to rehearse the Independence Day skit.

She forced herself to smile. The plan for a simple reading of the Declaration of Independence and other works had been embellished with patriotic songs, poetry, and recitations. Rehearsals were chaotic and treated more like parties than planning sessions.

Penelope waddled out of her room and went in search of the noisy rehearsal and the companionship and distraction it would provide.

"Yay, Penelope is here!" shouted scattered voices in the dining-room-turned-rehearsal hall. Polly bounced up to her, followed closely by Onofrio.

"Tell us who sounds better," Polly demanded. "I think I should recite the Emma Lazarus poem we learned at school, but Onofrio insists he should because someone told him it's about immigrants."

"She's not an immigrant," Onofrio said in a huff.

"You don't even know what the word means," Polly countered.

"Oh, *si*, yes I do. I come over the ocean in a giant boat. Some people when we got off yelled at us and called us dirty immigrants."

Both started reciting over each other and then looked to Penelope for arbitration. Around them the noise level increased. Children shouted at one another across the room, moved chairs and tables, and yelled out rehearsed lines that collided in air.

"Why don't you take turns and each do a few lines at a time?" Penelope asked, and winced at the off-tune singing coming from somewhere behind her.

"Oh," said Polly and Onofrio, and glanced at each other. "Why didn't we think of that?" Polly asked.

"Because you're too busy making noise," said Cornelia, who came in from the kitchen wiping her hands on her apron. "Misses Agnes and Fanny won't let any of you perform unless you learn to behave."

She turned to Penelope. "Did they wake you? You should be resting this time of afternoon. It's too hot for you to be up and about."

Penelope gave her a wan smile. "I can't stay abed or seated at my desk a minute longer. I came to check rehearsals and see how my sketches for the backdrop are being transformed to large scale. I hear they are in the barn."

Cornelia hesitated. She scrutinized Penelope's face.

"They're a big ugly mess," Onofrio butted in. "You better go fix them, Miss Penelope."

Cornelia shushed him. "Don't upset Miss Penelope."

Onofrio gazed upward with an exaggerated gesture. "She find out sooner or later. Better now than on the big day."

"Hmm, I better stroll over there," Penelope said. "I need to move a bit, Cornelia."

"Let me or one of the children to walk with you," Cornelia said.

Penelope refused. "You're all busy. I'll walk slowly and return soon." She cut off Cornelia when she started to protest. "You have enough to do here," she added, and glanced at Cornelia's unruly flock.

Cornelia ushered the youngsters toward the piano on the other side of the room as Penelope turned toward the door.

"What's wrong with Miss Penelope?" she heard Onofrio ask as she left the room.

"It looks like her sadness has come back," Cornelia said. "And it's up to us to help her do something about it."

• • •

Seeing the backdrops, Penelope winced. It was even worse than she'd imagined. She'd purposely made the sketches basic. But the enlargements created by the enthusiastic crew were askew with disorderly perspectives, varying scale, and unrecognizable renderings.

Let it go, she told herself. *They're doing their best and for a good cause.*

"Hey, should you be out here?"

Nate? She turned, and sure enough, there was Nate walking toward her from the other end of the barn, where he'd created a makeshift anthropology laboratory and storage site. Just seeing him lifted some of the sadness that weighed on her.

"I'm here to check on the scenery," she said. "But surprised to see you. I thought you'd still be out at the river. It's not even four o'clock yet."

"Came in early to get cleaned up for dinner in town at the Alloways'. Prof says he has news to share, something from one of his colleagues."

He peered at her. "That answers your question but you haven't answered mine. This barn is a minefield of objects to trip over. Careful!" He reached a hand to help guide her around a lopsided, rickety frame, from which hung a large canvas painted with something that might resemble a river and trees.

"Onofrio warned me I might be surprised at this, uh, scenery painting," she said. She waved a hand at the backdrop. Internally, she girded herself to hide the heaviness she felt and not let it show in her eyes. "So I walked out to take a look. Rehearsals were a bit loud, anyway."

"Uh, yeah, we didn't do such a good job."

"I don't know whether to laugh or cry."

"A bunch of us did what we could," Nate said.

"Did you even look at my sketches?" Penelope couldn't help but ask. She was both overheated and incredulous.

"Yes. We really did the best we could."

She pursed her lips and looked at him. She tamped down a sudden irritation. This was a small-town amateur theatrical. Not the Boston stage. The thought of Boston pushed the letter's contents to the forefront of her mind.

The letter, she knew, not the failed artistry before her, was the true source of her discontent. *Don't take this out on Nate and the others here,* she told herself.

"Oh. Oh, dear." She placed one hand on Nate and another on her stomach.

"What?! What is it? Are you having the baby? No! It isn't time yet!"

He quickly snapped out of his shock. Penelope felt his arms go around her in support, from behind her. She leaned back into him. His firmness, the feel of his breath on her neck, and the earthy scent of his clothes and skin enveloped her in cocoon of safety.

"I'm having pains," she managed to get out. Her hands gripped his arms as a contraction caught her breath.

"You sit down here, I'll go get Agnes and the other women." Nate guided her toward a stool. "No, come outside, I don't want you alone in here. Can you walk unsupported?"

"I think so." She took a few tentative steps, with Nate close by her side and one arm wrapped around her.

"It's too early." She turned frightened eyes toward him.

"I know," he said. "You'll be all right. You can get through anything."

His confidence bolstered hers. They made their way outside.

"Stay right here," Nate ordered. He darted back into the barn and brought out a bench. He placed it against the barn wall, where the overhanging eave provided a modicum of shade. He settled Penelope and bolted toward the Taylor log cabin and the orphanage, yelling loud enough to be heard into the next county.

Penelope tried to regulate her breathing as Agnes had taught her. The pains were erratic. They weren't regularly paced as

Agnes had told her expect. What was wrong? Something was wrong. It was too early.

She closed her eyes and prayed.

Nate returned first, out of breath from running. "They're coming," he said. "I turned back soon as I knew they heard me."

He sat down beside her and placed one arm around her with gentle care.

"I think the pains have stopped," Penelope said. She grasped his other hand and leaned her head back against the rough wood of the barn.

"That's good," he said. They both watched the figures of women running toward them.

"I think so." But a wedge of fear nudged itself into her. What if something terrible had just happened to her baby?

"My brave Penelope," he said. He raised and kissed her hand and lowered it as though it was breakable.

Penelope waited for the pains to return but nothing happened. She dared to breathe a little easier. The baby had almost four weeks to go. She wasn't ready. She had to make arrangements. Plans. She had to find a way to support them both.

Her heartbeat, which had started to ease back to normal, picked up again as the problems zoomed back into focus with force.

She closed her eyes and leaned into Nate. She wanted to stay there forever.

Agnes, Lupita, Cornelia, and Sisters Bridget and Rose were suddenly around her, all speaking at once. Seth and Alfredo stood a respectful distance away, ready to do anything needed. Nate rose and let the women take over. He gave Penelope's shoulders and hands a light squeeze before letting her go.

"The pains have stopped," Penelope told the women. She noted an immediate smoothing of some of the tension marking their faces.

"Thank God," Agnes said. "Seth, please get the stretcher

from when Alfredo broke his leg," She issued terse commands. "We need to get Penelope to the house immediately."

She spoke to Penelope again. "How far apart were the pains? Minutes? Seconds?"

"Minutes. But they were erratic. And they have stopped."

Agnes and Lupita glanced at each other.

"Was this the first time the pains occurred?" Agnes asked. She placed her wrist against Penelope's forehead to check for an elevated temperature.

"Yes."

"You're sure?"

"Yes, I think I would know." Penelope managed a weak smile.

"It might be false labor but we don't want to take any chances," Agnes said, and Lupita nodded her agreement.

"Don't move," Agnes said. "No, not a muscle. You're flushed and slightly warm. The men will carry you up to my house. From now on, you'll stay in Polly's bedroom. She can bunk at the orphanage for a while, in your room, if Sister Bridget agrees."

"Do whatever is best for Penelope," said Bridget.

"This was my fault," Cornelia fretted. "I shouldn't have let Penelope walk to the barn."

Lupita put her arm around the young woman. "Hush, now, you have been a saint to her for months now."

Penelope felt weak and more frightened than she let on. She wanted to tell them she'd feel most comfortable in her room at the orphanage. But maybe the move was just as well. She didn't want to be alone in her room when the baby decided to push its way into the world. What if the baby came before the doctor arrived? Agnes and Lupita had both given birth and helped others to do the same.

Despite the day's heat, the fright of near-labor had dashed Penelope with another cold slap of reality. First the letter, and now this. Her baby was soon to be more than just a precious jewel inside her. She had to be ready when her baby was.

"Coming through," Nate hollered as he, Seth, and Alfredo maneuvered a pallet to Penelope's side.

"I can get up, I just need a little help," she said, and started to push herself up.

"No, let me," Nate said, low, and leaned down. He and Seth inched the bench outward. Nate moved behind her and half-lifted her into a standing position. The other women stepped forward to assist her transition to the pallet.

"I'm afraid the wrong twist or turn could set off the pains again," Penelope said.

"Just be careful," Agnes said. "But I believe the danger has passed. Close your eyes and put yourself in the strong hands of these capable men."

Penelope nodded but remained tense. Everything had become so real. She lay in a haze of fatigue, worry, and weariness as the pallet swayed and shifted during the short journey.

She was soon alone again, settled in Polly's bright, sunny bedroom with instructions to sleep. She sank into the softness of the bed and lay quietly, still afraid to shift around much. Voices from conversations on the porch drifted in on the heavy afternoon air. Agnes sent Billy and Polly to the orphanage to get Penelope's personal items after Cornelia packed them. She shushed the men and shooed them back off to work.

"Only if you promise to tell her I'll return soon," Nate said. "I'm supposed to be at the Alloways' by now—the professor sent word he has news to share. Penelope will want to know. Tell her I'll be back to fill her in." She heard his footsteps pound down the porch stairs.

"Tomorrow," Agnes called.

"Can't I come back tonight?" he called back.

"No," Agnes answered, as the sound of his footsteps grew faint.

"Are you sure he's not the father?" Lupita asked Agnes. "He's beside himself more than Alfredo was when I had my sons."

"The closeness between them keeps growing," Agnes said. "I don't know if that's good or bad. I don't know much about the biological father or his relationship with Penelope. As far as I know, she hasn't corresponded with him while here."

Lupita huffed.

"I recognize that matchmaker look in your eye," Agnes said.

"The baby will need a father," Lupita said.

"She's supposed to leave the baby for adoption."

"We all know she has changed her mind."

"True," Agnes said. "I'm not sure it's a wise idea."

"You would leave your baby if it were you?"

"No. But I've seen it work for the best. I was left on a doorstep, Lupita. At the orphanage in New York. And might have died, otherwise."

"*Si, si,* I know," Lupita said. "Many times it's best for the baby to be loved in another home. I'm not convinced this is one of those times."

"Sorry I'm late!" Nate burst into the Alloway House. "Big doings out at Taylor Grove. Penelope gave us all a scare thinking the *bambino*—or *bambina*—was making its entrance."

"What! So soon?" Fanny was half out of her chair but Nate waved her back. "False alarm. She's fine. But it was a worry for a while. Agnes had us move her into Polly's bedroom."

"Thank goodness," Fanny said. "Help yourself to a plate. We just started."

Nate piled smoked ham, collards, a heap of rice and beans, and biscuits on his plate and sat down. "I'm starved," he said and dug in.

For a while, the only sounds were the clink of cutlery on

ceramic ware and the plunk of Mason jars being set down on the linen tablecloth.

"You doing okay, professor?" Nate said. "You're not your usual lively self."

Art adjusted his glasses. "You could say I have indigestion."

"Mercy! Why didn't you say something, Art?" Fanny was again half out of her chair. "Let me get you a mixture of saleratus and water."

"It's not the food, honey. And I wish saleratus and water could cure it."

They all stopped eating.

"May as well spit it out quick," Art muttered. He directed his gaze at Nate. "I regret to say that my, er, *esteemed* colleagues have decided your project has risen to the level of their importance."

"That means—what?" Nate asked in a cautious tone.

Art swallowed.

"They want control. They want to take over the next phase of the dig."

Nate leapt up.

"No way. They can't!"

"They can. The university funded the exploratory dig and will fund the extension if they're involved. You aren't a faculty member."

Nate stared at him, mouth open.

"But Professor Art, you are faculty, sort of. Your emeritus status must count for something."

"I'm a botanist. A retired botanist. My role in their anthropology department was always peripheral. Never as significant as the chair's or the scholars' whose research specialty is archaeology or anthropology. They won't leave the project under my oversight any longer."

Nate paced the length of the dining room. He stopped.

"Do they know about the theft?"

"Not yet. They're still agog over the news of the silver pendants."

"How'd they find out?" Nate stopped pacing and waited for the answer.

"You know I have to file regular updates," Art said. "Tempting as it was to keep the news to myself, in the interests of ethics, morals, and collegiality, I had to release all the information. And this was even before the human bones surfaced."

Nate grimaced.

"I know the drill." He started pacing again. "Can't you scare them off with tales of alligators and snakes?"

"That's not how academia works."

"There's got to be something I can do," Nate said, and threw his arms wide. "What? What can I do? I haven't published yet on what's been done so far."

"I see no way out unless you secure an outside grant or gain funding by a private patron. Something that will imply to my colleagues that your status has risen. With an understanding, of course, that the project would remain under their tutelage and artifacts would be sent to the university's museum."

"Well, where else would they go?"

"Some private donors want items for personal collections."

"So all I have to do is find private donors. How easy."

"If you brought in funding, my colleagues might be amenable to keeping you on as a junior associate."

Nate laughed but it sounded like a bark.

"I tried my best, son, to keep them at bay and let you conduct the research and reap the rewards," Art said. "They smell publication of new theories and the accolades and scholarly debates that follow."

"So do I," said Nate. "I won't give up without a fight."

The room silenced.

"Here, have a helping of persimmon cobbler," Fanny urged Nate. "You haven't tasted our famous persimmons yet. I preserved these from the last of the harvest. No problem seems insurmountable after you've had a good meal to sustain you."

The cobbler enticed Nate to sit down again.

"Delicious," he said between bites.

"You know, persimmons grow best in moist soil," Art said. "The kind you find close to the river where many of the mounds are. Places where alligators and snakes congregate. Ticks, too. There are wild boars out in those woods. Possibly a few panthers. I believe you were right, Nate. I was remiss in forgetting to mention those natural inhabitants to my colleagues. I must rectify that. In the interest of promoting better understanding of the sciences, of course."

CHAPTER 14

"$\mathcal{N}$ ate, no, Penelope's not ready for visitors." Agnes was growing exasperated at the energetic young man waiting impatiently on her porch a couple of days later. .

"I promise not to tire her out," he pleaded. "I need to see her, check on her, and bring her up to date on what I learned the other night. It dovetails with something we'd talked about a short while ago. A sort of business proposal."

"You want to discuss business? Today? You and too many others. The backstage artists want her advice on the scenery. Onofrio wants to keep his job as an Italian conversationalist. I want you all to go away and let Penelope rest."

Cornelia appeared behind Agnes in the doorway and gave a firm nod of agreement.

"She'd welcome my visit," Nate protested. "I know she needs to rest, but she likes to keep her mind active. Plus, I always manage to cheer her up."

The two women stood side-by-side just outside the door in twin displays of displeasure. Their positions blocked his access.

"Nate, a woman as near her time as Penelope may lose some

interest in other matters," Agnes said. "She's on bed rest in quiet surroundings until her doctor arrives from the North."

Nate's shoulders sagged almost imperceptibly before they squared into their normal firm position.

"Okay, you win. I don't want any distress to come to her or the baby."

Agnes and Cornelia's glances met. Each gave Nate an uneasy look.

"You're not telling me something," Nate said.

"It's true they're good friends," Cornelia said in a low voice to Agnes. "And it's true her spirits lift when she's with him."

"We can't take the risk," Agnes said. "The situation is too delicate."

"What?" Nate said. "I have a right to know."

"How so?" Agnes asked.

"She confided certain things to me. I feel responsible for her well-being."

"We all do, Nate," Agnes said. "That's why we're blocking your entry."

The trio fell silent in stalemate.

"She's not dying, is she?" Nate asked in a strangled voice.

"Good gracious, no!" said Cornelia. She blessed herself.

"I won't move off this porch unless you tell me what you're really worried about," he said. "There's more to this than lying quietly until the doctor arrives."

His earnest face and Cornelia's gentle prodding finally swayed Agnes.

"She has fallen into a deep melancholy that has us worried," Agnes said. "A year or so ago, she stayed several weeks at the Alloway House with family members for winter vacation. She was glum and quiet much of the time. We learned she was pining for a beau she'd been forced to leave behind."

"Yeah," Nate said, and his normally sunny face darkened. "I heard about that despicable so-called beau."

"When Penelope came to Persimmon Hollow this time, she was wrapped in a shell of shock about her relocation and situation," Agnes said. "She gradually emerged from that, as you know. We've seen her fight off melancholy from time to time but it hasn't been serious. This recent relapse was sudden and deep. She has been such a focused person all these months. The change is deeply concerning."

Nate did one of his usual pacing circles while he digested the information. He stopped.

"Did she get any letters from home recently?"

"I don't know," Agnes said. She looked at Cornelia. "Do you?"

Cornelia started to say no but halted. "Wait, I believe she did. It was on her dressing table. I saw it when gathering her things to send here for her stay with you, Agnes. I didn't pay it much mind. It must have arrived recently, just before her emergency. She's not one to pull out old letters. She files them away neatly."

"How were her spirits after that letter arrived?" Nate said. "I have a suspicion it might have contained unwelcome news."

"Why do you say that?" Agnes asked.

Before he answered, Cornelia interjected. "Her spirits started to droop soon after—had to be—soon after that letter appeared. I sensed a sadness when she came to the rehearsal room. That might be why she wanted to go check the scenery at a time when she usually stayed in and rested. And wanted to go alone, against my better judgment."

"I bet her family denied her request for funds," Nate said.

"Funds?" Agnes said. "Her family made a generous donation to the orphanage. The cost of her room and board hardly makes a dent in it. Why else would she need money?"

"To keep and raise her baby."

"Oh. Oh, dear," Agnes said.

Nate picked up the flat, newsboy-style cap he'd taken to wearing and adjusted it on his head. "If my assumption is correct, it makes my business proposal worth nothing more than the paper it isn't written on. I need to figure how to pivot. More importantly, Penelope has to make hard decisions. She doesn't need to make them alone. Wrestling with money woes is the last thing she needs to tax herself with. Would you send word the minute you decide I can see her?"

He turned and started to leave.

"No message for her?" Agnes asked.

Nate stopped, and turned. "Remind her I'm always here for her. Emphasize the *always*."

PENELOPE LAY on the bed and listened to the entire conversation through her open window. Humid heat drifted in with the voices. The breeze she craved had stirred only briefly in early morning.

Her inertia was so strong she couldn't stir herself to call out that Nate should come in. But his voice prodded a spark in her. She yearned to see him. She forced herself to push upward against the dull weight that melancholy draped around her, and turned to face the window.

"I heard every word," she called. She sounded like a mewling kitten even to herself.

On the porch, Cornelia and Agnes's eyes widened. Nate halted at the bottom of the steps, turned, and re-climbed them in one step.

"Wait, please, Nate, I'm coming outside," Penelope said. The effort to move was great. How much easier it would be to just stay put and wallow.

She swiveled ever so slowly and plopped her feet on the floor with as much determination as she could muster. By then, Cornelia had flown inside.

"Careful. Let me assist you."

"I'm not an invalid. Just give me a minute to pat down my face and arms with some water before we go out," Penelope said.

That done, she lumbered out to the porch, with Cornelia hovering nearby and Agnes flying into place on her other side. Nate perched on the edge of a chair. Concern and suppressed agitation mingled in his expression.

He leapt up when she came out the door and took a long look at her.

"Yeah, maybe you should be in bed and we should talk some other time," he said, and reached out both hands to her. Cornelia and Agnes stepped back.

"You're looking good yourself," Penelope replied in a hint of her former self. She let Nate lead her to the wicker settee and help her get situated. He sat down across from her.

She forced herself to smile, but felt flushed from the exertion of moving around in heat that had to be near a hundred degrees.

"Penelope, that's the first time you've smiled in days," Agnes said.

"It's my natural charm," Nate said. "She can't resist it."

Penelope looked up into his dear, handsome face and battled an urge to cry and bury her face in his shoulder. *Get a grip on yourself,* she ordered herself.

She reached to the side table and picked up one of the fans Fanny Alloway had left about the house for her use. With effort, she dug for her inner strength. She straightened her spine and squared her shoulders. She'd discovered by accident that good posture, for some reason, helped push back against her melancholy.

"It's mainly the sun and brightness all around, but I admit that you being here does have its benefits." She gave a feebly coquettish flick of her fan, then narrowed her eyes as she watched Nate's reaction. "I knew you would preen."

"Why not, when truth is spoken, even if the compliment was sparse," Nate said. He grew somber again. "Has your doctor arrived? Like I said, I'm from a large family and you look like, well, I mean, it appears your baby might come calling soon."

"We've plenty of womenfolk here to assist her," Agnes said. "I have to say, Nate, you're one of the few men I've known who doesn't get nervous around a very expectant woman."

"I've helped deliver a baby or two," Nate said. "Doctors are a luxury few can afford where I'm from. My mother and one of my sisters for years have served as neighborhood midwives. In the few cases of emergencies, they needed every available hand. On two occasions, those hands belonged to me."

He glanced at Penelope. "You'll have the best money can buy. So where is that doctor?"

"We're all asking the same question," Penelope said. "If he's not here soon, I'll ask Billy to run to town and send a wire. The calendar says I have only a short time to go."

Nate was silent for a moment and then exclaimed, "Maybe you'll have a July Fourth baby!"

"I hope he or she waits a day or two longer," Penelope said. "I want to attend the performance."

"First babies are often late," Agnes said. "Little Seth was a week late."

Talk lapsed, and the silence was filled by sounds of bees buzzing in the daisy-like flowers of Spanish needle plants blooming just beyond the porch railing. Somewhere in the near distance, a hawk cawed. Penelope felt a quietness settle over her and lift the veil of melancholy. Even Nate stopped fidgeting.

"You have a way of bringing calm to a man, Miss Gold," he said. His words pierced her fog. She reached a hand over to his.

"Truth is, Nate, you have a way of bringing me out of the inexplicable sadness that sometimes presses on me," she said. "Your exuberance, your optimism about life. It's catching, in a good way."

"And here I thought it was my powerful manliness," he said, and demonstrated a mock flex of his biceps. They all laughed. Nate was a handsome man—lean, toned, and strong—but muscular bravado had no claim on him.

He tossed his hat on the table, leaned forward, and clasped his hands between his knees. "Are you up to talking about the excavation?" he asked Penelope.

"Talking is about all I can do. I don't even have the energy to sketch. I'd love to hear the news. Anything to give me something else to think about."

Nate refrained from sending an "I told you so" look to Agnes, but she didn't need one.

"We'll leave you two to chat for a short while," Agnes said, and rose. "Housekeeping chores await me and Cornelia is needed at the orphanage."

The two women's shoes clicked on the porch floorboards as they departed.

"You're certain you want to listen to this?" Nate asked "It's a sorry story."

Penelope's gaze widened. "What's wrong?"

He told Penelope about the interference from senior academics, his lack of funding, and the stalled inquiry into the theft.

"Nobody can find out a thing," Nate said. "Either people don't know or they're not talking." He ran a hand through his hair.

"But that's all beside my main point. I came out here intent on swallowing my pride and asking for that loan you offered a while ago."

Penelope gave him a tight smile. "But you didn't ask. Are you asking now?"

He kept his gaze locked on hers. "No."

"So you must have heard my funding will be denied me. How? I haven't told anyone."

"I guessed after I learned your spirits drooped soon after you received a letter. Feel like talking about it?"

"There's not much to say. I received a clear message that if I don't follow the prescribed plan—*their* prescribed plan—my money will be withheld. My bank account in Boston would be frozen, so to speak. I wouldn't be able to tap any of my money there, and my annual income wouldn't be deposited there any longer."

"Well, we're a fine pair," Nate said. "Want to run away together?"

She almost laughed. "I wouldn't get far, fast. But it's actually a pleasant idea."

Something hummed between them, as evident and obvious as the gentle sizzle of the bees that had moved onto the spotted bee balm plants. Penelope shifted in her chair and broke the gaze. She looked out over the landscape. Nate slouched into the back of the chair and wiped his brow. A few minutes later, he straightened his back and leaned forward once more.

"You're not the type who gives up easily," he said.

"I see a gleam in your eye, Nate. What's churning behind those glasses? You're right, I'll not admit failure. But these past days have been exhausting. First the letter, then the scare of losing the baby. I felt like curtains blocked my perspectives and my feelings. The idea of surrendering to the original plan crossed my mind more than once."

He inched closer to the edge of his chair. "Have you thought of supporting yourself and the baby through your art? Or by giving language lessons?"

Her eyes widened. "Where? Here? How? I've not given serious thought to supporting myself by any means. I never had to. But I have to do something if I don't want to fold to my family's demands."

Anxiety uncoiled inside her. Nate took one look at her and was down on one knee by her side in one swift move.

"Not today you don't. Your mission right now is to take care of yourself and your baby. Do whatever Agnes and the other women tell you until the doctor arrives. My suggestions are a seed, a place to start when you're ready. Remember, you're not alone. You have me, them," he waved toward the house interior, "and everybody at the orphanage and more in town."

He stood up and walked over to the railing. He leaned his palms on it and gazed outward as though answers existed there.

"I'll think for both of us right now," he said. "When you're ready, you jump back in."

Quietly, Penelope rose and walked over to Nate's side.

He glanced down. She placed her hand over his on the railing.

After a few moments, Nate withdrew his hand so he could put his arm around her shoulder and pull her close. He placed his other hand atop hers on the railing.

Penelope gave in to mix of emotions his action stirred. Love, yearning, peace, a desire to stay with him, to remain forever in this hidden town and let the days roll together in a satisfying hum of love, work, play, and togetherness.

She let herself relax into him for support.

The squeak of the door behind them was followed by brisk taps on the floorboards.

"Time for Penelope to get back to rest," Agnes announced. "First, both of you come have a drink of cool water and a snack. Lupita's guava cobbler just came out of the oven."

A short while later, the sweet cobbler had revived Nate's enthusiastic nature.

"You're an amazing artist, Penelope. You could use your talents without going out in public. Solicit jobs through mail and advertisements."

The few bites of food Penelope nibbled had revived her, too, somewhat.

"Perhaps. I could use my initials, to avoid public association with my name."

"What's your middle name?"

"Millicent."

"There you have it. You could send discreet solicitations to publishing houses, geographic companies, scholars, who knows who else: 'Artwork by P.M. Gold. Botanical illustrations, sketches from photographs, etc. Serious scientific inquiries only.' Surely you have connections who could help distribute inquiries?"

Penelope liked the idea but couldn't think deeply about anything. His plan hovered over her, like something she wanted to grasp that was too far out of reach. She didn't answer him.

"Shut up Nate," Nate told himself aloud. "You're getting ahead of yourself. In due time, Penelope, we'll sort this out. Not today. The only due time for you right now is the one dictated by that baby."

"You need to focus on your concerns, too," Penelope said, ready to shift the attention off her problems.

"Yep, they're not going away, either."

He lifted his gaze from the almost empty dish. "A priest I know back home used to quote St. Francis de Sales when a situation looked bleak. Something about not trying to break difficulties but instead to bend them by using gentleness and time. We could try."

"Let's," Penelope said. The snack had made her sleepy again.

Agnes had come into the dining room when Nate was speaking.

"St. Francis de Sales also counseled patience," she said, looking directly at Nate. "Let's call upon that, right now."

"I can take a hint," Nate said, and glanced at Penelope's drooping eyelids.

He rose and came around the table. "Until next time," he said, and rested his hand on her shoulder. "Take care of yourself Penelope. I couldn't bear to lose you."

His words caused her eyes to fly open. She tilted her head back and looked up at him. "Nor I you," she whispered. They had eyes only for each other.

Agnes cleared her throat. Nate stepped back from Penelope.

"If it's all right with the gatekeepers, I'll bring you daily updates," he said to Penelope as he headed for the door. "Personally delivered."

"I'd like that," she said.

He grabbed his hat from the side table, plopped it on with a jaunty move, and gave her a goodbye grin that lit the room.

A few hours later, Penelope awoke from her nap with a realization so obvious she wondered how she'd overlooked it until now. Too much worry, she guessed. She arose with more energy than she'd felt in days and an eagerness to share with Nate what her mind had uncovered in sleep.

She waited impatiently for him to arrive the next day and was out on the porch before he reached it.

"Nate!" She waved to him excitedly. His face brightened at her reception.

"Hello to you, too!" he said as he bounded up onto the porch. He grabbed her hands for a moment and darted a peck of a kiss on her cheek.

Her lips curved upward.

"I've been waiting since late afternoon yesterday to tell you something," she said. "Here, sit with me." She patted the cushion next to her after easing down onto the settee.

"I awoke from my nap yesterday with a solution handed to me," she said. "When my family made its donation to the orphanage, they also set up a small local bank account for me. Here, in Persimmon Hollow and in my name. It contains funds for emergencies and incidental spending. I had forgotten about it."

He stared at her, slack-jawed, for a few long seconds. Then happiness spread across his face.

"Alleluia!" he said. "This makes my day. Just seeing your eyes sparkle again would have been enough. Knowing you don't have to fret about the future brings peace to my soul. Although you had me for a minute there. I can't imagine having enough money to forget about some of it."

His words reminded her of the gulf between their upbringings. And how it didn't seem to matter here.

"It's silly, that I forgot about the account," she said. "But my every need has been met, even my dressmaking bills. I have Josefa send them to my family's Northern bank. There's not a lot in the local account but it's enough for me to rely on temporarily. Enough for me to get settled and started on—on what?—on whatever the future holds. You're only half right that I don't have to fret. I just have a cushion on which to rest while I sort out my options."

"Best possible gift for now, I say," Nate replied. "I'll help you however I can. I want to see you and the baby happy and content with circumstances by the time I leave."

She tilted her head and glanced at him as though the realization that Nate wasn't a permanent fixture in Persimmon Hollow was something new.

"I guess I'd forgotten that, too," she said. "Or wanted to forget. Archaeological excavations don't last indefinitely."

"As it stands now, I'm here until end of summer. I won't be able to return here right away unless I get funding to extend and expand the project. And figure how to work around the pesky scholars higher than me on the academic food chain. I'll chart some kind of course. Don't you worry. I've no intention of waiting an entire academic year before coming back to see you. Something will arise. I refuse to give in to doubt."

The curtain that had parted over Penelope's gloom began to drape close again. Nate glanced down at her and she saw his expression shift.

He gently placed a finger under her chin and tilted her head up. "You remember what I said about always being available for you. No matter where I am. Here or back up North. You're not getting rid of me that easy, you know?"

She chuckled and sensed tension drain from him.

"Good," she said. She kept a grasp on her uplifted mood as they both relaxed into the cushions and watched late afternoon unfold around them.

TRUE TO HIS WORD, Nate bounded up the sandy path to the Taylor house every day, after work and before tackling his evening studies and writings.

"It's almost July," he said one evening, as he sat down on the porch and wiped the sweat from his neck. Sultry air hovered in the dusk. "Summer is racing by."

"It both is and isn't for me," Penelope said, and fanned herself.

"It won't be long, now," he said. "What's the word on the doctor?"

"I kept thinking, 'Surely he'll be here any moment,'" Penelope said. "I kept putting off checking on his whereabouts. But I feel fine, just tired. Not doing much sketching of the artifacts you bring or the others deliver. Onofrio is beside himself at my lack of progress. He'd rather I draw than make him talk what he calls 'fancy Italian.'"

Nate chuckled. "That's because he'd rather run artifacts back and forth to the site and here than do summer chores around the orphanage and grove. We have plenty of sketches already."

"To go with your article?"

"More than enough to submit with an article. I've been writing every night and making progress. Maybe you could help me with a title? I lean toward the awful. Leave it to me and the title will end up something like: 'Notes on an expedition on archaeological excavations on the northeastern quadrant of riverine property bordering the aquatic resources of the middle river valley of the St. Johns River.'"

"Oh, dear," said Penelope. "I can do better."

"Please and thank you."

"Although yours would work as a subtitle."

Thunderheads that had been building in the west collided and let out a boom, followed by a rush of cooling raindrops. The storm's force increased with the rapid intensity Penelope had come to expect in Florida. Nate helped Penelope up and toward the house, but not before a few raindrops and the accompanying wind kissed Penelope's feverish skin.

"That felt good," she said, as they hurried inside and closed the door. From the safety of the front room, they watched the rain fall in thick gray sheets and listened to the rattle of raindrops on the metal roof.

"I'm still surprised at how rainfall here goes from gentle shower to monsoon-like conditions in minutes," Penelope said.

"And then stops abruptly," Nate added. They both jumped at a loud crack of thunder. "Looks like Jupiter has put his seal of approval on our partnership," he said.

When Penelope didn't reply, he added, "You know, the Roman god of thunder and rain."

"Yes, but I favor the God of Agnes and Cornelia," she said. "His is a quieter mercy than your thunder god."

Nate crossed himself. "I may jest about mythical gods but none comes before my faith. Lean on Christ in all your needs, Penelope. He'll never fail you."

"I know," she said, as they lingered while Nate waited out the storm before departing. "I've seen how deeply faith is intertwined with life here. I no longer consider religion something people put on to go to services once a week. I'm studying the Catholic faith with Cornelia and Sister Bridget and preparing for baptism. There's just such a warmth, a...I don't know, I can't really explain it."

"No need, I get it," Nate said. "I'm happy for you. You mention this to your family?"

"Not yet. One thing at a time."

She put a hand over her stomach. "The baby just moved again."

Nate froze. "Do I need to get Agnes?"

"No." She stopped him from calling others.

"Check on the doctor, please," he urged.

"I will," she promised. "Maybe he'll arrive today."

THE NEXT DAY, the doctor still hadn't arrived.

Penelope carefully roused herself and let Onofrio escort her to the barn, where several older children were repainting the backdrops for the holiday presentation.

"Shhh, we no tell anyone," he said, as he checked to see if the porch and pathway were clear. "I snuck in here to get you, so you can be happy to see our paintings. Just a short visit, you'll feel better."

"I feel better already," she said.

She'd been in the barn less than half an hour before Polly came running with orders that she return to the house.

"For your own safety," Polly said. "They told me to tell you that. My mom and Cornelia can hardly believe you got out of the house without them noticing."

"What do you mean, for her safety? I keep her safe!" Onofrio protested.

"Yes, he's a fine protector," Penelope said, and put her arm around his shoulder. He shimmied out and went to inspect the backdrops.

"I had to move, Polly, do something, get out beyond the few rooms I see day-in and day-out. Even the porch felt like it was closing around me."

"Mom wants you to send that telegram inquiring about the doctor," Polly added. "Billy," she hollered to where the youth was on a ladder testing backdrop supports. "Mom said go to town and send a telegram for Miss Penelope."

Onofrio scrambled up from his inspection of a sky scene painted on canvas.

"No, me, I'll go," he announced, and glued himself to Penelope's side. "Billy, I take the telegram message to Mr. Clyde at the store," he hollered.

He looked up at Penelope and Polly. "Billy has to work on the farm. I heard Mr. Seth tell him they have to plow and plant field peas."

He turned large eyes upward on Penelope only. "I get delivery tip, yes?"

"You'll make a good businessman someday, Onofrio," Penelope said. "You already make a good businessman, I mean." She drew a small reticule from the pocket of her skirt and gave him some coins. "Here's enough to cover the cost of the telegram with some extra for your services."

He grabbed the money and started to run out.

"Wait!" Penelope called. "I have to tell you what to say!"

"Oh, right." He stopped in mid-step and returned to her, and fidgeted as he waited for her to pen a message on a scrap of paper.

A while later, he stormed into the Taylor house where Penelope and Cornelia were crocheting in the parlor.

"Miss Penelope! Miss Cornelia!" Onofrio skidded to a halt in front of them, out of breath. He leaned over, hands on knees, and breathed hard. "I run fast from where I left the horse in the barn."

"Gracious, what is it?" Cornelia asked.

"The doctor!" said Onofrio, between gulps of air. "The doctor, he left on the boat two weeks ago! On a big steamboat, but it hit another boat off the Carols, the Carleens, the..."

"The Carolinas?" Penelope asked.

"*Si*, yes. The Carolinas, and there was a big boom. The boat sank and I think everybody got off but the doctor, he broke his leg and no could walk and now he is in a hospital there because of his leg and because he swallowed water and almost drowned. Mr. Clyde, he read about it in the newspaper and saw the doctor's name and said he remembered about it when I give him your telegram paper that had the doctor's name on it. He said he didn't realize it was your doctor he read about."

"Lord, help us," Penelope said and gulped. Her trepidation about the birth loomed anew.

"Mr. Clyde says to telegram your family right away Miss Penelope, so they can send somebody else."

Penelope rose but sat down again because Cornelia had risen faster and was already getting paper and pencil.

"Go get yourself something to drink while I write down the message for you," Penelope told Onofrio. "Good job, young man."

The little boy straightened under the praise and he ran with loud steps and raised voice toward the kitchen, where he retold the entire story.

The baby moved again and Penelope felt like she—or he—was pressing some of her body parts out of place. Part of her was overjoyed each time she felt the new life inside her. Part of her worried whether she'd survive what lay ahead.

Focus on the joy, she told herself. She thought of Christ's mother, Mary, so young and betrothed but not yet wed, and held her image close to her heart. A warm, reassuring feeling flowed through her. She felt less alone in her journey.

She shared the experience with the other women when she joined them to say the rosary that evening. No one was surprised.

"LISTEN, EVERYONE." Agnes called the group to attention in the open compound behind the Taylor house. "Let's run through the recitations again. We have days—I said days, not weeks—until Independence Day. And I regret to say this is the sorriest lot of thespians I've ever had the misfortune to direct."

Her young charges—the orphans, Billy and Polly, and other local children, appeared on the verge of mutiny.

"Aww, it's too hot!" Polly complained. "Why don't we just stand onstage and hand out lemonade to everyone, instead. People would like that better than listening to us."

"At least we got the backdrop looking good," said Billy.

Penelope sat in the shade of a magnolia tree and watched the proceedings. Cornelia, who had started keeping Penelope within sight most of the day, helped Agnes with group direction.

Penelope stood, stretched, and eased her bulk back down. No position was comfortable. She wanted nothing more than to be delivered of her bundle of joy so that she could once again sleep easily and not have to run to the chamber pot so often.

She fanned herself as she watched the rehearsals. She had to agree the second go-around had resulted in vast improvements to the canvas backdrops' pastoral scenery.

But Polly was correct. Temperatures had skyrocketed and had started to dominate conversations. The Alloways proclaimed that such an extreme heat wave was unprecedented. Seth was concerned about the sudden cessation of daily afternoon thunderstorms. He'd started hauling water to the field peas, okra, and sweet potato crops. Lupita and the orphanage sisters stopped using their wood stoves and did whatever cooking was necessary on outdoor brick ovens.

Sister Bridget even broke out in hives from her habit on the second day of near-triple-digit temperatures. The sisters, Josefa, and Taylor Grove women were busy sewing lighter-weight habits for her and the other sisters.

The entire town of Persimmon Hollow came to a halt about noon each day, and didn't show signs of life until early evening.

Agnes surveyed her wilted performers. "Off to the spring with you all," she said. "Billy, Polly, keep an eye on the little ones and be back here in about an hour for lunch. Take just enough time for a cool dip."

The youngsters were gone almost before she finished speaking.

"They're right," Agnes said to Penelope and Cornelia. "How can we stage a performance if these conditions continue? Those children will be heated again by the time they get back here, and the spring isn't that far off in the woods."

How can I continue to live in these conditions, fretted Penelope, silently. The heat was so thick it muddled her attempts to chart a new future for herself. If she were to make a living from her art, she had to start writing for commissions. She agreed with Nate about that. Yet the idea hovered in a mist in her mind. She couldn't muster the energy to begin.

She wondered about Nate's whereabouts. His daily visits had stopped. "Has anyone seen Nate?" she asked Agnes as they strolled to the front porch.

"No, I thought perhaps you'd asked him to visit less so you could rest more," Agnes said.

"No. I can't move around without effort so I welcome visitors. I wonder where he's been." She felt the little one shift inside her. "Gosh, I wish this baby would come."

"I'm surprised we haven't heard from your family yet," Agnes said.

"It's not like them not to reply in an emergency," said Penelope. "Is Clyde sure the telegram wasn't damaged in transmission or overlooked on the receiving end?"

"It's possible, but I doubt it," Agnes said. "Clyde's a stickler for procedures and doing things by the book."

One of the cat naps that had become Penelope's habit started to steal over her. She eased down into her soft cushions on the wicker settee.

"It's just odd, is all." She yawned. "It's been too long. Perhaps the telegram got lost between the telegraph office and house in Boston."

She leaned her head against the high rounded back of the

settee and closed her eyes. She gave in to the pleasant heaviness and savored the smells of honeysuckle and Louis Philippe roses that floated in the air. *Just for a few minutes*, she thought.

When she opened her eyes again, it was almost dusk. And seated in chairs in a semicircle in front of her were her grand-mother, stepmother, and step-cousin, all sharing the same straight-lipped expression.

Penelope blinked. "Am I dreaming?"

"No," said her grandmother. "You're not. And we've come to take you home as soon as you're fit to travel."

CHAPTER 15

*B*efore Penelope could process what was happening, Cornelia came hurrying up the pathway from the orphanage. She nodded to the newcomers but walked over to Penelope and kept her back turned on the visitors.

"I sat here with them until Vespers," she whispered as she adjusted the pillow behind Penelope. "They wouldn't leave until you awakened. They're staying at the Alloway House."

She straightened and spoke louder. "Are you hungry, Penelope? Need assistance of any kind? I'll let Agnes know you're awake." She bustled into the house.

Penelope returned her gaze to the three fixed stares upon her. She had the irrationally funny thought that the row of disapproving looks was enough to bring on her labor.

"How nice to see you," she finally managed to say, pulling on lifelong lessons in etiquette.

"And you, dear? Both of you?" her matriarch grandmother asked, with a glance up and down her swollen figure. "Is it common for women here to show themselves in public when *enceinte*? We assumed you'd be sequestered in your orphanage quarters."

"This house isn't what I consider public," Penelope said.

Her stepmother sniffed. "People in town kept stopping us to say congratulations."

Penelope stifled the urge to smile. They looked so out of place, so citified and upper crust, dressed as though waiting for an opera to begin.

"We couldn't find another doctor willing to journey to this rustic place on short notice," her stepmother said. "So the three of us came to ensure your well-being. How are your art studies and language lessons proceeding?"

As if on cue, Onofrio came tearing around the side of the house and into the front clearing. He skidded to a halt when he saw the semicircle of women dressed in what went far beyond Sunday best in Persimmon Hollow. Then he galloped up the porch stairs and clomped over to Penelope. His hair was mussed, his pants had a tear in the knee, and his once-white shirt was soiled with streaks of sandy dirt. The sand reached as far as his cheek and forehead.

"Who are they? Why are they here?" he asked Penelope in Italian.

"*La mia famiglia,*" she replied. "*Qui per una visita*—to visit me." To her family, she said, "The language lessons are going well, as you can hear."

This time she did smile.

Onofrio's appearance and familiarity had wrought tight lips from her relatives. He stared at the visitors, then at Penelope, then at the visitors again, as though he couldn't make the pairings fit as a whole.

"A street urchin? Really, Penelope," said her stepmother.

Onofrio glowered. Penelope put a hand on his thin arm and drew him closer to her. She watched her guests' eyes widen as the boy plopped down beside Penelope on the settee.

"There are no urchins here," said Penelope. The frost in her tone could have cooled the heat wave. "Only loving families, lovable orphans, and the kind sisters and novices such as Miss Cornelia who just checked on me."

"And the generous family who helps fund the charitable institution," her stepmother said.

Penelope closed her eyes. Of course she'd never be allowed to forget that her family paid the orphanage to house her. To take her off their hands.

"I mean the Taylor family that offered the land and built the orphanage, the warm Gomez family that helps keep Taylor Grove running, the holy sisters, and—"

"Careful, Penelope, you'll become one of them if you keep taking their side," her step-cousin interrupted. "You sound as if you like it here."

Cornelia came out looking for Onofrio. She beckoned him away from Penelope and withdrew with him to the far side of the porch.

"Of course she doesn't like it here," said Penelope's step-mother. "She's only here until she can return home without hanging her head in shame."

"Actually, I've grown fond of the people and the place," Penelope said. "All of them."

She rose. She couldn't and wouldn't deal with any more of their displeasure.

"That young fellow over there speaks better Italian than any of you ever heard from your language instructors," she said.

"So does the entire north end of Boston," her step-cousin replied. "It doesn't mean I fraternize with anyone there."

"You should get back to town before dark," Penelope said, ignoring the comment. "I'm in need of rest. Thank you for calling."

They didn't like the dismissal, she noted. Heavy with child or not, she would stand firm and stand up for herself. Her months in Persimmon Hollow had given her new strength she wasn't aware had developed until she called upon it for help.

"Penelope," her grandmother began to say. Her nostrils were pinched.

"Tomorrow." Penelope held her off. "I'm fatigued, as you must be after your journey."

Onofrio pulled away from Cornelia and came to stand next to Penelope, his hands fisted at his sides. Cornelia drifted over and stood on the other side of Penelope.

Penelope's stepmother and grandmother exchanged glances. *Ah, a* détente *in their decades-long battle for power,* Penelope thought. Her step-cousin was the first to rise, as though she couldn't bear to stay a moment longer.

"Onofrio, would you please get Billy and ask him to take the ladies back to town," Penelope said. He ran off and Cornelia started to steer Penelope toward the house door.

"I'm her companion and overseeing her welfare, and she must rest now," Cornelia said in a gentle but firm voice. "The child is due any day now."

"And not a moment too soon," said Penelope's stepmother. "The sooner this is over, the sooner we can resume our lives as before," she added, with a meaningful glance at Penelope.

PENELOPE LAY ABED, wide awake, and heard the grandfather clock in the parlor chime twice. She couldn't get comfortable, no matter how she propped the extra pillows. She rose, lit the kerosene lantern, and rinsed her face and arms with the tepid water in her washbasin. It provided momentary relief from the thick air.

"Penelope!"

She stepped back, startled at hearing Nate's loud whisper amid the night sounds of frogs and cicadas outside. He conveyed an urgent sentence in the shape of one word.

She peered out the screened window but didn't see anyone.

Her corner room faced the front porch and side of the house. The moonlight shadowed a breezeless summer landscape.

"Where are you?" she asked in loud whisper.

"Over here, by the trellis. Are you well enough to step outside for a few minutes?"

She looked at the trellis that extended the line of the porch a short distance from the house and supported a thick growth of moonvine. The shadow of Nate's shape emerged from behind the heart-shaped leaves dotted with round white blossoms the size of bread plates.

"Yes, I was awake anyway," she said. "Is something wrong?"

"No," he said, and came closer to the side window so they could lower the volume of their whispers.

"Nate, it's hardly the right time for a house call." Irritation came fast these days, she found. But Nate didn't answer. She peered more closely at him. He appeared not to have slept and his face sported a stubble she'd never seen before on him.

"I'll be right out," she said.

She wrapped a shawl around her and padded out to the porch as quietly as she could. Nate climbed the steps with silent footsteps.

"Nate! Where have you been? It's like you fell off the planet."

"More like I fell backward into another world," he said. Penelope stared at his distraught face. Her cheerful, optimistic, ambitious Nate seemed to have met demons poised to destroy him.

Nate helped Penelope settle into the settee. He sprawled in a chair opposite hers, then leaned forward with his elbows on his knees and forearms dangling down.

"I was pacing outside the barn when I saw the light go on in your room," he began. "I ran up here. I have to tell you—the excavation site." He stopped. She nodded at him to continue.

"I extended the west side and started digging there."

Penelope wondered why it was so urgent to share that fact.

"Forget it." He rose. "What am I doing, dragging you out in the middle of the night. Nobody can untangle the ethics of this mess except me."

Bewildered, Penelope watched him.

"Nate, don't pace, you'll wake the whole house," she said. "Settle down. You look drained. It's too hot for the strenuous work you're doing out there. On top of the financial strain and the pressures of the senior scientists, it's too much. It's sapped you. You're not yourself."

She wasn't sure he listened. He had stopped, half-turned, and stared at the moonflowers whose velvety petals shone with reflected light. Their luscious fragrance drifted on the night air.

"Maybe they saw this exact type of flower." His voice was lower, softer.

Penelope was ready to suggest he see a doctor.

"Nate, it's past two in the morning, it's hot, and you need to recover from overwork and burdens. Perhaps you should go to your bunk in the barn—or lay outside if that's cooler—and get some rest. Join us here for breakfast at, say, seven o'clock. We can talk then."

He took off his glasses and rubbed his eyes with a weary gesture. He put his spectacles back on.

"I'm not ill, Penelope. You don't need to write me a prescription for milk and naps."

"Oh, Nate, you're not okay, anyone could see that."

"Penelope, I dug up a complete skeleton."

CHAPTER 16

*P*enelope let out an involuntary gasp, covered her mouth with her hand, then lowered it. Perhaps she'd misunderstood him. It was late and she, too, was overtired.

"What did you say?"

"You heard me. A full skeleton. Actually, two of them. It appears I found some kind of ritualized burial ground. They were laid out side-by-side, with small bowls next to each of them and some evidence of trinkets. Everything was orderly, not like the loose bones. They're at a lower stratum than anything I've dug yet. Older than the other things I've found."

Penelope looked around to make sure no one else had awakened or overheard their conversation. Only the sounds of cicadas, frogs, and crickets kept them company.

"What did you do with them?" She was seized by the enormity of the discovery. "This is exactly what Billy spent weeks out there making sure you didn't find. Do you think he knew?"

"No. He's wary of the whole project because of what he learned from Tustenuggee. But he finally bored of policing the site after discoveries ebbed a while ago. He and the other young people drifted off to other pursuits. Sightseers haven't braved the scorching temperatures recently. It's been quiet there. Just me, and sometimes Onofrio and a few others."

"Has anyone else seen what you unearthed?"

"No," he said. "I reburied the skeletons after I took measurements and made rough sketches. I even camped out there the first night. Penelope, from the layout of the land and the way the skeletons were placed, I think there may be more. I may have stumbled on an ancient cemetery."

"What are you going to do?" she asked. "Finding pendants and pieces of pottery is one thing. Even loose human bones. But this…"

"That's just it. This could make my career. This discovery is in another stratosphere from silver pendants, a bird effigy, and a stolen vessel no one is able to recover. Think of the theories that could be advanced from knowledge gained from analysis. But…"

He stood again and started pacing. "At the same time, I'm troubled about disturbing a sacred cemetery. A place the ancients likely considered an eternal resting site."

Penelope could almost feel his inner turmoil. She hated to see Nate mired in a conflicted mess. She wanted his success as much as he did. But not at the wrong price.

"I want to pray about this," she said. She grabbed Nate's hand and tugged on it as he paced past her. He stilled his incessant movement.

"We need the Lord's guidance," she said.

"That we do."

She recited the Lord's Prayer in a quiet murmur. Nate joined in.

"'Lead us not into temptation' is the phrase that's staying with me, Nate," she said, after the prayer ended and they sat in silence for a few minutes.

He didn't reply.

"Listen, I understand how such a discovery would ripple

through the antiquities community," Penelope said. "I've been among audiences who flocked to such lectures in Boston. At the same time, we've all heard Billy's talk about Tustenuggee's beliefs, about the sacredness of his ancestors' burial places. More than once."

Nate looked glum.

"I can't disagree with his belief, Nate. We treat our cemeteries with reverence. Why wouldn't other cultures do the same? And the ancients who came before them?"

Nate sat back down. He shifted in his chair. "It's ancient, for sure. Nobody knew it was there. It's not like anyone tended the site out there."

"True," Penelope said. "But it's still a cemetery."

Nate rubbed his temples. "You're almost preaching to the choir, Penelope. I felt—I don't know—something—when I camped out there the other night. Early in the project, I spent a few nights out there. Something felt different this time. Not a presence. Not ghosts. But, as though I wasn't alone."

"Part of the communion of saints I'm learning about?" she asked.

"Maybe," Nate said. "Adds another level of sacredness to their resting place. I'm hesitant, Penelope. Not sure what to do."

"The Nate I met back in January might not have asked these questions," Penelope said. "He was one of the most determined and ambitious men I'd ever encountered."

Nate half laughed. "I work around fierce competitors. Guess I absorbed some of their attitudes. Being away from them woke me up to how much I'd almost become like them. Most will stomp on anyone or anything who gets in their way, hesitates, stumbles, or falls. I've never done that. Never will. But my ambition to succeed is strong."

"Your good heart is one of the things I lov...like so much about you," Penelope said.

She was glad Nate was too preoccupied to notice her slip of

wording. Did she love him? Yes, she did, she thought, as she sat inches from him. *Not something to think about now, Penelope,* she told herself. Her baby shifted inside her as if in agreement.

"Here's the problem," Nate said, and leaned forward again. "I don't have a cushion to fall back on, Penelope. The only way I can go is forward. That means announce the discovery, remove the bones, study them, give them to the university, and publish my findings."

"You sound like you're trying to convince yourself."

"Maybe I am."

"Maybe things will look brighter after some sleep," she said. Penelope's eyes were starting to droop. The thought of sleep was inviting. She tried to stifle a yawn, but failed.

"You need to sleep, too," Nate said. He got up and held out his hands to her. "I don't have to make a decision tonight. Just talking with you gives me hope things will work out."

He took her by the elbow and guided her toward the door. They heard the muffled chime of the clock inside ring three times.

"I'll pray that a resolution be found that works for all," she said, just before opening the door. "One for you and one for me. And an extra one for me, especially after what happened last evening."

He gave her a quizzical look.

"My surprise visitors," she said. "Late yesterday, my grand-mother, stepmother, and step-cousin showed up here. They're determined I'll return home with them as soon as possible."

"Send them back. You don't need that pressure, Penelope."

"You tell three stubborn Boston society ladies to do anything."

"Well, then, it's a good thing you share that stubbornness."

For the first time in their hour together, both Penelope and Nate smiled.

. . .

BY LATE THE FOLLOWING MORNING, Penelope prayed for more than a safe delivery of her child. She prayed to be taken to the childbed as soon as possible, to escape the dour presence of her uninvited guests.

"They're so disapproving, they're sending her spiraling backward into the melancholy she's worked so hard to overcome," a vexed Cornelia said to Agnes as they walked to the orphanage for midday prayer in the chapel.

"They hovered around her at the breakfast table, then followed her outside," Cornelia said.

Agnes sighed. "I saw. They allowed her no space, no quiet, no peace. I'm trying to hold my tongue. They're her family, after all. But they've brought the chill of a Northern winter with them."

The women settled themselves on a chapel bench and waited for the sisters.

"I've searched for charity but I'm wrestling, Miss Agnes, I really am. Three times I've been on the verge of telling them to let Miss Penelope be. If it's not one thing, it's another. They even harangued her about the antiquities sketches. Told her she's to return home with painted Italian landscapes for display at a private showing."

The door opened, and, as though she had heard them discussing her, Penelope slowly walked into the chapel, a hand on her stomach.

"She looks like a Madonna," whispered Cornelia.

"A feeble one, right now," Agnes said. She rose and lifted her wrist to Penelope's forehead as the young woman joined them on the bench. "You're pale. Are you feeling all right? No pains? You didn't walk over here yourself?"

"I'm weary, is all," Penelope said, and gave them a wan smile. "I crave peace, more than anything. As you can imagine. Onofrio showed up for language duties but I asked him to escort me here. My relatives even objected to that. They almost came with me. When I explained they'd be participating in the Catholic Divine Office with us, they found excuses to stay behind."

"You're in the right place at the right time," Agnes said. "Here come the sisters."

Sisters Bridget, Rose, and their companions made little sound as they entered the chapel. They conveyed greetings through inclined heads.

Penelope gave thanks for the serenity that flowed over her in the small, sacred space. She thanked God for leading her to a faith that fed her soul. She prayed that he stay close when she sprang the news of her pending conversion to her oh-so-loving family.

For they will no doubt find displeasure in that, too, she thought, in the internal monologue she couldn't quite turn off. Behind it all lay the heavy knowledge of Nate's momentous discovery.

Minutes later, Sister Bridget began the recitation of the prayers, hymns, and psalms that were becoming familiar to Penelope.

When she heard the psalmody words, "God, come to our assistance, Lord, make haste to help us," she felt her inner resolve strengthen. *Help me, Lord, and help Nate too,* she prayed. *Together, if possible.*

CHAPTER 17

$\mathcal{N}$ate's good mood had resurfaced by the time he knocked on the door of the Taylor house on Independence Day.

"I'm here to escort two of my favorite ladies to the festivities," he said. Agnes ushered him into the front room and left him with Cornelia. Penelope hadn't yet appeared. He looked around. "Is she well enough to go?"

"She says she's ready," Cornelia said. She glanced over her shoulder and lowered her voice. "Most of us feel she ought not to travel, even just the two miles. But she's adamant. Told me she won't stay here while everyone else goes to town. I think she fears her relatives might come here to spend the day. We'll need to keep an extra eye on her."

"You have my word."

Penelope's skirts rustled as she came into the room. She smiled but it couldn't mask the worry and fatigue that shadowed her eyes.

"I'm looking forward to this," she said, then stopped, put a hand on her belly, and let out a breath. She gave a little laugh. "All is okay," she said as Cornelia and Nate took quick steps toward her. "No need to jump into action. But let's go before it's not okay."

Cornelia cringed. "Are you certain you won't change your mind? I'll stay here with you."

"Me, too," Nate said. "Seen one holiday event, seem them all."

"No. I won't miss the youngsters' performance. Nate, you even tore yourself from the excavation for the day."

She wondered if he'd told anyone else about his latest discovery. She guessed not. He'd likely wait until town was back in its normal routine. For his news would surely stir things up.

"Who knows what people we might meet today," Penelope continued. "I heard people are coming from all over. Maybe there will be publishers interested in academic essays. Business investors who want inventories sketched instead of photographed. Philanthropists seeking new archaeological projects to fund."

"You dream on," Nate said. "My goal today is to learn more about the folks who frequent Persimmon Hollow and the surrounding towns. Could give us some leads about the theft. It's at such a dead end. It's like it never happened."

"Is anyone checking antiquities collectors?" Penelope asked as they made their way outside. "That bowl has several identifying marks, even aside from its obvious turtle shape."

"Professor Art says important collectors rely on local middlemen," Nate said. "He's compiling a list of collectors who might be nosing around, but the process is maddeningly slow."

He guided Penelope through the sand to the wagon. "Enough work talk. It's a holiday." He helped her step on a wooden box and up into the wagon. She settled herself against pillows he and Cornelia arranged.

"I'll be fine in the back," Cornelia called and hopped in. Penelope couldn't wait until she was nimble again. She closed her eyes and savored the feel of the sun and breeze, despite the heat. She could sense the intensity of the day's brightness behind her closed eyelids.

Nate inched the horse along so slowly, so as not to jostle Penelope, that it took them an hour to travel two miles. The reverse debarking procedure got underway, with pillow padding removed from around Penelope and her feet steered toward the box step.

Safely down, she looked around at the activity one block north of Persimmon Hollow's main intersection. The west side street, Indiana Avenue, was blocked off to carriage traffic. No horses, carts, barouches, or bicycles were allowed past barricades. Instead, they were parked up and down the main boulevard. People milled in thick crowds on the side street and in between the parked conveyances.

She, Nate, and Cornelia made their way along the closed street. Red-white-and-blue bunting hung from windows and doors of the shops and offices that lined the brick-paved road. The bank on the corner, the druggist, numismatist's shop, attorney's building, shoemaker, even the new café that wasn't yet open for business, all sported patriotic decoration. Beyond them was the courthouse, with a wide grassy park across the street from it.

The showstopper was the canvas theatrical backdrop with the giant painted scenery. It was draped for all to see on the top of the courthouse steps. Ropes tied each side of the backdrop to the massive columns that supported the portico. At the bottom of the steps, at street level, a small stage had been set up. A podium sat atop it, draped in bunting.

Across the street, a brass band played bright tunes in the shade of an elm in the park. The spicy smell of barbecue hung in the heavy air. Around the perimeter of the grassy area, and up and down the street, vendors under the shade of umbrellas and awnings displayed wares for sale. Penelope saw everything from a peddler's wagon open to display pots and pans, to a small table, behind which a tiny woman wove intricately patterned pine-needle baskets.

"Beautiful, the backdrop is absolutely beautiful!" an enthusiastic voice shouted behind them as they strolled into the park. Penelope turned to see Fanny and Professor Art, Eunice and Clyde, and a few of the instructors from Persimmon Hollow Academy who'd stayed in town to test the idea of a summer term.

"My dear, I saw what that backdrop looked like only a couple of weeks ago," Fanny said, "It's like a miracle occurred." She opened her wicker bag and withdrew two fans, one of which she handed to Penelope.

"For you, should you have need," she said, as she began fanning herself. "Which I'm certain you will, in this heat. If you need to rest, you just go to the house. Walk along the side of the courthouse and cross the street diagonally. You'll see the house about a block beyond."

Penelope opened her mouth to say thanks but closed it. Her relatives were at the Alloway House. She had no intention of going there.

As if she read her mind, Fanny added, "Your relations left a while ago but gave no indication of their plans."

Penelope was relieved. She was happy to be part of the exuberant crowd but was already growing weary of the sticky humidity and noise. Tensions with relatives would have been most unwelcome.

At the same time, she had the oddest sensation of energy and verve. Her spirits were buoyant despite the minor irritations. *The excitement of the day is contagious*, she thought.

"Your relations declined to attend," Fanny continued. "They said they could hear the festivities quite well from the parlor and porch, and already had their fill. I'm sorry they chose not to attend."

"I'm not," Penelope said. At Fanny's shocked expression,

she hastened to explain. "They wouldn't have a good time. This isn't their preferred, ah, leisure activity. My grandmother doesn't function well in noisy places. The dust and smells would annoy my stepmother. My step-cousin wouldn't want to soil the bottom of her dress."

Nate hung back during the exchange, and Penelope noticed he and the professor didn't converse. Usually, they had their heads together pondering theories and comparing notes on antiquities. Not today. They stood several feet apart.

When the four older people wandered off, Nate and Cornelia maneuvered Penelope toward a heavily shaded corner of the park.

"Best seat in the house," Nate declared, as he set up a small wooden stool he'd carted with them. Penelope's legs ached, and the seat was a welcome relief. She ignored pointed stares at her condition.

"I'll go find the rest of the Taylor Grove clan and check on the children," Cornelia said. "And will bring back some lemonade." She hurried off, oblivious to the looks from people unfamiliar with the garb and headgear of the Franciscan novice.

After a while, the heat, noise, and the weight of a full-term baby pushed aside Penelope's usual calm. She let out a long sigh and stopped fanning herself. Nate grabbed the fan and flapped it energetically around her.

"What's taking Cornelia so long?" he said. "Are you hungry? Thirsty?"

"I probably should eat a little bit," she said without enthusiasm.

"Be right back," Nate replied. He bolted into the thickening mingle of people. Children ran every which way, firecrackers popped, the brass band clanged, and someone at the podium shouted over the raucous crowd. The sun stood overhead, and the heat no longer felt as welcoming as it had a while earlier.

"There you are! For mercy's sake, Penelope, why are you out

in public? Have you become as commonplace as the rest of the people of this town, what is it called? Parson's Hill?"

Her stepmother's querulous voice preceded the quick-stepped emergence of the woman from the crowd. She marched up, closely followed by Penelope's grandmother and step-cousin.

Penelope wished the recitations would begin to spare her any conversation. She looked up and stared at the "Trio of Doom," as she had taken to calling her unwelcome visitors.

Only her grandmother had a shred of honest decency in her. But she was also the strictest of the family in terms of propriety. Penelope considered the other two women opportunists. After Penelope's father died, her stepmother had begun putting on even more airs.

Penelope chafed at the way appearance and social standing were so important to her grandmother. But she respected her. She lived according to her high morals.

It was to her grandmother she now spoke.

"This town is named Persimmon Hollow, grandmother," she said. "There's quite a collection of settlers here, from many states and several countries. They've carved a new town out of the wilderness and it's still maturing. Boston, once, was wilderness."

"Thank goodness it no longer is, my dear. I hope you have grown to appreciate the benefits of civilization during your exile here."

Penelope had done no such thing. Quite the opposite had occurred. Today was hardly the day to try to explain, though.

Nate jostled his way back through the crowd, holding aloft a large paper bag whose aroma revealed the chicken within. Cornelia was behind him with lemonade.

"Here, got you some chicken and Cornelia has the drinks," Nate said, and then looked at the out-of-towners. "Ladies, good day to you. I'd bow if my hands weren't full."

The three visiting women stared as he withdrew wrapped

paper bundles from the greasy bag. Penelope attempted to balance one of the bundles on her lap and unfold it. The aroma of fried chicken saturated the air. Her step-cousin wrinkled her nose and frowned.

The shriek of a whistle broke through the noise and the crowd quieted momentarily. Finally, the man at the podium had everyone's attention. Penelope sipped her lemonade but set aside the chicken. She felt full despite not having eaten in several hours.

"Welcome to the Persimmon Hollow Independence Day Extravaganza!" said the speaker. The band's drummer thumped his instrument for emphasis.

"We open our program with a patriotic reading of the Declaration of Independence by the youth of Taylor Grove and our very own St. Isidore's Orphanage South."

Cornelia hurried off to help Agnes guide the performers, who presented near-impeccable recitations of the document and a few poems. The band launched into "The Star-Spangled Banner" and the crowd roared its accompaniment. Halfway through the song, Penelope regretted drinking the lemonade. It had given her stomach cramps.

A half hour and several musical selections later, she realized her cramps had nothing to do with lemonade. Her baby was coming. She reached over and tugged Nate's sleeve. He looked away from the makeshift stage and at Penelope just as she grimaced. The pains were worsening. The noise, smells, and activity around her dimmed. Her body took command. Nate dropped everything and jumped to help her.

"Don't tell them," she said and indicated her relatives with a nod of her head. Having grown bored with the small-town program, they had stepped away to peruse the vendor stalls. Nate nodded and waved frantically at Cornelia to return from where she stood with the Alloway and Taylor families near the stage.

In what seemed like seconds, Nate and Cornelia each had a

gentle but firm grip on Penelope's arms. They shuffled her toward the other end of the street and soon were swallowed by the crowd.

"I'm okay, I can walk," Penelope fretted. "It actually helps." Neither Nate nor Cornelia let go of her. They also spoke over her as though she were no longer coherent.

"She'll never make it back to the grove," Nate said.

"Oh, I was afraid of this. I didn't want to say in mixed company, but we had a sign a few days ago when the baby shifted inside her," Cornelia said.

"Can we go to the Alloway House?"

"No," said Penelope, but it came out as a gasp because she was hit with a pain just as she opened her mouth.

"Her relations are staying there," Cornelia said.

"Take me to Taylor Grove," insisted Penelope.

"How far apart are the pains?" Nate asked. "Cornelia, I'm not out of bounds. I assisted at a couple of births when my mom needed help. She's a midwife."

"I'm glad to hear that," Cornelia said. She made a sign of the cross. "Agnes saw what has happening. She and the others will be along right behind us. She didn't want to draw attention."

"I don't know how far apart they are," Penelope said. "Quite a few minutes, maybe. Not too close. Well, maybe."

"I'll time them," Nate said, and pulled out his pocket watch.

When they reached the wagon, Nate picked her up without asking. Cornelia made a bed of blankets and pillows for her in the back of the wagon, and then scooted beside her.

"You just pray with me and all will be well," Cornelia said.

"I hope so," Penelope said, and gripped her hand as another pain clamped down on her. Nate inched the horses out of the crowded parking area. Penelope's fears increased with each cramp and jolt of the wagon. "Pray that we make it in time," she croaked.

Cornelia crossed herself again. In the distance, the crowd

sent up a cheer about something, the band started playing again, and firecrackers spurted and crackled.

"You'll have yourself a Fourth of July baby," Nate said. "The birthday will always be a day of celebration."

A MEWLING CRY awoke Penelope from a half-slumber. Her baby! Her precious little girl! She reached out, awake as never before.

"Here she is, your jewel of a daughter." Agnes laid the little one into Penelope's arms. A fierce, protective love surged through Penelope as she nuzzled the baby's softness, inhaled her baby smell, and marveled at her tiny, perfect body.

The endless previous day of walking and resting and walking and resting and finally, finally, pushing one last time against pain that stole her breath and left her half-delirious, all receded before the miracle she held.

She remembered little except that it had been dark and hot when she first held her daughter, knew that all was well, and succumbed to exhaustion.

"Mercy, she is perfect," said Lupita, who'd come in from the kitchen at the sound of Agnes's voice. She knelt beside the bed. "Thank you, Lord, for her safe delivery. May this little one always be under the protection of you and your Blessed Mother."

Next to arrive, as Lupita rose, were Cornelia and Josefa. The baby went from one woman to the next. Agnes checked her diaper, Lupita and Cornelia prayed over her, and Josefa gave her tiny kisses.

"My turn," Penelope said, but she smiled.

The room quieted as the others watched Penelope cradle her baby, who stopped fussing. The little mouth formed a tiny yawn.

"Blessed Mother, oh Lady of Guadalupe, we seek your intercession for what is to come," murmured Lupita.

"What do you mean, what is to come?" Penelope asked. She tried to shift herself to a seated position but gave up. Weariness crept over her. She wanted everyone to leave and let her sleep with her baby at her breast.

Agnes's dress rustled as she moved closer to the bed. "Penelope, perhaps it's best you don't hold her too long. It will be easier when you leave and she stays here. You won't form as strong a bond."

Agnes drew in a breath before she continued. "Your relations are adamant. They were here for quite a while last night. They expect their original plan to be carried out."

Penelope pulled the baby closer. "No. That's their plan. Not mine."

The other women glanced one to the other.

Penelope looked each in the eye, in turn. "I know it won't be easy. I accept that. Nothing you or my relatives say will make me change my mind."

"By God's grace, I can't keep a baby from her mother," Agnes said, as much to herself as to Penelope.

"Have you decided what to name her?" Cornelia asked.

"Grace. She's perfect and a gift from God."

"Yes!" Agnes and Lupita and Josefa all exclaimed.

"A beautiful name," Cornelia said.

"And now we need to stop blabbering and let this new mother get some rest," Agnes announced. She ushered everyone out of the room.

Morning sunlight filtered around the edges of the drawn curtains and a warm breeze filtered through. The baby had fallen asleep. Penelope released a contented breath and sank into sleep again.

In the other room, Agnes looked out on the porch as she adjusted the front curtains against the sun. "Oh, dear," she said. "Poor Nate. Look at him."

Lupita, Cornelia, and Josefa looked over Agnes's shoulder. There, stretched out on the porch floorboards, was Nate, asleep to the world.

The caw of crows passing overhead roused him as they watched. He opened his eyes, blinked, and looked around until his gaze landed on the women staring out the window.

He bolted to his feet, eyes wide and hair tangled, and felt around on the porch table and chairs for his glasses. Finding them, he smashed them on his face.

"How is Penelope? What time is it? Where is she? I don't hear anything. Is there a baby yet? Can I see her? Penelope, I mean. Is it a boy or a girl?"

His words tumbled over one another, and he stumbled over the nearest chair, the one between him and the window.

"You'd think he was the father," said Lupita in a low, clucking voice.

"Penelope is doing beautifully," Agnes said through the screened window. "Yes, we have a baby, a little girl that Penelope named Grace. We didn't want to wake you."

"Can I come in?" He pressed his hair down and adjusted his wrinkled garb.

"Just for a minute. They're asleep."

He bounded toward the door so quickly his footsteps thudded across the wood floor.

"Quiet!" said all four women in loud whispers.

"Ooops, sorry," he whispered and opened the door without making a sound. He tiptoed in, closing the door behind him with an almost imperceptible click of the latch.

"Just a peek for now," Agnes said. "Come back this evening. Have dinner with us. You can visit longer then."

She trailed him and hovered by his side as he pushed open the partly ajar bedroom door. He stood in the doorway, silent for once, and gazed at the sleeping mother and child.

Joy and love suffused his face when he turned toward Agnes. Then he blinked once, twice. "Got something in my eye," he mumbled and stubbed his finger at his eye behind his glasses.

"Uh, huh," said Agnes, and steered him away so as not to disturb Penelope and Grace.

Nate let out his breath when they got back outside. "They're beautiful, both of them. Grace, what a perfect name."

He glanced at his watch and stuffed it back in his pocket. "Dinnertime, huh? I'm going to have a hard time focusing on work today."

"You'll survive," Agnes said. "On your way to the excavation, would you mind stopping at Clyde's Mercantile, Stillman's Nursery, and Bight Furniture and sharing the good news?"

"I'd be happy to!" Nate said. "Past time for me to get out to the river anyway. Will you tell Penelope I was here and give her my best?"

"Yes, and also that we pushed you out and that you'll be back later."

The women heard him whistling as he headed toward his horse and wagon and then rattled down the drive.

LATER THAT DAY, Penelope was awake and resting when she heard the voices of the Trio of Doom. She shifted to sit up, leaned back against her pillows and drew Grace into an embrace. Her grandmother, stepmother, and step-cousin knocked on the frame of the open bedroom door and entered as though at home.

"How inappropriate," sniffed her stepmother without saying hello or how are you. "You shouldn't be bonding. Why isn't that baby in the hands of the nuns at the orphanage?"

"Because I'm keeping her," Penelope said. "Say hello to Grace Gold."

The loud intake of breaths of the three visitors was so uniform it sounded as one.

"You'll be a ruined woman," her stepmother said.

"And you'll ruin my reputation and the rest of the family's, too," complained her step-cousin.

Her grandmother, meanwhile, said nothing. She gazed at the baby. Penelope wondered what her protocol-loving grandmother was thinking.

"You and the baby are well?" her grandmother finally asked.

"Never felt better," said Penelope, but it was a brave front. She'd awakened from a nap with an unwelcome heaviness starting to press down on her. Why did melancholy rear its head now? At such a time of miracle and new life?

Her grandmother didn't need to hear any of that. Or her step-mother or step-cousin. They would dismiss her as weak. Nate, he would understand. So would Cornelia.

But the two people who'd become her closest friends weren't nearby. She stared at her three relations crowded into Polly's small bedroom, a room given up to her with pleasure and care. Emotions that her inquisitors lacked.

"You realize the consequences if you insist on pursuing your foolish notion?" her grandmother asked.

"How could she not?" her stepmother interrupted.

Fear and stubbornness squeezed Penelope's heart.

"I will manage."

Her grandmother didn't answer, merely raised her eyebrows.

"I don't see how," her stepmother snapped. "You know my thoughts about this ridiculous idea you've embraced. I've tried to make allowances for your erratic behavior, but this is simply too much. What shall you do, return to Boston with a baby and say you found it on the street corner in Italy?"

"It's a she, not an it," said Penelope. "Her name is Grace."

"Well, you and Grace better get used to poverty, for that's where you shall slide," her stepmother said. "You cannot return to Boston as a single woman of good family, with a baby in tow. The entire family's reputation will be sullied, not just yours."

Penelope didn't reply. She understood the social mores. She would defy them, or at least circumvent them, for the sake of her daughter.

"What is the status of Herman, distasteful though his name is to me?" her grandmother asked. "The family can bring pressure on him to marry you. There would be scandal, of course. But with time and a relocation of your small family, the ripples would fade."

Penelope shook her head. "I don't know and don't care to know. He didn't reply to my early communications and I long ago stopped inquiring. I want nothing to do with him."

"That's his child you're holding," her stepmother reminded her.

Penelope closed her eyes and a sigh escaped her. Her body screamed for rest and her emotions weren't far behind. Had these women forgotten the rigors of the childbed, or did they just not care?

Her eyes flew open in surprise when her grandmother came to her defense.

"We'll discuss this at another time," the family matriarch said. "Enough of our reprobation. The child and her baby need support right now."

The words stunned Penelope. Her stepmother and step-cousin gaped at the elderly woman, then moved toward the door.

"Penelope, you're tired and not thinking clearly," her step-mother said. "We'll endure another few days in Persimmon Hollow in hopes you'll reconsider your impulsive decision." She cast an annoyed glance at Matriarch Gold, who returned an even colder one.

A light tap rapped at the door frame and Agnes peered into the room.

"Perhaps you'd like to keep your visit short, for our new mother's sake," Agnes urged. They all heard the underlying iron in the suggestion.

"We're just leaving," Matriarch Gold said. The three visitors glided out of her room, heads high, followed by Agnes, who closed the door behind her with a gentle click.

Penelope spent the rest of the afternoon dozing, feeding, and cradling Grace. Just before evening, a short but heavy rainfall blew through and cooled the summer air. She inhaled the earthy scents that sprang from the moistened ground and drifted through the window. Oh, how refreshing, the smell and the feel of the rain-kissed earth and air.

The change lifted her, body and soul, and drew her from bed. Grace had awakened but was asleep again, and Penelope placed her gently in the cradle someone had placed in the room. How thoughtful they all were.

Lupita came running from the kitchen. "I heard you moving around," she said. "Should you be up? How is the baby? Are you hungry?" She wiped her hands on her apron and kissed Penelope and smiled at the baby.

"Now that I think about it, yes, I'm kind of hungry."

Grace awakened and looked around with wide eyes.

"I'll bring you some milk and a slice of pie," Lupita said. "We won't tell anyone you had dessert before dinner. Our little secret."

She returned with the snack and something extra. "A little something I made for the baby." She gave Penelope a baby blanket knitted in blue and pink from the thinnest, finest yarn. "And this." She reached in her apron pocket and withdrew a rosary. "See, it is made of pressed rose petal beads, and the center medal is an image of Our Lady of Guadalupe."

"They're beautiful, Lupita. Thank you."

"I knitted the blanket and Josefa and I dried and rolled the rose petals and made the rosary. They're our special gifts to you as a new mother: a blanket to show the warmth of Our Lord's love and protection, and a rosary to help you stay close to Our Lady."

The starkness between her first post-baby encounters with her own relatives and with this loving woman she hardly knew, settled deep into Penelope's heart.

"You have no idea what this means to me," Penelope said. "And to her," she added, looking at Grace.

"If I may ask, please pray for our Josefa, who yearns for a little one. I see the new sadness on her face each month. She and Ben will be good, strong parents. I know it's not for me to question God, but still, this emptiness is hard to understand."

Penelope remembered the conversation when Josefa said she waited longingly for a baby. The young seamstress hid her sorrow well. Josefa had shown nothing but friendliness and happiness about Grace.

Lupita helped Penelope back into bed and placed the milk and pie on the side table. She picked up Grace and settled her into Penelope's arms.

"Rest while longer. The men are still in the fields, Agnes is at the orphanage, and I've shooed the youngsters away. Later, if you feel able, you and the baby join us at the dinner table for a few minutes. We've invited Cornelia and Nate. Oh, you don't know! We found Nate asleep on the porch early this morning and we let him in to take a peek. Ah, the man, he was so overjoyed. He's a good man, that one."

Lupita's last words stayed with Penelope long after the housekeeper left. They were in her mind that evening when Nate arrived and loped into her room with restrained eagerness she could almost feel. Cornelia trailed him by a few inches, radiant with joy and much quieter.

"Penelope!" Nate called out. "Grace! Thank God you're both okay. Can I hold the little one?" He squatted down by the side of the bed and peered into Penelope's eyes.

She wanted to reach across and kiss him. She wished he was the father of little Grace. She wanted to say so many things to him. Instead, she parted her lips and surprised herself by managing only a few whispered words.

"I'm fine—Oh, Nate, I'm so glad you're here." And

suddenly she began to cry. They were tears of joy and release and frustration and, just, *everything*.

Cornelia grew alarmed and started to pull Nate back but he resisted. "I'm here, for both of you, always," he said to Penelope and smoothed her hair. He pressed a finger to his lips and then to Penelope's. "Always."

Penelope gripped his hand and regained control of her emotions. With a tenderness that didn't surprise her, Nate picked up Grace as though she were a piece of fine porcelain and rocked her a few times before setting her back into Penelope's arms. She held Grace in one arm and laid her free hand on Nate's arm so that he stayed near. They gazed at each other without speaking.

Cornelia stepped back as far as she could without actually leaving the room.

CHAPTER 18

*H*ow could a tiny baby require so much attention? Penelope soon realized she'd need long-term help. Two weeks of pampering and assistance from the women of the grove, orphanage, and town made that clear.

Even with help, her world had shrunk into a jumble of baby feeding, diaper changing, baby rocking, eating, and sleeping that rolled day into night and back again. She was no longer sure what day of the week it was.

Nate's visits, morning and afternoon rest on the porch, and the routine of family mealtimes helped mold time into a structure. Nate's goofy antics over Grace warmed her heart and delighted everyone else.

Then her relatives visited. It was the first time they'd been to Taylor Grove since the day of Grace's birth.

The brief encounter was strained and unsatisfactory as they crowded into her bedroom. Her grandmother was reticent. The others wanted only to know when Penelope would be ready to travel North with them. All three ignored Grace, although Penelope did catch her grandmother's surreptitious glances toward the cradle.

"I don't know when I'll feel ready for the journey," Penelope said. "If you don't mind, I'd like to sleep now."

"Women no longer spend a month in bed after childbirth," her stepmother said. "Start spending more time up and about. Plan to leave here in two weeks. That'll be four full weeks since birthing and should be sufficient. I'll make the travel arrangements. The sooner we all get away from this dreadful heat, the better. And you need to get away from that baby."

Penelope closed her eyes and made no response. Her eyelids fluttered open only after the sounds of footsteps and rustling dresses faded.

Her stepmother's insistence brought nagging concerns flooding back from the corners where Penelope, in her new mother haze, had banished them. She did have to make plans. Where and how would she and Grace live for the long term? The baby awoke and began to fret.

THE FOLLOWING WEEK, Penelope left Grace with Cornelia and the other women and took a much-needed stroll around the property. The late afternoon shadows had dropped a hint of cooler temperatures over the filtered shade cast by the longleaf pines. She inhaled the rich scent the sun baked out of the evergreens. How she'd grown to love the woodsy forest smell.

The barn doors were wide open. Penelope veered toward the structure and hoped Nate was there. She missed their long talks and hours together. He'd been limiting his visits, giving himself only enough time to hold and marvel at Grace, ensure Penelope was regaining her strength, and make sure she was smiling when he departed.

Sure enough, there he was, hunched over the work table in the back. Penelope made her way through the dusky space.

Nate looked up when her shadow fell over his shoulder in the long, slanting rays of late afternoon sun. His face brightened and he scrambled to his feet.

"How's that baby?! How are you?"

"Grace is thriving. How could she not, surrounded with so much love and care?"

"But you? What about you?"

"Just lovely. I mean it."

He peered into her eyes but didn't voice any questions, although she read them in his gaze. Instead, he drew out the other chair at the table and helped her sit down.

She recognized some of the artifacts and a cluster of new-to-her pieces. "Fill me in on what's been happening."

Nate exhaled loudly as he sat back down. "A lot."

"More burials?"

"Evidence that more exist, although I haven't dug to find them. The word is out. Crowds are coming around, even in this heat. Onofrio is in his element again."

"I wondered why he wasn't hovering around me and the baby," Penelope said. "He popped in one day and tiptoed around the cradle with wide eyes. When Grace awoke, she was fretful. When she started crying, he bolted out with his hands over his ears. Yelled one of his cheery goodbyes to me, 'See you later, Miss Penelope, you got lots to do here!' I haven't seen him since."

"He's been staying by me," Nate said. "Billy told Tustenuggee about what we unearthed and the man now camps at the site, day and night. I guess that's good in a way. We've come to know each other over the past few weeks... Forced proximity."

Penelope discerned mountains left unsaid.

"What about you, Penelope, really. How are you truly doing?"

"Well, I'm relieved my loving relations decided to take a side trip to St. Augustine. They'll be out of my way for days. Last week, they all finally visited Taylor Grove again. My stepmother insisted I prepare to travel soon. I didn't answer them. They finally left."

Nate groaned.

"Then I learned from Fanny they'd gone to St. Augustine and told her they'd return in a couple of weeks," Penelope said. "They apparently think I'll obey their orders if they give me more time. You know, leaving the baby and returning North with them? Which I've no intention of doing.

"But I can't stay at the grove forever. The Taylors and Gomezes and the sisters and Cornelia have been overly generous with their hospitality. It's time for me to move forward. I've been thinking. I'd like to run an idea past you."

"I'm all ears." Nate turned toward her with undivided attention.

"I expect to earn some income from my art, but let's face it, it won't be enough for a life of comfort for me and Grace in a large city." Penelope fingered the edge of the excavation ledger's open page. "But, that income and the money in the local bank will be enough for us to live in a simple manner here."

"You're thinking of staying in Persimmon Hollow?"

"Surprised?" she asked.

"Sort of, at first thought," he said cautiously. "It's a fine idea. But it could be somewhat limiting in terms of earning income."

"The local bank account contains enough to cover me for a good six months if I'm frugal. That gives me time to secure other income, such as from art commissions. Also, come the winter season, I can tutor visitors in language and art. Maybe locals, too."

Nate thought for a few minutes and then gave a nod.

"You'll achieve anything you set your mind to, Penelope. I support your every step."

Shadows dimmed the barn further as the sun dropped in the west. Nate rose and lit the kerosene lantern and set it in the center of the table. He sat back down.

"I should get back," Penelope said. "I can tell by the angle of those shadows it's almost time to feed Grace."

Nate helped her rise. "You know you have the backing of the people here, not just the itinerant archaeologist who has to wander North soon."

He walked with Penelope toward the doors. She didn't want to think about a Persimmon Hollow without him in it.

"You're certain about staying?" he asked. "This region is still a wilderness."

She leaned into him as they emerged into the soft evening air and started walking toward the house. He kept an arm around her shoulder.

The heavy sweetness of night-blooming jasmine mingled with the woodsy pine scent around them.

"I know it's not Boston." She inhaled deeply. "It's not a bad place. Growing fast but still quiet and peaceful. Good people."

"Except the ones who steal artifacts. I'd worry more about you and Grace if I didn't know how much you keep your wits about you. And by how you're surrounded by protective people. But a frontier isn't the safest place for a woman to live alone. And you have to admit opportunities for culture and enrichment are limited."

"You forget the Academy," Penelope said. "It's stellar. Perhaps I can teach there in the future. As for now, I plan to hire a live-in companion to help with Grace. And I'll be protected, Nate, between the men and youth here and in town. I'd rather be happy and accepted in a frontier town than shunned in a cultured city."

They stopped walking and faced each other, two intelligent, stubborn, determined people.

"I keep repeating that you'll always have my support," Nate

said. "But I won't always be physically here to give it. Especially not now, not after finding ancient burials. It's the kind of discovery that can catapult me into a permanent university faculty position. We both know there aren't any universities in Persimmon Hollow."

He kicked at a clump of wiregrass.

"Something I've always wanted," he said. "And now that it's coming within reach, I'm not as happy as I thought I'd be. Not happy at the idea of compromising sacred beliefs, not happy about leaving here."

Penelope stopped walking, leaned away and tugged on his arm. "It's your dream, Nate. You'll find a resolution that works. Are you going to rework your paper to include the burials?"

"No, not this article," he said, after a moment's hesitation. "It's finished. My theory doesn't rely on the existence of burials for support. I'm ready to type up a draft. Then we can decide what sketches will accompany it, if you're feeling well enough to take a look."

"I'd like that," she said as they neared the porch steps.

"First, I need to run up to the Academy and see if I can borrow a typewriter," he said.

"Yes, that would help," she said, and chuckled. It felt good, this focus on something other than her own gnawing needs. She waved to Cornelia, who sat on the porch with the baby, who was in a carriage draped with mosquito netting. Penelope picked up Grace and kissed her cheeks, which grew chubbier by the day. Nate added a peck atop her little head. He held aside the netting as Penelope lowered Grace back into the carriage and readjusted the thin fabric.

"It's at the top of my list, first thing tomorrow morning, I'll go see the principal," Nate said.

. . .

THE NEXT AFTERNOON, Penelope was on the porch when she saw Nate lug a typewriter to the barn. His shoulders were slouched and his walk slow. She watched as he went into the barn, came back out a short while later and started walking toward the house.

Something was terribly wrong.

"I see you got the typewriter," she said as he slouched into a chair on the porch.

"And more than I bargained for."

He cast her a somber look. "Eunice wanted me to teach a course in archaeology and anthropology in the fall. Said they're intent on expanding the Academy from primary-secondary to college level. Said my course could help them launch the idea."

Penelope noted he used past tense. He said Eunice *wanted*, not *wants*. Nor did he look happy about the offer.

"I had to turn it down, of course," he said. "I'll be back up North. I have to be. I need to lecture, even before publication of my article. Publication and public lectures at big venues up there will be springboards to the next level of my career. I want to end up in the classroom during semesters and in the field at other times."

Penelope maintained a neutral face but raised an eyebrow.

"Uh, Nate," she said. "Do you realize what you just said? Eunice offered you a place in a classroom."

Nate grimaced.

"Like I told Eunice—who asked the same question— spending next semester here would throw my plan out of order," he explained. "Excitement about the discoveries would wane."

He winced. "Her reply to me was harsh," he continued. "She said, 'You mean, your plan for landing at a more prestigious institution more befitting of your excellence?' Those were her exact words."

Nate had the decency to flush as he relayed the exchange to Penelope.

He ran a hand through his hair and adjusted his glasses. "You know how pressure on me mounted when Professor Art's colleagues decided they wanted to take over site work. Penelope, I either return North to secure funding or risk losing any advantage I can grasp."

Penelope chose her next words with care. "Nate, there's much in Persimmon Hollow and the Academy worth your while. Except the prestige. Yet. It'll come in due time."

"You're probably correct," he said. "But the timing isn't right for me. Enough about me. Tell me about Grace. Any new movements, coos, smiles?"

Penelope glanced inside the window to where Grace lay asleep in the cradle in the front room.

"Come, see for yourself," she said.

His face lightened when they went inside and he drew near the baby. Grace awakened at the sound of their footsteps and Penelope picked her up.

"How can your family be immune to her charms?" Nate asked as Penelope eased the baby into his arms. "Are they still in St. Augustine?"

"Not sure. If so, they'll probably be back any day now." She sighed. "I'd best be ready with my reasons for remaining here and a detailed plan to back it all up."

She stared out at window at the homestead landscape, lush with summer growth. Magnolias, persimmons, palms, pines, and oaks grew in profusion beyond the cleared area that marked the boundaries of the homestead's main buildings. Silvery gray Spanish moss drooped down from oak limbs that formed a canopy over the entrance road.

Penelope took Grace, who had started to fuss. She held the baby close and prayed. When she opened her eyes, her own troubled gaze met Nate's tired one.

"Take me out to the excavation tomorrow," she said. She had

a deep, sudden need to be back among the activity and surroundings of something bigger than herself.

"Tomorrow?"

"Yes. For a couple of hours. I can be away from Grace for a little while and the ladies here will dote on her. Yes, let's go. It'll be like old times. Something we both need right now."

A hint of the old Nate kindled in his eyes.

"I'll bring the wagon around first thing in the morning."

CHAPTER 19

*P*enelope stood outside and watched the next morning as Nate and Onofrio waved goodbye to Seth at the barn door and started off in her direction.

"Chief archaeologist and his chief assistant, at your service," Nate said as they pulled up out front. Onofrio scrambled out before Nate could and assisted Penelope down the porch steps and into the wagon.

"He's so happy you're coming with us today he camped overnight in the barn, pestered me every time I tried to write, and then woke me before dawn," Nate said. Penelope noticed his grin toward the boy was fatherly. Some of the tension had drained from him.

"*Si*, Miss Penelope, the sisters and Miss Cornelia said it was okay for me to stay in the barn just one night," Onofrio chattered. "I saw a giant owl fly in and out! Oh, and Miss Cornelia said remember we stop and get her this morning. That's why I stay with Mr. Nate. To make sure he not forget. Oh, and I build boxes for Mr. Nate! For his stuff."

"Small artifact boxes," Nate explained. "Kept him busy. I

actually managed to get some work in between showing him how to measure and nail."

Penelope wondered if Nate realized how much he and Onofrio looked—and acted—like father and son. Probably not. But she certainly did. An image of herself, Nate, Onofrio, and Grace as a family flitted through her mind. And stayed.

They stopped to get Cornelia at the orphanage. Onofrio curled up in sleep before they'd driven off the grove property.

"Here we are," Nate said as they reached the mound.

"You're gonna be mighty surprised, Miss Penelope," Onofrio said as he sat up and rubbed his eyes. "Things changed."

"They sure did," Nate said, and took her arm to escort her up the winding trail.

The slow journey upward was more of a challenge than she'd expected. She almost kissed Nate when he tugged a folded camp chair out of his pack and set it up for her a short while into the walk. Onofrio ran ahead.

Moisture from the river's closeness brought freshness to the breeze, and the mingled scents of pine and oak acted like tonics. She inhaled and felt rejuvenated.

After two more breaks, the three adults reached the top.

"Gosh, it looks so different," Penelope said. "You go ahead and start work. I'll rest here a few minutes in the shade and then walk over." Cornelia moved a distance apart for the prayer time Penelope had learned was called Terce.

Penelope surveyed the scene before her. The main excavation area had been enlarged. The primary corner where Nate had first uncovered artifacts was roped off. The strata were smooth and undisturbed. The project focus has shifted to the far side of the excavation, where much of the additional digging had taken place. Adjacent to the work area, a tent was set up. In front of it sat Tustenuggee and Billy.

Nate headed over to the tent. Onofrio dragged Billy to the far side of the mound top to show him an unusual growth on some trees.

"Have you seen any of this yet, Cornelia?" she asked when the younger woman concluded her prayers.

"No, I stopped coming up here when you did."

Tustenuggee was talking to Nate, who'd squatted down on his haunches at the edge of the pit. After a while he got up, jumped into the pit, and turned toward Penelope.

"The burials begin there," he called to her and pointed to a disturbed area of soil that hugged the exterior wall of the project site. "You can see where I covered them up."

She couldn't, not from her vantage point. She hurried over with Cornelia.

Nate looked up at Penelope from a few feet down inside the pit. His eyes were wide and alive with restrained patience. It was the Nate she'd come to know and love. He was back, if only temporarily.

His tone was hushed. "I've done preliminary samplings outward from here. Far as I can tell, this is the edge of a significant burial mound. I suspect there might be more than one time period, because there's a sizable distance between these two burials and where I've found evidence that others are located."

"Do the professor's friends know any of this?" Penelope asked.

"I hope not."

"So do I," said Tustenuggee.

Nate dropped his head forward, then tilted it back up.

"I think the professor told them only that a few bones had been discovered, in addition to artifacts. His last report was done before the full burials emerged. But bones and precious metal pendants were enough to put them on my trail."

"To think, people lived here so long ago," Penelope said. "I wonder what their lives were like. Can you uncover the one skeleton you re-covered so that I can make a quick sketch of it? I have a pad and pencils in my day pack."

Nate stood up and looked at Tustenuggee.

"My friend here and I have gone round and round on protocol, Penelope. I want to excavate, take specimens north for study, arrange for display in a suitable museum, and build on my discovery by writing, teaching, and lecturing. And do it before the newly interested academics get their hands on my find. That's what I want to do."

"And I want to leave them to their rest," Tustenuggee said. "Would you let your ancestors be treated the way you suggest?"

"They won't know," Nate said. "How long have they been lying here? Hundreds, thousands of years? Think what we can do to further knowledge of ancient peoples and civilizations by studying them."

Tustenuggee didn't answer.

"And so it goes," Nate said to Penelope and Cornelia.

"I might be hesitant if someone dug up graves of past generations of Golds," Penelope said after some thought.

"But you'd allow it, right, if it could further the study of science?" Nate asked.

"This is sacred ground," Tustenuggee said. "Ancestral ground."

Cornelia, meanwhile, had knelt by the edge of the pit, blessed herself, and said a silent prayer. The others noticed when she rose and brushed sand from the knees of her habit.

"I almost wish you hadn't done that," Nate said.

They all looked at him, surprised.

"Because a part of me understands what Tustenuggee says and you just reinforced it. Not exactly what the scientist side of me wants to see."

"Perhaps exactly what you need to see," said Penelope. Nate stalked off and circled the grounds with long strides before stopping back in front of them.

"We need at least a few sketches, done *in situ*. I'll uncover the burials so you can do that. Then I'll re-cover them until we come to some solution. Are you willing?" He looked at both Tustenuggee and Penelope. She gave him a positive nod.

"The less disturbance, the better, but I see no harm in a brief uncovering if done with respect," Tustenuggee said. "I'll pray first and afterward."

Penelope was fascinated by the prospect. Sketch the remains of an ancient person? Few men had such an opportunity and fewer women. Nate retrieved the camp chair and Cornelia brought over Penelope's art materials.

They bowed their heads while Tustenuggee prayed. Penelope heard the thump of Onofrio and Billy's footsteps come closer and halt. Their voices fell silent.

Afterward, the men and boys carefully removed the dirt covering one of the burials. Cornelia crossed herself and the others followed suit. Penelope wasted no time. She began to sketch at the first sight of bone.

For a while, only the sound of pencil etching across paper vied with the noise of cicadas, frogs, songbirds, alligators, and the occasional call of a hawk or a heron.

"There's a welcome dearth of visitors here today," Nate remarked.

"Billy and I let it be known in town that work has stopped," Tustenuggee said.

"Word had spread fast about the burials," Billy said. "We figured it'd get around quick that work has stopped, too. I told people there were only two and they were dug up and gone. And that we searched hard but didn't find more."

"Not taking any chances, though," Tustenuggee said. "I'll camp here as long as necessary."

"But you can't stay forever," Nate said. "We already know thieves operate in this area. The minute I'm gone and you pull up stakes, some pothunter will start digging. It'd be safer to remove the bones."

Penelope looked up from her pad. "I can't help but think we should leave them in peace."

"Thieves who pick up a scent won't stop until they've mined their quarry to exhaustion or until they get caught," Nate said.

He stopped and looked around at each one of them.

"But I might have a solution. What if we dig up and relocate these two graves? Far enough away to make it appear everything is gone from here? It might be the only way to protect them. We don't actually know for certain that others exist."

"Nothing would be necessary if you had stayed away from here to start with," said Tustenuggee. "But you speak the truth. Still, it bothers me greatly to disturb these ancestors."

"It's too late to not disturb them," Nate said.

To Penelope, he looked as though he were ready to relocate the entire mound, shovelful by shovelful, beginning that second.

"If we were to remove everything, where would the reburial be?" wondered Cornelia. "We'd have to arrange services."

"What if we reinter the skeletons over there, at the edge, with a proper ceremony," Penelope suggested, and pointed to an undisturbed area far outside the excavated area. "If anyone asks, we'll keep to the story Tustenuggee and Billy already spread in town. The bones will be gone, as they said, just not very far away."

Nate looked hard at her and then picked up the thread. "We could make the new spot look undisturbed. And mark it in some way so Tustenuggee and others can keep an eye on it."

Tustenuggee offered a terse agreement and Billy and Onofrio promised to help him check the site as often as he wanted them to.

"No one knows you've found evidence of a larger cemetery," Penelope reminded Nate. "When you return next summer, everyone here can help you decide next steps."

Next summer. It sounded so far away.

Nate's gaze caught her own. She sensed he also had a hard reminder about time and distance that would soon separate them. His eyes wore a tinge of regret.

She swallowed a lump in her throat. "Or, you could stay here and do as Eunice suggests. Teach a course at the Academy. Be close by in case you're needed."

"You know I can't do that."

She was about to ask why, but Onofrio piped up.

"He can't take that job because it won't pay enough for him to take care of you and the baby," he said. "I heard him tell Mr. Seth."

Penelope took a step back in surprise. She looked at Nate but he'd already turned away and grabbed shovels.

"Get to work, boys," he called to Onofrio and Billy and held out shovels to each. "Got a lot to do if we're going to relocate the graves and make the new area look like no one ever stepped foot there." He picked up his shovel. "Help me find an appropriate spot?" he asked Tustenuggee.

For Penelope's remaining time at the site, Nate found a way to ward off any attempt she made to question him. She knew there'd be no chance on the ride to town. They'd agreed earlier the boys would drive the ladies back in late morning and then return.

Onofrio's comment echoed in her mind all the way back to Taylor Grove. She turned the family picture it formed over and over. Onofrio kept appearing in the image. She felt an extra rush of love. Her heart was joyful at the possibility, remote though it seemed to be.

"Bye, boys, bye, Cornelia" she called and waved farewell when they dropped her off at the Taylor house. She could hear Grace fussing as she hurried inside. A package caught her gaze as she passed by the table where mail was placed. She stopped, briefly, to check the return sender address. The package

contained tracings from the Peabody Museum Library's antiquarian books, the ones that were to help her and Nate identify
the turtle bowl—the one that had been stolen.

CHAPTER 20

anny Alloway invited the Taylor Grove families and some others to Sunday dinner at the boarding house with the Boston Golds, who had returned from their visit to St. Augustine.

"They're at a bit of a loss, waiting for Penelope," Fanny confided to Agnes as they worked in the kitchen. "And I'm at a bit of a loss, trying to entertain visitors in August. Even river excursions are hot and buggy."

"At least there won't be a lag in conversation, not with the mix of people you've invited," said Agnes. She opened the door to the tin-lined wooden ice box and took out cold chicken and a dressed salad of white acre peas.

"Remind me to remind Seth we need more than just the one icebox at the grove," she commented. "How did we ever get along without these marvels?"

"That icebox is a miracle of modern times, just like our new school," said Estelle Wade as she walked into the kitchen.

"Estelle, hello!" Agnes and Fanny said to the Alloways' former cook, now principal of a new school in a nearby neighborhood.

"How's your new cook working out for you?" Estelle asked.

"Nobody is as good as you but she's learning," Fanny said. "She's not here today – illness in her family. But I've taken to heart your suggestion that we add an assistant cook permanently instead of only when needed. Lessens the burden all the way around. We're looking for the right person."

"My eldest girl is ready for a real job," Estelle said. "Long as she can make her hours fit around her schooling."

"Done," said Fanny.

"How is the school doing?" asked former schoolteacher Agnes. "The sisters tell me it's becoming a central place in your community."

"Wonderfully and yes, it is," Estelle said. "Only the church has more prestige. The Ku Klux tried to scare us just once. The sisters and I ushered all the children and many adults into the building. We sang hymns as they rode up and milled around outside. They left after a while without making any trouble."

Agnes stopped mashing sweet potatoes and set down her wooden spoon with more firmness than usual for her.

"And here I was bothered by how schools are segregated. How dare those men!"

"From what I hear around town, your school has the support of Persimmon Hollow," Fanny said. "The community embraced the idea."

"Apparently not everyone," Estelle said. "No mind, we're not backing down."

"Amen," said Agnes, and added more cane syrup to the potatoes. "We're here to help whenever needed."

"Us, too," Fanny said. She finished plating the chicken and picked up the platter. Agnes and Estelle grabbed other bowls and pitchers.

"Agnes, where is Billy?" Fanny asked as they moved toward the dining room. "I need him to empty the icebox's drain tray before the melted water overflows. Art usually does it but his arthritis is protesting."

"Billy's free hours are spent guarding the excavation. But I know a small orphan who'd be glad to take on icebox duty as a regular job, provided you pay."

Fanny laughed. "And I know who that lad might be. Art would be delighted to hand over the job to him. Complains about his aches and pains every time he has to do it."

They entered the dining room smiling, and encountered a room full of gloom.

THE THREE GOLD visitors from Boston huddled at one end of the table. Nate stood and fidgeted like an edgy panther in the corner opposite them. Professor Art sat at the head of the table, brow furrowed.

Lined up on one side of the table were Penelope with the baby, Cornelia, Seth, and the Gomezes—Lupita and Alfredo.

On the other side sat Eunice and Clyde, and Polly with Seth Jr.

Aside from the toddler, who kept reaching for the salt and pepper shakers, everyone else watched pointed stares travel between Nate and the Boston Golds.

"Mom, Fanny, Estelle, hi!" Polly called as the smiling women entered the room. "Thank goodness you're here. Food's here, everyone, you can stop shooting darts at each other and enjoy some brotherly and sisterly love."

"Polly!" Agnes flicked an unspoken reprimand to her daughter with her eyes.

Polly turned an innocent gaze toward her. "You won't believe what just happened in the parlor. But you're about to find out 'cause they carried the argument in here."

"I wondered why everyone was at the table already," Fanny said, as she put down platters. Agnes and Estelle added their dishes to the table. All sidestepped to avoid the pacing Nate as they found and took seats.

"You have to give it back!" Nate demanded of Penelope's step-cousin.

"Indeed not. How dare you?" The woman's pointed chin inched upward.

"Someone tell me what's going on," Fanny ordered. "I won't have this meal sullied by inconsiderate manners."

All gazes flew to Fanny, better known for soothing tempers and placating the disgruntled than for issuing demands.

Penelope raised her head from the baby and broke the stillness.

"My step-cousin has purchased what turns out to be the stolen turtle bowl. In St. Augustine."

"And she won't give it to us," Nate growled.

"It was a valid purchase from a reputable dealer," said Penelope's step-cousin. "I intend to donate the item to a museum in Boston."

"She's trying to attract the attentions of the museum's curator," whispered Polly to Agnes, who'd sat down next to her.

"The artifact was stolen from the excavation site, my dear," said Professor Art to Penelope's step-cousin. "Museums won't purchase an item that doesn't have clear provenance."

"I have papers to prove the provenance and they say nothing about your excavation," said Penelope's step-cousin. "Can you prove it's from your river site?"

"We have etchings that were done at the site," Nate said.

"Which proves nothing," interjected Penelope's stepmother. "I suggest you stop trying to berate us."

Penelope's grandmother remained silent.

"Well, this is a fine mess," said Fanny.

"You're not kidding," said Nate. "Where's the nearest lawyer?"

The Persimmon Hollow denizens looked at one another as though they'd not ever considered the thought.

"You don't have one in town?" asked Penelope.

"Er, we did have two permanent lawyers but one relocated to Jacksonville because there wasn't enough business here. The other spends the summer up North," Fanny said.

Billy appeared in the doorway. "Oh, boy, just in time to eat."

"Yes," affirmed Agnes, and raised her hand to prevent anyone from continuing the conversation. "I think I can speak for Fanny by saying we'll discuss this after dinner. In the parlor or on the porch, when the weather—and the tempers—have cooled. Right now, we should give thanks for the blessing of this food."

Grace began to fuss. It wasn't yet time for feeding. Penelope checked the baby's diaper. All was well. Yet the little one fretted and her small face scrunched up and she started to howl.

"Ah, yes, just what we need now," said Penelope's stepmother.

Penelope rose but so did her grandmother.

"May I?"

Penelope was so surprised she stopped short, and just stood there, in front of her chair, the baby's pitch increasing with every second.

"Ouch!" complained Billy, and put his hands over his ears.

"You were there once," Polly said, and bounced the happy Seth Jr. on her knee. He reached to grab a napkin.

Matriarch Gold held out her finely clad arms and took Grace. The baby stared at the unfamiliar face and screeched. The men in the room began to eat. Even Nate had sat down at the sight of the chicken piled on the platter.

"Come, walk with me," Matriarch Gold said to Penelope, who followed her out of the room in mute surprise.

"I see no resemblance to that man Herman in this child," her grandmother said as they walked back and forth in the parlor to quiet the baby. Penelope had taken the Grace back in her arms and patted her back as she rocked her.

"I've thanked God for that," said Penelope.

"Leaving a child behind can be difficult."

Penelope stiffened. Had her grandmother pretended concern in order to corner her?

"But sometimes that's best for both the child and mother."

"Grandmother, I won't leave her. I can't."

The older woman didn't respond.

"Could you have left either of your babies?" Penelope asked.

Matriarch Gold closed her eyes briefly. "No. But circumstances were different. I was married and my husband had the means to support us. If you stay here, as you indicate you may do, what will you live on?"

"I don't require much. Just enough to provide for a simple life until I secure teaching or art commissions."

"Penelope, be realistic."

"I am. More than you can imagine."

Grace had quieted and nestled contentedly in her Penelope's arms.

"You're not accustomed to this pioneer life. It requires rigor."

Penelope laughed. "Which I've learned I have."

Matriarch Gold stared at the baby. "She is beautiful."

Penelope had never seen her grandmother act so—human.

"Oh, yes, I think so too, of course!"

"You may be surprised to hear this, but a part of me is loath to leave my first great-grandchild in the hands of strangers."

"Then why insist on going through with the original plan?"

"Because it's what's best for the family."

"No," Penelope said, and inwardly marveled at her own gumption. No one questioned the family matriarch. "My plan is what's best for the family. *My* family."

Her grandmother drew in a breath. "I'll consider it only if

you agree to marry Herman and move to a city where the child's history won't be known."

"You'll consider what? Agreeing to let me keep my own baby?"

"Agreeing to provide income." Her grandmother made it sound like a business deal.

"I will starve before I marry Herman, even if he was interested, which he isn't. You don't know the all of it, grandmother. I spared you some details. But I've since shared them with others here so you may as well hear them, too. He forced himself on me."

"I didn't say I like the man," her grandmother said, but her face looked pained. "He is the child's father. People have married for lesser reasons."

Penelope ground her teeth and halted. "Grandmother, perhaps you didn't understand me. Herman raped me. Then tried to force me to lose the baby."

Her grandmother blanched but betrayed no other outward reaction.

"You would force me to spend my life with such a monster?"

"No. I wasn't aware."

"Well, now you are. Pardon me for trying to keep my humiliation under wraps. And no, before you ask, I won't press charges or bring him to trial. Not only because the scandal would smear the family name. Mainly because of the harm it would cause to Grace's reputation."

Her grandmother nodded her head slightly.

"But I will consider living my own life."

Her grandmother had now started to make the little circles on Grace's back. Penelope moved her fingers so she'd have room.

"I realize you're not thinking clearly right now, Penelope. I still believe you should reconsider your decision and think about leaving the child behind. You will be able to start anew and put this difficult chapter behind you. Trust me, in a decade or two, you'll be glad."

"It's too late for that," Penelope whispered, and kissed the top of Grace's head.

Her grandmother assessed her through narrowed eyes.

"You are throwing away your life."

"Oh, no, grandmother, I'm gaining a new one."

"As you wish, then."

"That's it? Good wishes?"

"Yes. You'll have need of them."

With that, her grandmother walked in a starched rustle back to the dining room.

Penelope pushed aside the knot in the pit of her stomach. She had lost her appetite. She'd eat later. She knew her way well around the Alloway parlor. She headed straight for the highboy desk in the corner.

She placed the now-quiet baby in the cradle Fanny always kept in the room. She moved the cradle next to the desk chair, settled herself, and drew out writing materials. A chill passed over her as she recalled sitting in this very seat once before. It seemed so long ago that she'd written letters of longing to Herman while on the family-imposed vacation to Florida. A vacation done expressly to remove her from his presence.

If only she'd listened. If, if... She pushed the intrusions aside. The past was done and she couldn't change it. She needed to move forward.

She dipped the pen in the inkwell and started writing the first of what she knew would be many letters of inquiry to schools, scientific institutes, professional organizations, and book publishers. She detailed her abilities, rates, and interest in accepting artistic commissions for botanical and scientific illustrations. She signed her name as *P. M. Gold*. Let the respondents think she was a man if it would garner more commissions.

She was still there an hour later when she heard the swish of silk again. Looking up sideways, she saw her grandmother walk back into the parlor. The others trailed after her. She waved off the questions and concerned expressions she read on many faces. "I wasn't hungry and the baby stayed quiet here," she said.

"Join us on the porch for coffee and tea," said Fanny. Nate started to come over to Penelope but her grandmother nudged him aside. His expression turned mulish. Penelope sent him a muted plea to let it slide, for now.

"Go, I'll be out in a minute," she said, addressing herself to the group but looking and speaking to Nate. He grudgingly stepped outside with the others.

Matriarch Gold strolled over to the desk and read over Penelope's shoulder.

"I believe you are as hard-headed as I am, my dear," the woman finally said.

Penelope tightened her lips together. She missed her grandmother's hint of a satisfied smile.

PENELOPE CLOSED the desk as noise drifted through the open windows from the porch, where everyone seemed to be talking at once. She rose and went to the nearest window.

"Hush!" she declared. "I just got the baby to sleep again. You'll wake her."

The voices, some of them heated, lowered.

"Can you come out? You'll want to be part of this conversation," said Nate.

"Go. I'll sit with the baby," said her grandmother.

Her grandmother would never cease to surprise her. Penelope walked outside, where the warm, humid night reflected the heated topic that dominated the evening.

The stolen turtle bowl sat next to two kerosene lanterns on the wicker table. The interplay of light and shadows made it appear as though a spotlight glowed on the ancient piece of pottery.

Nate spoke to Penelope's step-cousin. "Will you at least tell us where and how you came upon the bowl?"

Her answer added few details that could help solve the mystery of the theft. She had seen the item on the shelf of a reputable antiquities dealer in the Ancient City.

"I was taken by its obvious age, the pattern of the design, and the story that went with it," she said. "The dealer said he was told the item came from a place called Ten Thousand Islands in the far southern reaches of Florida. That it had belonged to a people named the Calusa and had been used only for ceremonial purposes. I assumed the associate curator at the Peabody Museum —a personal friend of mine—would appreciate its addition to the collection there."

Nate glanced at Professor Art before speaking.

"Unfortunately, it's all a lie," Nate said. "There are at least four people here who saw me reconstruct that vessel from shards and pieces unearthed at the riverside excavation site."

He alternately crossed his arms over his chest and used them to emphasize his words.

"Days after I finished reassembling the bowl, it disappeared. It was stolen. Now it reappears fifty miles north of here with a false tale that's miles longer than that. The Ten Thousand Islands are hundreds of miles to the southwest. The Calusa didn't live around here and that design isn't associated with them. It's more closely associated with the pre-Columbian Mayaca, who lived along the river here thousands of years ago. We learned that because Penelope sent etchings to your esteemed Peabody Museum and they replied."

No one spoke.

"I'm afraid your curator friend won't be interested when he learns of the false provenance," added the professor.

"I paid quite a sum for it," said Penelope's step-cousin. "I can't afford to lose my investment."

Penelope almost snorted.

"The dealer ought to be prosecuted," said Nate.

"Unless he didn't know it was stolen," said Penelope's step-cousin.

"Oh, mercy, like I said before, this is a fine mess!" said Fanny. She reached for a fan off a wicker side table and waved it over her for a hint of air in the stagnant evening.

"We still haven't gotten to the bottom of the theft, either," Nate reminded everyone. "How did the bowl get from Persimmon Hollow to St. Augustine? Who was responsible? That's where the prosecution starts. But all I care about right now is having that bowl returned to me."

"All I care about is leaving this town and getting back to civilization," said Penelope's step-cousin.

"We leave as soon as arrangements can be made, whether Penelope joins us or not," said Matriarch Gold, who'd walked out carrying the baby.

"You can't take the artifact with you." Nate started to look worried.

Penelope's step-cousin studied him.

"I'll consider selling it to you."

"Fine! How much?"

"Three hundred dollars."

She may as well have said three million.

CHAPTER 21

*O*ver the next few days, Penelope used almost every free minute to sketch the bowl from several angles and in the finest detail possible. She wanted to finish quickly. She expected her family wouldn't provide much warning about their departure. They'd show up and demand she relinquish the bowl that instant because they had a train to catch.

Every time she thought of that, she felt an urgency to pick up her pencils and ink pens and create the most intricate artistic record possible.

But she remained astonished at how much care a month-old baby required. Even with Agnes and Lupita's help and with Cornelia serving as temporary helper for a few hours each day.

"So much care, for such a tiny being," Penelope exclaimed one morning at breakfast, to the chuckles of Agnes and Lupita.

"I don't know what I would have done without everyone. I still sometimes feel that night is day and day is night."

"You still need to take it easy," Agnes said. "I'm not sure you're ready to move back to the orphanage yet. Stay here a little longer. Rely on us."

Penelope nodded her grateful assent. She was, for the most

part, exhausted. Exhausted by the baby, the tension with her family, and the August-in-Florida heat that sapped every living thing within its grip.

The screen door banged open. "Halllooo, anybody home?"

"In here, Nate," called Agnes. Footsteps bounded across the front room and into the kitchen.

"How's my favorite baby?" Nate said and, after waiting for Penelope's okay, lifted Grace from her lap. He held her up, cooed over her, and made goofy faces until the baby smiled.

"Success," he said, as he handed Grace back. "I needed that."

"Coffee?" Agnes said, and put a full cup in front of him without waiting for an answer. Lupita followed with a plate. "You're lucky, there are some scrambled eggs and sausages still warm on the stove."

Nate smacked his lips and made a show of flicking open his napkin. "This is heaven compared to what we're eating out there. Cornbread and fresh fish are good but not for every breakfast, lunch, and dinner."

"You're staying at the site round-the-clock?" Penelope asked. "I just assumed I was asleep by the time you returned to the barn each night."

Nate answered between bites. "No, I've been out there. I've come to appreciate Tustenuggee's vigilance but he can't shoulder it alone. Especially now that we know the thief or thieves operate some kind of resale network."

"I heard Professor Art talked you out of securing a loan to buy back the bowl," Penelope said. Agnes and Lupita had risen from the table and gotten busy at the stove and sink.

"You mean buy back what is rightfully mine? Yeah, he did." Nate focused on his food until he'd wiped the plate clean.

"Did you also hear about what I told your step-cousin?" Nate asked.

"No," Penelope said. "We've had no communication since dinner at the Alloways.' Delaying the inevitable, I suppose."

"Well, I told your step-cousin we—me, the prof, anyone who wants to help—would attempt to get her money back in exchange for the artifact. That the effort would be lengthy and uncertain. That if she insisted on keeping the bowl, we'd have to get the law involved."

"Oh, dear," said Penelope. "Did the whiff of scandal have any effect?"

"Your stepmother and step-cousin huffed about impropriety. Your grandmother asked them whether an old piece of pottery was worth sullying the family name in public. Said the bowl wasn't even much to look at."

Penelope smiled at the mental image of her grandmother issuing one of her forthright comments.

"But nothing was resolved," Nate said. "Your step-cousin only agreed to let me 'borrow' the bowl for you to sketch because your grandmother ordered her to do so."

Grace began to fuss.

"Oh, she needs to be changed," Penelope said and started to rise.

Nate stood too. "I need to get back out to the site. I only came into town only for a change of clothes. I'll bathe in the river."

"Watch out for alligators," she said.

"Don't worry, we do." He looked at Grace again. "Bye, little one. He planted a kiss on his fingers and then atop her head.

Then his hand came up under Penelope's chin. He used the other to help her cradle Grace. Penelope tilted her head toward him. His kiss was lightning-fast at first and then slower and richer...and over before she was ready to relinquish savoring his touch. But, oh, how right it felt.

She stepped back and cradled Grace with both arms.

"I love you, Penelope," Nate croaked. "And, Grace, too. And that small, pesky boy who I know you love, too."

"I—we—love you," she whispered. "So does Onofrio. One

step at a time, we'll get wherever the Lord is sending us. Together."

"How can I think otherwise?" Nate said. And he bolted before she could respond.

A FEW DAYS LATER, Cornelia held the padded and wrapped turtle bowl as carefully as Penelope held Grace as Nate drove them into town, through it, and out toward the railroad.

"You know I have to give it to them," Penelope said. Nate's frown dipped a little lower and the crease between his eyes got a little deeper. Good thing she sat between him and Cornelia on the wagon bench, she thought. Nate might never let the artifact out of his hands if he got close enough to grab it.

"I know, but I don't have to like it."

"Soon as we can prove it's ours, I mean *yours*, it'll be returned. My family may be haughty but they are law-abiding."

Cornelia took Grace and stayed in the wagon when they reached the Persimmon Hollow train station. Penelope grasped the package in one hand and Nate's helping hand with the other, and stepped down. Shoulders back and posture straight, she walked to where her grandmother, stepmother, and step-cousin stood amid trunks and carpet bags. She glanced back once. Nate leaned against the wagon, arms crossed.

"You are welcome to return to us at any time," her grandmother said as Penelope drew near. Penelope noted the invitation hadn't been extended to include Grace.

"Thank you," she said as formally as the offer had been made.

She held out the packaged bowl to her step-cousin. "You're still intent on taking this?"

Her step-cousin pursed her lips together in disgust. "Oh, that stupid thing. No. The professor mentioned he 'might' have to relay the full story to the entire antiquities community if I went ahead and donated the bowl to the museum. 'Scientific integrity demands that provenance be examined from all angles,' he said. 'Especially when an object's past might be in question,' he said. He was certain my curator friend would insist on such procedures.''

Penelope stared at her, tucked the package tightly under her arm, and silently praised Professor Art.

"Your step-cousin's full name might even show up in newspapers if the subject became controversial," her stepmother said. "At the very least, the family name would circulate as part of any story disseminated among antiquities collectors and aficionados. They do like to gossip."

"Mabel acts quite admirably in leaving the item here," Penelope's grandmother said. "She deserves thanks for such generosity."

"Yes, oh, absolutely," Penelope said, and looked at her step-cousin. "I'm certain Nate and the professor will refund your loss as soon as they're able."

"They better."

The women stepped back as the train chugged into the station. It stopped with a screech, clank, and puffs of smoke. Penelope exchanged dutiful cheek pecks with her relatives. A slight tug pulled at her as she watched the three others climb the steps and vanish inside the passenger car. Porters lugged their trunks to the baggage car. Her past life was leaving, for good. She waved as the train departed and watched its progress until it rounded a bend and was swallowed by a forest of longleaf pines.

For a long moment, she felt utterly alone.

As disagreeable and difficult as her relations could be, they were still her family. Especially her grandmother. And Penelope had refused to stay united with them.

Nate would be gone in two or three weeks. Cornelia would depart soon after to spend part of her novitiate at the Sisters' motherhouse up North.

Penelope plodded her way back to the wagon in a slow march. Her shoulders no longer felt as firm, nor her back as straight.

Doubts about whether anyone would mail a request for an artistic commission nagged at her. The emergency family funds at the bank wouldn't last forever.

Nate let out a whoop.

"The bowl! You have the bowl!"

Penelope looked into the dear, dear faces of Grace, Nate, and Cornelia. Nate's expression went from euphoria to worry.

"What's wrong?" He was by her side in seconds. He took the package. Cornelia hurried over and pressed the baby into Penelope's willing arms.

"What did they say that upset you?" Nate said. "I'm glad they're gone."

Penelope leaned her head down on top of Grace's. Her shoulders shook as she made an attempt to quell the sobs welling up inside her.

She slid into Nate's strong grip as he angled her gently into his arms. Cornelia's whispered prayer added more balm to her anguish. Grace's warmth and beating heart reminded her why she'd chosen her route.

She wanted to stay forever in that circle of love that enfolded her. And knew she couldn't. *Oh, Jesus, help me, please, on this journey*, she prayed.

A WEEK LATER, Penelope sat at the corner table in the empty orphanage dining room and laid out five sketches of the turtle bowl. Nate stood and hovered over her shoulder.

He let out a low whistle. "Nice."

"They still need a few finishing touches," she said. "But I'm happy with them."

Nate had dragged in boxes of paperwork from the barn. He

and Penelope sorted through them and attempted to make a paper layout of his proposed article.

He sat down and started to pair images with text he'd typed up from field notes.

"You've got the makings of a substantial article here," she said as she surveyed the pages.

"All I have to do is decide how best to organize the flow of the presentation," Nate said, getting up. He sorted and paired text and images and soon had several tables covered with papers to reflect his organizational outline. Penelope followed and marked identifiers on the paired items so they wouldn't get mixed up.

She glanced up at the clock. "We'll have just enough time to clean up and get the room in order before the older children come in to set the tables."

They worked with quiet intensity until a strong breeze arose in the previously quiet afternoon. Penelope readjusted the netting over Grace's pram, where the baby rested.

"Darn wind," Nate said, and reached to stop a set of papers from flying off a table.

A stiffer gust blew through the open windows. Within moments, thunder cracked, lightning blazed, and rain fell with such force it obscured the view out the window. Breezes whipped through the room.

Grace started to cry and Penelope knelt beside the pram and protected the baby from the wind. Papers danced and flew faster than Nate could grab them. By the time the fast-moving rainstorm passed by, the baby was squalling and the paperwork was in disarray.

The sun came back out and made the raindrops atop leaves glisten and sparkle.

Penelope picked up Grace, rocked her, and stared at the mess with Nate.

"I've got the page layouts penciled in my sketchbook," Penelope said finally. Nate continued to stare at the jumbled paperwork.

"Back to organizational square one," Nate said finally when Grace quieted. He started to pick up and reorder papers. Grace's good mood was restored and Penelope laid her in the carriage. She glanced at the clock and helped Nate pick up the scattered pages. At one point, his arm brushed against hers. She stilled, too aware of his nearness.

He glanced down at her. She was conscious of how her tilted face reached his chin, and she traced his jawline with her gaze. He was close enough for her to see the gold flecks in his blue eyes. Those eyes were hungry and she knew the sustenance they sought wasn't the kind quenched by food or drink.

Suddenly his lips were on hers. Strong, firm, and telling stories he never uttered in words.

A loud clatter followed by an "oops" and some giggles jolted them apart. Three girls who'd entered the room gave them shy hellos and focused on setting the tables.

Penelope looked at Nate, unsure for a moment what to say or do.

"What Onofrio blurted out to you the other day? It was true," Nate said in a low voice. "You're all mixed up in every plan I've set for the future. I can't separate you from them."

"Neither can I, not anymore," she said.

"Will you wait? For me to be where I need to be before asking for your hand?"

She parted her lips. Part of her would be happy to start from right where they were. But she didn't say that. She knew Nate needed solid footing and foundations to support his happy attitude and bold confidence. And she needed him to be like that.

He misread her silence. His expression shuttered and he moved away almost imperceptibly.

"Nate," she said, and smiled as she drew him back toward

her. "Yes. You know the answer is yes. Grace and I—and Onofrio—will wait."

THAT NIGHT, Penelope prayed the rosary as Cornelia had taught her. By the end of the five decades, she felt settled and calm. She looked at Grace, asleep in her cradle. Penelope smiled and thanked God.

She'd contemplated her religious conversion deeply and had reached her decision after much prayer. It felt right. As right as keeping Grace and staying in Persimmon Hollow. As right as loving Nate and waiting for him. As right as bringing Onofrio in as part of their new family.

For the first time in recent nights, thoughts and concerns didn't crowd Penelope's brain when she crawled into bed. *All shall be well*, she mouthed silently, echoing a phrase she'd heard the sisters and Cornelia use. She fell into a deep, untroubled asleep.

THAT SUNDAY, Penelope sat in the welcoming embrace of the Taylor Grove and orphanage community under the shade of a live oak tree outside Persimmon Hollow Catholic Church. A hint of the early morning's relative coolness lingered, but just a hint. Enough to say autumn would someday arrive.

"I can see why they call these the dog days," Nate said, and waved a palm frond that sent a breeze over Penelope and Grace.

Agnes and a few of the other women slathered soft bread with fresh muscadine jam and passed out the simple repast. Conversation quieted as the churchgoers filled stomachs empty from fasting since midnight. The aroma of fresh coffee brewed on a small fire a good distance away drifted close as cups of it were distributed.

Penelope chose a cup of the cool spring water from a crock

in the back of one of the wagons. Nate put down the palmetto fan and gulped coffee as though it were in short supply.

"I'll put Penelope's work against the best work of any illustrator out there," Nate said as he told the group about her sketches for his article.

"If only customers could hear that," Penelope tried to joke. "It's too early for letters of inquiry to make their way to me, but I'm wondering if I should have included more samples than I did in my solicitation letters."

"It's a tough business, like mine," Nate said. He looked at Sister Bridget. "And yours."

"Doing the Lord's work is everyone's business," said Bridget. Her smile lightened her words. "We're especially happy that Penelope has grown to feel our faith enough to embrace it."

Warm wishes and welcomes flowed around Penelope.

"What are you converting from?" Nate asked.

"I was a lukewarm Congregationalist. My family is religious in name only. I still have a lot to learn, but Grace will be baptized during Father's next visit. We discussed it just before Mass. I'll be baptized when I finish my studies. I look forward to the day I can receive the Eucharist. The sacrament seems to bring so much to all your lives."

"As it will to yours," Sister Bridget said. "It brings Christ into your heart."

"Feeling the Lord's presence always helps me," Nate said. "I need him more than ever right now, too. I'm debating traveling to St. Augustine and grilling that antiques dealer for more information. I can't rest until that theft is cleared."

"Do you have time before you leave?" Penelope asked. "It would take you away from site work." *And from me*, she heard her inner self say.

"That's why I'm hedging," Nate said. "A quick trip to St. Augustine would take, what, about a week?"

"Two weeks, minimum," Seth said. "You don't want to push your horse too fast or hard."

"I'd take the train," Nate said. "The horses will thank me. Riding isn't my strongest skill."

Turning serious once more, he continued thinking aloud. "I can delay my return North into September if necessary. I can't forget that an artifact from here ended up in St. Augustine with a tall tale attached. The dealer can at least describe what the seller or sellers looked like."

Penelope's heart squeezed at the idea of losing him for some of his precious remaining time. But she kept silent.

"When I get back, I'll still have a few days left at the excavation before heading North for good," he continued.

His voice trailed off. His gaze found hers. It told her what her own conveyed back to him. Parting would be a challenge neither wanted to face. Not yet.

"Hey, I've got a great idea!" Nate leapt up. "Penelope, come to St. Augustine with me. Bring some sketches. The antiquities dealers may need some drawings done or know of others who do. It's called the Ancient City, there's got to be archaeological work being done up there."

Penelope was intrigued. But how could he possibly think his idea was practical? It was so wrong on so many levels.

She saw that his comment awoke everyone from the languid stupor the Florida August morning had brought on.

"What do you think?" he pressed.

"I think that, although a good idea, it's not something I could undertake."

"Why not?"

"For one thing, St. Augustine is already full of artists. The city's art colonies are famous."

"They do landscapes, not scientific work," he said.

"And propriety does come to mind, Nate."

Easy laughter rippled through the others around them.

"It wouldn't be the first time I flouted it," Nate said.

"And there's a small thing known as a baby."

"Bring her with us!"

"She's barely seven weeks old. Nate, there are just too many obstacles."

He sat down on a downed tree limb, momentarily dejected.

"Much as I wish I could make the trip," she added. She'd already breached several proprieties herself, she recalled.

"But I couldn't leave the baby and she's too young for the journey" she said. But part of her yearned to go. She'd be with Nate, could explore work opportunities and see the historic city she'd heard so much about.

"We'll care for little Grace at the orphanage if you wish to make the trip," Sister Bridget said. "We always keep tinned baby formula on hand in case infants end up in our care without notice. We'd also give leave to Cornelia to accompany you. The Sisters of St. Joseph have a school and orphanage in St. Augustine. I'm certain they'd extend hospitality to all of you. Cornelia could tour their facilities and learn procedures that may benefit us here. I could telegraph and alert them of your pending arrival."

"Sister Bridget!" Penelope exclaimed. "You would do that?"

Nate beamed. "Thank you, Sister!"

Bridget replied with a nod. "We work with the tools God gives us, even if we don't initially recognize them as such."

But now that the trip was possible, conflicting emotions washed over Penelope. She pulled Grace closer. Leave her baby for a week or more? Even with the most diligent care, Grace couldn't possibly receive constant attention in the busy orphanage. No, she wouldn't go. Not to be with Nate or help with his detective work or even to secure the commissions she so desperately needed.

"I'll—I'll think about it," she said.

"I must be losing my powers of attraction," Nate joked. But

Penelope saw mixed hurt and understanding in his gaze when he looked at her holding the baby.

Agnes walked over and put a hand on Penelope's shoulder. "I think I understand," she said. "I know what it's like to leave a precious child behind, even temporarily."

Agnes directed a questioning glance toward Lupita. Both looked toward the far end of the churchyard. There, Josefa tossed a ball gently with some of the younger orphans. Lupita looked at Agnes, nodded, and smiled.

"We have another suggestion for you to consider," Agnes said to Penelope.

She leaned in and spoke in a quiet voice so that her words didn't carry.

"You know how much Josefa aches for a child. Grace would be by her side every minute if you let her care for the baby while you're gone. Josefa would be overjoyed to care for her."

"Oннннн, Penelope, you have no idea how happy this makes me, so very, very happy." Josefa gushed as she cradled Grace in her lap in the parlor of Agnes's house at Taylor Grove. Nearby, Agnes and Lupita hovered over the young seamstress, who handled Grace as though born to be a mother. Josefa was all smiles.

"With Ben off on a trip, and no little *niñas o niños* of my own yet, I am blessed to look after this precious gem," Josefa said. "So beautiful!" She lifted Grace and met the baby's face with her own, and gave the little one a kiss on the nose.

Penelope saw the love pouring from the young woman. Grace was in good hands. Josefa had decided to close her sewing shop for the duration and to stay with her aunt and Agnes at Taylor Grove.

"In case I have any questions," Josefa said. "Business can

wait. August is a slow time anyway. You stay in St. Augustine as long as you want."

Josefa gave a delighted laugh when Grace reached for her long braid, which hung loose and over her shoulder. The baby had taken instinctively to the young woman.

Penelope wasn't prone to impulsiveness. The thought that came to her seemed more like divine intervention than rashness.

"Would you consider being Grace's godmother?" she asked Josefa. "She's to be baptized during Father Kenny's next visit to town."

"I'd be so honored. Do you mind if I make the christening outfit, as a gift? I will stitch it while she sits by my side."

Penelope hadn't considered a special outfit. It wasn't within her constrained budget.

"I'd be delighted," she said.

A deeper friendship took root before Penelope departed. But she ached when Billy and Onofrio brought the horse and wagon around to drive her, Nate, and Cornelia to the nearby town of Orange City. Only there could they could catch the train that went eastward toward the coast, where they'd connect with the railroad to St. Augustine. The train out of Persimmon Hollow was on a different rail line.

She knew the baby was in good hands, but the temporary separation was hard before it even began. Josefa distracted Grace and the baby didn't glance Penelope's way as she tiptoed out the door. Her heartstrings tugged as she took one last look. Then the strength of and closeness to Christ she was gaining from her newfound faith rushed to support her. Catholicism was as rock-like as the others had promised her it would be.

CHAPTER 22

The journey to St. Augustine was one of both endurance and beauty.

Penelope soon drooped despite the parasols that shielded her and Cornelia from the sun as the horses lumbered through five miles of sand to Orange City. After they boarded the train, she fell into a fitful sleep as the rail car rocked through pine forest and across swampy lowlands.

New vistas unfolded when they reached the coast and sat in the shade of the depot to wait for the connecting train. The sun seemed sharper and brighter. The sand under Penelope's feet was bright white. She sniffed. The air was damp, with a tangy scent both salty and fresh. In the distance, an open, gentle river lapped against a low, clear shoreline.

"So different than the St. Johns River," she commented. "There aren't as many trees hugging this river. How close to the ocean are we?"

"Couple of miles?" Nate guessed. "It's on the other side of that strip of land that's on the far side of the river."

A shadowy line dimmed the day's bright sun and the three travelers looked up at the same time.

Cornelia crossed herself.

"Whoa!" Nate exclaimed.

Penelope stared with her mouth open.

The door to the depot opened and a laughing station manager came out.

"Guess you've never seen pelicans before," he said.

"They look prehistoric," Nate said.

"Another of God's miracles," Cornelia said.

Penelope stared at the unusual giant-beaked birds as they floated through the air in a line toward the water.

"A scholarly type who passed through here on his travels told me pelicans are a sign of love and motherhood, and sacrifice, too," the station manager commented. He looked at his watch. "Main reason I came out was to say your train will be here in ten minutes. Enjoy your journey and come back soon!" He went back inside.

Nate stood close to Penelope. Her arms and heart ached for Grace…love and motherhood and sacrifice. She had embraced all three at once. Would that she could feel light enough to fly.

The rail cars arrived to carry them the next leg of their journey. The heat again made Penelope drowsy. She nodded off until the squeal of brakes signaled their arrival in the Ancient City.

She forgot her fatigue as a horse-drawn carriage carried them along King Street into the heart of the city at dusk. She stared at the majesty of the Ponce de Leon Hotel. She'd heard people back in Boston gush over their stays at the luxury resort.

Their driver guided the horses southward on St. George Street. Two blocks later, they drew up in the quiet yard of the Sisters of St. Joseph convent and school. After the fancy adornment of the hotel and its nearby buildings, the plain, quiet convent and school grounds were a striking change. And a welcome one to Penelope. She, Nate, and Cornelia disembarked and stretched.

"I'll go announce us," said Cornelia, "and beg some dinner for us."

She returned with that, and more: an offer of accommodations they had hoped would be forthcoming. After dinner, they each were shown to small rooms accessed via an arched and pillared walkway that wrapped around a courtyard. In the center of the courtyard was a statue of St. Joseph and a fountain, surrounded by curved stone benches that formed a semicircle.

Late that evening, Penelope stepped outside and strolled the courtyard pathways and walkways while she prayed a rosary to thank God for their safe trip, and to beg the Lord to keep watch over her precious baby.

THEY FOUND the antiquities dealer easily the next day on the other end of St. George Street. The main thoroughfare of King Street was a dividing line for St. George Street. To the south were quiet blocks and peacefulness. To the north, the area transformed into a bustling tourist center filled with shops, restaurants, and boarding houses. The separation was accented by the town plaza, a rectangular park situated between the two lanes of King Street.

"Here, right where the sisters said it would be," said Cornelia as they stopped in front of a narrow storefront.

They entered the dusty store. Artifacts and antiques were piled so high in the window displays that they blocked the daylight. Shadows bounced off walls and around the small pools of illumination from dim indoor lights.

Nate carried the folder that contained sketches by P.M. Gold, including one of the turtle bowl.

"Ah, yes, I remember that piece quite well," said the proprietor, an elderly man with a long white beard. He held the paper inches from his face.

"It was illegally traded," Nate said.

"You don't say? Well, I reckon I don't believe that. I run an upright business, son. And you waltz in off the street and make accusations. I won't have it."

"Please, hear me out," Nate said. He laid out the saga.

"I have the artifact back in my possession," Nate said as he finished his recitation.

"Then why are you here?"

"To solve the theft. We don't know how the bowl got from Persimmon Hollow to St. Augustine. And," he added, "to ask if you or anyone in your industry might have need of illustrations by the same artist who produced these drawings for me."

"One thing at a time," said the man. He limped over to a file cabinet and shuffled through papers for what seemed an eternity.

"If you don't mind, I'm going to walk back to the plaza and visit the cathedral," Cornelia said.

"We'll meet you there after we're finished," Penelope said, and kind of wished she were going, too. She sneezed as dust shifted when Cornelia opened the door and closed it behind her.

Long minutes later, the man came back to the counter with a folder. "Uh huh, yes, that's right, yes, it figures," he spoke to himself as he sorted through the contents.

"Now, Mr. and Mrs....what did you say your name was?"

"Russon," Nate said in a rush. "Mr. and Mrs. Russon." Penelope looked at him, opened her mouth, and then closed it. Penelope Russon. It kind of had a nice sound. But she was here to promote P.M. Gold. She settled the thoughts whirling through her mind and paid attention to the proprietor.

"It was like this, see, I was out of town." The man launched into a slow, lengthy summation. "Summer ain't the swiftest time in this business, you can imagine. Had a young relative mind the store, seeing as how he expressed some interest in learning the business. He made the purchase. I had my suspicions about the story that came with the bowl the minute I saw it. This here item," he waved a hand over the illustration that Nate had placed face up on the counter, "had obviously been put together from pieces fairly recently." He tapped his temple. "I can tell things like that just by looking after so many years."

He slid Nate's paper to his nose again, and then placed it down. "Had quite a row with that grandson of mine because he fell for the story they told him. The Calusa!" The man snorted.

"The only redeeming point of the whole incident is that he got it for a bargain," the proprietor said. "Which I told him should have woke his suspicions about the bowl. Young fellers who were selling it asked such a low price they had to be amateurs. Well, live and learn, I said, after I got done hollering."

Nate leaned over the counter. "Do you know what 'young fellers' sold the bowl? Do you have any names in that folder?"

"Lemme see now." The man scratched through the pile again. "Yep. I remember. Was happy to unload the bowl to some tourist who acted like she got a bargain. Hmmm. Here's the name. The buyer was a Miss Thorn-Gold and, heh, heh, she got herself a bargain and we got double our money. She paid a full one hundred dollars. Looked like she could have forked over a lot more."

"The nerve of her, trying to charge you three hundred dollars to buy it back," said Penelope under her breath to Nate.

"What's that you said, Missus?"

"Oh, nothing, sir," she said. "Please, continue to confer with my, uh, husband." She blushed when she said the words. Nate cast her an amused glance.

"Sir, does it say who the initial seller was?" Nate could barely contain his anticipation.

"I'm looking, hold on. You young folks today, always in a hurry. Take your time. Look around. Might find something."

Penelope was doing just that when she heard the proprietor say. "Ah, here, we go. The sellers were John and Lon McLean. Brothers, I think."

"Never heard of them," Nate said. Disappointment edged his words.

Penelope hurried back to the counter. "Me either."

She and Nate exchanged exasperated looks. To have come so close, only to end up stymied by unfamiliar names. Who were the McLeans?

"Does it say anything else?" Nate asked. "Place of residence? Age? Occupation?"

The proprietor shook his head. "Just says 'South Florida' as their address. Nothing more. Yup, something shady about the whole deal. Glad you got it back."

"I don't suppose you'd refund us the money paid by the woman who bought the bowl from you?" Nate asked. "She's related to my wife. You know, a refund to compensate for the trouble that arose when the woman learned it was a stolen artifact."

"You suppose right. Got my own living to attend to."

Penelope stepped outside and Nate was halfway through the door behind her when he stopped.

"Wait," he said, and called back to the proprietor. "Do you need any illustrations, or know of anyone who does? P.M. Gold is accepting commissions. The rates are reasonable and the work is outstanding."

"That it is. Sorry, but I'm set right now. It's a slow time of year. Check with the Army officers at Fort Marion, the fancy types at the Ponce Hotel, and the historical society folks at the Oldest House Museum."

The sand in the street hindered Penelope's steps as she and Nate made their way toward the plaza on King Street in the high heat of the day. They met Cornelia outside the cathedral, but she opted to return to the convent rather than continue trekking through the city.

"Surely, there are people in Persimmon Hollow who know

the McLean name," Penelope said as she and Nate walked north along the bayfront toward the fort.

"Yeah, and at least we have a name," Nate said. "But that shop owner could have given you a few commissions in exchange for holding tight to his ill-gotten cash."

"I'm keeping my hopes up," said Penelope, even though she was beginning to wonder. A main antiquities provider in the Ancient City didn't know of anyone needing illustrations. That didn't bode well for anything turning up elsewhere. Especially not in summer.

"It'll be interesting to see the fort." She attempted to lighten the mood.

"Let's go, Missus," said Nate, "and make the best of it."

A laugh escaped her. Somehow, with Nate by her side, she had a feeling they would.

FORT MARION WAS massive and almost vacant.

"If you'd been here back in the '80s, I'd have had plenty of work for Mr. Gold," said the presiding officer after inspecting the illustrations Nate displayed. "Had near about five hundred Apache here."

"Say that again?" Nate blinked.

"Warriors, wives, children—about five hundred—were confined here for some six months. Pitched tents out there in the courtyard, even one of Geronimo's children was born right here. Was named Marion."

"I would have loved to sketch that scene," Penelope said.

"Oh, you draw?" the officer asked. "Artists like to paint scenes of the southeastern watchtower with the bay in the background, especially at sunrise. You're welcome to set up atop the fort battlement whenever you'd like. Might have company from the Artist Colony at the hotel. You folks in town for a while?

What brings you here? Honeymoon? This isn't the usual tourist season."

Do we look that much like a married couple?, Penelope wondered.

Nate took the opportunity to put his arm around her waist and draw her close. She felt a laugh bubble up but maintained her dignity.

"Several reasons, but right now we're drumming up business for P.M. Gold," Nate said.

"And visiting with the Sisters of St. Joseph to collect insight for the Sisters of St. Francis, who have an orphanage in Persimmon Hollow," added Penelope.

"The sisters from St. Joseph schooled the Apache children here," the officer said.

What sketches the scenes would have made, Penelope thought. Had anyone recorded history-in-the-making visually? She'd never seen any renderings, and it had been more than ten years now.

"It appears our visit is several years too late," she said.

"Afraid so, at least in terms of artistic commissions," the officer said, and tipped his hat to them as they departed.

"You can let go of me now," she teased Nate as they passed through the main gate of the coquina-stone fort and over the wooden drawbridge that spanned a grassy culvert. He immediately released her.

"I kind of got used to it," he said, as they strolled across the grass toward the street.

"So did I," she admitted.

"And I liked it," he said, and slowed his steps.

"So did I." She spoke in a lower tone that forced him to put his head near. Their steps slowed to a halt, and they turned to face each other. Nate put his hands on her waist, and she didn't push them away. Her breath began to grow constricted.

"Would you consider it, Penelope?"

"Consider what?"

"Marrying me now instead of later."

"I...we...now?" She put her hands on his arms. She wanted Nate, wanted to be with him. But waiting for him and marrying him now were two different things. Marriage would move their relationship to a different place. Marriage would include...she fought off a rising panic as an image of Herman's twisted face and his violation of her flashed in her mind.

She shoved the memory behind an imaginary curtain. She'd draped that curtain when the thoughts kept intruding after the incident and finally had threatened to overwhelm her. Bit by bit, she'd managed to render them less harmful. And the prayers and training she was learning as part of her religious studies had given her new means of coping. But underneath, the wound wasn't yet fully healed.

"Yes, sooner than later," he said. "I know we talked about waiting, about getting more established first. But the more I'm with you the more I don't want to be without you. And I hope you feel the same."

"I do," she said slowly. "You know, I'm part of a package," she said, inching the conversation to safer ground. "Two for the price of one. Actually, three. I know you want to give Onofrio a permanent home as much as I do. Nate, I want to adopt him."

"Make that 'we' want to adopt him. I can't imagine life without him anymore. Or you. Or the baby."

"But neither of us has any money right now. I mean, that's why we're here to begin with."

"Any other excuses?" He gave her a sad smile and released her.

"No! I mean, that's not it." She dropped her hold on him.

"What is it, Penelope?" They had started walking again. "You were frozen with fear for a moment there. I can't even make a joke about my charm in light of the look that came over you. Is the idea of marriage to me that distasteful?"

"Oh, Nate." She put a hand on his arm again and tugged so he'd stop walking. This was Nate, not Herman. Nate, her closest confidante, the man she loved. She owed him the truth. She owed herself as much.

"Nate, you're so much more than a friend."

"I kind of had that impression."

She danced around the conversation, unsure how to explain her feelings.

"There's no good way to say this," she said finally. "I fear that the incident that led to, no, that was the reason I ended up with a baby, well, I fear it damaged me." Her words trailed off.

Nate watched her with a concerned wariness.

"Tell me, if you want," he said in a soft voice.

"I'm afraid it ruined me for, well, you know, conjugal relations." Her words sounded stiff and awkward.

He stopped her with a gentle finger to her lips, which sent her insides aflutter.

"You were traumatized by hatred, Penelope. I offer you love, and as much time as you need to realize the difference."

"You're serious?"

"Despite my general enthusiasm for life and zest for new endeavors, I usually am."

"I love you, Nate, so much, but I need to think about this," she said. "You've kind of caught me by surprise."

"You and me both, Miss P.M. Gold," he said, and took her hand and swung it between them as they start to stroll again.

"I'm not sure when everything changed," she said. "Gradually, over the months, I guess. I suddenly realized how much I care for you, how much you mean to me. How much I love you."

"I fell in love with you the first day I saw you, Penelope Gold, seated on the porch at the Alloway House on my first day in Persimmon Hollow. And it's only gotten stronger since then."

. . .

"EVERYONE SEEMED to think we are married, so I proposed," explained Nate that evening to Cornelia and the Sisters of St. Joseph as they all sat in the convent's parlor. Everyone began to *oooh, ahh,* and congratulate them.

"She hasn't accepted yet," he added.

Cornelia sent a bemused look toward Penelope.

"I expect she will, in due time," Cornelia said.

"Am I that much an open book?" Penelope asked. But she couldn't contain the flush of happiness she felt. "I expect you are quite correct," she added.

Cornelia explained to their hostesses how she'd been Penelope's companion. "I watched Nate and Penelope's relationship develop over the past several months," she said. "I guessed they'd reach this point long before they realized it."

The happy atmosphere lingered as Nate and Penelope wandered down to the bayfront a short while later. The moon rose low over the water, an oversized orb that cast a silver glow over the dark water and the low, barrier island beyond.

"It's so beautiful, I feel I should whisper," said Penelope as they stood on the water's edge and watched the moon dominate the horizon. She snuggled against Nate and inhaled the earthy scent of the riverside mingled with his familiar scent of soap and outdoors.

"Just think, the ancients who lived here might have watched the same scene," Nate said, and pulled her closer. "Lovers might have stood here just like we're doing. Might have done this." He lifted her chin with his hand and gave her a long, slow, gentle kiss.

She sighed with pleasure. "Something about being here, kissing you, seeing this," she swept her arm to indicate the starlit sky and shine of the moonlight that rippled through the velvet night. "It's magical. Makes me forget my worries. It's perfect."

In the far distance, a baby cried.

"No, it's almost perfect," she added. "Oh, Nate, I miss Grace so much."

"I do too," he admitted. "I know you do. We'll get you back right away."

"We're in some kind of dream world here," she said, and broke away from his embrace. "Something about this city." She hugged herself.

A horse and buggy clip-clopped behind them on the river-front road, and an owl hooted. Somewhere, a woman laughed amid the chink of glasses.

"We're forgetting ourselves," she continued. "You have to find a publisher for your article. I have to find a place to live and secure a living. You have to deal with the bones and find funding. And get back to your job. We have to learn who the McLean brothers are. And here we stand, acting like children grabbing at candy because it's sweeter than what we left behind."

Nate stuck his hands in his pockets. "Right on every score," he said after a while.

"Let's enjoy the moments we have now," she said, and moved closer to him. They stood side by side. The moon grew smaller to their eyes as it continued its ascent, and its silver glow narrowed.

Penelope stretched in the beautiful night air and glanced upward. "Look!" she said. "Nate, all the stars. I'm finally getting to look at stars with you."

"I knew this day would come," he said. He moved behind her and wrapped his arms around her as they gazed at the lights that painted the sky. For Penelope, the moment was as brilliant as the sparkle of the cosmos above.

THE NIGHT's magic had evaporated by the time Penelope, Nate, and Cornelia traveled back to Persimmon Hollow under a glaring sun the next day.

"Not a single commission," Penelope said as they boarded the train. "No luck at the fort, or at the historical society, or at the Ponce de Leon. Have to say, that hotel's grandeur lived up to the descriptions I've heard. You'd think I could have secured something there."

"At least we have the names of the thieves," Nate said.

"And my baby will be back in my arms later today," Penelope said.

Hours later, she hopped out of the wagon as soon as it halted at the Taylor house, lifted the hem of her skirt, and ran toward the porch. "Grace! Mama's home!"

Josefa and the baby, followed by Agnes and Polly, came outside. Grace smiled at Penelope as she ran up the steps.

"Oh, my baby," she took the infant and hugged, kissed and rocked her. "Oh, how I missed you." Grace gurgled. Nate came up behind Penelope, put an arm around her shoulder, leaned in and kissed Grace.

Agnes's eyebrows rose and Josefa clasped her hands together in front of her heart. Polly narrowed her eyes. "What's up with you two?" Polly asked.

"They're deciding if they're betrothed," said Cornelia.

"Which is the best news that resulted from the trip," said Nate, and he plopped in a chair.

"Up," said Agnes. "You can sit inside. Join us for dinner. We're just getting ready to eat. I won't let you get away until I learn about this almost-betrothal."

Penelope looked up from the baby. "Nate's getting ahead of himself," she said, but her eyes were merry and her lips curved upward.

"It's the only way a man can win," he said, and bounded up from the chair.

"I've taken risks before and this one seems to have everything in its favor," Penelope said. The smile she gave Nate made clear she was saying more.

"Yahoooooo!" Nate said, and beamed.

"Another wedding I'll have to get dressed up for," Polly groaned.

"Yes and I'll make sure you look beautiful," Josefa told her. "You're old enough now to be thinking of beaux."

Polly didn't come back with one of her quick retorts.

"Unless perhaps she's considering a vocation?" Cornelia said.

"Unless I'm certain we should be talking about the travelers," Polly said in a loud voice. "How was your trip?"

Penelope went into her bedroom to feed Grace. Nate and Cornelia filled in the Taylor and Gomez families about the journey. Penelope rejoined the group to share a meal of ham, fried okra, and zipper cream peas. Agnes cried for joy and Lupita thanked Our Lady when Penelope shared how much she and Nate wished to adopt Onofrio.

In the glow of the happy news, Nate glanced at Penelope and then put down his half-eaten biscuit. "There is one more piece of news," Nate said. "I wanted to wait until Penelope had rejoined us before speaking of it."

He took another bite and swallowed. "We learned the name of the men who sold the stolen bowl to the antiquities dealer in St. Augustine. Not sure if they're the ones who committed the theft or are part of a ring. Or if they gave their real names to the dealer, who said the men acted like amateurs."

The table talk quieted.

"Do any of you know a John or Ron McLean?" Nate asked.

Lupita's fork clattered when it fell from her hand and hit the plate.

"Uh oh," said Billy.

"Oh, dear," said Agnes.

"I'm afraid we do," said Seth.

CHAPTER 23

*E*veryone stopped eating. Smiles vanished.

"You got wrong information," Billy proclaimed. "The McLeans would never do something like that. I know them. They help us at harvest times."

Penelope watched Seth and Agnes convey some kind of silent message to each other.

"The family is in severe economic distress," Agnes said slowly. "They were among the people who received money we raised during the Independence Day benefit."

"That doesn't excuse thievery," Nate said.

"They're not thieves!" Billy yelled.

"Son," Seth said to Billy, and the youth quieted.

"The McLeans are good youths in a family facing hard times," Seth said.

"If what you learned is true, I have to say only despair could have driven them to such a crooked path," Agnes added.

"Why would the dealer lie?" Nate said. "He showed me and Penelope the inventory papers on which their names were written."

No one had an answer.

"Well, we should get the law involved and question them," Nate said. "I want them arrested if they're the culprits."

The room grew even more still.

"Wouldn't that be the normal procedure here?" Penelope asked. It seemed so obvious.

"Actually, not always," Agnes said.

"We'd like to first speak to them privately," Seth said. "Would you consider letting us intercede? Get to the bottom of this for you?"

Nate leaned back in his chair. "And let them go their merry way as though nothing happened? I'd rather they learn a lesson."

"Oh, they will," Agnes said.

"We're not suggested you look the other way," Seth said. "We're suggesting we handle this without hauling them off for inquiry or, worse, jail."

"We don't want to deprive their parents of desperately needed help," Agnes explained.

Nate gave Penelope a questioning look but she was as uncertain as he appeared to be.

"I've always benefited when listening to advice of the people here," she told Nate.

"And something tells me nobody at this table would help me find these two boys," Nate said. "I don't seem to have much choice. And I know the Taylor word is good."

"You won't regret it, Nate," Agnes said.

ALL TOO SOON, it was time for Nate to head back north.

"If I don't get out of here I won't have a job to return to," he told Penelope a couple of weeks later as they lounged on the Taylor porch. Onofrio stretched out on the floor planks, watching anole lizards scamper up and down the railings. He'd taken to staying close as possible to Nate.

"I've stretched out my time here as long as I could," Nate

said. "But I'm not leaving until this little princess is baptized on Sunday." He cast a fond gaze over baby Grace seated in Penelope's lap.

"And Onofrio will wear a suit for the occasion," Nate said, a little louder. "The one I bought him at Clyde's Mercantile."

"Okay boss, if I have to," Onofrio said. "But only for church. Then I change when we all go outside!" He chuckled at his own determination.

Melancholy twisted in Penelope. The four of them were already like a little family. Yet they weren't. Not yet. She grew wistful.

"Onofrio, Grace, and I will be here, waiting for you," she said to Nate. "How could we not be? The Sisters of St. Francis, the Taylors, the Gomezes, Josefa and her husband, and each of the Alloway sisters all offered me and the baby a place to stay."

"And I am stuck at the orphanage the whole time you go away," Onofrio said to Nate.

"I'll be back before you know it, son," Nate said, but Onofrio released an exaggerated sigh. Nate stood up and stretched and Onofrio did the same, copying his every move.

"I've decided to go stay at the orphanage again, for a while," Penelope said. "I'll be able to get ready for our future. More importantly, it will allow me to stay close to Onofrio."

The little boy's face lit up.

"He's going to help me find a house rental, study my catechism, and keep track of art commissions," she added. "When you return, all three of us will be here for you—a ready-made family—father, mother, son, daughter."

Onofrio stared with growing awareness and a hint of disbelief.

"What son?" he asked.

"Would you like that, Onofrio, to live as a family with me, Miss Penelope, and baby Grace?" Nate asked him.

Onofrio didn't answer with words. He barreled head-first into Nate and hugged him with a fierce grip.

"YOU'RE KIDDING? You're not kidding?" Nate stared at Professor Art when they met outside Persimmon Hollow Catholic Church that Sunday, as the community gathered for Grace's baptism.

"How could my last day in town be any better? Baptism, and now this news!" He looked around for Penelope. He had to tell her. It was unbelievable.

His eyes rounded wide when he saw her. He loped to where she and the baby waited just inside the entrance to the church.

"You both look like angels," he said.

"Josefa is the angel," Penelope said. "She dressed both of us. I wouldn't have gotten anything finer—or even as fine—from the best dressmakers of Boston." She held Grace up with both arms so he could see the baby's long christening dress.

Nate whistled, which drew Onofrio's attention from where he sat, clad in his new suit, with the other orphans. He gave a cheery thumbs up to them. Nate and Penelope waved back.

"Listen to what Professor Art just told me," Nate said as he turned back to Penelope. "The senior scientists have changed their mind. 'Someone' mentioned mosquitoes, alligators, panthers, even uncertainty as to the validity of the suspected burials—that was a tough one on my credibility, I admit. But I can go back to my job without fear of losing my spot out here. I'll return as soon as I find funding."

His last words hung like a heavy weight.

"Money. A necessary evil," Penelope commented.

"Got to have enough to live on," Nate said. He straightened his shoulders. "And to support a wife and daughter and son, and hopefully more to come, Mrs. almost-Russon."

Penelope returned Grace to the crook of one arm, and took Nate's hand with her free one as they gazed at each other.

"Oooh, look at the lovebirds," said Polly as she bounded in the door with the rest of the Taylor Grove clan. "How are you going to stand being apart?"

"It won't be easy," Penelope said. "But we have today."

"And we aim to make the most of it," Nate promised.

Moments later Father Kenny arrived, the church filled, and Penelope carried Grace to the baptismal font, followed by the baby's godparents, Josefa and Ben Stillman.

Penelope wished the day could last forever.

"I'LL BE BACK AS SOON as I can," Nate said. His face was glum. He showed no eagerness to board the train. He kept one hand around Onofrio's shoulder and the other on Penelope's arm.

Onofrio pressed against Nate's side. Penelope had placed her hand atop Nate's and held it with a tight grip. She didn't want to release him to the train that was clanking loudly into the station. Cornelia stayed back, under the overhanging roof of the station house, with the baby.

"I'll miss you so much," Penelope whispered. She hadn't spent any time in Persimmon Hollow without Nate nearby. She felt as though a part of her were departing.

"I already miss you," he said.

She rested her head on his shoulder. Then stepped back from him and forced a smile.

"I'm not accustomed to public displays of affection," she said.

"Italian families like to show their love, so you better get used to it," he said. "Right, big guy?" He knelt down on one knee to meet Onofrio at eye level. "You be good and pay atten-tion to Miss Penelope, you hear?"

Onofrio gave a solemn nod. Penelope had never seen the boy so quiet.

Nate gave the boy a kiss on the top of his head and then stood up. Before Penelope realized it, he'd cradled her face in his hands and brushed her lips with his.

The train stopped with a hiss. Penelope and Nate stepped apart. This time, Penelope was the one who put a hand around Onofrio and drew him close.

"You make sure Miss Penelope plans a big, fancy wedding," Nate said to Onofrio.

"Okay, boss," he said, and Penelope saw that he was trying to be brave.

"And you keep him and the baby safe and happy for their new daddy," Nate said to her.

"All aboard!" shouted the conductor. "Train's leaving in five minutes."

Nate began to inch his steps backward. He lingered as long as he dared. With one last look of longing, he scrambled aboard as the train started to inch forward.

Penelope felt hollow as she stared at the train moving off in the distance. She turned at a tender touch on her arm. Cornelia had placed Grace's baby fingers there. Penelope took the baby and cuddled her with one arm, while keeping Onofrio tucked beside her with the other.

"Come, you look tired," Cornelia said. "Let's go back."

"I miss him already. I hadn't expected parting to be this difficult."

Cornelia smiled. "He's a good man."

Who will make a good husband and father, whispered Penelope to herself.

CHAPTER 24

A month later, Penelope listened to the rivulet of
rainwater that dripped off the metal roof of the
orphanage. It fell in a small stream along a gutter and splashed
into a small cistern outside the window. Overflow splattered
onto a drain basin of crushed shell. The rain shower was
ending, but the grayness of the day fit her mood. Even Grace
had been fussy, but the afternoon rain had finally lulled her to
sleep.

Penelope sat at her desk and tried to focus on the copy of the
completed journal article Nate had mailed to her. She'd already
read it once. It was good. Very good.

Once published, the article would put Nate in demand for
lectures. She could visualize audiences in drawing rooms, clubs,
and lecture halls agog at a brash young scientist's supposition
that primitive societies in Florida were more complex at an
earlier time than anyone gave them credit for. Nate's career
would benefit.

And that would bring them one step closer to being together.
She decided to inquire about family connections to the lecture
circuit in Boston. It was time her family knew about her plan to

marry Nate, anyway. Penelope moved the article aside and began a letter to her family.

She kept the letter brief and as formal as her grandmother would like. She had two things to say: one, she had promised her hand to the archaeologist son of Italian immigrants, and two, she was converting to the Roman Catholic faith.

She requested names and addresses of Boston leaders and organizations that might be interested in booking a lecture based on Nate's article. She was certain the article would soon appear in a reputable journal, despite the rejections he had written that he was receiving.

There. Done. Her relatives would understand, finally, that she was serious about her decisions. They could stop alternately demanding and wheedling her to follow the original plan.

She pushed the window curtain aside and looked out to see if anyone was around to take the letter to the post office. No one, even though the rain had dwindled to misty droplets. Just as she let the curtain fall, movement caught her glance. Penelope looked out, then frowned.

Two thin youths in faded coveralls walked as if headed for a gangplank on a pirate ship. Seth Taylor walked between them. No one appeared happy.

Seth noticed her and waved, then beckoned her to stay there. The three walked over to her window.

"Just the person I hoped to see," Seth said. "I'd like to introduce John and Lon McLean."

She stared at the two gaunt youths. They had faded hair and skin and none of the verve of Billy, despite being of similar age. Both gave her quick "how'dos" and kept their eyes downcast. No wonder the grove folks had stalled on involving the law in the theft.

"I'll be right out," she said. She tiptoed out so she wouldn't wake Grace. When she got outdoors, she stood by the window so she'd have a clear view of the baby inside.

"We met with the McLean parents," Seth said. "And have their authority to enforce reparations in the form of free labor until you and Nate feel adequate compensation has been made for the bowl theft."

"That would be fifty dollars' worth of labor each," Penelope said.

The boys visibly flinched. *Dear God,* Penelope thought, *how can anybody here, myself included, take these boys away from a family that needs their brawn just to trap their next meal.* At least that's what Polly and Billy had told her, in a private conversation some days back.

"We're right sorry we took that pottery, miss," said Lon McLean, the taller of the two brothers. "It were wrong, we know. We were hurting for money to pay for Pa's medicine—he's been sick, our pa—and to get the store-boughten goods Ma's in dire need of."

The other brother, John, spoke up. "We aimed to fetch that bowl from St. Augustine when we had the money and put it back where we found it. It weren't going to be gone long enough for anybody to miss."

"Honest, it were so darn ugly we didn't think anybody would care," Lon added. "We figured nobody would buy it from that antiques store before we earned enough to fetch it back. Sounded like a right good idea at the time."

Penelope stared at the boys and wished Nate were back. Once he got over his astonishment at their description of the bowl as ugly, he'd likely find mercy in his heart...as she was finding.

"Mr. Russon, the archaeologist, is out of town right now," Penelope said, to stall for time while she decided how to handle the unusual situation.

"We sure got the message about what we done," Lon said. "We shamed our pa, our ma, ourselves, and we disappointed folks in Persimmon Hollow. We are most truly sorry."

A slow anger started to burn through Penelope. She could get a check from her family for double the amount these two owed and no one would blink. Yet these young men were a half-step from starvation. So poor that they stole—"borrowed"—to help put food on the table and care for their parents. Now they were ready to forfeit wages for however long it took to work off the equivalent of a hundred dollars in chores.

"When Mr. Russon is away, I have authority to act on his behalf," she said. "Tell me, what do you feel is a fair exchange to compensate for your theft?"

The boys looked at each other, at Seth, then back to Penelope.

"Lord only knows," said Lon. "Do you mind if we think on it a while?"

"Not at all."

He pulled a harmonica out of his pocket and started to play while he and his brother walked over to sit in the shade of an oak.

"Seth, I understand why everyone counseled us let the community handle this case," Penelope said. "I can't—I won't take a thing from those two. I understand why you said they took a wrong turn out of desperation."

Seth watched the McLeans. "That's why we asked Nate to wait before taking action," he said. "If it ever happens again, well, they had their chance. I'll be the first to call the law. But they must pay, in some way, for what they did."

A strain of harmonica music, clear and pure, soared from the tree area. Lon let loose with notes that caught the small band of listeners by surprise. John tilted his head back and started to sing a mournful ballad.

"Good gosh, he's using his voice like an instrument," said Penelope. "Hits every note. And so does Lon on that harmonica."

The tune, and the one that followed, drew the workers from

the grove, and the women from the house. Onofrio, headed out to empty icebox trays for the customers he'd lined up along the Alloways' street for his after-school job, halted the pony he rode.

When the McLeans stopped, Penelope applauded with enthusiasm.

"How much do you charge to perform?" she asked, when they came slogging back over toward her.

"Charge?" said Lon. "You mean make people pay cash to hear us? No, ma'am, we don't charge." The boys glanced at each other.

"Well, if you haven't come up with an idea for remuneration, I've just found it," Penelope said.

The boys grew quiet again.

"I'd like you to perform at my and Mr. Russon's wedding. That's likely not for several months, so you go back to your regular routine and remember to save a few hours to entertain."

"We'd play anyway if you were wanting us to," said Lon. "For free."

"Where I come from, musicians are paid. If you play at our wedding party, you'll have earned more than enough to pay back what you owe. We'd pay you the difference."

The boys stared at her, but she saw understanding and hope in their tired eyes.

"We're right happy to oblige by making music," said Lon.

"There's one more slight requirement, though, and it's one we can start on right away."

The boys looked crestfallen, as though a dream too good to be true had ended up exactly that, too good to be true.

"I've got some free time on my hands with Mr. Russon away. If you come to the orphanage once a week for the next several weeks, I'll help you develop a plan for earning money from your music. The work's not steady but it pays well, and you'd be able to bring extra cash into the family."

"You can help us figure how to do such?" asked Lon.

"Exactly that."

Their faces went from gloom to dawning awareness of what might be.

"Since you're here, we shall begin today. Meet me in the dining room in fifteen minutes."

The day's gray overcast no longer bothered her. She walked briskly back inside and set down the remarkable happenings in a letter to Nate. She knew he'd be delighted.

BY LATE OCTOBER, Penelope wondered why she hadn't heard from her family. Even a curt refusal to discuss anything would have been customary, as would lectures on her life choices.

Adding to her concerns, Nate's letters were a stream of one publishing rejection after another. Editors kept telling him his theory upended current scholarship and needed support from big names in the field. She could feel his disappointment a thousand miles away.

"Do you think Nate is sharing this struggle in letters with the professor?" Penelope asked Cornelia as she helped her fold her spare habit, towels, and other linens for the novice's stay at the motherhouse up North.

"Maybe not. He probably doesn't want the professor to know he's not achieving his career goals as quickly as he wants."

"I hadn't thought of that," Penelope said. "I'll miss our chats, Cornelia. And Grace will miss you. I hope you get to return soon. You'll do well up there. I could see you as a Mother Superior someday."

"Oh, not me," she said. "Not unless God wills it. Now, Polly, she would make a formidable Mother Superior."

"Polly? Is she considering religious life?"

"Not that I know of. But I've suggested it to her. She has what it takes."

"But does she want that life?"

"It's more a matter of, has she heard a call to it?"

Penelope laughed. "I can't really see Polly as a religious sister. She's too stubborn. Pushes every boundary that she can. And obedience is hardly her strongest trait."

"Polly will forge her own path, no matter what she decides," Cornelia said. "There, that's it." She closed the buttons on her fabric satchel. It looked so spare and limited. A memory of trunks piled high before ocean vessels came to Penelope's mind. It seemed a million years ago.

"Are you sure you have all you need?"

Cornelia smiled. "More than I need."

"Well, then, let's get you to the train station, Sister Cornelia," she said, with an emphasis on the word *Sister*.

But no one had anticipated Onofrio's reaction. He wailed like a waif and clung to Cornelia. The boy was so bereft the others finally grew concerned.

"She's only going to be gone a couple of months," Penelope repeated when they'd returned to the orphanage from the train station. "She'll be back."

He squeezed his eyes shut and gave a vehement shake of his head. "That's what they all say. That's what my momma say. She'll be back. She never come back." He wailed, then wailed louder. "Mr. Nate go, Miss Cornelia go, what next, you go too?!"

Penelope folded the ten-year-old into her arms, and glanced up at Agnes, Polly, and Sisters Bridget and Rose, who'd all formed a protective circle around the little boy.

"His mother died," mouthed Sister Bridget to Penelope.

Penelope nodded in understanding.

"She told him she'd be back when she was being taken to the hospital, where she died," Agnes whispered into Penelope's ear. She nodded again.

"Onofrio," she said, and held the boy out from her at arm's length. "I have a project to keep us busy but I need strong help. Would you help me teach Grace the Italian language?"

"That little baby!?" He was surprised enough that he stopped crying. He looked at Grace seated in her baby carriage, watching Seth Jr. toddle around the yard.

"You're silly, Miss Penelope."

"Maybe sometimes I am. How about if you apply yourself to your lessons and write letters to Sister Cornelia?"

His lower lip started to protrude. "I can't write good."

"I'll help you," Penelope said. "We could write them in Italian and English. Each letter, both ways. That would help me with my Italian lessons. And maybe Cornelia would start to learn Italian if we send some of the Italian versions to her."

"Oh, *mamma mia*, that will never happen," Onofrio said and slapped a hand to his forehead. "I try so hard but she can't remember the first word." But his despair had lifted slightly and the women relaxed. He responded further to the smiles and care they showered on him.

"We won't know until we try," Penelope said. "Set a schedule with the sisters and let me know when we'll begin. You know how I like to keep myself busy."

"You are a hard lady boss, Miss Penelope."

"You'll thank me someday," she said.

"You're beginning to sound like a Persimmon Hollow matriarch," said Polly. "Just what we need. Another one."

"I'll take that as a compliment," Penelope said.

CHAPTER 25

$\mathcal{P}$enelope gradually began giving art lessons at the Academy and soon had a regular class. She and Onofrio wrote letters once a week and had language lessons on two other days. She added English and math lessons to her work with the McLean boys. And she arranged to offer language and art lessons to tourists at the town's Railroad Hotel once the winter season began.

She and Grace became a familiar sight as they moved from orphanage to classroom to town visits. Grace thrived on all the cuddles and kisses she received. Penelope ignored the raised eyebrows she occasionally encountered.

The McLean parents protested they couldn't pay for learning and wouldn't accept charity. Penelope sent back word that attending lessons was part of the boys' payment for the theft. Everyone accepted the arrangement.

One day in mid-November, when Penelope sat on the Taylor house porch and visited with Agnes, Lupita, Josefa, and the children, an unfamiliar horse and buggy came clip-clopping along the long driveway. She had an uneasy feeling as it neared the house. It was larger than the typical town buggy and its sheen and the horses' equipment gave it an air of officiousness.

"Greetings, gentlemen," said Agnes to the two men who got out. "Welcome to Taylor Grove. How may we help you?"

Penelope didn't like the look of the two. They dressed like Pinkerton agents she'd seen up North.

"If they're looking for the McLean boys, they'll have to listen to me," she said in a low voice to Josefa, who sat next to her on the wicker settee and rocked Grace on her lap.

"We'd like to see Miss Penelope Gold."

Penelope froze. Agnes didn't even blink. Quietly, Lupita and Josefa got up and moved so that they blocked the visitors' view of Penelope. Josefa propped the baby on the edge of the table and fussed with the infant's clothes.

"Please present your identification, gentlemen," Agnes said. The men complied and she turned her back to them while inspecting their cards. She lifted her eyes, looked at Penelope, and grew pale. Then she whirled back around.

"She doesn't live here."

"We were told she does."

"You were told wrong. I'm Mrs. Taylor and I know who lives in my own house."

"Apologies, ma'am," said one of the men. "We're sorry we bothered you. Would you happen to know where she lives?"

Agnes hesitated. Penelope knew Agnes would rather walk over hot firewood than lie.

"Can you please tell me why you seek her?"

"We're here on orders of her family, ma'am. We're to take her back to Boston, under restraint if she won't go willingly."

"I see," said Agnes. "With or without her baby?"

"No one said anything about a baby."

"You understand that I can't be an accomplice to your activity."

"No, we don't understand. Her family is concerned for her mental condition and wishes her to return home."

The lone call of a mourning dove in the distance broke the unnatural stillness. Even the baby and Seth Jr. were quiet.

"I'm sorry, but I must ask you to leave," Agnes said.

"As you wish. Good day, ma'am. Just know that we don't give up easily. If we learn she's anywhere on this property, we'll be back. With the full force of the law, if necessary."

Agnes gave them a curt nod.

Penelope released a long slow breath as they left.

All gazes on the porch focused on Agnes, who'd eased down in a chair.

"Were they really Pinkerton agents?" Josefa asked in a whisper.

"Yes," Penelope said. Dread coursed through her. "No wonder I never received a written reply to my last letter to my family. The reply was hand-delivered."

"What are we going to do?!" Polly spoke for them all.

"Right now, say a rosary," said Agnes.

PENELOPE MADE up her mind quickly. She wouldn't put Taylor Grove and the orphanage under suspicion or ask them to lie for her. The agents would find out soon enough that she lived on the property, if not actually in the Taylor house. And that she'd hidden in plain view on the porch during their first visit. She knew the company's reputation. The agents wouldn't stop until she was delivered into the family parlor on Beacon Hill.

That evening, she wrote out a list of her meager options and weighed the benefits and detractions of her idea to flee to St. Augustine, to the convent there or to a boarding house or hotel. The imbalance of negatives made her hastily devised flight plan seem ridiculous. But nothing else came to mind.

Grace whimpered. Penelope changed the baby's diaper and

steeled her resolve in the face of the adorable infant. She had to keep herself and Grace safe.

She flew to her trunk, pulled out a smaller valise, and started to cram into it an overnight change of clothing for herself and as many baby items as would fit. She heard footsteps in the hallway and shoved the valise back into the trunk. She sat down quickly atop it and put Grace in her lap. Then she answered the knock came on the door.

"Come in."

"Penelope, do you wish to join us for early evening prayer," asked Sister Bridget.

Penelope did, but she couldn't.

"The baby's a little fussy right now. I'll stay here and do the readings myself. I'll try to join you later for the Night Office."

Bridget gave a slight nod and left.

Penelope thought quickly as she took out the valise and tried to fold and fit more than it could carry. The perfect time to leave was when the sisters were at prayer, orphans at prayer or play or chores, and all of the Taylor and Gomez clans winding down their work day. She needed only to get to that train station in Orange City.

She checked her small purse. She had enough cash for tickets and a couple of days' rations and rent. Thank goodness she had started to withdraw small sums from the emergency bank account to keep close at hand. She prayed the Sisters of St. Joseph would take her in temporarily, that they wouldn't turn her away if she landed on their doorstep.

But how to get to the train station? Then, with an internal thud she could almost hear, she remembered the train for the coast departed at mid-morning. And here she was, ready to flee at dusk. She had no choice but to wait.

Her thoughts swirled as she sat down and fed Grace. If she brought the idea to Agnes or one of the sisters, they'd insist that she stay, that they were all in this together. But they weren't. And she wouldn't. She penned a note for Onofrio, telling as much as he'd understand and promising her return and assuring him of her love.

With a heavy heart, she fell asleep fully dressed, Grace snuggled by her side. The valise sat open on the floor. The next morning, she walked to the Taylor house with a firm foot.

"Going somewhere?" Polly asked, when Penelope walked into the kitchen carrying Grace and the valise. Agnes and Lupita looked up from the stove. Seth and Alfredo, finished with breakfast and about to head out to the groves, stopped before reaching the door. Billy kept shoveling food in his mouth.

"I don't wish to impose, but I must," Penelope said. "Could Billy and perhaps a few others to take me and Grace to the Orange City train station. I'm going to St. Augustine."

Billy looked up and whistled. "You're running from the Pinkerton dudes?"

"Dudes," said Polly dismissively. "You sound like one of the cowhands on the big ranch outside town."

"No, I sound like I'm up with the times, unlike you. It's a new word."

"Please," said Agnes. "Penelope, sit. Think about this. You should stay here."

"I heard those agents at the mercantile yesterday, asking questions of everybody who walked in," Billy said. "Clyde near about had a fit."

"No. I won't put everyone on this homestead in danger by hiding me," Penelope said.

"We'll figure something out," Agnes said. "Polly, run and get Sisters Bridget and Rose."

"Okay, but don't leave until I get back 'cause I want to join the getaway ride!" she called as she ran out.

"I realize I'm asking a lot," Penelope said to Agnes. "But I must go. I don't want to put your family, the Gomezes, the sisters, and everybody else at the orphanage under the scrutiny of the Pinkerton Agency. I hope to put myself and Grace in the care of the Sisters of St. Joseph. I'll send word as soon as I reach them."

"You can't travel alone," Agnes and Lupita said at the same time. Seth and Alfredo had sat back down at the table.

"You're set on this plan?" Seth asked. When Penelope said yes, he looked at Agnes, who shook her head no.

"There's truth in Penelope's words," Seth said. "It's actually safer for her to leave Persimmon Hollow, as long as she can do so undetected."

"Thanks for understanding," Penelope said, and her shoulders relaxed. She sat down but refused the breakfast Agnes offered. She was too keyed up to eat. But the cup of warm tea with honey she sipped helped smooth the jagged edges of her nerves.

"All right, if you won't stay here, we need to get you to the train right away," Agnes said. The small group huddled at the table and talked over each other as they suggested and discarded various candidates for wagon drivers and travel companions.

"No, Billy, I don't think you and Polly are old enough to make the journey to St. Augustine and back alone," said Agnes as Sisters Bridget and Rose entered. A few minutes later, they were trailed by Polly and Onofrio.

"I told you to stay at the orphanage," Bridget said to the little boy. But he was in such a frenzy of worry he didn't hear her. He raced to Penelope.

"Miss Penelope, there you are! I go to your room to say hello and you are gone! I worry. Where is Miss Penelope? Where is Baby Grace? Are they gone like Miss Cornelia. Poof? Like Mr. Nate? Poof? Just like that. And then I find your note! Oh, *mamma mia*, you are gone too. No, Miss Penelope. No!"

He hugged Penelope as though afraid to let her go. "But I

know the whole story. Polly told me. I go with you." Penelope hugged him and smoothed his hair.

Bridget looked around the room. "I was about to say Rose and I would be happy to accompany Penelope and the baby to St. Augustine. We'd love to visit with our sisters in Christ at the convent there. The other three sisters can manage the orphanage here for the short time we'll be gone. Perhaps Onofrio could be one of our male guardians on the trip to the Orange City depot and then again when we return."

The youngster now raced over to the Mother Superior and gave her one of his hugs. "Nobody mess with you with me around!"

"Indeed," Bridget said. "And I doubt anyone will mess with two religious sisters as they journey with a young mother and baby," she added to the others in the room.

"There goes our chance," Billy said to Polly as Bridget's suggestion gained approval.

"Can we at least go on the Orange City leg of the trip?" Polly asked Agnes and was overjoyed at the positive response.

"Well, let's go then," Billy piped up. "We have to get them to the train." He looked at his dad, who'd risen from the table.

"I'll take the reins," said Seth.

"I'll work the fields so everything looks normal here," Alfredo said.

The mismatched group rattled into town with Penelope and the baby hidden in the back of the buckboard wagon behind barrels and blankets.

"Get down," hissed Polly. "We're passing the main corner and I see the two agents over at the livery stable."

Penelope slunk down even lower and prayed the baby stayed quiet.

"Morning!" yelled Billy in a cheery voice, in general to the people who were out and about. "Taking the sisters to the train."

Seth gently increased the horse's pace. They just made it.

The train was at the station when they arrived and platform activity had already quieted down.

Seth, Billy, Polly, and Onofrio scouted the area and gave Penelope a thumbs-up sign. Polly took the baby while Seth helped Penelope and the sisters out of the wagon. Billy grabbed their valises. Quick as they could, the group hastened to the first open door they saw on the train.

"Hurry!" said Polly.

"This way," said Billy to Penelope, who kept her head down and covered with a veiled hat. They all walked onto the car, checked the other seats for suspicious faces and then settled Penelope, the sisters, and the baby.

The train started to move, then stopped. Polly and Billy bolted off but Onofrio stood rooted by Penelope's side. "I go too."

"No, my little one, you be good and make sure my room and my things stay safe at the orphanage, okay? I'll send you a telegram soon as I get there later today. You'll meet us here at the station when we return."

He dug in his heels. The train inched forward again and stopped. Seth hopped aboard and with a few steps picked up the boy. "A man has to make hard choices sometimes, Onofrio. Right now, we need all hands at Taylor Grove."

Onofrio was too wary of Seth, whom he didn't know very well, to protest. But Penelope's heartstrings tugged as the little boy's sad gaze latched onto her until she could no longer see him and the others on the platform.

Penelope sat back, loosened her hat, rocked the baby, and prayed.

PENELOPE'S TELEGRAM didn't come until the following day. Onofrio had refused to leave the mercantile. He'd spent the night on the floor, flanked by Clyde's aging dog Lumpy, who was up in years but still did guard duty. Polly and Billy stayed, too, to keep an eye on things. Clyde found the lot of them already awake when he opened for business the next morning.

"Telegram will be firing up soon, I promise you, young feller," Clyde said to Onofrio.

Onofrio sat on the pallet, knees drawn up, and said nothing. He was wan and his face tear-stained.

Sure enough, the first telegram to arrive was from Penelope. Onofrio snatched it and read it in a halting voice as he sounded out the words.

"She made it!" he announced. "She and the sisters are with the other sisters. The baby is fine. She sends her love to everybody. Oh! Especially me! Look, right here, she put my name."

His small face brightened. "Maybe I could be a telegram man like you Mr. Clyde, when I grow up."

"That's a possibility," Clyde said.

"You make good money at it?" Onofrio asked.

"Onofrio!" Polly said. "You don't go around asking people such questions."

Clyde put up a hand.

"Son, a man never asks another man about money. You ask something like, 'So, can a man make a living at that job?' or something like that."

"Okay, I get it. So, can a man make a good living at a telegram job?" Onofrio parroted.

"He can, but not enough to live on. I advise you to have one or two other jobs too."

Onofrio nodded like a little man. "That's good. I don't want to stop working for the ladies with ice boxes and for Mr. Tustenuggee who lets me help him fix the roof of his chickee house. You know who I mean, the man who is Mr. Nate's friend."

"I hear my name."

"Mr. Nate!" Onofrio's shout was loud enough to be heard for blocks.

Nate stepped forward to the hellos of the others and hugged Onofrio.

"You all right, son?" Clyde asked Nate. "You look a little peaked."

"Fine as ever," said Nate. "It was a long trip."

Something in the way he spoke cautioned the others not to pry into his sudden appearance.

"Been to see the professor yet?" Clyde asked.

"No, want to go see my darling girls first," said Nate.

"They're not here," announced Onofrio.

"I know, young guy. They're out at Taylor Grove. That's where I'm aiming."

"No. They're not there."

Nate's drawn face grew even more somber.

"Where are they?"

"It's a long story," Polly said, and put a hand around Onofrio from behind him and covered his mouth to keep him from blurting out Penelope's location. "And enough has been said out in the open here. Come back to the grove with us."

"What are you talking about? Why the secrecy?"

The door opened again and the Pinkerton agents walked in. They stepped forward with grim countenances. Billy signaled to Nate to keep his lips sealed.

"We'd like you to spread the word," said one of the agents to Clyde without so much as a hello. "Anyone who aids and abets the flight of a person we're contracted to find has to deal with the wrath of the Pinkerton Agency. We don't recommend it."

Nate opened and closed his mouth and looked like a fish for a moment.

"Any telegrams come in?" one of the agents asked.

"Against the law to show you fellows any telegrams," Clyde said.

"We are the law, when we want to be."

Behind them, Onofrio folded Penelope's telegram into a tiny package and put it in his mouth.

Clyde didn't miss the action.

"Take a look around gentlemen. You'll not find any telegrams."

"I'M GOING AFTER HER," Nate said. He paced an oval in the Alloway Boarding House parlor, where he'd quickly rented a room from Fanny.

"Hush, you don't know who's listening, with the windows open," said Polly, who had followed Nate across the road from the mercantile to the house, along with Billy and Onofrio.

"I will not hush," said Nate.

"You must," said Fanny with uncharacteristic firmness.

"Come back to Taylor Grove with us," said Polly. "We have a lot to tell you."

He looked from one face to the next. "This is ridiculous. We're in Persimmon Hollow, not prison."

"Nate, listen," said Billy, sounding very grown-up. "Polly's right. We won't talk here."

"Okay, okay," said Nate. "I'll go out there just long enough to learn what I need to know. Where is she? Anything could happen to her and the baby."

"They're fine," Polly whispered. She looked out the open windows to make sure nobody strange was near the house. "She's with the Sisters of St. Joseph. She and the baby are fine! We got a telegram."

Onofrio pulled out the damp, wrinkled telegram he'd shoved into his pocket after leaving the mercantile. "See, here."

Nate ran a hand through his hair as he read the short notice.

"Let's go. Let me grab my papers and bags upstairs."

"You can leave them here," said Fanny. "Art would be delighted to read any writings you brought. He's over at the Academy. Can't stay retired. Once a professor, always a professor."

Nate blanched.

"What's wrong?" Fanny asked. "You went pale for a moment, then you flushed. Goodness, I'll tell Art not to touch anything."

"No, it's not that," Nate said. "I appreciate his review of any of my work." He signaled to the young people and stalked toward the door.

"May the Lord watch over you," said Fanny, twisting her hands in her apron. "We'll all be happier when those Pinkerton gentlemen depart. They make us all nervous."

"Speak up," said Nate the minute they were in the wagon and on the road.

"Can't," said Billy. "It's like those guys have ears everywhere."

"I can't believe all of you are running scared. Don't expect me to believe Seth Taylor is quaking, or Alfredo Gomez."

"Nobody is 'running scared.'" Billy said. "Dad says we have to stay quiet to protect Penelope and the baby. Rumor has it those agents you saw at Clyde's Mercantile hired lowlifes from down by the river. We don't know who's listening and reporting our words."

"I don't like the sound of any of this," Nate said.

"Neither do we," said the three youngsters.

Nate drummed his fingers on his thigh the rest of the trip.

"Nate, thank God you're back!" exclaimed Agnes, who rushed out to the porch when she saw the wagon come up the drive. "Hurry, come inside."

Nate got the full story within minutes. Billy, Polly, and Onofrio remained, for once, subdued.

"How did you get word and get back down here so quickly?" Agnes asked.

Nate pressed his lips together.

"Are we sure the agents have no idea she and the baby are in St. Augustine?" he asked.

"So far," said Agnes, but she gave him a quizzical look. Nate was known for openness, not for avoiding questions. "But if they pay off the station master and conductors, or show them a photograph of her—oh, yes, they have been doing that—someone is bound to talk."

"When's the next train to the coast? I've got to go to her."

"Tomorrow mid-morning. That train leaves once a day. As does the connection to St. Augustine."

"Stay here overnight and I'll take you to Orange City," said Seth, who'd entered the house mid-conversation. "Billy and Onofrio, you'll join us. Wear old work clothes. You'll be our lookouts, to make sure no one follows us or trails Nate onto the train."

The boys swelled with importance. Polly pouted.

"Sorry, honey, we need the trip to appear as though we're journeying to a field job," Nate said.

"Stupid rules," Polly mumbled.

Agnes gave her daughter a hug and continued talking with Nate.

"After you arrive, you might want to spend a night at a hotel or boarding house to make sure no one is following you."

"It's that serious? She can't just refuse to go with them?"

"It's that serious. They have her family's money and power on their side."

"I'll use a night in the hotel to determine next steps," he said, as grim as anyone had ever seen him. "Thanks for the overnight here and the drive tomorrow. I'm sure those agents are watching the Alloway House, trying to guess who I am and if I'm connected to Penelope in any way. They'll get no satisfaction from me."

CHAPTER 26

"Why, Nate Russon! What a surprise! Come in." The Sister of St. Joseph on door duty let him into the convent's public area. "You must be looking for our sweet Miss Penelope and her baby, right?"

Nate was ready to bolt down the hallway and search for them himself.

The sister wasted little time. Moments later she knocked on the door of one of the rooms that faced the courtyard.

Penelope opened it. She blinked against the sunlight.

Nate? Was it really Nate?

"Oh! Oh! Nate!" She flew into his embrace. He wrapped his arms around her and pulled her into a tight hug. He kissed her face, the top of her hair, her hands. She let herself relax for the first time in days. Just having Nate near her made everything more bearable.

Behind her, Grace began to cry. Penelope took Nate's hand and dragged him in behind her. The sister propped the door wide open with a chunk of coquina rock for a doorstop. "Don't let me be hearing this door close," she said and smiled as she walked off.

Penelope tended the baby and Nate sat down in a chair. "Thank God you two are safe."

"Thank God you're here," she said. "How did you find out? I can't believe word got North so quickly."

"It didn't. I found out soon as I arrived in town. Those agents will never touch you because they'd have to get past me first. Which won't happen."

He reached over and kissed Grace.

Penelope waited to hear more about why he'd returned to Persimmon Hollow so much earlier than expected. Nothing was forthcoming.

"Did you get funding to expand the excavation?"

"No."

"You must have sold the article, then, right? Oh, I don't mean to babble, Nate. I feel safe here, but this is quite a mess."

"Penelope."

"You don't appear excited for a man who just got an article accepted for publication."

"I didn't."

She rose and sat on the edge of the bed, opposite his chair. She laid Grace down beside her and kept a hand on her.

"Something is wrong and it's more than my situation. Tell me, Nate."

He took off his glasses, set them on the bedside table, and rubbed his eyes. Then he put his spectacles back on.

"I was fired."

Penelope's eyes went wide. "Whatever for?"

"Well, not really fired. They had no basis for that. My research and archival work have been stellar. No, they reorganized and no longer had a position for me, or so they said."

"You think that was an excuse?"

"I know it was. As I left the conference room, one of my buddies came running after me to be sure I knew the 'real story,' as he put it. Let's just say some of the established scholars up there are vindictive. Archaeology is a competitive field, Penelope. Some of Professor Art's so-called friends weren't happy to be called off the hunt down here. And they don't like that I'm the one pushing scholarship forward with my theories. Some of them retaliated."

Penelope sucked in her breath.

"I suspect that's why the article hasn't found a publisher yet, either," Nate added. "The men in the field's elitist group are extremely powerful with many connections. Way more powerful than I am."

"I imagine so. No wonder I received no answer to my inquiry home about people to contact for lecture opportunities in Boston," she said. "I didn't understand the lack of response. I was certain experts there would jump to book you for an appearance. How odd. You're no threat to those colleagues of yours. Why should new theories worry them?"

"Apparently, I'm enough of a threat that some want me out of the way."

"The injustice bothers me," Penelope said. "Polite bullies are still bullies."

"We'll tackle my woes later, Penelope. Right now, we have to figure out how to deal with the bullies after you."

"Stay here until my money runs out, is the only plan I've developed," she said.

"I studied the problem last night," Nate said. "Stayed at a boarding house on a side street and made sure no one followed me over here today. I can get those agents off your trail."

"How?"

"By marrying you."

She gave him a perplexed look. "We've already discussed our wedding, Nate. It won't be for several months. I doubt the sisters here would extend their welcome mat that long."

"No, I mean right away. Today or tomorrow. Soon as we can find a justice of the peace."

"That's impossible, Nate. Our wedding has to be in church. We need to meet with the priest first. The banns have to be published. I'm not even baptized yet. So many plans have to be made. Agnes and Lupita will have a fit if they're not involved in the organizing. And I want Cornelia as my bridesmaid. Can religious sisters be bridesmaids?"

Nate watched her with love in his eyes.

"You don't have a job," Penelope said. "I haven't a spare cent. Nate, we can't start out like this."

He leaned forward. "We have to. Here's the plan. We marry before a justice of the peace as soon as we can. The Pinkerton agents won't be able to touch you then."

Penelope frowned.

Nate held up his hand. "They won't know the marriage is in name only. We'll continue living as before. Lord knows I have to leave and find work. We'll celebrate with the Sacrament of Matrimony after you're baptized and Father Kenny approves and the banns are published and as many preparations are in order as you wish."

"I won't consider myself married until we do things properly, in church," she said.

"But the Pinkerton agents will. They can't take a wife from her husband, no matter what the wife's family says."

She looked at him with her lips slightly parted.

"It's the best way I know to save you from them," Nate said.

"Nate," she whispered, "I'm not ready for marriage."

"It won't be marriage as you expect. I mean, yes, by law, we'll be married. But nothing will change in our lives until we get that blessing. Consider it a betrothal like in biblical days."

He stared long at her when she remained silent.

"I can guess the other reason for your hesitation," he said.

Grace had fallen asleep and Nate leaned forward and gently took both Penelope's hands in his. "Even after we seal our marriage in the eyes of God, you have my word you'll have as long as you need to feel comfortable. About anything and everything."

Penelope felt heavy with emotions swirling inside her.

"Personally, I think you're getting quite a bargain in me," Nate said and grinned.

His comment succeeded in lightening the mood.

"Oh, Nate, I'm getting so much more."

A FEW DAYS LATER, Nate escorted Penelope, who held Grace, down the steps of the train at the Orange City station. Seth, Billy, Onofrio, and Polly waited and waved from the wagon.

"No hiding this time," said Nate, as he settled Penelope and Grace in the back of the wagon and sat beside them. Onofrio scrambled to sit close to Penelope's other side. She put a free arm around the little boy.

As they rolled into Persimmon Hollow, Nate called out a loud hello to the livery owner and to Clyde, whose stood in the mercantile doorway.

"Are you trying to provoke the agents?" Penelope asked.

"I'm trying to get this over and done with, Mrs. Russon."

They stopped at the Alloway House for a break. Nate was escorting Penelope, Grace, and Onofrio up the walk when the Pinkerton agents came running toward them from the corner.

"Halt right there," they yelled.

Penelope turned away from them to protect the baby. Nate stopped but kept a tight hold of her arm. Onofrio glared at the agents. Fanny and Art came out from the house and Clyde and Eunice hastened from the mercantile across the street. The others from the wagon drew near.

"Remand this woman to our care," said one of the agents to Nate, while ignoring Penelope. "We are authorized to return her to Boston."

"Is that so?" asked Nate, eyebrows arched.

"You arguing?" the other agent asked, and took a step toward them.

"Gentlemen, there's nothing to argue about. My wife and children and I will now continue strolling toward the front door of the Alloway House. Good day."

One agent stepped in front of Nate and blocked the way. The other stepped behind them.

"What did you say?" asked the agent who faced Nate.

"You heard me."

"Let me see the papers."

Nate made a slow process of taking the paperwork from his pocket, unfolding it, and showing it to the agents.

"You gentlemen do know that unless I give my consent, you cannot take my wife anywhere. Let me say it right now, I refuse consent. In case you didn't hear, *I refuse consent.* Now please step out of our way."

The agents shifted aside and glowered but made no attempt to stop them. Minutes later, Nate, Onofrio, and Penelope were safely inside, with Grace still asleep in Penelope's arms.

"Did I hear you say you are married? You got married?!" Fanny's voice pitched high as she rushed around. "Mercy. We must celebrate. Wait! Does anyone at Taylor Grove know? Oh, dear, this was sudden."

"Quick thinking on Nate's part," said Seth.

Eunice came running in. "Married?"

"Wait!" Penelope held up her hand. She and Nate explained the details. Baby Grace continued to sleep through the ruckus.

"So, you see, we plan to continue our lives as before. Nothing will change in living arrangements or anything else until we're married at Mass at Persimmon Hollow Catholic Church," Penelope finished.

"Oh, dear, Clyde rode out to the grove to tell them soon as he heard Nate talk to the agents," Eunice said. "I expect they'll be here as fast as their horses will bring them."

"You can count on that," said Seth.

"I'll prepare refreshments," Fanny said.

Agnes and Lupita showed up at the house a short while later.

Onofrio stuck close between Penelope and Nate as everyone talked around and over them as the story was told and retold. Grace, by now awake, gurgled and chortled in Penelope's lap while Agnes's little boy stared and tried to figure her out.

"And, to make our new family even more perfect, I want everyone in town to know what the grove families already know —Nate and I also have a son," Penelope announced.

The chatter stopped as though cut off. Penelope, Nate, and Onofrio exchanged grins.

"I've talked with Sister Bridget and we're starting the necessary paperwork so that Nate and I can adopt Onofrio right after we celebrate the Sacrament of Matrimony," Penelope said, and reached down to hug and kiss the boy.

Clearly pleased, he nonetheless squirmed away from her. "You like?" he asked the adults who were all offering congratulations and patting him on the back. "I keep them out of trouble!"

After the laughter quieted, Penelope explained how the next months would unfold for her, Nate, Grace, and Onofrio. She and the children would stay at the orphanage and Nate would board at the Alloway House while pursing work opportunities.

"And finding us a place to live as a family," Nate added.

"There's a lovely cottage that just became available a couple of blocks from here, on a street off the boulevard," Fanny said. "It's between here and the Academy."

Eunice cleared her throat. "An ideal location for a professor of anthropology."

She suddenly became the center of attention.

"Don't look so surprised," she said with feigned affront. "Don't any of you wonder why I'm in the middle of town on a school day? I came down from the Academy soon as I learned

Nate and Penelope were due back. I offered Nate a part-time teaching position a few months ago. At the time, the Academy didn't have the resources for me to offer more. Donors have come forward since then. Perhaps Nate will consider a full-time slot."

"This is too good to be true," he said.

"In Persimmon Hollow, sometimes 'too good' really is true," Eunice said.

"You'd continue to live here at the Alloway House until the wedding, of course," said Agnes to Nate, as though she were orchestrating their life. "Penelope, if you hire a companion, you could live at the new house if you wished, to make it easier for your art and language pupils to reach you, and you to reach them."

Nate and Penelope exchanged glances.

"Buying a house is quite out of the question at the moment." Penelope spoke first. She tried to keep her voice light. She read in Nate's expression the pain he felt at their precarious finances.

"I know the owners," Seth said. "They'd be happy to let you use the house until a mortgage could be arranged."

"Right, let's be real," said Nate. "No owner would agree to that."

Agnes crossed the room and planted a big kiss on Seth's cheek and then looked at Penelope and Nate. "Yes, we would."

Slowly, the meaning of her words sank into Penelope. Nate took hold of her hand and kissed it. She looked up at him. The others in the room receded from their view.

"So, when do we all get married?" Onofrio asked, breaking the moment and squirming his way between Penelope and Nate.

"We'll telegraph Father Kenny today and find out what is required," Penelope said to Onofrio. "We have a lot of work to do so we can get ready. I'm not baptized yet. And you can't just run out on the sisters without notice! Plus, we have to fix up our new house. It'll be months. But they'll go fast. We'll be busy."

"Good thing you have me to help," Onofrio said.

"And to love," she said, and pulled Onofrio close for a kiss.

"Our second wedding in Persimmon Hollow Catholic Church," said Agnes. "The first was Josefa and Ben's. Oh, I can't wait!"

"Penelope, you can expect a visit from Josefa likely within hours," said Lupita. "She'll want to start on the dress right away."

Penelope and Nate gazed at each other as everyone started to talk at once again. Penelope sat down again and cradled the baby. Nate put his arm around Onofrio's shoulder.

"The ancients had the right idea, Penelope," he said. "They chose this place for a reason. We each chose it for a reason, too. Could be we're here to stay, just like they were."

"I hope our roots go down as deep," she said.

"They will. I love you, Penelope Gold Russon."

"I love you, Nate Russo. *Russo*, not Russon. That's only your professional name."

Nate's look was priceless.

"And we love you, Onofrio," they said in unison to the little boy. "And our little girl."

"We've grown a family, one of the heart," said Penelope. "The best kind to be."

EPILOGUE

*A*lmost a year later, on a perfect October day, Penelope, Nate, Onofrio, and baby Grace stood as a family in front of Father Kenny after the formal wedding Mass. He blessed them with prayers for a long and happy life.

The one-room church was full. Nate's boisterous and loving parents, siblings, in-laws, grandfather, and assorted cousins, aunts, uncles, nieces, and nephews packed into five pews. Upon arrival in town, they had embraced Penelope as one of their own as only an Italian family can do.

Across the aisle, Penelope's grandmother and a handful of other Gold relatives sat stiffly. They had signaled defeat after the Pinkerton debacle. Her grandmother had even begun depositing a small amount of money each month into the Persimmon Hollow bank account. Upon arrival in town for the wedding, she'd acknowledged Nate with chilly but proper manners.

The Persimmon Hollow families squeezed into every other available space. Their joy was contagious. Penelope's live-in maid and companion—Sister Bridget's recently arrived cousin Margaret—still couldn't get over the full story of Penelope and Nate.

"And to think I called her 'Miss Gold' the whole time I've been at her employ!" Margaret Murphy shared her shock with all who'd listen. "And with Mr. Nate gone from town for research all summer, well, I had no idea. Not even when he came back! I thought he came to the house a lot because of that article he got published with her sketches in them. Thought maybe they were working on more. They were in a fine state of happiness over that paper being printed in such an important magazine. You can see it sitting out on the parlor table, *The American Antiquarian*. Anyway, I felt right smart myself because I finally figured he was her beau. And then, to learn the whole story about them!"

"In the Lord's eyes, that's all he was, a beau, until today," Sister Bridget reminded her.

"Yes, yes, I know, but, ah, such a love story," Margaret said.

Read Margaret's story in the novella Trust in Love

Father Kenny called everyone's attention back to the front of the church.

"Please welcome Mr. and Mrs. Russo and their beautiful children, Onofrio and Grace."

Everyone applauded and Billy ran outside to ring the steeple bell loud and long. Grace decided enough was enough and started to cry. Onofrio loudly started to soothe her.

"You tell big brother what is wrong and I fix," he said in a loving voice that told Penelope that brother and sister would have a strong bond. She met Nate's gaze, which held promises of delights on many levels. She knew she was ready for anything that might come her way in this unusual marriage that had woven such different threads together. She never felt more certain about anything.

Nate reached across the top of the children's heads and gave

Penelope a gentle kiss. His eyes spoke deeper meanings. Hers returned the same.

The four of them started down the aisle and reached the outside door just as Billy stopped ringing the bell and bounded back up the steps.

"Hooray, you're done!" he said. "I'm starving. Let's go! I can't wait to chow down on good fixin's and listen to the McLeans play some music. I'm ready!"

"So am I," said Penelope.

THE END

ABOUT THE AUTHOR

Gerri Bauer is the author of three Persimmon Hollow novels and two novellas. She also writes short stories, biographies and other nonfiction, and blogs about life in pioneer Florida. A former journalist, she also worked in university communications. Learn more at gerribauer.com

ALSO BY GERRI BAUER

~

At Home in Persimmon Hollow

Persimmon Hollow Legacy Book 1

2015/2021

~

Stitching A Life in Persimmon Hollow

Persimmon Hollow Legacy Book 2

2016/2022

~

Trust in Love

A Persimmon Hollow Novella

2018

Circle of Light

A Persimmon Hollow Christmas Novella

2023